The Hunter Overture

Josh D Sanders

The Hunter Overture

To both Crystal Livingood and Kareem Miskel for keeping me sane through this entire process. I don't think anything I've done would have been possible without the help of these two wonderful people.

CHAPTER ONE

A small remote township in central Missouri. It lay along Interstate Forty-Four west of St. Louis before reaching Springfield. A patch of highway known to some as the *Slasher Belt* for the names of towns and general ambiance of the area. Teens are probably not safe having any kind of sexual contact anywhere near these small bastions of evil. St. Robert, Conway, St. Cloud, Sleeper, even Devil's Elbow were some of the names on signs along the interstate. Each one could be the setting of any mindless slasher movie from the 80s or 90s. It was easy to picture any one of their downtowns having a store specifically selling masks and murderous implements to anyone who walked through the door over six feet tall and having a bad mental state.

Immediately off the ramp for this particular town, there stood a sign pointing East into the dark distance. The sign read simply "Cemetery." The road wound off into the distance and up a hill before disappearing over the crest. There had been bright red taillights seen there, but there never seemed to be the accompanying headlights later. The road led down over the hills to the cemetery, which laid in the low area between the rolling landscape. On one of the nearby hills, overlooking a resting place as old as the town itself, stood a lone figure gazing down on the graveyard. The breeze blew gently through her short hair. She kept it cut to about her ears and it rose from the front to the back. Her hair was a rich red and hung straight down the sides of her unmoving head.

The wind blew warm around her, but only her hair showed any sign of movement. Bright green eyes peered steadily upon the site which loomed below. Her face was locked in a mask of fierce intensity. That same concentration held her body tight and unmoving, but not rigid. There was no fear or anxiety in her posture, merely deep concentration and focus. She resembled a large cat watching an animal move through its territory before deciding on which action to take.

Her facial features were sharp and angular as offset by her short hair. Severe would have described both her features and demeanor at that moment. Dark clothing clung tightly to her long and muscular frame. She stood six feet three inches tall and had the build of an athlete at the peak of her game. Though she didn't look like a body builder, she gave a definite impression of strength and power. Standing there she looked much like a comic book hero in her tight clothing, though she lacked a distinct costume to make her memorable. She did, however, successfully fight the artist's impression of cocking her hips to one side or sticking her butt out. Flat dark boots held her feet warm and firm as heels would have been ridiculous.

On each of her thighs was strapped a Colt model nineteen eleven, forty-five caliber pistol. She had brought very little gear for this particular job. Not much would be needed to finish this one successfully. She'd been hired by a local man to go after two targets. They were rogue wizards who had kidnapped his daughter. Now, she was being held for ransom. Their mistake was built directly into their poorly thought out plan. They had taken the daughter of a member of the Neolithic Consortium, a powerful wizard collective. His connections had allowed him to find and hire the woman standing on the hill. Her name was Autumn Graves and she was a bounty hunter.

Autumn tended to avoid standard work. There was no sport in catching bail jumpers when you have superior power and skill. There was also less profit to be had from regular work. She tended to work pursuing wizards, beasts, and other extraordinary prey. The field was in demand and there were few players on that front. Autumn's skills were in demand enough that she made a reasonable income.

She had set up a meeting at five in the morning in the graveyard below. Since midnight she'd been watching the spot from her vantage point on the hill. As she had suspected, the two wizards had shown up early to prepare the area for her arrival. She watched intently during their entire preparation. Her plan was to act early and end the night sooner, but they had not brought the girl. They were smarter than she had given them credit for. She would have to wait and play the game.

Leaving her car away from the road, she had hoped

not to alert them to her presence before she was ready. With twenty minutes left, she returned to her car preparing for the act she'd have to play. The first objective was to retrieve the girl. After that, she was to make the wizards pay for what they'd done. She'd interpreted that to mean kill them. She had a plan for the situation though she had hoped not to need it. It seemed that no one ever wanted to take the easy road in these situations. Changing into the middle-class clothes she had brought, including a mid-thigh length skirt and a polo shirt with low buttons about a size or so too small, was step one in her elaborate plan. The rest of the plan was get close and kill them. Very elaborate.

She pulled out the case the parents had given her. There was supposed to be two million dollars and a spell book the parents owned. Autumn had no clue what was in the spell book, but she assumed it was more important than the money. Wizards seemed to value books more than money most of the time, though she had seen them use the books to get money. The case was sealed shut and it had been filled with paper enough to approximate the weight of the money. The seal was magical. She was to tell them the keyword to unlock the case when she had the girl. This allowed her to play dumb about the contents.

She trekked down the path to the cemetery arriving a few minutes early. Walking slowly into the clearing, she would allow them plenty of time to see her. There was no value in causing them any surprise yet. A voice boomed into the clearing for all around to hear.

"Drop the case."

She dropped it at her side and raised her arms.

"You're not Clarence," the voice continued. "Where is Clarence?"

She raised her voice higher in pitch, since her natural voice was rather low for a woman. She had her stereotypes, as well as anyone did.

"Like, he sent me," she said to the empty graveyard. "I-he-I'm his tennis coach."

"I'm sure you are. And I'm sure that's all you do for him," the voice continued to fill the clearing.

"Hey! I'm a good teacher. Like, I could have played pro."

"I'm sure, Honey," the voice continued trying to sound menacing. "Where's Clarence?"

"He said this was, like, something he shouldn't do."

"Yeah? Can't even come get his own kid, can he? Guy has to send his bimbo mistress instead," boomed the voice before it changed slightly. Possibly, because someone else was actually speaking. "Hey! Are you the kid's real mom or are you even old enough?"

Laughter boomed out through the spell over the clearing. There were definitely two people laughing. The illusion it created was quite creepy. Horror movie directors would have killed for that effect.

"No! I-he-we're-" Autumn pushed herself to cry. Acting was often required in her line of work and she was fairly good at it. At least good enough to stay alive. She dropped to her knees and put her hands over her face in case her skills weren't good enough. "I teach Katie too. He thought she'd feel better if I, like, picked her up instead. Daddy might be scary, and she likes me... a lot."

"For fuck's sake, I believe you," came the voice loaded with condescension. "Stay there and stop

7

crying. We'll come make the exchange… Jesus."

She wiped her face clean and stood up. She was very careful to make a show of it all. A worrying thought hit her because she had not bothered to wear make-up and they might be expecting her character to be. It was too late to think of a good story, so she'd have to roll with it should it come up. Right as she was done, two men walked into the clearing in front of her. Both had a look of smug superiority on their face as they walked. Neither of them had a girl with them.

Shit.

They walked over and stopped a few feet from Autumn. She had to keep the act up for a while still. The longer it went, the more risk of being caught in a lie. Both smiled as they looked her up and down. The man on the right had a perverted look in his eyes as he stared directly into her cleavage.

"Hey," she said indignantly. "My eyes are up here."

"Yeah? Who cares? Your tits are down there. Your cup size is probably higher than your IQ anyway. I'm rich now, how 'bout you show 'em to me?"

"Hey," the man on the left said. "Let's be sure we are rich first. Stand back from the case, bitch."

She took two steps back. She'd taken a huge gamble on her disguise since she couldn't carry her forty-fives on her. There would be no way to conceal them with what she wore. The Pervert on the right stepped forward and picked up the case. He had more than a little trouble lifting it with his gaunt physique. Autumn couldn't help but smile inwardly at the trouble he was having.

"Shit, Phil, this is heavy."

"Of course, it's heavy, you dipshit," Phil responded.

"Did you think that two million dollars would be light?"

"No, but I've never lifted this much before. I didn't think it'd be this heavy. Jesus, man."

"So," Autumn broke in. "Where's Katie?"

"Well, now," Phil spoke first. "We have to count the money and authenticate the book, don't we? That's going to take a while."

"I'm supposed to take her home. Like, tonight. That's what Mr. Bradshaw said."

"Well," the Pervert broke in. "Maybe you could come with us. Might be able to speed up the whole process. I could show you a couple good pay-to-win games that would help me stay focused on all that counting."

The Pervert couldn't help but laugh at his own cleverness.

"Dude," Phil spoke over the Pervert's laughter. "We have the case. Just tell her, so we can get going, alright? We'll leave while she's crying. When we're done you can go get all the pussy you want."

"Fine," he said as he reached into his pocket and pulled out a small box. With utter disdain the Perv tossed the box down in front of Autumn. She saw blood all around the box and understood immediately. Reaching down slowly, she lifted the box. Carefully, she opened it and looked inside to find a small ear.

"You-" she dropped the box and bent her knees.

"Yeah," Phil spoke matter-of-factly. "We need parts for some of the spells we intend to perform."

Autumn's face changed. The change came instantaneously and was complete. Phil seemed to notice that something had was different. Before he

9

could speak or react in any way, Autumn rolled forward and latched onto his left leg. Phil instinctively covered his genitals.

"Nope," Autumn smiled, held his ankle down, and struck the inside of his left knee. She felt the joint snap and left Phil to collapse.

"Fuck!" Phil screamed as he fell to the ground. The Pervert darted to his right into the cemetery leaving his friend entirely to the wolf before them. He moved with the urgency of a boy who had been bullied most of his life. Some people used that past influence to change the world for the better; others suggested sexual assault.

Autumn grabbed Phil's right arm and broke his elbow over her own arm. He screamed again.

"Move from here and I'll kill you."

With that said she sprung up and moved off after the other man. She knew they had been preparing and she assumed that they had set some traps in case things went awry. She'd have to be very careful to watch for and avoid whatever they had planned. Wizards, at least smart wizards, always tried to build in advantages for themselves.

Her first act was to get off the main path. She assumed he had moved down the path that held the most advantage. She moved off and walked through the graves. Once off the path, she walked a bit faster. He couldn't have prepared every possible option. No one was that good. She didn't run since she was sure he'd be slowing down soon. This guy was no athlete.

Soon, a distinct feeling of being watched crept over her. Looking around for his position, she continued her steady pace between the graves. She had moved out toward the outer edge of the cemetery and found there were trees all around. She couldn't see where he'd gone from her current position. Looking up, she saw the trees had been trimmed up in an attempt to prevent climbing. Most groundskeepers tried to prevent kids from coming into graveyards at night. It was a losing battle, but they tried.

The lowest branch sticking out was twelve feet or so, in the air. Having no other way up, Autumn crouched a bit and leapt fifteen feet or so straight up to a strong branch of one of the nearby trees. From her branch, she surveyed the landscape and saw the Pervert on top of a monument. He was staring at the tree she had leapt into in shock. Obviously, he'd seen what she'd done, and fear was gripping his imagination. She watched him as he stood and began to scramble down off the monument. He must have taken a while to get on the top in the first place.

The monument was about twenty-five feet in front of her and only a few feet below her position. Autumn crouched on the branch and waited. He moved down carefully and prepared to leap to the ground. He was taking care to be able to leap away from the base. Making some quick mental calculations Autumn leapt forward slightly before he did. She led him by a second and reached his position while he was still a couple feet from the ground. With her angle and a well-placed push kick, she shoved him back toward the base of the monument while she sailed away.

After a flip, Autumn landed in a crouch with her left fist on the ground looking forward at the Perv. He flopped back and hit the concrete. Hard. His head and body rebounded forward. When he touched the ground, blue fire leapt up all around the base of the monument, a solid four-feet-thick, flaring to four feet in height. He scrambled as fast as he could, but he had to exit through the fire to earn his freedom.

She could feel the heat herself as she stood back away from the bright flames. He wasn't in the fire for long, but his clothing and hair had already caught. As quickly as he could, he stripped down to his boxers, but his hair was burning off and his skin was already red and beginning to bubble from the burns. Some areas of his skin were already starting to peel off. His screams were loud.

Autumn walked toward him slowly as he worked to put out the last of the fire and tried not to cause himself too much pain in the process. Once he got the last of the fire out he turned to look at the woman who had caused this to happen. She was quite a bit taller than him to begin with and he looked smaller still, as he was naked and hunched in pain.

"Please," he whined. The pain must have been horrible. Autumn reached out and, with one quick and smooth motion, broke his nose.

"Please, what?" her voice was flat.

He clutched his nose, "stop!"

He was almost blind at this point from pain and fire damage, so he never saw her kick coming. She hit his knee square and strong. It snapped back with a satisfying crunch and a grunt.

"No," Autumn replied.

He fell to the ground again. He was no longer screaming. His fear and pain had taken over and he was trembling. He didn't want to die, but his imagination was running rampant with ideas on the

disfigurement she could cause. That and pain were far
more real to him than actual death at that moment.

"Take the money," he said crying. "Go."

"Is that it?"

Autumn stomped down on his stomach splitting the
skin and exposing the muscle tissue to the open night
air. He was losing a lot of blood.

"Did you show mercy?" she asked. "She was a
child. Tell me where she is now."

"You'll kill me."

"I could have killed you at any time. This can go
on for a long time still. You can't win this, and I
won't stop."

He cried. Sobbed really. His body shook as he
truly understood what was happening.

"Please don't kill me."

"Where… is… she?" Autumn's patience was
running short.

"Please-" Autumn stomped down on his throat
ending his plea. He could no longer talk or breathe.
The look in his eyes said that he understood these
facts. He clutched at his throat as though he could
find a way to open the passage for air. Skin came
away under his fingers as he dug, but there was no
salvation to be found. She turned and walked back to
the clearing.

Autumn reappeared in the clearing. Phil had pulled
himself over to a gravestone and was seated propped
against it. It didn't appear that Danielle Metcalf cared
much that her final resting place was being used as a
seat. Autumn strode over to him with purpose. Phil
motioned like he might be casting some spell or

another. She stopped in her tracks and watched what he was doing. He looked confused. His mouth continued to move as nothing happened, so she resumed walking in his direction. When she drew close enough she knew why his spell hadn't worked, he was praying instead. Autumn knelt down beside him.

"Where's her body, Phil?"

"At home: 1221 University Ave. Apartment D. It's a basement apartment. I didn't start this to hurt anyone, honest. I just wanted to use magic. I-I was really good at it. It was the only thing I was ever really good at. I'm not really smart or anything. Not like other kids I went to school with. Scott was meaner. We were both picked on our whole lives, since we were kids. We thought that, with magic, we wouldn't be picked on anymore. That's all. I never shot up a school or bombed a plane or nothin. It all just got out of hand. That's all. I didn't mean nothin. I-I'm sorry."

"Yeah? Are you really sorry?" Autumn asked him. "Did society really push you to do it? You want that story on the news? Maybe a book deal? How about a movie? You already cast yourself in your mind?"

"No," Phil whimpered and looked down. "I just... I realize what I've done."

"Oh yeah? A kid who hadn't done anything to you or anyone is dead. Now you expect me to give you credit for an epiphany? This isn't a movie, Phil. The end credits won't save you from what you've done."

"Please. You can't," he was crying. His fear was palpable. "You need me. I have magical barriers all around the apartment and if I don't take them down

14

you'll never get in to find her."

"Your death will take care of that. You think you're better than your friend and those people you were talking about: the school shooter and the bomber? Well, you're not," Autumn spoke sternly. "You're right there with them. You've gotten really good at justifying your actions, Phil. You've been doing it with each step further down the road you've gone. So did those people. You see yourself as the hero of your own story, but you're really the villain of Katelyn Bradshaw's. All villains see themselves as heroes, Phil. The problem you ran into is that Katie's story had a far more powerful hero: me. That's what this all comes down to. Nothing more."

Autumn placed her hand on his chest and pressed him against the grave stone behind him. He fought with all the strength he had left, but he found her strength as absolute as a baby finds an adult's. She slowly increased the pressure as she felt his ribs bend and then crack under the pressure. She felt the beat of his heart as his sternum pressed against it, causing Phil intense pain and fear. She didn't stop pressing until she felt his heart stop beating and her hand curled around his spine. She could never be too cautious when it came to wizards.

CHAPTER TWO

Autumn grabbed the case and walked back to her car, away from the carnage in the cemetery and stripped off her costume as she strode. She hated wearing that kind of attire, but its effect could prove uniquely useful sometimes. She cleaned her hands and arms with the shirt to take care of the excess blood leftover from tonight's work. When she reached her car, she popped open the trunk, then inserted the case and removed a personal bag. She had more reasonable clothes to wear inside the bag now that she could be more comfortable. Her shirt was off already, so she slid on a black hooded sweatshirt she'd picked up at a concert she had attended the year before on a job. It proclaimed that amusement was required. How whimsical.

She wriggled out of her tight skirt and slipped on a pair of loose sweat pants. She rarely applied any effort to dress well unless work required it. Fashion really made no sense to her. She didn't downplay her appearance on purpose, but she generally wanted to avoid attention and her appearance tended to create difficulty. With her hood up over her head, she mostly drew attention for her height. At that point, with her muscular build, many people could assume she was a man and not look twice.

A memory returned to her of a night when a drunken guy had made a mistake thinking she was a man. He had really wanted to take home the guy she had looked like. She chuckled to herself as she thought about what she needed to do to finish the night's work. Her laugh sounded empty and felt hollow. The rest of this night would prove to be extremely difficult for many people. Autumn tended to maintain an aloof nature toward other people she met or worked with. In fact, her attitude came a little too easily in regard to others. She tended to have trouble connecting with people and made little effort to change that in any work relationships.

She packed away her now very bloody costume and squared away everything into her trunk so that nothing showed out of the ordinary. She was driving a base level Toyota Corolla currently. With all the abuse her vehicles took on any given job, she rarely put much effort into picking anything. Price and some basic functionality were usually the only factors in her buying decisions. She plugged the address into her GPS and looked at the route it showed to their apartment building. They were in a pretty low rent district judging by all the manufacturing that surrounded the small residential area. She guessed that if they had succeeded in tonight's endeavors they would have instantly moved to a better neighborhood.

The route she ended up taking was not the neat and clean direct route her GPS unit described. Computers didn't understand caution and surveillance. Autumn circled the block first to get a better idea of the surroundings she would be dealing with. It was low rent, but there were signs that some of the building owners were taking steps to improve the area somewhat. It didn't appear as bad as she had expected. She slowed as she passed the building to get an idea of which windows were to the basement. The entrance for Apartment D was in the rear of the building. That was very fortuitous for her. She pulled her car into the back lot and stopped so as to block most outside views of the back door she'd be using.

Carefully, she approached the stairwell that led down to the steel door leading into their apartment. She was not as confident as she had sounded before that all the spells would have been removed by the death of the caster. She knew of items that had been enchanted properly which kept their enchantment long after the spell caster died. She didn't know all that much about magic or its specific rules. Since Phil had not argued with her, she had thought that her assumption was correct. Looking at this stairwell she was not nearly so sure. She had been on the wrong side of a bad assumption before.

"Well," she spoke quietly to herself. "I can see no other way to check."

She had her right hand wrapped around the grip of her forty-five and her left arm up to guard and open the door. There was some hope that there would be a warning first should any of the spells have remained active. She slowly walked down each of the six concrete steps.

Nothing happened.

She reached out to try the door.

Holding her breath.

Nothing happened.

She relaxed. No defensive spells yet. This would be the easiest part. She gripped the knob and gave it a sharp push. The door frame on the inside cracked and gave way to her insistent entrance. She had rarely found any door that could keep her out if she wanted in. Once inside, the apartment was dark and rather spooky looking. These guys had taken themselves, laughingly, too seriously as only lifelong nerds could. Thick drapes covered the small windows of their basement apartment. The room was almost totally dark, so she searched the wall until she found a switch.

The room was instantly bathed in red light from a Gothic-looking, wrought-iron, overhead fixture that hung a bit too low with the already low ceiling. The mood and ambiance continued around the room. Autumn was in awe of their conviction to decoration. She stood in a small living room and first noticed there was no TV. She didn't see a computer either. No electronics she would have expected from their age group. Maybe this was their dedicated spell room. Maybe they thought this shit would help them pick up girls. She couldn't be sure what those two were thinking at any given time.

There was a table that covered one wall almost entirely. On it she saw a multitude of instruments and ingredients for magical rituals. Here she found the serious work being done. There was no doubt that these two were into some form of very dark magic. There were many sharp objects, bones, and even small animal corpses on the table. The corpses appeared to be fairly fresh. Some of those parts might have been used in whatever traps they had planned for Autumn in the graveyard. She avoided touching any of the liquids or other items. Curiosity would do her no good when it came to this table.

The living room was quite cramped with all they had crammed into it for work. There was also a door to a kitchen and a hallway leading off the small room. Autumn checked the kitchen quickly, but then headed down the hallway first. There she found doors to two bedrooms and a bathroom along the short walls. As she came to the end she heard soft noises coming from one of the bedrooms. She still held one of her pistols at the ready and swung the door open. She found a soft night light switched on in the room and quite a surprise to go with it. There was a young girl in a large dog kennel next to the bed against an outside wall. The girl was about Katie's age but, from what her father had said, this girl was too small to be Katie. She was also black, and Clarence didn't seem to be that progressive.

The girl was a mess. She looked drugged and utterly terrified. Whimpering quietly and glancing up, the girl gazed almost dreamily as she heard Autumn enter. Realization shot through her like electricity and drew her out of her dreamlike state. She began to make muffled noises and rattle the kennel furiously. Autumn saw that she had a kind of fashioned muzzle on so that she couldn't bite or speak. There was no way for Autumn to know how long she had been in that cage or in this hellhole.

There was a shiny padlock on the kennel door keeping the girl contained. Autumn put one hand around it and tugged down. The bottom of the kennel gate gave before the lock did and the door swung open from the force. The girl was quite wary, but she appeared glad to step out and stand up fully for the first time in a while. As she stood Autumn realized that she was completely naked, so Autumn yanked the blanket off the bed and wrapped it around her small frame. The girl was quite thin. Too thin. She probably hadn't been fed well during her captivity if at all. Autumn had no way to tell how long it had been since the girl had last eaten. She figured the girl should get some kind of medical care as soon as she could manage.

Autumn looked over the muzzle to see how it was attached. It had been fashioned out of leather and fit fairly well. She guessed it had been made specifically for this girl. Maybe she was a fighter and a biter. Good for her. She saw that, once again, a shiny new padlock was attached in the back to keep it locked in place. Autumn pulled out a small knife she kept in her pocket. It would be easier on the girl to cut the straps than to try and break the lock. The sight of the knife caused the girl to writhe so Autumn had to grab her tightly with her left arm so she didn't cut her accidentally.

The muzzle fell from the little girl's face and she turned to look at her savior. The girl's eyes were bloodshot and one of them was black. Her lip was split and there was dried blood around her nose. She had bruising around her body and arms. Yeah, she was a fighter.

"What's your name?" Autumn tried to sound kind as she asked.

"Clare," the girl spoke after a cough. Her voice was raspy from disuse.

"Well, Clare, let's get you something to wear besides that blanket. I'm certain that I don't have anything that will fit you."

Clare was not even five feet tall and hadn't reached a hundred pounds yet. Tight fitting for Autumn was still a large.

"He kept my clothes in the closet." Claire's voice was improving rapidly. She seemed to be recovering well also. Autumn sensed a strength in this little girl. Maybe too much strength for a girl who appeared to be under ten.

"Good," Autumn said, as she walked over to the closet and opened it. Inside she found a lot of T-shirts and a couple dark robes. She also found one hanger with a small T-shirt and a pair of pants. She pulled it out and handed it all to Clare. After that she turned around to give the girl the first privacy she may have had in a while. Clare spoke from behind her.

"Thank you. Are you with the police? Are my parents coming?"

"No, I'm private," Autumn said not knowing how to explain what she did. "I can work to get you home, but I have to find the other girl first."

"Oh, her," her voice became quiet. "I have something terrible to tell you."

"I know. I still have to take her to her parents."

"He kept threatening to do the same to me. It was horrible," she said as she began to cry.

"Well, he didn't. You get to go home. Dressed yet?"

"You're not very nice, you know? I'm scared."

"And she's dead. Are you dressed yet?" Autumn had little patience for domestic affairs. None of it felt natural to her.

"Yes," she sounded meek. People had probably treated her softly until this ordeal.

"Follow me. I need to check the other rooms."

"She's in the kitchen. They cleared out the fridge to keep her in it. They made me help with the whole thing."

Autumn walked to the kitchen. She did a quick visual check on the other bedroom and the bathroom to make sure there were no other surprises before walking down the hallway. She found a messy room that had nothing of interest to anyone but the now dead occupant. She had no desire to go digging through his things. Clare refused to enter the kitchen. Autumn opened the fridge to see a young blond girl folded carefully into the fridge at the base. One final surprise caught her eye as well. There was an even smaller boy packed in on top of Katie. She turned to address Clare who was still at the door-way.

"Here," she tossed her keys to Clare. "Go to my car outside. It's the blue Toyota right outside the door. Get the trunk open for me."

Clare darted off, glad to leave the grizzly scene of this apartment. Autumn lifted both children into her arms. She'd have to find a way to find the boy's parents, so they could get some terrible news. She was surprised that two human bodies could feel so light and delicate in her arms. So little mass in either of them. Something seemed worse because of that. Life not lived, perhaps?

Outside she found her trunk open and Clare in the

passenger seat crying. She carefully loaded both bodies into her car. The whole time she worried she would break them. She closed the trunk and climbed into the driver's seat. Her night still had a while to go. First on her docket was to find the family who had hired her and deliver the terrible news.

CHAPTER THREE

It was early still though the night felt long. The sun was barely touching the landscape on the lower areas. The streets were empty and the town still dead. Autumn's mind was locked firmly on the two kids in the trunk and their parents. She never felt comfortable in her own skin when a job turned sour. No one ever liked to fail, and Autumn very rarely did. This time she'd been called in too late. Usually, when things went sideways, it meant that an item wasn't retrieved, or money was lost. This time it meant someone's life.

To be realistic people died in her line of work all the time. Often, she was responsible for that occurrence, but that was when it was acceptable. The two sleazy wizards tonight had found out first-hand what that was like. Even collateral damage occurred and could be an acceptable part of the job as long as the objective had been achieved. Results covered a lot of messy details. Tonight, however, Kaitlyn had died, and the job was solely to rescue her. Mr. Bradshaw was not going to be happy with that result.

Autumn had made it clear to Clarence that this was

a very real possibility, but he hadn't listened. Parents never listened. He had treated her warning like the fine print on a loan application or a terms of use agreement. He was sitting in his warm home, drinking some whiskey, and waiting for his daughter to come running into his arms. Powerful people were never prepared for the truly terrible to happen. In their world people had the power to avert tragedy. It made no sense that two rogue men could destroy their safety and comfort so totally. Clarence would be glad to know that the men responsible had met truly horrible ends, but he'd still blame Autumn for Katie's death.

Autumn drove to the address she had been given to return Katie. The neighborhood was nice, if a bit redundant. All the houses looked too similar for her tastes. This kind of middle class show-of-wealth held no interest for Autumn. She had seen power, true power, and it rarely resided in places like this. She began to wonder if Clarence could afford to pay her the agreed upon price. These neighborhoods were full of people who spent their last dime and credit trying to keep up the appearance of wealth. She backed into his driveway so that prying eyes could not see what in the trunk.

"Wait here," she told Clare.

"I'm scared," the young girl said meekly.

"Nothing will hurt you here," Autumn opened her door as she spoke. "This place is safe."

Autumn stood up out of the car and walked up the short path toward the front door. The subdivision was so bland that she began to wonder if she had the right house. The lights popped on as she approached, so she assumed this was the place. Stepping onto the

small cement porch she knocked on the door.
Somehow, using a doorbell felt out of place. It would
emit a cheery tone that would betray the night.
Standing there unmoving, she waited to see how this
would play out.

The door flew open and Clarence appeared...
looking down. His expression slowly switched from
joyous to confused as his eyes raised to look up at
Autumn for answers. Standing about an inch or two
shorter than her, his face betrayed how much agitation
that fact added to his emotional state.

"Where is she? Oh!" his expression turned hard.
"You want your money first. No way. Not until I see
my daughter. Haven't we suffered enough?"

Autumn nodded and held her arm out toward her
car with her palm upturned. Clarence led the way as
they walked toward her vehicle. When Clarence
caught the outline of the girl in the front seat his whole
body jumped of its own volition. He hurried in front
of Autumn to the front of the car while she continued
to the trunk. She knew what was coming, so she made
herself useful by opening the trunk and preparing for
what was next.

Clarence froze in his place when he got a good look
at the girl in the front seat. She refused to look at him
or even show that she knew he was there. He could
see that she was crying. He shot a look back at
Autumn and his heart dropped out of his chest to
another realm of existence entirely. Autumn held her
gaze steady over the open trunk lid showing no
emotion at all. Slowly, Clarence plodded toward the
rear of the Corolla. All his strength had drained from
his body in record time. He was now running on

autopilot.

He turned the corner, froze in place, and then dropped to his knees. He was destroyed in that one glance. A single instant had changed his life and character forever. The garage door behind Autumn opened and Mrs. Bradshaw walked toward them. She seemed to be less hopeful from the beginning that things would turn out like a movie. Clarence noticed her approach and quickly stood and rushed to her. He tried to keep her from looking into the trunk at the gruesome image. The chivalry seemed more for his protection than hers.

However, a mother will not be kept from her child, no matter the circumstances or forces standing against her. Autumn lifted Katie from the trunk carefully in both arms and brought her into the garage. Slowly, she walked the few steps, making it all feel like an abridged funeral march. Autumn held her so easily that it served to enhance how frail the girl looked. Like a tiny bird who fell from the nest too early. This one had not been ready to fly.

Katie's mother touched her face in stunned disbelief. The shock served to protect her from reality, however, at that moment of truth, the situation became real. All too real. Mrs. Bradshaw wailed and slid down to her knees. Her tears poured from her eyes as the world around her was lost to the swell of emotion she felt. Autumn slid Katie into her mother's arms. She felt that was where she belonged at that moment. Mrs. Bradshaw held her tight, as her body was wracked with emotional tremors.

Autumn looked at Clarence. His reaction she was ready for. He'd made the next leap since his wife was covering grief. There were fires of rage burning in his eyes. He stared at Autumn seething with rage begging for a target. She'd encountered this before and she'd expected it here. All she could do now was wait to see how he chose to proceed.

"How could this happen?" were the first words out of his mouth.

"It was a kidnapping. Bad things happen when bad men try to hurt people. Even the ones you love," Autumn's tone and volume never changed. She remained emotionless to his outburst.

"You were supposed to save her," Clarence said, flailing his arms. His rage requiring a frenetic outlet of some kind.

"True," she replied. "Or bring her back. You knew this was a possibility when you brought me in so late."

"You should've been faster," he said as the situation declined to its terrible ending.

"Stop," Autumn said calmly and held up her right hand. "We're not doing this now. This outcome was always a possibility. They were dark wizards with a distinct purpose. We can stand here and try to sort out blame all day long, but that won't change anything that has already happened. The fact remains that I did the job. Hate me if you want. Pay me and I'll leave."

"Pay you? Ha! You won't get one red cent from me," he said puffing his chest out.

"Big mistake. You're emotional right now. I understand. Don't make another one."

"You'll hear-"

He never finished. Autumn's hand shot forward and lifted him up by the throat. She stood with Clarence in her outstretched hand three feet off the ground. Her eyes were locked on his now and the rage had transferred from him to her. Fear had entered his eyes.

"Pay me," she said, again in a flat tone. This time there was obvious signs of emotion behind her tone waiting to break free. "I just left two wizards dead tonight and I won't hesitate to make it three if you push me any farther."

Clarence nodded as much as he could in the position he was in and Autumn dropped him. Mrs. Bradshaw had come around enough to see what was happening. Maybe his attitude had roused her from her grief.

"Pay her, Clarence. Katie's been dead for a long time. Just pay her and send her on her way."

He looked back and forth between the two women. He felt powerless. It was written on his face. That was really his problem. No one liked to feel powerless over their own life and this was a man who was a big fish in a small pond. He was used to making others feel powerless. It would have made him feel better and helped him regain his composure to push Autumn around a bit. Clarence simply wasn't that powerful. He would never be that strong and he could feel it.

"Fine. Where's the case?" he said trying to maintain some show of strength.

"Here," Autumn reached into the trunk and pulled out the steel case. She dropped it in front of him and stood there waiting. She was done giving him any space to be an ass. He picked it up and walked off into the house. The two women were alone outside for a time, but Katie's mother took no notice. She had said her piece and was back to her daughter again.

Clarence walked out of the front door and motioned Autumn over that way. She walked over waiting to see what he would do next. He held the case out to Autumn. She didn't take it.

"Open it," Autumn's voice was firm.

"It-"

"Just do it," Autumn spoke flatly, with face was set firmly.

Clarence opened the case and turned it for Autumn to see. She reached in and took out the bundles of cash. She never took the case.

"Can't trust a wizard."

"Cunt!" Clarence spat venom at her as he spoke.

"I'll give you that one. It's been a hard night. I've done my part and now I'm leaving. Track me and I'll kill you. Come after me and I'll kill you. Got that?"

Clarence set his jaw hard. This was a hard pill for him to swallow and Autumn was giving him no space to posture. And she had no intention of changing that to suit his fragile ego.

"We won't," he said and took a long hard breath.

"Thank you for finding Katie," her mother spoke up. "What will you do with the boy and the girl in the front?"

"Take these two to the hospital and drop them. She needs medical care and they'll work to find their parents. The authorities can handle the rest from here."

"Okay," Mrs. Bradshaw said. Her face was red and puffy. "Thank you. But please, one woman to another, leave. This is hard enough as is and seeing you isn't making this any easier."

Autumn did not respond. There was nothing to say.

31

She closed her trunk and pulled out of the driveway. She searched for the hospital on her GPS and left the subdivision. What a train wreck this night had turned out to be.

CHAPTER FOUR

Autumn was on her way across town toward the hospital along the purple line her GPS had mapped out. She had decided early against going to the police because they would further complicate this whole situation. This town had worn out any charm it had, so she was ready to be out and on to her next job. Anywhere else would be preferable to this place right now. Angry wizards were something Autumn preferred to avoid whenever there was no profit in dealing with them. A small voice spoke up as she drove.

"Where will you go?"

She thought about that and realized she had no place to be at that time. She had no job to take or even a prospect. She was currently held down by no obligation at all. Her options were open, and she could go anywhere. Simply drive off into the distance and go wherever the road took her. Take a vacation of sorts. Go somewhere away from dead children and mad wizards. It was often advisable to take a little time after a job turned sideways like this one had.

Travel somewhere comfortable and relaxing. Possibly warm with sand and warm waves.

"After you leave us, what'll you do?"

It hit her that the small voice was coming from her small passenger. She had almost completely forgotten that she had any live cargo.

"Away," Autumn said both to the girl and herself.

"But where?" the little girl was insistent.

"Why do you care?"

"Who will save the others?" the little girl was quietly crying again.

"What others?"

"The men who had me worked for another man. A scary man. He said there were other kids in other places like us. Don't they need to be saved?" she spoke through her tears. Autumn listened while the little girl tried to collect herself. She was making a plea to Autumn the only way she knew how. Autumn could see a strength within her. She was still being rational after everything that had taken place.

"I'm no hero, kid," Autumn finally responded after a moment of silence. "I was paid to rescue Katie. She died in the process and now that it's done, I'm done. Got it?"

"But the others'll be scared... like me," she said fighting back the tears. Maybe she had read that Autumn didn't like the crying. "You can save them and stop the bad men. Just like you saved me."

"Kid, there's something you need to understand," Autumn spoke as carefully as she could. She had no experience with children. "There are always bad men in this world. No one can stop them all. To many people, I'm a bad guy. Can you understand that? It all depends on what you want in life and how you plan to get it. All you can do is look out for yourself and try to help the people you care about. This is no longer my business."

The girl couldn't hold back the tears any longer. She wasn't bawling like a kid with a scraped knee. No, she was softly weeping in the passenger seat for the lost children of the world that she now understood far better than any child has any right to.

"I am trying to help people I care about," she continued to cry. "I can't save them."

"Then stop caring," Autumn replied curtly.

"Why," Clare said after a moment. "Why did you save me? Why not save some other girl? What did I do?"

"You were there when I showed up," Autumn's tone remained unaffected. "Nothing more."

"That can't be all. It can't be. Mommy said that God has a plan. She said when God closes a door he opens a window."

"Kid, your mom's an idiot. There's no great plan. No savior of us all. Life happens how it happens. You were there and still alive when I showed up. I was hired to come get Katie. It was chance, circumstance, luck, random, whatever helps you to deal with the fact that shit happens in this world. Be happy that someone hired me and that you lived longer."

The was a pause in the conversation. Autumn thought it was all over and they could drive in silence. She had no idea how to handle this kid. What did she want? Autumn couldn't run around saving everyone all the time. That didn't make any sense. Real heroes died. That was part of what made them heroes. She had no intention of running like mad until she died trying to save anyone she could find. She'd leave that to the plot of bad movies.

"What about the demon?" Clare said quietly. She had stopped crying again. Maybe she had run out of tears. She seemed defeated and weary. Something that seemed very out of place on such a small girl.

"Demon?" Autumn asked.

"The big bad man said that we were supposed to help him bring a demon to the world."

Autumn thought about that one for a moment. She'd been told about that kind of stuff before. This was why... well, it was why she had been made in the first place. That's what the team behind her creation said. She had been an experiment to see if mankind could create something that could take on this kind of stuff. Of course, that really made no sense, but that was what some guy in a lab coat had said. She generally found that she didn't trust guys in lab coats. Did she have some reason to be involved in this now if that was true? Did she care?

"You probably misheard him," Autumn finally responded. "People don't play with demons. That's just ridiculous. It was just something out of a book or nightmare."

"He called it a 'lesser god.' He told me that it was like a demon or something," her voice was intense when while she spoke. "He said it to me the only time he spoke to me. 'You'll be part of history.' That's what he told me. You're strong. You could fight it and save us all."

Could she? This all seemed so crazy. Maybe she

should at least hear the kid out. With the whole story she'd probably find all sorts of holes and make-believe stuff that would let her go along her merry way. At least then she could say she had listened. Might make the kid feel better. Autumn pulled into the empty parking lot of a diner that was still closed. She turned off the car.

"Okay, kid, tell me the whole story about this man and the demon."

"He came to them a while back. I'm not sure when," she seemed to perk up now that Autumn was listening. "I wasn't there when he first showed up, but I heard them talk about it. He gave them money and stuff. He told them he needed kids for something he was doing. They were happy working for him and stuff. At least they said they used to be. He told them he needed a live one. They complained a lot that he was too picky. They kept getting kids and he kept saying no. Katie was going to be one of them. They were sure she was the special one.

"They had picked me up before Katie, but they were certain she would be perfect. One of them told me they might keep me for themselves. He also said the only thing saving me was that they were waiting for 'Him' to show up and see who he liked. I don't know how long we waited. I never could see a clock or anything. One day the big bad man showed up. He came in and there was a lot of yelling. He seemed really mad about something. He came in and looked at Katie and told them she wouldn't work. They got mad too. Then he saw me. He bent down and looked at me really closely."

"What did he look like?" Autumn managed to ask.

Clare took time to think. She seemed set on helping as much as she could. Her face scrunched up as she tried to put her memories into words.

"I couldn't see well with the mask they had on me. He had black hair all over his head and face. His eyes were scary. He was kinda fat and dressed in a suit."

"Okay, go on."

"He looked at me really creepy, before standing up and telling the other two I might work. They seemed happy about that. Before they all left the room, he bent down again and told me: 'I'm going to summon a lesser god and you're going to help. You like that? You'll be part of history.' After that he left. That's when they got the idea to use Katie to get that book. The really scary one said they could take care of the bad man with that book. He was angry that the bad man said Katie wasn't right, so they killed her."

"That's how he said it?" Autumn asked. "He called it a lesser god?"

"Yeah. Just like that. He smiled when he saw me and then told them I might be privileged. I never forgot that moment. He looked really scary. I don't want to help bring a real monster here. The guy was, like, dirty and slimy, but clean. Like Jafar in Aladdin. He told them that if I was lucky I could help him with his plan. He said he'd rule the world.

"I was scared, but I couldn't do anything. That felt so long ago," Clare was trying to keep her voice even as she told the story. "They killed Katie and spent a lot of time yelling about 'Him' after that. I could tell they were scared of 'Him,' like I was. Then you came. You said you beat up the bad men and then saved me, so you must be really strong. Can you stop him? Can you stop the bad man? Please? You just gotta."

Autumn was lost. None of that made any real sense to her. She didn't know enough about magic. As far as she could tell there were no demons or gods or any of that. Maybe he was telling stories to scare a kid. He could be performing some magic that would make him more powerful. That seemed to be a real possibility. She simply couldn't tell what was true and what was the nightmare of a very terrified child.

"Kid, this is all above my pay grade," Autumn finally spoke. "I can't do anything about something that powerful if it's even real. I'll contact people who can do something about it, though. They'll look into it and find out what's best to do. Okay?"

The girl didn't look convinced. She had it in her mind that Autumn was a real hero. That wasn't Autumn's problem, however. She'd say something to someone and tell them where the girl was. That was the most she could do. She looked at the clock and saw that they had been talking for over half an hour. How had that taken so long? She started the car and left the parking lot. There wasn't much left in the trip to the hospital, so it only took ten more minutes.

The hospital was located outside of the main town. Autumn guessed it served all the towns around this one. It wasn't far out, but it was fairly busy. She guessed that there were enough people in the area to keep an emergency room hopping most of the time. When she pulled into the lot for the emergency room she saw a few people gathered there. Clarence was among the crowd.

Shit.

Her car was barely stopped before she was out of it

striding toward Clarence. This shit had to end here.

"You son of a bitch. I told you what would happen if you came after me."

"Wait!" he looked and sounded panicked.

A man standing slightly behind him stepped forward.

"I'm Thomas Karn of the Neolithic Consortium. I wish to apologize for Clarence's actions and talk to you. We have a job for you."

"Was this shit planned? How could you all have gotten here so quickly?" Autumn was hot and suspicious.

"Only partially," Thomas replied calmly. "We found out yesterday that you'd been retained by Clarence. We had him let us know how things were going because we wanted to hire you after you had finished with him. I'm from Chicago, as is my team," he said motioning to the people standing around him. "We were prepared to transport in whenever Clarence called me. My team is keeping us protected from both attack and eavesdropping. This isn't exactly how we prefer to do business, but you are hard to find."

"I'm listening," Autumn wondered what the NC could possibly want. They had a lot of power available to them and very deep pockets. She guessed that Clarence had contacted them when she had left, but she never expected to actually see them. It could pay very well to listen to what he had to say. It could also be a terrible trap.

"We've been following a cadre of rogue wizards. You stumbled on the outskirts of their group thanks to Clarence here," Thomas shot a quick glance toward Clarence as he spoke. "We believe that they're trying to summon a great and terrible beast to our world."

"Yeah, a lesser god," Autumn said casually.

"What? You know?"

"I hear things. What's the pitch?" Shit. She thought the kid might have been right.

"They know all our agents and will be on the lookout for our involvement," Thomas continued. "We'd like to hire you to infiltrate the group, stop the ritual, and kill the wizard at the top of the whole thing."

"You think I can just waltz in and stop a demon?" she asked.

"No, not at all. Stop it before they summon the demon. We're willing to pay you one million to go and kill the man in charge and another million if you should have to kill any powerful cohorts who could still pull off the spell and stop it from being replicated by anyone else. No matter what we want Andrzej Christos dead."

"That's quite an offer," she had to keep her eyes from popping at a number so high. "Sounds to me like you have no intention of paying. Am I supposed to die in the process? I'm opposed to suicide missions on principle."

"Not at all," Thomas didn't bat an eye as he spoke to her. He seemed to have expected her response. "This is worth the money. I've already spoken with Alexander DesChanes. He approved the payment and the hiring of you. I'm authorized to give you half a million up front so you can get whatever you need to pull this off. No restrictions. Do whatever you think is necessary. You have total carte blanche here."

"You've got five hundred grand on you? How

stupid do you think I am?" Autumn said sure this had to be a trap now.

"No," Thomas said smiling. Once again, he was ready. "I have an account number and a lock box key for you. In the box you'll find the money for you in cash. It's in St. Louis in a bank we control. Will you take the job, Lindsay Brown?"

She thought about the risk and the reward. Both were very large. Two million was more than she had ever made before. Hell, five hundred thousand was more than she had ever made for one job. That amount must mean that the danger on this one was serious. She was confident but had no illusions that there were things out there more powerful than she was.

"I've got nothing else to do," Autumn responded with a shrug. "Will you take care of the kids in the car? One's alive and the other is dead."

"Yes, Clarence already informed us about the other children. We'll see to it that everything is taken care of and you will not be involved in anything that has transpired here. You are safe."

Autumn heard a car door open and saw Clare run across the space to her. When she arrived, she latched onto Autumn's leg in the most powerful hug the little girl could manage.

"I heard what you said," Clare said with renewed tears. She was smiling this time. "You're going to stop the bad man."

"Kid, why do you have so much faith in me?" Autumn asked, exasperated by dealing with children.

"Because," she said beaming up at Autumn. "Wonder Woman never lets the bad guys win. You're a real-life Wonder Woman."

"Kid, that's fucked up. These guys will find your parents. Go home and stop believing in Wonder Woman."

A woman from the crowd broke off and came to retrieve the girl.

"I'll always believe in you, Lindsay."

The woman led the girl off toward the hospital. She still needed to be checked out by doctors. She probably had numerous things wrong with her beside believing that Autumn was some kind of superhero. Thomas pulled an envelope out of his coat and handed it to Autumn.

"This has the key and the account number in it that you'll need. Thank you for your help."

"Just come through with that money when this is over."

Autumn took the envelope and walked off toward her car. She had been in such a hurry she hadn't turned it off. She climbed in and rolled up the passenger side window. They had already removed the young boy from the trunk, so she was free of any obligations here. Or she would have been, but she had agreed to take another job. She drove off into the rising sun in search of adventure and demons.

CHAPTER FIVE

Autumn filled up her car with fuel. First thing on her mind was to secure the payment and be certain this was a legitimate job. It was hard to believe that the Neolithic Consortium would try to fake her out, but rich people get and stay rich by finding ways to make and keep money. She couldn't assume that they were trustworthy simply because they were powerful. She set off on the road to St. Louis and, hopefully, wealth beyond anything she had ever known.

As she drove she thought more about the Consortium. They were an old and powerful organization according to what she knew. The NC was both an organization of wizards and a collection of business interests. The whole thing, both sides, was controlled by a man named Alexander DesChanes. His business holdings made him one of the very wealthiest men in the world. That would be power enough for most men, but Alexander wanted more. The NC was also the largest single collection of wizards on Earth. They helped to bring order to magic... as controlled by Alexander DesChanes.

Autumn knew of them and had heard even more. She had never worked directly for them, though she had been hired by wizards who claimed membership like Clarence. There were so many rumors about them and their control over the world. They were connected to the Illuminati, the Masons, the New World Order, and even the old gods. They controlled every government on the planet depending on who was talking, and every economy was influenced by their hand. Almost any conspiracy theory known had one member attributing it all to the Neolithic Consortium. They stood astride the world as both angels and demons.

Autumn had no opinion on them and didn't care to form one outside of their ability to pay their bills. Two million dollars would buy her a lot of freedom to do what she wanted and go where she wanted. After she had struck off on her own, she had lost all connection to any but her own resources. It was very difficult to build the pool needed as an independent without something to start with. That being said, Autumn has never liked working for anyone else. From basic jobs to the military, she had never enjoyed being someone else's tool. After she was changed they had expected her to work for them. She had a different idea in her head. No one would rule her future.

Autumn hated to think back to her past. There was little value in it, but as she drove her mind turned back. She remembered her days in the Marines and then in SEAL training. She had loved the challenge and physical training, even the structure. The work had been challenging until she had the realization that she was nothing more than an asset to some commander. She was then offered a chance to be much more and took it. A shady group had taken her and changed her in almost every way possible creating something new. She truly hated to think about those men in lab coats.

The sun rose higher as the morning wore on. The day was showing signs of heat already. Midwestern summers could be so unpredictable. She knew that it would be hot, but anything else was going to be a surprise. She still had hours left to travel before she reached St. Louis, but she didn't waste them reflecting on the past. If the money was there as promised, then she had a job to do. Judging by the pay she had to assume that this guy was both powerful and dangerous. She was supposed to find and stop him however possible.

Of course, killing him was the easy answer.

Or was it? Killing a wizard was always a difficult proposition. She'd done it many times of course, but it was tricky, and Andrzej sounded like he was powerful and had an organization under him. She had taken care of that before as well, but it always served to make things far more complicated. There were bound to be other wizards involved and any one of them could be a difficult task requiring planning. That was all before the possibility of a demon entered the equation. Autumn had no magical power.

Well, that wasn't entirely true. She had no understanding of spell work and she couldn't cast any spells or enchantments, but that was not the limit of her power. Those men in lab coats had enhanced her. They had enhanced her body both technologically and magically. The procedure was one of the worst memories she had. The group had been trying to study magic scientifically and believed that they could create something new through a mixture of the two. Autumn was an experiment.

A successful one.

She had been recruited, but she had volunteered as soon as she heard the pitch. Despite their explaining, there was no way to truly understand the proposal ahead of time. The doctors had replaced much of her musculature tissue, as well as her bones, with materials vastly stronger than what was in her body to begin with. Her ligaments, tendons, and cartilage had to go as well. She still didn't fully understand what they had done or what the new mixture of biological and technological in her own body was. What she knew was that before she had been at peak human capability and now she was super-human.

A procedure like that should have killed her. In fact, it had killed every person who they had tried it with before. They had used a magical ritual to keep her alive during the overhaul of her body. Somehow, unlike those before her, Autumn had absorbed the magic along the way, further strengthening her and her connection to the enhancement. She now healed faster, and her skin seemed to be much stronger. She had never found her total physical limits and really didn't know how to test them well. Was it possible that she had magical abilities? Maybe. The Neolithic Consortium could probably help her answer some of those questions.

Of course, any group that offered to help always wanted something in return. Quid pro quo. With

Autumn they would surely want to add her to their asset sheet. The NC would of course want to study her and once they knew what she could do, they'd want to use her. She was tired of being under anyone's control, so those questions would have to wait. She had always been cautious of easy answers and that one really made her think.

It was probably best that she not allow herself to be under the control of anyone either. Who wouldn't want the answers she had inside of her? If what she had heard was even slightly true, the Neolithic Consortium might even be the people behind the men in lab coats. Someone had to have funded them and given them their ability to work. The NC had the knowledge, power, and resources to make something like that happen. Now that she thought about it the answer seemed obvious. Did they know? Thomas hadn't known her name. Or was he playing a game?

The bank could make for a phenomenal trap location. Maybe they were the ones who had funded her creation and they wanted her back. She hadn't gotten that feeling until now, so she was less inclined to believe it. Driving alone along the Interstate made for a perfect scenario for paranoia. It was a real possibility, but she thought it was an outside possibility. Intricate traps were more the realm of movies and stories. If they had wanted her it would have made more sense to grab her at the hospital with overwhelming force. Either way, the idea of their involvement with the men in lab coats was all too plausible.

Best to stay independent. She still worked for other people, but she controlled what jobs she took and how she operated. The difference was slight, but very important. Autumn refused to be caught in a situation where she was stripped of choice. These were her abilities now and she would be the one to decide when and how to use them.

Again, she found herself reflecting on the past. Back to the present.

Once she knew that the money was hers she'd contact the number given in the envelope and get the rest of the details. Of course, she would take some time to check those for herself. She had learned the hard way that she never wanted to follow blindly. It might behoove her to find a magical hangout in St. Louis after she arrived. That might provide her with information independently of the NC.

Autumn had always felt most comfortable on her own, even when she was young. She had never been much of a team player. Fewer people involved meant fewer people to fail or betray her. She felt best when she had no one to depend on and no one had to depend on her. Much of her life had been spent amassing power and skill. It was most comforting to rely on her own abilities than anyone else. Moving parts meant weak points.

She was no Wonder Woman.

She drove on in silence through the growing Missouri heat. The Interstate wound around and through the hills and mountains showing her a beauty she never took the time to notice. Autumn continued to fight her own memory as she drove to find her greatest adventure yet.

CHAPTER SIX

Autumn stopped at a local diner on her way into St. Louis. It served as an easy spot to regroup and prepare for the day ahead. She was hungry, and she might have to spend the day dealing with both wizards and bankers. She wasn't sure which was worse, but everything about that sounded awful. After placing her order for eggs, ham, toast, and a cup of coffee she pulled out the envelope again that Thomas had given her.

There was no writing on the outside and the contents were surprisingly banal considering what they were to lead her to. The key was small and brass. The handle was round and engraved on it was a simple 35. There were no other markings on the key. She saw no brand or even a warning not to copy. Hell, the key didn't even have the usual hole in it to fit onto a keyring.

There was also a small slip of unlined white paper, maybe two inches square. One side of the sheet had ten digits on it in the form of a phone number. She assumed that the number would put her in contact with

Thomas Karn. She'd call that number only after she
had the money in hand. There was no reason to tip her
hand or give them any more knowledge of her
movements than they already had. Her physical
location could be the last bit of information they
needed. There still stood the chance that this whole
business was a setup for her. The antipodal side
contained a name and a series of numbers.

Old World Travelers'.

That was no bank she had ever heard of before, but
she figured that was to be expected. It made sense that
the Neolithic Consortium would have its own banks
for its own people. They owned many banks,
according to what she had read, and controlling the
bank wizards used would give them further control
over the magical world. Mages probably had different
banking needs than other people, but separate systems
were inherently corruptible. All the more reason
Autumn never wanted to join that world entirely.

Autumn's food arrived, and she ate disinterestedly.
She was looking for the location of this bank she'd
have to find to get the money. The eggs and ham were
passable, but she ate mostly for the sustenance. The
coffee was strong, and she enjoyed that well enough,
but she couldn't live on coffee alone. She had tried,
and it had never worked.

To find the bank she'd taken her phone out and
powered it on. She kept a smart phone for the utility
of it, but didn't leave it on when she wasn't directly
using it. She never used the number that was attached
to the account that she paid for. Shifting that number
every month or two as she used the phone provided
her with another wall of security. For that purpose,

she used an app that let her create a different number to give out. That number she could burn much faster than the main number. She could then use that number for any of her communications. She also burned the main number once or twice a year.

The phone itself had been commissioned to be built by an engineer she had known. It used the basic Android operating system, but it had no connection to any specific carrier. This allowed her to use different providers in different places with different numbers. At some point in the future she would look into having another one built, but this one was still functioning well, and she liked it. The whole system allowed her to stay off the grid when she wanted to be off the grid without losing the information accessibility.

She found the location of the bank and plotted a few different courses to get there. She never liked to fully rely on a device for anything. Best to see the map and know alternate routes should something go awry. This job had been, so far, quite easy. Too easy. She knew that would be changing soon and she wanted to be prepared. Finishing her food, she left cash on the table for the bill and a tip. She'd find a good spot and stakeout the bank for a bit before she actually entered. Never trust wizards.

The bank was downtown not far from the baseball stadium. Though she would have liked to watch it from before it opened until some time after, she wasn't early enough for that, and waiting for tomorrow would waste valuable time. She parked a few blocks away and walked closer to the bank. Surveillance was easier the smaller an object the watcher could be. She could find a good spot to hide without a car much easier. She kept the hood of her sweatshirt up despite the heat. It made her a bit conspicuous, but without it she was more suspicious still. She had not seen many people enter or leave the bank for the couple hours she had watched. She figured this was not a bank open to the general public.

Time to move.

Keeping the hood down and her hands in the front pocket she walked toward the door. She was curious what security they would have at a bank like this. No one on the street noticed her movement toward the bank. Somehow moments like this always felt bigger than they looked when they were happening. She knew that she was embarking on a grand new case, but everyone else was going about their own Friday normally. The people walking by had no clue who she was or what it was that she did. Would their reactions be any different if they had known that she had brutally killed two wizards that very morning? Two young men whose lives were open in front of them?

Right inside the bank there was a guard and a large metal detector. That seemed to be too simple. Autumn had a lot of metal in the replacement parts in her body. So far it seemed that the magic helped mask her from other detection, but this was a wizard bank. What different methods might they have? This might not even detect metal. Or it could detect more than metal alone. Would they find out this simply?

"If you could lower your hood, please," the guard said as he pointed to a camera on the wall facing her.

Autumn hated cameras. As much as possible she avoided both still images and videos. No one needed to have a lasting record of her actions or her appearance. She had caught an ex-lover using a hidden camera at one point. It cost him all his library of recordings, three computers, two cameras, and the comfortable functioning of his right leg. Fortunately, that had been before cloud storage.

She lowered her hood and stepped through the device.

Beep Beep Beep

Shit!

"Ma'am, could you please empty your pockets?"

Of course, she hadn't emptied her pockets before walking through.

Autumn stepped back. She pulled out her keys, some change, and a small wallet. The guard motioned her through again. She held her breath as she stepped through the machine again. Nothing happened this time. Tragedy had been averted... this time. Now she had to move on to the next hurdle. She took the items and returned them to her pockets before walking into the lobby.

The lobby was small, but very lush. The only clients this bank dealt with were VIPs. She now figured this wasn't even open to the general wizarding public. The few employees made no secret of the fact that Autumn looked like no one's VIP. In her sweatshirt and sweat pants she appeared to be physically revolting to many of the people in the room. Her soft shoes made no noise on the shiny marble floor as she strode over to the first desk she reached. There was no wall of tellers here, only a small grid of wooden desks, each with a professional behind it ready to help each customer. Each proper customer that was.

Autumn approached the first desk where the woman didn't look like she was repulsed by the look of tennis shoes. She stood by the desk while she waited for the impeccably dressed woman behind it to notice her. The woman looked up at her showing no sign of the shock the rest of the room conveyed. In fact, she showed no sign of any emotion at all. She watched Autumn for a moment before motioning her to a chair before the desk. Autumn sat.

"How may I help you?" she said in a voice that was rigid and properly mannered like a Victorian woman's voice should be.

"I need to get into a deposit box you have here in the building."

"Do you?" she asked. "Well, what is your family's name?"

"It's not my father's," Autumn responded ready for a problem. "I have a key and a number."

"I see. Look," the woman folded her hands on her desk as she spoke to Autumn like a child. "This is not a normal bank. We don't allow just anyone to have an account or a box here. There is no room behind me with a table and a wall of boxes to keep a will or other banal documents. Are you certain you have the correct bank?"

"Look, Bitch," Autumn's mood jumped when she heard the woman's tone. "I have a key and an account number given to me by Thomas Karn. Do I need to put your head through one of these walls before I speak with someone important enough to handle my request?"

The woman jumped, "just a moment." She scurried

off as quickly as she could while retaining her dignity. She disappeared through a door on the left side of the room. The people at the other desks looked her way as discretely as possible. No one intended to make a scene, but that was very unusual.

Autumn thought she had fucked it all up perfectly. The woman was probably off to get security to have this ruffian removed. People like her didn't handle physical threats well and Autumn didn't handle people like her well. She sat in the chair and waited for the inevitable moment when large men would walk out and ask her kindly to leave before the police were called. In her current mood it would be an ugly scene. She'd see to that.

After a few minutes the woman exited the same door behind a small man in an extremely expensive suit. Autumn knew nothing of fashion, but figured he had paid more for that than she had paid for the Toyota a few blocks away. He walked over to her desk. Autumn stood as he approached. She wasn't fond of receiving threats sitting down. He wasn't tall, but he still showed surprise when she stood to her full height. Only a little though.

"Ms. Brown, I presume," he did not offer to shake her hand. "I was told that you were coming. They failed, however, to tell me how lovely you were."

"Can we skip this dance?" she sighed. "You know why I'm here. Can we just do whatever it is we have to do?"

"Certainly. Come with me," he turned as he spoke and walked off to the rear and right side of the small room. She saw a small railing around a hole that had a spiral staircase leading down. He began to descend the staircase and Autumn followed. She kept her eyes open for any tricks that might come her way.

They traveled more than two floors down with no landing or sign of floors. They finally broke out of the small vertical tube into a long dark hallway. There were weak lights between doors at an even interval along both sides of the hall. He walked down the hall to a lone desk that sat at a four-way intersection. He turned back to her when he reached the desk.

"Your account number is a map to the door matching the number on your key," he said calmly explaining as he would how to unlock a car door. "The contents of that room are none of my business. This is where I leave you. Find your door and the contents inside. After you exit the room and the door is locked you will see signs leading you to the exit. Thank you for your patronage."

He walked back down the hall they had used to enter toward the spiral staircase. She watched him ascend the stairs. The moment he rose above the ceiling the stairs disappeared revealing an identical long dark hallway into the distance.

Shit.

She was alone and trapped now in the catacombs of a wizard bank in Missouri. Had they intended to trap her she had walked right into it.

CHAPTER SEVEN

Autumn was stuck. There was no mistaking that.
If there was a plan to have her eliminated, then she
had walked right into it like some pathetic rookie. All
four of the halls leading from her position looked
identical. The only thing she could think to do was
move forward with finding the door. This could be
normal. Maybe wizards enjoyed doing their banking
in dank dungeons.

Fucking wizards.

She walked over to the desk sitting in the crossroad.
There was a spotlight emanating from no source above
illuminating the desktop. On the desk was a small pad
of paper, three sharpened pencils, and two pens.
There was also a chair pushed under the desk. She
pulled out the envelope and emptied the contents onto
the desk. The key was still a simply key. She could
see no additional information there. Instead she
focused on the account number.

N3 W1 N2 E1 S3

It had always looked like an odd account number, but now it made some sense. Autumn was assuming that it was a set of directions leading her around this maze to a door somewhere. Nowhere on the paper was there listed any kind of starting point. That was the problem with most treasure hunts, really. The best directions in the world were useless without a solid starting point. Autumn decided to consider the desk and this juncture the starting point. It made sense and it was the only option she really had in front of her.

She studied the directions before she left her position. It looked like the directions doubled back on themselves at the end. If not for the magic she had already seen, she would have thought there was a mistake. These halls were probably oozing with enchantment. She had no clue what would actually happen when she walked away from the desk. Her only choice was to follow the directions perfectly. Fortunately, her time in the military had made following contradictory orders commonplace.

She then turned and studied each of the hallways. One of the halls had a glowing **N** over it that seemed as straight forward as a wizard would ever be. Seeing no more sense in waiting, she struck off in that direction with purpose. The first hall felt shorter than it should have been. She tried to count the doors on her left as a way of noting how far she had come but the number felt slippery. Somehow, she couldn't remember if there were three or five when she arrived at the next crossroad. She looked back, but she couldn't see the previous crossroad anymore. Looking forward again, she decided to count that as one, so she would need to go two more. There was room for interpretation, but a decision had to be made. If she didn't find what she was looking for she'd try to follow these directions backwards to the desk.

On the third juncture she had only three options including back. One of the options was left so she kept moving with the plan. One more juncture forward. This hallway felt very long. She was certain she had passed seven doors? Eleven? The next juncture had four options again, so she turned right. There was no longer any demarcation on any of the halls. Getting lost here would be exceptionally easy. She may have managed it already.

Two more long hallways later and she reached a spot with three options again. This felt different from the previous junctures. Autumn realized that she had been walking on a downward slope for a while now. This area felt cooler like caves do. She had no idea how far down she had walked or if she was even still under the bank. It was easy to lose track of time and space underground. The faint lighting remained the same and the halls were all identical aside from the length. At least she thought that was a varying point.

She turned right again. The grade down here was steep enough that she could not help but feel it. Somehow the hall looked the same though she could feel gravity pulling her forward as well as toward the floor. The magic here was apparent. Wizards may live in the same world, but they made sure to keep one of their own that others didn't want to be a part of. The hallway felt like the longest one yet. She reached another crossroad. Again, she had four choices.

She turned right again and hoped she had followed everything correctly. She was coming to the realization that backtracking was probably impossible. The paths felt almost alive. Things were changing as she moved. Time had completely slipped her grasp. Thirty minutes or three hours she had no idea. She walked forward. Her directions showed no other turns only three more junctures. Between the first and second the land leveled off again. She continued to the third juncture. She had wondered how she would know what to do here, but the answer was before her.

This spot was not a crossroad, but a cul-de-sac. She walked into the middle of it and saw that it was ringed with doors. The clearing had an octagonal shape and the doors on the walls numbered from thirty-three to thirty-seven. She pulled the key out of her pocket and figured it would fit only thirty-five. That door was located directly in front of her. The lighting here was the same with a faint glow between each door.

Upon further inspection she could see that the doors appeared wooden. They were rounded like castle doors in fairy tales with no window or opening through which to see inside. She stepped to the middle door and saw that it was marred with only a keyhole, iron hook, and the number thirty-five. The door looked very old and unused. This whole area had the smell of great age.

She slid the key into the lock and it fit easily. Despite the age this lock felt well maintained. The key turned smoothly, and she heard heavy tumblers move. Pulling on the hook the door moved with but a faint whisper of effort. There was no creaking or rusted sound at all. The room was still completely dark when she looked in. It didn't look like a dark room in a house, but the dark found a hundred feet underground. There was no light penetrating the doorway at all. She could believe that before her was a solid wall of darkness that was impenetrable.

Taking a deep breath, she stepped inside the all-encompassing darkness. As she passed the doorway she saw that there was a glow inside the room that appeared to be on all the time. It was brighter in here than in the halls. Again, she couldn't see the source of the light, but it would be easy to read or write in this room. Once she fully passed the doorway the door shut of its own accord.

Shit.

She whipped around to catch the end of the movement and hear the lock. She was still wary of a trap, but this was all feeling like the eccentricity of wizards. There was a keyhole on the inside of the door as well. She decided against trying it now. She could imagine too many magical limits that could exist if she started to panic. If they wanted her, she was there now. No reason to panic. She turned back to inspect the room.

There was a desk like the one in the hall and a spotlight on it as well. This desk had the same pad and writing utensils, as well as a stand magnifying glass. There was a high-backed chair in one corner and the back was covered with a grid of small doors like she had entered but only twelve inches tall or so. Each had a small iron ring on it and all had some kind of writing on it. She glanced over them but could not make out the languages. Some looked like languages she knew of, but nothing she could read. A few seemed to be of a language she had never seen before. Something out of a fantasy book maybe. The was one

door with English writing on it. It glowed and said
HUNTER on it.

She decided to try the one she could read. Might as
well. Nothing else made sense and there was no one
here to stop her. When her hand touched the iron ring
she heard another lock release in the door. It swung
open easily to reveal a briefcase that was larger than
the door she had opened. As she saw it now, the
opening had to be at least two feet square. She pulled
the case out and put it on the desk. She looked in the
opening and saw that it was back to its original size
and there was nothing else there. After a moment the
door swung itself shut and the writing was like the
rest, unintelligible.

Wizards.

The case was metallic in appearance and heavily
built. Each side had a combination lock with four
rollers zero through nine. She tried the latches, but the
case was locked. What the fuck? How was she
supposed to open the case? Was this the reason she
had been given the phone number? Was there yet
another puzzle before she could open the case? This
was becoming tiring.

She looked at the slip of paper again but saw no
combination. The numbers on it were the same as
before. She looked the case over and even checked
the pad of paper on the desk with no luck. Of course,
there was probably some simple spell that would have
unlocked the case. Some kind of tool, keyword, or
something that would make this all easy.

Fuck it.

Autumn went with the direct approach. She
grabbed the case on both the top and bottom around

one latch and gave it some gentle encouragement.
One side gave with a crack. She switched to the other
side and repeated the process. She had to avoid
spraying the contents around the room. Inside she
found stacks of hundred-dollar bills. There were two
hundred stacks of hundreds in the case.

She pulled one of the stacks out and flipped through
it casually. All the bills were hundreds and they all
appeared to be authentic. It was looking like she was
going to be properly paid. It also looked like she was
about to accept a very dangerous assignment.

Autumn decided she had been in that dank dungeon
for long enough. She was ready to see some sunlight.
She closed the case but found the problem with her
method of encouragement. The case would no longer
latch closed. She didn't think it would be a good idea
to leave while trying to keep it closed. That seemed
like a recipe for losing a lot of her money. Instead she
bent down and ripped the legs off her sweat pants
turning them in to shorts. She then tied the case
closed with the material.

Long legs make for long ties.

She stepped to the door with her rigged case in hand
and slid her key into the lock. It opened again with an
easy turn and she looked out from the room. Here she
could see out into the hallway fine. The barriers must
have been a kind of security feature. Once she
understood, some of these things made a lot of sense.
She walked out into the pale light into the hall. The
door closed before she could grab the key. Once the
door closed, a spiral staircase appeared in the middle
of the clearing. He had said that a sign for the exit
would appear. Seems he had been correct.

She climbed the steps for an indeterminate number of floors before coming out of the exact same staircase she had entered before. Wizard work was always so convoluted. She was already done with magic and this had only begun. She had to get out of this bank… now. She strode across the floor toward the entrance receiving as many or more stares then before as she was now clad in very tiny shorts. The guard smiled at her as she walked out the front door.

Of course, he did.

CHAPTER EIGHT

Once out of the bank Autumn walked to her car. She kept her hood up though she was showing lot of leg. She got into her car and placed the case in the passenger seat next to her. She decided to leave this location and go to a new one. There was still some doubt in her mind that everything here was legitimate. She drove around a bit until she found a spot in a large parking lot near Union Station. Once parked, she pulled out the slip and her phone. She powered it on and typed in the phone number on the slip. The phone almost didn't ring before it was answered.

"Lindsay. Did you get the case?" It was Thomas as she had expected.

"Yes."

"Good. I assume, then, that you want the combination? It's-"

"Why?" Autumn asked without thinking.

"You've looked at the case, right? You saw that it was locked?"

"Oh, yes," she replied.

"Well, I had assumed that you would want to open

it. The money is there, but I want you to count it so that you know that we have held up our end."

"I have."

"Oh! Fantastic," Thomas sounded almost giddy. "Sorry, I didn't think you'd figure out the combination. I thought of that one myself. I love prime numbers. You're quite surprising."

"What are you going on about?" she asked him. "I just broke it open."

"What? That was a steel case with a reinforced lock. How did you break it open? What did you use?"

"My hands. Now, I was hoping that you might have some more information to go with this money."

"Um... yeah," he hesitated and sounded nervous. "I-I do. Your hands? Jesus. So, okay, we think that Christos is based in the St. Louis area though we don't know exactly where. There's a local branch of the Consortium there that can help you with anything you need. The bank manager, James, will be your contact. He's aware of the situation and the importance of your mission. He has been told to help you with anything you need."

"Wait, you know that he's here and you have boots on the ground?" Autumn asked suspiciously. "Why not just kill him? Why do you need me to be some sort of secret agent?"

"We know what he has planned, and we think that he's located in that general area. That's a far cry from knowing where he is," Thomas had recovered his calm. "We need someone that isn't connected with the Neolithic Consortium. He knows most all our people or at least he's has been able to figure them out. We also need someone inside so that we can be sure that he is the one behind it and that he doesn't have any cohorts that could complete his work should he disappear. We'll achieve nothing if he dies, but his second can simply move and start over."

"You want heads as proof they are dead?"

"Jesus! No," he exclaimed. Autumn smiled at his shock. "Damn! The guy wears two rings at all times. They're silvery but not made of silver. They're magical and there's writing on them. Bring those to prove that he's dead."

"So, if I break up the party I get the other half mil. If I take out the ability for anyone else to ever replicate this work, then I get the second mil?"

"That's the deal," he replied calmly. "Take out anyone you think could finish his work. This ritual can't be completed. This is deadly important."

"I gather," she said growing tired of the whole conversation. "So, what do you know about his operation?

"We mostly know about Christos. He comes from humble beginnings, so now he likes to live it up. He has money now and throws it around fast. We still haven't found out where it all came from. We've assumed he has been a mage-for-hire and possibly helped with some massive heists. We know he's been willing to kill. We figure he has killed a few Consortium members."

"Is he powerful with magic?"

"We assume so, but we have heard conflicting opinions. Information about him has been shaky at best," Thomas sounded frustrated at his lack of knowledge. "We think he's very new to the scene.

No one is entirely sure where he comes from. We have an entire file on him that you can get from James. There's a lot of misinformation here, but he keeps showing up in the St. Louis area. Surely you can find a way to get close to him. We don't know when the ritual is happening, so you may want to assume that you have little time."

"Is that it? Anymore more news to give me?" Autumn asked him with a hard sardonic edge.

"We are aware that this isn't going to be easy. That's why we are willing to pay you so much. We can't afford to move slowly or try multiple people. We need to get him on the first try. You're our only shot here."

"Don't worry, I'll get your boy."

"Thank-" Autumn ended the call before he could finish. She then shut her phone down and put it away. She didn't want them to be able to track or contact her on their time. She'd decide when contact was to be made. It was time she found a place to stay and got some work done.

Autumn drove toward the river. She figured she might be doing a lot of work downtown so it might help to have her base of operations there. If he was throwing money around, he would probably do it at the high-end places. She had no idea how bad the commutes here were, but she'd rather not find out. She ended her search when she found a Drury Inn near the Arch. The location was well placed, and she figured, with the money she was making, she could afford to stay at a nicer hotel. It would also go with her image should she need to appear as a high roller.

Going to see James from here would be easier, though she doubted she would. James could have information, but chances were better that his job was to keep tabs on her and keep the NC informed of her movements. Thomas had already told her that their information was spotty and inconsistent. What good would it do for her to go get more bad intelligence on the subject. She had an idea how to handle someone like Christos.

The staff was not happy with her clothes. Well, the girl at the desk wasn't. The bellhop at the door couldn't get enough. He slowly worked to keep her in view as long as he could until the girl at the desk sent him off. She probably thought that Autumn was a sex worker or something. She used a prepaid credit card to book the room since places like this don't accept cash without a card. She'd pay cash when it was all over so that there was no paper trail. Any trail she left, no matter how faint, meant she could be tracked. She knew that mages had additional methods, but she didn't know what they were. Best, she thought, to avoid as much as possible. She was using her Lindsay Brown ID for this job. That was the identity she had been on when she was hired by Clarence for her last job. She'd change after this one since so many people knew of her involvement.

She carried her own bags to her room. Having brought the bag, she had packed for the last job and the steel case, there wasn't much to carry. The bellhop was not happy about her independence, but the girl at the desk seemed to enjoy Autumn's choice. She'd have to think of something to do with all this money since she was worried about when she left the room.

She took the stairs up to room three-seventeen.
Autumn had never been a fan of elevators. She'd use
it if she had to, but only then. The halls looked newly
remodeled and it all smelled of the powerful cleaning
products used in these hotels. She was used to it, but
that was a big reason they could never feel like home.
No hotel smelled like home.

In the room she decided to change her clothes after
she took a long hot shower. It had been many hours
since her last shower and she had killed two people
and handled corpses since then. She felt a little grimy.
The amenities were fairly nice, so she treated herself
to a bit of spa treatment. As she was showering, she
realized that she was tired as well. It had also been
quite a while since she had last slept. She figured that
the best time to make first-contact with the seedy
magical underbelly of St. Louis would be that night,
so she could allow herself some time to sleep.

She had heard of Imo's Pizza before and people had
told her that it was quite good. She put in an order for
a pizza and continued to get cleaned up. Pizza
delivery was a great boon in her line of work. The
food was easy to keep and provided a meal in a nice
hand-held package. She ordered a pizza large enough
to provide her with a quick meal when she woke up as
well. Pizza had to be one of the most utilitarian meals
on Earth.

She paid the guy in cash when it arrived and sat on
her bed to eat. It was good, but not the best she had
found. Things rarely seemed to live up to whatever
hype they received. When she was done, the rest went
into the fridge provided by the hotel. They had put a
few items of their own in it that she could have... for a

cost of course. These high-end hotels seemed to be the pettiest when it came to the nickel and dime expenses. She figured it best to fleece the rich people anyway though it probably wasn't them that paid the true cost for any of the things left out as traps.

Finally, she lay down on the bed to get some sleep. She couldn't allow herself a full night, but a few hours would assure that she was in good shape for whatever happened. When she woke up she'd begin work and try to take down Andrzej Christos.

CHAPTER NINE

It was dark outside when Autumn opened her eyes again. She looked over at the clock on the night stand and it placed the time as seven thirty-five. That left her some time to get ready and find some spots she could check for her target. She needed to find where she was going and get ready to go. She'd have to come up with a way to get in as well. Infiltration could be the hardest step of the whole process.

As she showered again, ate, and dressed, she tried to decide where to go and how to handle the first night. She needed to get close enough to the top that she could find out who the players were and get a shot at them. She would also have to find out how far along they were. Autumn had no desire to fight some demon or whatever it was that they wanted to dredge up. At minimum it was probably some kind of powerful beast.

She had done some research on her phone during dinner and came up with some wizard hangouts. She could visit those, talk to people, and try to get into the organization from the bottom. That would take a while and she could waste months trying to get high enough to find out what was going on. She needed to get to the top and those guys rarely hung out with the grunts. They tended to go to exclusive clubs where only other wealthy and powerful people congregated. Karn had said the Andrzej liked to throw his money around, so a flashy VIP spot was probably in his wheelhouse. She was not one of those wealthy and powerful people but climbing the ladder from the bottom might never get her where she needed to go.

There was another option. Exclusive clubs had another way to get in. A kind of back door used by people very interested in getting close to wealth and power. She guessed that Christos would use the money method to climb the ladder. Autumn did have money, but not nearly enough to buy her the prestige to get into one of those places as a guest. She was, however, a gorgeous and exotic woman. Rich men seem to love those. Women were the one accessory that all those men wanted but had the hardest time getting. She could get dressed to the extreme and try her hand at getting in and then close to Christos. Time to take advantage of his own chauvinism.

She had no fancy clothes on hand and even if she did, she had little fashion sense. Autumn had never taken the time to learn how best to dress on the high end. She could fake it well enough, but that would require something better than anything she owned. Her best faking usually involved buying things she was told worked together and not deviating from that.

An idea hit her, and it seemed like the best option she had. She called the front desk and hoped.

"Front desk, how can I help you?" the voice

sounded like it belonged to a young man in his twenties. Perfect.

"Hi. This is Lindsay in three-seventeen. I have a big favor to ask. Is there a place nearby where I can buy a nice dress so I can go out?"

"I think most everything is closed by now," he sounded hesitant.

"Please, I can make it worth the time of anyone who can help me," Autumn poured on what little charm she had. "The airline lost my luggage and I'm supposed to meet some people tonight. This could mean a really big part for me."

"Let me see what I can do," his voice changed ever so slightly. "I may know a guy."

"There is something in it for you too if you can make this happen."

She hung up the phone and put on a sweatshirt and jeans. That was really about the only things she had left to wear that weren't covered in blood. Hopefully, the desk employee was greedy, sleazy, and well-connected enough to make this all happen quickly. Autumn didn't want to wait for the next day to get her supplies. Time might mean no demon.

Twenty minutes later her room phone rang.

"Hello."

"This is Max at the front desk. A guy I know works at a store not too far away from here. He said he'd take a chance opening the place after hours for you. But it has to be soon."

"Great," she didn't have to fake the joy in her voice. "I'll be right down," Autumn hung up the phone and grabbed a few bundles of cash, her fake ID, one of her Colts, and stuffed it all in a laundry bag from the room.

She took the stairs down and walked over to the front desk. Max was there and visibly surprised when he saw the woman he had been talking to. It took him a moment to collect himself once he realized. No doubt he had heard her husky voice and pictured a very different woman. She waited while he realigned his world view. During that time, she could see that he was also adjusting what reward he would accept.

"Well?" she asked finally.

"Sorry," he said with a big smile on his face. "The guy is sitting over there in a chair. He'll take you there. He said that the store has really good stuff and that he can help you pick out anything you need."

"Good. Thanks," she said as she turned away and slid a hundred across the counter to Max. He snatched it up off the counter quickly hoping that no one saw that on any of the security cameras.

"You're welcome."

Autumn walked across the lobby to the skinny kid sitting in a chair far too large for him. He stood up as she approached. The boy looked increasingly nervous as her distance from him decreased.

"Hello," he said and stuck his hand out like he was meeting a car dealer.

"Hi. Let's go. I'm in quite the hurry," she never took his hand.

"Yes, ma'am."

He walked in front of her leading the way to the store. He seemed far more comfortable once she took control. The walk to the store was rather short and they didn't pass conversation as they walked. Autumn had no desire to make a new friend or encourage anything he might be thinking. The store was small and unassuming, but the ambiance seemed upscale. He led her around to the back of the building. There, he unlocked the back door and waived her in first while looking around.

"Pete!" they heard as soon as he closed and locked the back door.

"Shit. Wait here," he muttered and hurried forward into the main part of the store. Autumn followed and found a wall to lean against with a view, but out of the general line of sight in the store. She wasn't ready to be seen yet. There was a strict woman in comfortable clothes standing in the middle of the sales floor with her hands on her thin hips. Pete walked up to her slowly. "Hi, Elizabeth. How can-"

"Can it. What bullshit is this?"

"I was trying to help a very nice lady who's in trouble," Pete sounded entirely submissive.

"Yeah? Help her what? Rob me?"

"No, she needed clothes and wanted to buy things. I thought I could make you some money."

"Yeah? Well," she called to the back where Autumn had remained unseen. "Bitch, get out here and talk to me. I want to see the skank my employee brings in after hours."

Autumn walked into the room and stared at her without speaking. She wanted to see how this would play out. Elizabeth turned to Pete.

"She must be fairly expensive, Pete," Elizabeth continued drilling into Pete. "Come on, what decent woman carries her things around in a laundry bag? You coming into my store at night to get your dick sucked?"

"No, she los-"

"Look," Autumn finally spoke up completely disregarding whatever Pete had to say. "I asked to come here. I need some decent clothes, I have money, and I don't have a lot of time."

Elizabeth never looked up as she spoke.

"Were you going to keep all that money, Pete? Were you robbing me?"

"No! She was just going to tip me well," Pete couldn't hold up under her barrage. "Max already got his money."

"Oh good," Elizabeth rolled her eyes like a cartoon character as she spoke. "Of course, that twatwaffle is involved in this business. Get the fuck out of here. I'll deal with you later. I'll take care of this *lady*."

Pete scurried out the back feeling like a mouse the cat had forgotten to eat when it fell asleep. Elizabeth turned to Autumn with fire still in her eyes. Autumn continued to look at her with the same casual indifference.

"So," Elizabeth spoke with a high stern voice. "What's your story?"

"I have money and lost luggage," Autumn kept it short. "I want shoes, a dress, a bag, the whole deal."

"You can't afford me."

"Try me."

"Two hundred just to open," Elizabeth said not missing a beat. "You buy from my top-shelf inventory. No clearance shit. You don't spend enough, and I end this whole thing. Take it or leave it."

"I don't want your trash anyway. I'll pay if what you have is worth it."

Puffing her chest out and squaring her shoulders, Elizabeth took up the challenge. She looked like she planned to kill Autumn with quality. No one had tried that method before. Maybe it would work.

"Worth it? You wouldn't know quality if it bit you in the cooch. Well," she motioned Autumn over with her head. "Get your Amazon ass over here. I got clothes here that will make you look human. That's how good my stock is."

Autumn smiled. She was going to like this bitch. She followed orders and walked over to see what Elizabeth had planned for her. The small woman stood there with a tape measure. She was actually tapping her foot impatiently like a schoolmarm. Autumn couldn't help but feel the authority radiating from her.

"Well...?"

"Well what?" Autumn was confused.

"Take it off. You want fine clothes I need proper measurements. I do this right. Period."

Autumn stripped and stood there waiting. She was beginning to think that Elizabeth was enjoying this.

"Well then," there was surprise in Elizabeth's voice. She walked over and began to carefully take Autumn's measurements. She had a small pencil and notepad that she recorded it in. She would measure and remeasure from slightly different angles. Her hands were quick and smooth from years of practice. Though she didn't look very old, she had varied and abundant experience. Autumn had never been measured so thoroughly in her life.

After that was over she began to show Autumn dresses in her size. This went on for a bit though

Elizabeth kept reminding her that there was precious little in her size. They finally settled on one dress. It shimmered green to match her eyes and hair. Autumn liked the dress because it showed off her figure and that would be more important tonight than her eyes. She needed to wow people from the very moment they saw her. Elizabeth seemed to pick up on this and worked it out very well. She did a great job.

There were heels and a bag that Elizabeth picked out. She said that they matched the dress best. The heels weren't especially high.

"A slight heel's going to lift your ass and stick your tits out there in everybody's face. Can't go too high, though. It might make those men all too insecure if you're too much taller than they are. I think it makes their dicks look smaller to them."

She was extraordinarily profane for a fashion shop keeper. Another quality about the woman that Autumn found enjoyable. Finally, she stood back and looked at her creation.

"Not bad," Elizabeth said almost to herself. "You want help with your make-up as well?"

"I think it's fine. I don't need any."

"No, no. I know the look you're going for and those women always have very carefully done make-up. Without it you'll look out of place. Come upstairs to my place," she put her small hand on Autumn's wrist. She looked smaller by comparison. "I'll help you as much as I can."

They walked up the stairs in the back room to a small apartment where Elizabeth resided. It was obvious straightaway that Elizabeth lived alone. The apartment was neat and tidy but had an air of a lonely woman. Autumn wondered what kept her from dating. The living room was sparse but what furniture she had looked quite rich. She saw no pictures of family, friends, or a boyfriend. There were a couple paintings on the walls that matched the feeling and colors of the room perfectly, but that feeling was slightly cold. The mood was displayed amazingly. She was as good a decorator as she was a dresser.

Once there she led Autumn to her bedroom where Autumn saw more evidence of her loneliness. There were no pictures of a guy or evidence of someone sleeping over. She saw no men's clothing and there was no trace smell of sex. There was a bed, a large chest, and a vanity with a mirror. She had Autumn sit down at the dresser, so she could better reach her face.

"I dress some models for shows I have been a part of, so I have some extra colors here. Hopefully I can match your skin tone," Elizabeth said pulling out a large box and beginning to dig through it. "You have a very unique look."

Elizabeth spent another half an hour working carefully with make-up that Autumn had never seen. Again, she took her time but worked deftly and efficiently. She created the exact glamorous look Autumn had hoped to achieve. When she looked in the mirror she was amazed at the work that Elizabeth had done. Her face was transformed ever so slightly, but Autumn couldn't tell there was make-up at all. She had an amazing talent that Autumn had never even thought about learning.

"You look amazing," Elizabeth gave Autumn her first straight forward compliment. "I'd love to use you as a model if you're ever looking for work."

"No."

"Fine. I can see that you're no fun," she had a small smile on her face. "Let's go downstairs then and settle this all up. I do still intend to charge you. I'm not some stupid man who'll give everything away when I see some big firm tits."

"I had assumed you would," Autumn was also smiling.

Elizabeth led her back downstairs and to the register at the front of the store. She wrote everything up and took more of the cash than Autumn had expected, and Autumn had expected this trip to be expensive. Fortunately, she could afford her. Autumn threw in four hundred for Elizabeth's time for the quality of service.

"Carrying all that cash is dangerous. You should consider getting a card. You afraid of banks?"

"Some of them, but I think I'll be just fine," Autumn responded playfully.

"Somehow, I bet you're right. Well, remember me and come back if you want anything else. With more time I could tailor something to fit you even better."

Autumn smiled and left out the back door. It was time to head for the club she had chosen. There was one club she thought would have the best chance if Christos was out tonight. Play time was over. She had to go to work.

CHAPTER TEN

Autumn walked off toward the club she had picked out earlier. It was the highest on the list of elite clubs in the city that she could find. Of course, there would be at least one other wizard club that was more exclusive, but that one would be by invite only. She'd have no way to find or get into that one. Her best hope was that Andrzej was not yet that high on the list of elites. Those clubs usually tried to exclude people like Christos who bought their way into higher society so blatantly.

Walking in heels, even the short ones Elizabeth had picked out, was difficult, but Autumn's car would give her away as someone who didn't belong. She had to maintain an air of superiority and mystery or this would never work at all. Toyotas didn't have the kind of prestige she needed, and she didn't have time to hire a limo service. She'd have to rely on her looks and acting ability. Once she was within a block, she worked to get into character.

She added more swing to her hips and tried to be sure there was a lot of bounce in her step. She turned the corner and saw the entrance with a cordoned off area guarded by a large bouncer. There were no lines outside of wizard clubs. Either the bouncer let her in or she'd have to move along. No waiting list. It wasn't safe to allow an angry wizard to hang around thinking of a good spell to cast on the building or people passing by. She was sure there was a scarier bouncer inside who could wield some serious offensive magic. It was possible the man standing there served a dual purpose, but she had not heard of that occurring many times.

Autumn strutted up to the door showing no sign that she even acknowledged the man at the door. The large man moved to place himself between her and the rope that barred entrance. He stood taller than she did, but only by two inches. He was broad enough to cover a standard doorway. She guessed that he was a College football player and amateur MMA fighter. He moved like someone who had been in a few fights and knew how to handle himself.

"Can I help you?" he spoke with a deep bass and wore dark glasses despite the lack of light outside. She could see the rippling evidence of the time he spent in the gym. His dark skin and broad shoulders added to his intimidation factor. The proprietors had chosen him well for look alone. She assumed that he could back it up as well.

Autumn chose to use her normal voice. Deep and sultry would probably get her farther here than a bubbly cheerleader. She couldn't really do much voice work. She had never had the knack for impressions or impersonations. He looked to be on edge a bit already by her height and body style.

"Hello," Autumn said maintaining a straight face. She worked to affect a slightly bored expression. "I was asked by Mr. Christos to meet him here tonight. I hope that he has already arrived. I do not like to be made to wait."

"He has already arrived, but he never mentioned any guest."

"Fine," she turned to leave. "This place looks boring anyway. Tell him that you turned Lindsay away when he asks. He will be very disappointed."

"Wait. Wait," he stepped forward and placed his hand on her shoulder. She didn't react as she normally would have, but instead turned back around without any violent act. "I wasn't expecting you," he said with concern in his voice. Autumn guessed that he had run afoul of Christos before and that had not gone well for him. "Sure, come on in. No one will complain even if you're lying about being his guest." He moved the rope and even opened the door for her.

"Thank you," she said and sauntered in, flashing him the barest of smiles as she went by. She guessed that Andrzej brought many women here attempting to impress them. The inside was a clash of multiple different bars brought together with an audible clunk. To her right was a dance floor with bright lights and a DJ spinning his own mix of the top hit songs. Many people were dancing and carrying on there. To the left was a long wooden bar with some booths and large TVs. One had a baseball game on while another showed a sports commentary show.

Autumn looked up and could see onto the second floor where there was an old stage like out of an old movie with a big band and a crooner singing. Magic was the only way a club like this could be assembled. Magical barriers had been erected that kept the sound between them to a minimum. There was just enough sound that, if someone was close, they could hear enough to know if they wanted to enter. This allowed the one club to cater to many different tastes, leading to many different demographics in the same place. She also saw a high number of security people moving throughout the club to keep all these different mages in line and in place.

The sports bar seemed like the only place downstairs that she could stand, so she decided to start there. As she walked over she realized that she had nothing smaller than a hundred-dollar bill on her. That was not a problem that she usually encountered, so she had not been prepared with a contingency. Hopefully, that would not draw too much attention from the wrong people. Or maybe, the wrong people were exactly who she wanted to entice. Walking up she drew immediate attention from most of the patrons. There were many attractive women at the bar, but none she could see who looked like her. The bartender stood attentive waiting for her order.

"What can I get for you?"

"Long Island Iced Tea," she said focusing on his eyes. She wanted to leave an impression. Somehow, she needed to find someone who could supply her with quick answers.

"Yes, ma'am," he saluted and hurried off to make her drink. She watched him get the bottles and make a real show of mixing the drink. He even flipped some of the bottles showing off as much as he could. Autumn could see that he had a real knack for mixing drinks, but his enthusiasm detracted from the effect. She hoped he was as good at the actual mixing as he was the show of it all. Long Islands tasted terrible when mixed incorrectly.

"Here you go," he made a flourish of presenting the tall thin glass to her. "That'll be twenty-five."

"I don't bother with anything less than a hundred," she said with snide disinterest putting her hand into her bag.

"That doesn't sound safe," he said, maintaining conversation.

"Gerald, let me cover it," a man said before she could pull out a bill. "Put it on my tab." The voice came from her right. Autumn turned to look at her mark. "Hi, I'm Aiden. How are you?"

Perfect.

"I'm fine," she let a thin smile form. "Thank you."

"No problem. I haven't seen you before. Are you new to the city?"

"Yes," Autumn said taking a drink from her glass. "I came because I heard this was the club to see in St. Louis. Is that right?"

"Sure is," Aiden smiled as she continued to focus on him. "Are you a member of the NC or are you a Fringe?"

"Private," she gave him another small coy smile. No sense letting on that she wasn't a wizard yet... or ever if possible. "I was hoping to find a man."

"Oh?" his smile was so wide she could see his gums.

"A specific man..." she continued. "Or at least more information about him."

"Oh," Autumn kept her smile internal as his

diminished. She could feel the sleazy desperation radiating off him already. "So not just entertainment, huh? Pity. Well, I probably know him. Ole Aiden knows most everyone worth knowing."

"Yeah? You're my man, then."

"So, who is this lucky bastard who has the attention of such a lovely woman?" Aiden asked continuing his smile.

Autumn fought back the urge to wretch, "Andrzej Christos."

Aiden's expression changed. He became serious and leery. That name had a great effect on each man she had spoken to so far. He must be quite the showman to have affected people so strongly. That, or he was a legitimate threat.

"That guy? Why're you interested?"

"Someone told me that he was deep into some heavy casting that would interest me greatly. You don't seem to be one of his many fans."

"He comes in here all high and mighty throwing his weight around," he recovered his swagger a bit as he spoke. "Guy keeps saying he has the path to some ultimate power like some Marvel movie villain. Guys who want to talk power all the time are no fun at all. Just boring. I think he's just trying to get the attention of the NC. Probably wants money or membership. Guys like that are all show and shit. Got to be compensating for something."

"Sounds interesting," Autumn said taking another drink. Gerald had done a wonderful job mixing her drink. That or he added no alcohol at all.

"You're just like every woman," the last of his smile fell off his face. "Only interested in power, money, and bad boys. Women never want a nice guy who'll show 'em a good time and be good to them. Just find some dude to treat 'em like shit and friend-zone anyone decent."

"True, and as long as you hold to that doctrine you'll always have Lefty and Righty to keep you company on your many lonely nights."

"You bitch!" He froze after saying that. Autumn had grabbed his left wrist. She could feel the bones and soft tissue flex under her vice-like grip. Only his pride kept him from crying out in front of the rest of the bar.

"You've lost the right to speak by being a whiny brat who never grew up," Autumn spoke softly, but knew that he heard every syllable she spoke. "I'll ask you one question and if you answer correctly and quickly you'll get your hand back. If you fail I will break it and move on to someone worthier to speak with me. Nod if you understand."

Aiden nodded and began to sweat visibly.

"Where is Christos? I want to speak with him. Nod if you understand the question."

He did.

"Now, I want you to answer me. Keep it concise and on subject. Where?"

"He's on the second floor in a booth in the back," Aiden's voice cracked a bit under the strain. "He calls it his seat. The bartender up there can point him out."

"Good. Now, you think about your attitude and why you're alone," she let go of his wrist and walked off in one cool motion. Aiden grabbed his wrist and tried not to cry. To calm his pride, he'd have many more drinks and concoct an elaborate story about the beautiful woman he had encountered in the bar that night. Autumn couldn't care less.

CHAPTER ELEVEN

Autumn ascended the stairs as conspicuously as she possible could. She wanted everyone to see her. Especially Christos and his party and she had no idea who they were, so everyone was the goal. She walked over to the bar hoping to draw as much attention to herself as possible without having some kind of massive wardrobe malfunction. This time she waited at the bar while people watched. The bartender wasn't nearly as interested in helping her as the one downstairs. She had entered the barrier for this bar at the top of the stairs and could hear the music from the stage. The band was playing a tune in the style of a Las Vegas lounge act with the singer playing the part. Autumn couldn't recognize the song.

Finally, the bartender walked over to her with the intent of giving service. His face showed no awestruck wonder at the beauty before him. Maybe Autumn was not nearly as attractive at higher elevations. Good thing this wasn't in Denver. Truthfully, the whole ambiance up here seemed more refined and sophisticated. She was still beautiful, but his tongue stayed in his head.

"What are you drinking?"

"Nothing. However, I'd like to be drinking a vodka martini," Autumn kept her face impassive during the exchange. "More importantly I'd like to be drinking that martini in the presence of Mr. Christos. I was told that you were the man who could make all my dreams come true."

"Well, then, let me see what I can do," he said and walked to the end of the bar. There he stopped and spoke with a thin and well-dressed man for a moment. The thin man then strode off and made a bee-line for the back of the bar and a round booth situated in a corner. The booth was bathed in a soft light that didn't make it very easy to see any details from where Autumn stood. She saw that the thin man had a short discussion there and then returned to the bar.

After a second brief discussion with the thin man, the bartender returned to Autumn with no drink. "Your presence has been requested by Mr. Christos. Your drink will be brought out to you at his private table."

Paying no more attention to the barkeep, Autumn glided from the bar across the room. Her performance from that moment had to be perfect. She made certain to show no attention to the other patrons in the bar or the help. As she walked she kept her eyes locked on Andrzej. Once close enough she could see that his gaze was locked on her as well. Good.

Upon reaching the table she stopped and struck a pose with her hand on one hip she jutted out from her side. She kept her gaze on Christos as she stood silently, allowing everyone to get a good look at her.

He made no attempt to hide his lustful looks. She was glad to have that effect when it counted. Finally, he spoke with a deep rich voice. His accent showed signs of both his Greek and Romani heritage. He made no effort to hide that accent.

"Wonderful entrance, My Dear. Truly wonderful. To what do I owe this singular honor?"

"Your reputation alone drew me to meet you," she smiled slightly as she spoke. "I heard that you were here, and I simply had to meet the man I had heard so much about."

"Did you?" he spoke with a large smile on his face while he gestured next to himself. "Well then, have a seat by me and let us have a conversation."

Andrzej was a stocky man. Some might say meaty. He was seated so Autumn wasn't certain about his height though she would have guessed around five-nine. His shoulders were broad for his height, giving him the look of an old-time gangster in his dark pin stripe suit. His hair was a dark black with powerful product keeping it straight. His natural curl, however, refused to give up the fight quietly.

His skin was light while still not being pale, while his face showed signs of the many battles puberty had won on that battlefield in his youth. He kept the damage covered on most of his face with a dark and full beard and mustache. Autumn had expected a more olive tone to his skin, but she wasn't an expert. His eyes were dark and deeply set inside his face. He had a very specific look and it played to his wizardly type well. He knew how to cultivate an image, and that might have included staying out of the sun to keep his skin lighter.

He also matched the description that Clare had given Autumn of the 'big bad man.'

Autumn grabbed a chair and took a seat right opposite him to start. It was time to play the game. She knew that she had but one chance to get this right or her cover would be gone entirely. She was too unique to try again as another identity. She had to earn or win her way into the fold quickly so that she could continue her work.

"Why sit there, My Dear?" Andrzej asked. "Come over here with me. The booth is far more comfortable."

"Not yet," Autumn said defiantly. "You have not earned that honor yet."

"Earned it?" his eyes lit up as he spoke. "A game?"

"A challenge. Your reputation may have drawn me here, but the rest is up to you and your personality. Few get this far so easily. None go further without effort to prove their worth."

"Wonderful," he laughed. "This, my friends, this is a woman to be fought for. She falls at no man's feet. Take note because women such as this are why men advance our society to the fullest. Scientific achievement, magical accomplishment, power grasped from chaos all to earn the admiration of women such as this." He smiled broadly as he held court over his loyal minions. Each sitting there worked for him or had something to gain from being in his presence and good graces.

"So, Dear, what is your name? Let us begin with the most banal information before moving on."

"Lindsay Brown."

"Sad, truly sad. No, no, no," Andrzej shook his

head slowly. "Such an exotic woman deserves and equally exotic and lovely name. An orchid would lose its mystique were it called a mum."

"My parents probably agree with you, but they were neither exotic nor sophisticated. Lindsay was the furthest limits of their imagination."

"No matter, My Dear. It is what you do with yourself that truly defines who you are. Humble beginnings can lead to the most amazing people," Christos gestured large with his hands and arms as he spoke. There was a strong sense of stage presence in everything he did. "Take myself. My parents traveled with a Romani clan around the Greek isles and mainland for most of their lives. They brought me to this country for the chance at a better life. And once they got to the promised land of the American shores, do you know what they did? Traveled with another Romani clan. They had no ability to see a way out of the paltry existence they had known their entire lives."

"So, you know what it is like to be treated like a freak?"

"My Dear, I have been called everything from a common thief to a witch. People fear what is different. The Other. However, those harsh lessons gave me the strength to stand up and take power. To take the things I want that society would never give me. Growing up Romani in this world makes you an outcast amongst even the outcasts. I had to become stronger still to even survive."

"How strong?" Autumn asked with a coy smile. "Could you beat me in a test of strength? Arm wrestling perhaps?"

He laughed loudly and melodramatically.

"Lindsay, Dear, I have spent a life of hard labor. Even without magic there is no question of my physical prowess. You are a fit woman that, I'm sure, many men along the way have allowed to win. However, I never allow someone to take a victory from me. Surely, you see that you cannot win."

"I don't believe you. Prove it," Autumn said as she put her arm up on the table and allowed a cattish grin to overtake her face.

"That's fine," he smiled and put his arm up to demonstrate. "But I cannot reach you from here. There is a large table between us. You will have to move closer if you wish to pursue this."

Here was her chance to give Andrzej a victory of sorts. She moved into the both so that they could lock arms. By the look on his face he had considered that a victory and he was counting. She was curious what he could manage without magic. His pride may force him to use magic, but she would feel it kick in and know herself.

Andrzej took off his expensive coat and made a show of flexing and loosening up. He placed his arm on the table bent into position. His arms were corded with thick muscle and Autumn could see that he hadn't lied about the life of manual labor. She put her arm up and grabbed his hand. His expression became slightly uncertain when he saw that his hand was no larger than hers.

Autumn pretended to move his arm and look it over. The whole time she was examining his ring. He did indeed have a silvery ring on his hand. The metal shined as if it had been polished carefully right before she had seen it. The writing was faint, but noticeable.

She couldn't place the language, but somehow it looked familiar. She wondered if she had seen it in a movie or if another language was a derivative. It was written in script and she couldn't even make out the alphabet used. Surely it was some magical language.

"Nicholas," Christos piped up when Autumn was done inspecting his arm. She could see that he had enjoyed that. "If you could get us started on three."

A man with him grabbed both of their hands and made a show of checking for cheating. He held them there as he began to count.

"Three. Two. One. Go!"

Autumn felt him pull and felt a boost from his sudden spell. Liar. She waited a moment to allow him to struggle before slamming his hand down. Andrzej's face showed pure shock and the small cry that left his throat matched that perfectly. Gasps circled the table.

"Amazing," he said perplexed. "How?"

"My secret," she replied with a wry smile. She pulled her arm back, but made no movement to change the new seating arrangement. "So, I hear you've achieved your position and goals without any help from the Neolithic Consortium."

"Indeed, I have. Just as I've gotten you to move closer to me."

"So, it seems you have," she smiled and finished her drink. Andrzej motioned for another round including hers.

"The Neolithic Consortium has courted my membership. Alexander DesChanes himself expressed his personal interest. I knew then as I know now that they would merely suppress my true power and potential under their membership. I do not need their help as they have nothing to offer. I know what I want, and I go after it. With my willpower and tenacity, the world cannot help but yield and bend to my will."

"What is it that you want?"

"That, My Dear, is my secret."

"Is it now?" Autumn asked allowing a small smile to overtake her expression. "You seem like a man who holds secrets from people you distrust only."

"There are many of those people."

"Do you count me among their number?"

"There we share something else," Andrzej said firmly. "My trust is something to be earned."

"What if I said that power and ambition excite me?"

"Don't you seem to be very interested, now. I think I may have been deemed worthy."

"Maybe," she said carefully playing the game. His reaction here could tell her a lot.

"Maybe? I will not be toyed with," his voice rose as Christos became visibly angry. He was not accustomed to being told no and so hated it like a spoiled child. Autumn should have expected such anger. She would have to work quickly.

"You are well on your way, but anything worth earning is worth working hard to get. Your trust and mine, as you said. However, I assure you that I am worth the wait."

"True," he seemed to calm down as she worked to massage his ego. "My Dear, no woman such as yourself has entered my life in a long time. Forgive my outburst and let us continue to chat."

The conversation continued for some time.
Christos' attention was soon drawn away to the rest of
the party. He enjoyed oration and this collection
listened attentively as he pontificated on every subject
that was raised. It seemed that the night had returned
to the flow of his normal nights out. Autumn was
relieved when the spotlight fell off her. She didn't like
talking that much. It was also easier to maintain
character when she could melt into the background.

As the conversation continued, so did the drinking.
It quickly became obvious that Andrzej took pride in
his ability to drink. He seemed to take pride in
everything he did on any level. Autumn watched him
play two separate drinking games, as well as continue
to drink for pleasure. After the arm wrestling she was
certain he was using magic to bolster his abilities. He
was showing off and cheating was a small price to pay.

Good.

"So, My Dear, tell me of your parents. I wish to
know more about the people who brought you into the
world," he said at a low point in the conversation.

"There is little to say," she had to think fast. She
had not taken the time to construct a full background.
She hadn't expected the conversation to go deep about
her. "My father worked in a factory and my mother
was a secretary. My childhood was very banal."

"I see," he said nodding his head. "I must say that I
understand little of a banal childhood. My parents
traveled with the clan making money how they could.
My mother was a wonderful woman who did readings
for people. She spent much of her life devoted to
learning the art of prophecy, though that is truly hard
magic to master." He motioned for another round of

drinks. He was settling in for a sermon.

"My father never had any magical talent. He was a laborer for the clan. He also spent time cleaning up messes and doing the clan's dirty work. He was never in charge, but he felt the weight of those who were. My father was a limited and angry man, but my parent's love was written in the stars. I was an unruly child with my curiosities and magic. He did his best to control me, but he had little imagination beyond the old ways. He did the best he could.

"My mother was truly a saint. She wanted nothing more than to help the people she performed readings for. She spent so much time with those people trying hard to grasp the most elusive of magics. Sometimes she spent days and nights with marks trying to properly help them. She would come home at all hours exhausted from her studies and work."

The waiter brought the next round of drinks. Andrzej always bought his drinks as rounds. He seemed to loath the idea of drinking alone. Autumn figured that he hated doing most anything in his life alone. He seemed the type who would always have people around.

"There was an old woman in the clan who taught me magic. My mother was busy with her own studies and prophecy is no magic for children to learn. We called the woman Babcia. My mother told me it was a Greek word for grandmother. She acted as a grandmother for the children of the whole clan as most of our real grandparents were dead. I was very young when my parents came to America, so the clan here has always been my true family.

"I had no formal education growing up. It's hard to

go to school when the local sheriff comes at three in the morning to run off the *gypsies*," he said the word with true hatred. That was not a term he took lightly.

"I know very little of the Romani," Autumn tried to keep him talking. He was many drinks into the night. She wasn't sure what his limit was, but she wanted as much from him as she could get.

"Thank you, My Dear, so many people use that word because they hear it in movies and books. They do not understand how much hatred it draws. People have never cared about the Romani. We are one group that will never have a movement started. My people spend too much time trying to hide what we are to stand up and take what we deserve."

He took a long drink and thought for a moment to himself.

"We traveled all through my childhood. My mother and father were always working hard. Mother made most of her money doing personal readings for men as we traveled. She was very good at controlling men and getting what she wanted from them. She was quite beautiful and soft spoken. Her devotion to magic and her family was unshakable. Though her time spent away meant I didn't see her often. My father took the brunt of the law. He spent many nights in local jails and dealing with the clan's legal issues. I would go long stretches without seeing him either. He was so angry with the way the world treated his people.

"Babcia was my constant. She taught all the children. We learned of the world around us and what was expected of us by the clan. She tried to teach us all magic, but I was especially talented. I had my mother's genes though they never let me try prophetic magic. I was told that was not for me to learn. I offered to help Mother with her readings, but I was told that was work for special women like her. She wanted me to achieve grander things."

"It sounds like those women truly shaped your life," Autumn stoked the fires a bit.

"Yes. Women teach us all how to live better. Men have a responsibility to keep the world from destroying them. That's why my father bore the brunt of the outside world and its fury. My father knew that my mother was gentle and caring. He never wanted harm to befall her. He was harder on me, but he knew my potential. I had to be strong. One day I was to take his place in the clan."

"Did you? Did you take his place in the clan?"

"That, My Dear, is a sad story. When I was a teen my father was killed by the police. They came into our camp and tried to arrest him for murders they couldn't solve. So often they would blame us for anything they couldn't easily solve. In this case they arrested my mother and killed my father. Babcia had died the year before, so I ran off. I knew that my parents would want me to achieve greatness. I had to avoid arrest or being sent into the system for children. I never wanted to lose my heritage."

He looked down as these thoughts filled his head. Autumn could not tell if he was grandstanding or truly feeling for his lost family. She thought it best to play along either way. She reached out and put her hand on his. He looked at her and smiled.

"Enough of this dour discussion," he forced a smile to his face. "Let us have another round and lighten up."

Andrzej ordered another round and began coaxing people around him to tell jokes. Autumn once again faded into the background to listen. She had learned quite a bit this evening.

After a few hours more, the party seemed to be dying down. Most of the patrons had left the bar, alone or in groups, for greener pastures elsewhere. Andrzej's table was winding down from the late night and massive alcohol consumption. His friends were all tired, drunk, and not having fun anymore. Autumn decided that she had gotten all she could, and it was time for her last play.

"Andrzej, I believe it is time for me to find my hotel room."

"No, surely we're still having fun."

"Of course, but I never stay until the fun is over. I would rather be the one to end it with my departure."

"Surely, you will accompany us to our next venue," he pleaded. "This spot has grown dull, I agree." The rest of the party groaned. At least the ones who were still conscious did. Autumn's careful drinking and physical enhancements made it very difficult for her to become drunk, though she feigned some effects of alcohol to be safe. "Your presence has made this night the most interesting in many."

"We have only just met. You have fared very well," Autumn stood as she spoke. "We will meet again. Of that I am certain."

"Of course, My Dear," he said. Autumn could see that he was very aware of social cues. She could also see that he'd not always been powerful, lending credence to his stories about his youth. "I look forward to the next time I'm in your presence."

As she stood the party stood with her where possible. Christos made a show of bowing and kissing her hand. Autumn had to keep her skin from crawling as he did. She walked away carefully making certain to keep her motions the same as long as she could be in view. It would be tragic to blow her cover after she had gotten so far. She felt certain that if she broke character someone in the club would inform Andrzej of that fact.

After she was outside she walked back toward her hotel. She walked a block away and turned a corner before she opened her bag and put her heels in it. Bare foot in the city was preferable to those monstrous shoes. Why do women subject themselves to such torture for fashion? She also pulled her phone out of the bag and a small slip of paper she had found earlier. She powered on her phone and dialed the number written under the letter *E*.

After two rings it was answered by an attentive voice. "Lindsay?"

"Yes," she smiled when she recognized the voice.

"Did you have a fun night?"

"I did not but I hope it's not over," Autumn said to the pleasant voice.

"Oh? Well, maybe it isn't, but I would prefer your hotel room."

"I'm at the Drury nearby in room three-seventeen."

"Well, I just woke up so…"

"I'll be in my room in ten minutes. I'll be naked in ten more. Five minutes after that I'll start with or without you."

"Aren't you the pushy bitch?"

"And you love every bit of it. That's the deal."

"You won't start without me," Elizabeth ended the call. Autumn couldn't help but smile as she turned her phone off again. She continued to walk to her room after checking the time. She was on the clock and the rest of this night might actually be enjoyable.

CHAPTER TWELVE

The next day Autumn woke up around one in the afternoon. She had woken up briefly when Elizabeth had been getting ready to leave. Autumn had watched her prepare and gave her a kiss before falling back asleep. When one rolled around she returned to the waking realm to find a small note on the nightstand. On one side of the folded paper she saw *Lindsay* written in small exacting print. She opened the note to see what the critical review was of her performance the night before.

Lindsay,
Last night was a lot of fun. Some of us must go to work, however. I'll be thinking about you all day at work. Please, feel free to contact me at any time while you are in town. I would greatly enjoy keeping you company on any lonely night.

Elizabeth.

Xoxo

Autumn smiled while she read the short letter. Usually, anyone she took as a lover grew to hate her distance. It was still early, but she had chased men off before in the first night. She realized how much she'd like a repeat performance soon. Autumn's smile faded after a moment. She thought too far into the future, which made her flash back to the past. She thought of the ritual and procedure. She continued to question how human she really was anymore.

When men pull out many of your original parts and replace them with technologically enhanced upgrades do they remove humanity? How much is removed with each change? Was this how someone felt when they had a prosthetic arm or leg? Of course, that would leave someone as still mostly human. At some point during the process had they removed too much of Autumn's humanity? If Autumn's Toyota was a Toyota shell full of Chevy parts would it still be a Toyota? There had been other internal effects aside from the increase in strength, speed, endurance, and recovery.

She had been told before, by more than one partner, that she didn't "feel real." She was glad, at those moments, that she had never told them the details of the procedure. Would they have reacted like the village folks toward Dr. Frankenstein and his monster? She had never told any of them the true nature of it, but she had constructed a story about an accident and a lot of work that she had to have done. Even without that knowledge many had reacted poorly to one aspect of her or another. Though she tried to write them off as jealous, proud, stupid, and the like, none of it changed that they could tell that she was different. That had made her conclude that she could never have something long lasting. She further embraced her job and tried to tell herself that was why she had to be alone.

Elizabeth seemed to have potential. She had loved Autumn's size and how hard she had felt. Her strength and musculature had seemed to turn Elizabeth on. Her intensity and competitive nature had fueled the night instead of detracting from it. There was no complaint of Autumn "not feeling right." This one seemed to have the potential to last for a bit of a longer run. Autumn, however, would not allow herself to become hopeful for anything beyond temporary. That would be ludicrous.

Autumn shook herself from her self-indulgent reverie. She put her personal feeling aside to prepare for the job she still had to perform. Autumn hadn't given Andrzej any contact information, but that had been part of the game. She had to depend on his desire and ability to hunt her down. Autumn put the over/under at nightfall to hear from him. She chose under. She had faith in his ability to stalk her.

She showered and prepared herself for a day of regular shopping. There was very little left that she could wear in public and she probably had many days of work left. She should no longer have to dress to impress so much. It was still possible that he would have more club nights, but she hoped she could find a way to be more utilitarian. She had some hope that she could end this quickly once she was in deep enough to learn the truth.

Once she was clean she put on her sweatshirt and jeans again. That was about all she had left, and she had grown tired of wearing it. There was no way she'd wear the dress from last night to go shopping today. Once she was all set she made sure she had enough cash to cover her day and left the room. The case with her money had been placed under the dresser in her room with the TV on it. She figured few people would try to lift the dresser to find her case. Walking to the front desk, she asked the very proper woman there where she could do some shopping for clothes at a good price. The woman was helpful and gave her the names and locations for a few malls in the Greater St. Louis area.

Autumn collected her car and drove to one the woman had called The Galleria. She had said it was a very popular destination. Judging by the state of the parking lot that had been correct. Autumn parked in a distant spot and walked in. Shopping held no fun for her; at least this kind of shopping didn't. Employees gave her pointed looks when she constantly asked for larger sizes of what was on the shelves. Shoe stores tended to be the worst for this size problem. Autumn preferred to shop in men's shops because they had bigger sizes and utilitarian clothes, but that brought a whole different set of problems. Of course, she couldn't go into men's shops for bras and underwear.

Autumn did what she could to keep the shopping trip short, but it still took a few hours. She could never trust sizes and had to try everything on. She was shopping for most everything possible so there were no shortcuts. She needed some clothes that could handle some action, so she couldn't simply buy everything in sizes large enough to be loose. Best not to leave a lot of handles if she found herself in a fight. There was also the consideration that clothes had to be able to conceal her firearms.

Finally, she exited the mall with many bags filled with the things she would need for the next week or so. At least she had enough to do some laundry now instead of shopping for everything new. If this went beyond that she could shop as needed only. Short trips were far more palatable than these long shopping trips.

On her way to the hotel she picked up fast food once she realized she was hungry. She had wanted nothing more than to leave the mall right away, so she hadn't eaten there. The mall itself, with all its patrons, had begun to feel claustrophobic. At the hotel she carried everything in to meet a porter at the door. She was about to tell him to shove off when he mentioned that he thought she had a message at the front desk. Autumn gave him her bags and walked to the desk.

The girl at the desk was still the same proper and professional woman who had told her of the Galleria. She was watching Autumn walk over to her with an extremely fake smile on her face. Her opinion of Autumn seemed to have dropped further still over the course of the last few hours.

"Lindsay Brown," Autumn said to her. "I believe you have a message for me."

"Yes. A very…" she searched for the correct word to use. "Unsavory man left this for you. He seemed very adamant that only you see it. I hope he is not staying with you here," she said, fighting hard to maintain her required smile.

"That's none of your damn business." Autumn took the note and returned to her room. She figured that she owed herself some money from the bet.

When she arrived at her room the porter was leaving.

"Everything is on the bed, ma'am. Your sandwich in on the dresser," his smile felt far more genuine.

"Thank you," she gave him a ten. All this kindness and thoughtfulness was bought and paid for. She could at least understand this system well. She wondered if at some point she could pay them to forgo all the happiness and sweetness. Could she buy straight faces and no greetings?

She closed and locked her door and looked at the note. It seemed that he'd managed to find her, unless this was some odd random message. She hoped that last night had paid off and enticed Christos to pursue her. She was banking on his naivete. There was no other way to find out but to open the envelope.

On that plain white envelope was printed "Lindsay Brown" in fine exacting fashion. The whole thing had a feeling of magic about it. She continued to look it over without opening the letter. Wizards could be a very tricky bunch. She wasn't sure but figured that opening this letter could trigger many different types of spells to activate. Autumn knew that fire would break the spell, but to do it she would have to burn the note. She had heard from someone before that running water could wear away a spell over time, but that would also destroy the note inside. She couldn't think of any way to deactivate a possible spell without causing damage to the underlying letter. Ingenious

The Hunter Overture

method of spell delivery if that was indeed what this was.

Finally, she decided to rely on the safeties she already had in place. With her act and her fake ID, she hoped that any spell aimed at her specifically would be mis-targeted enough that it couldn't take hold. Any kind of tracking spell or identifying spell would require a good target. An offensive spell wouldn't, and neither would a simple enchantment of the note and envelope, but she couldn't be one hundred percent safe all the time.

She tore open the envelope and nothing happened. She paused for a moment expecting some kind of light show and realized that she probably wouldn't know if something had happened no matter what. Time would tell if she had been hit with something. She pulled out the letter and flipped it open. This was hand-written by someone with careful script. She wondered if it might have been Christos himself who had written it.

> *Lindsay,*
> *Last night was refreshing. Most women I meet I find to be a bore after any amount of time. You were exciting and quite challenging. Please do me the honour of accompanying me tonight. I will send a car for you or your declination at nine. Please dress casually as there is no reason for formality where we will be going. I await your company with bated breath.*

> *Andrzej*

"What a sanctimonious asshole. At least I'm in," she spoke to herself as she walked to the bathroom. She dropped the letter and the envelope into the sink after she lit both of fire. Were either of them enchanted to track her or anything else this would take care of it. She had what she needed, so there was no reason to ever leave a trail.

Casual dress at nine tonight. That sounded more her style. She wondered what kind of plans he had in mind. Surely, it wasn't another night-club if he wanted her to dress casually. Maybe, he was going to try and impress her by giving her a tour of his entire operation. That would make this all very easy. He might be planning to attack her in some way. If he learned anything that made him feel she was a threat, he could be on alert. Or maybe he thought he was going to get laid. She would have to wait until nine to find out.

She could better plan for events to take a rough turn since she didn't need to dress formally. She had no good way to hide a gun on herself with most formal wear. Especially, when she needed to dress to look good. Curves don't look as enticing when there were holster bulges. Tonight, she could carry and hide it well. That should help her even the odds should it all go sideways.

The alarm clock in her room showed five-thirty. She turned her phone on and sent a message to Elizabeth. She had mentioned last night that she preferred text messages to phone calls. Autumn completely agreed.

-Hi there. I have some time tonight. Would you like

dinner?-

After she sent the message she began to search her bags for something to wear. She'd try to dress to cover dinner with Elizabeth and a night out with Andrzej. This was starting to feel like a weird sitcom that she would hate to watch. After a few moments she checked her phone again.

-Well hi. :) I'd love dinner. I'll pick you up in 10?-

-Perfect.-

Autumn turned her phone off and chose a pair of jeans and a green top that exposed her abs. She then put on a waist coat over that leaving it open in the front. The coat was loose, so she could use it to hide one of her forty-fives under her arm. One major benefit of her size was the ability to hide a large gun on her frame. She put her wallet in her pocket and the phone into a pocket on her coat. She couldn't stand carrying a purse. If she needed a bag, a backpack made far more sense, but that didn't have the same acceptable look. Fortunately, short hair required very little care. She forgot all about the food she had picked up for lunch.

She walked downstairs and out into the lobby area of the hotel. She saw a small car parked in front with Elizabeth in the driver's seat. Autumn walked quickly across the lobby out of excitement. She was genuinely eager to see this woman again. She folded herself into the passenger seat and pushed the seat as far back as the little car would allow.

114

"Sorry. My car is quite small."

"That's fine," Autumn said with a slight laugh. "So are you. It fits. Let's get some food and talk."

"Your wish is my desire."

Elizabeth pulled out and drove off toward their second date.

CHAPTER THIRTEEN

They drove quietly for a time. Elizabeth knew where she was going and Autumn was along for the ride. Autumn had never had any problem with silence. She spent much of her time alone and there were occasions when her silence had kept her out of trouble. She had a natural aversion to people who run their mouth to fill space. Ever since she was a child she found silence to be her natural state of being. That's why it struck her as odd when Elizabeth finally spoke.

"So, are you shy now?"

"No, I just see no reason to speak when I have nothing to say."

"I see," Elizabeth said with a determined tone. "I guess I'll get this conversation started since you won't. So, do you like Asian food?"

"For the most part, yes."

"Good. I know a really good Mongolian Grill where the staff will leave us alone to talk. The food is pretty good too. I hope you are up for more conversation than this."

"I'm sorry if I gave you the idea that I don't want to

talk to you," Autumn said tugging slightly at her shirt. She had dressed to impress but found herself slightly uncomfortable. "I spend a lot of time alone and forget how uncomfortable others are with silence."

"I guess I'm being a bit of a defensive bitch," Elizabeth commented with a chuckle. "I don't want you to think I do this kind of thing all the time. I'm not even sure what kind of thing this is."

"Let's just see what happens. I hate labels."

"Fair I guess," they finished the trip in silence. Autumn felt a little bad that she was making Elizabeth uncomfortable, but she didn't really know how to fix it. She didn't know how to act either. When they reached the restaurant, it was six. They were seated in a back room per Elizabeth's request. There was a lag in service, but it was worth it for the privacy. Once their drink orders had been taken, they finally joined the line to pick out their food. Autumn had never been to a restaurant like this, but she liked it. She picked out each item she wanted to be in her stir-fry and never had to speak to a soul about her preferences.

Elizabeth spent her time in line watching the other customers stare at Autumn. She could understand why. Autumn was a truly unique woman. She also began to see why Autumn would remain silent. No matter who Elizabeth looked at they were openly watching Autumn. The women looked jealous and distrustful while the men looked lustful. Elizabeth had never met a woman like Autumn in her life and it seemed none of these people had either.

When they returned to their table Autumn took time while they waited for their finished food to look at the woman across from her. Everything looked different in the light of day… and vertical. She had not paid as much attention to her when they were in her store. Elizabeth was a small woman. Tiny really. She was shorter than Autumn, but most people she met were.

Her face had sharp angles that led to the severe librarian look she had. Her icy blue eyes and blond hair tied back aided the severe look she seemed to cultivate. Her limbs and frame were compact and thin. In the light of day, she looked fragile though Autumn knew that wasn't the case. She dressed very well if a bit plain for a woman running a top-of-the-line clothing store. Autumn was a bit taken aback by how different the two of them were physically. She was also taken by how attracted to Elizabeth she was.

"So," Elizabeth began the conversation again. "I've never met someone in the manner we met. I don't do that kind of thing normally. Do you do that sort of thing often? I had to fire Pete for what he did. I thanked him and gave him five hundred bucks too."

"Did you?" Autumn found that she was smiling at her. "Very mixed messages to send a young boy."

"He'll get over it. He wasn't a very good employee anyway. I thought he would never do anything good until last night. Does that sound desperate?"

"No, it doesn't. And no, I've never done that before either," Autumn said adjusting her shirt a bit again. "To tell you the truth I wasn't even sure it'd work."

"Being with a woman?" Elizabeth asked.

"No," she was almost insulted until she saw the wry smile on Elizabeth's face. "The shopping thing. It was a bright idea I had suddenly."

"Ah, okay. I can't believe this is all happening."

Autumn paused, "Is that your reason? Is this some

sort of crazy bucket list thing?"

"No, no. Sorry," Elizabeth blushed slightly. "You're... I... I was just so taken with you so immediately. I've never met someone like you before. Really."

"You keep saying that. Others have before. In fact, everyone says that at some point after meeting me. I know that I'm different. That's why I've developed some trust issues."

"I bet. I've watched how people look at you. I was watching people here while we were getting food. I bet you feel like you're on display sometimes."

"Yeah? I've seen you watching me too," Autumn said quietly.

"I know. I'm trying to convince myself that this is all happening for real. People like me don't find people like you," Elizabeth was still nervous as she spoke. It all seemed to be coming out wrong.

"Is that so?" there was suspicion in Autumn's voice.

Their food arrived steaming hot. The server set down two large bowls in front of them and a refill for each of their drinks. Silence hung over the table while the server was there. She must have felt like an invader. They both tasted their food. Autumn quite enjoyed the creation she had gotten.

"Look," Elizabeth spoke. "I'm fucking this up majorly. I don't mean to be an asshole. Let's try another line of conversation. What do you do for a living?"

"Nope," Autumn said flatly.

"What? Why?"

"Okay, my turn to ruin things." Autumn put her fork down and pierced Elizabeth's eyes with her gaze.

Their eyes held the lock as if they were magnets.
"Simply put: I'm lying to you and I have to keep
doing it for a while. I can't tell you what I do or why
I'm doing it. Hell, Lindsay isn't even my real name.
I'm sorry, but for both of our sakes I must keep many
things about myself secret. I do understand how this
must sound to you."

"That is quite a hard pill to swallow," Elizabeth
looked down at her food as she spoke. "Will I ever
know?"

"I think I'd like you to. I do think I know that
much," Autumn broke her stare and looked down.
She felt more vulnerable than she had in a very long
time.

"I see," Elizabeth looked up to see Autumn looking
at her food and returned to her food to think and
escape for a moment. They both returned to eating in
silence. Each wondered while they ate if there was
anything here that could work on any level. Elizabeth
took a drink and looked Autumn in the eyes. She held
the gaze and for the time she seemed to be digging
into Autumn's soul. Autumn began to suspect magic.

"Okay, Lindsay, I'll buy in," Elizabeth finally said.
"You're too amazing for me to walk away from just
because it might be difficult. I'm not open to the
world. I guard myself carefully. People assume that a
gay man knows fashion well, so they'll shop at his
store. People think that a lesbian is some plaid
wearing dyke who drives a truck. They refuse to take
fashion advice from her. I have feelings for you,
Lindsay, and I want to take the risk. I think you're
worth it," she paused. "What's wrong?"

"I want to hear you say my real name," Autumn

said with a shaky voice. "Hearing you call me Lindsay just doesn't feel right at all. It's hollow. I just realized how much I want to hear that. However, I know that it will go poorly for both of us if I break character even for you."

"Then don't," Elizabeth said firmly. "I think you're someone very special and I don't want you doing anything you're not comfortable with. You can tell me when you feel it's the right time. You've been protecting yourself for much longer than I've known you."

Autumn was amazed. No one had treated her so honestly and well since her parents. People always want to further their agenda. That brought back some memories she thought were completely under control. She fought hard to push those back. Elizabeth would not yet understand.

"Thank you, Elizabeth. I don't want to break that trust. Truly. You keep telling me how amazing I am, but you need to give yourself far more credit."

"Well, I never thought we could give each other so much gratification in public without having the police called," her smiled beamed out at Autumn too beautifully not to be true. "Let's get to know each other as much as we can. What would you like to know? I'm an open book."

"Why the fashion industry?"

"Well, I've always been a bit of a girlie girl. When I was young, adults always said I was pretty and gave me attention. I liked that, of course. Then when I hit high school and college my knowledge and ability got me into all the prettiest girl's dressing rooms."

"You perv," Autumn laughed, and Elizabeth joined

her.

"I thought you had figured that out last night."

"That was this morning," Autumn said with a warm smile.

"That was amazing is what it was. Are you an athlete? Not career, just in your spare time and past."

"I was. I've always been athletically gifted."

"I'll say," Elizabeth said with an audible wink.

"Quiet you. I was in sports all through school. I've trained in martial arts and I've always worked out. When I was eighteen I joined the Marines and excelled until I had the chance to join the SEAL program. I spent some years as a Navy SEAL before I moved on."

"Jesus. No more?" Elizabeth asked with a look of shock on her face.

"That's the wall."

"Quite an amazing resume. I assume I'll be seeing the theatrical release soon. I can't wait to see them cast someone who isn't nearly as beautiful. No wonder, though. You're built like Wonder Woman."

"You're the second person to say that in as many days."

"Another love interest? Should I be jealous?" A nervous looked clouded over Elizabeth's eyes.

"A little girl. She seemed to think I was a super hero."

"Nah. You need a costume for that. You seem uncomfortable enough in the shirt you're wearing."

"I wore it to impress you," Autumn said not telling her about keeping up a look for Andrzej tonight. She hadn't realized how uncomfortable she was when she was. She would be fine once she was playing the part tonight, but she felt different around Elizabeth.

"Well, it's working, but I can't picture you in brightly colored spandex."

"No?"

"Well, not in public, at least. My pants are too lightly colored for that," she winked. Suddenly she reached into her purse. "Oh! Here." She gave Autumn the four hundred-dollar bills from the store.

"What's this for?" Autumn took the money.

"After our night last night, it felt too much like prostitution to keep that money."

"I see," Autumn said with a smirk. "Glad to see that I maintain my record of never having to pay for sex."

Elizabeth flipped Autumn off.

"So, are you out? What was it like in the military?"

"Truthfully? You're the first woman I've ever been with."

"No way!" she puffed out her thin chest with pride. Autumn approved. "I turned you? Just call me Amazbian. How did I manage that?"

"You asked," Autumn said simply. "I found your number and it sounded like a good idea. I've never really thought about it before. Guys have always pursued me, and they were fun enough. It was just so easy and that's how it seemed it was supposed to be. Some women have asked before, sure, but you were my first."

"Well, I hope I'll be your second too."

"Probably, but it won't be tonight. I have work things to do."

"Woah! Your whole demeanor just changed drastically. If that has to do with work you must do some scary shit."

"Maybe, but don't go trying to find out," Autumn said trying to bring the light back to her face. "There's a side of me that you should never see even if you learn more about me. I-I don't want you to see parts of my life. There are things I don't want to see in your eyes when you look at me."

"I think I agree with you."

"Sorry, but on that note, we should probably head back."

"Oh," Elizabeth looked down. "Do we have time to make out in my car a bit? I really want to get my hands on you again."

"Well, let's pay the check and get going."

CHAPTER FOURTEEN

Elizabeth dropped Autumn off two minutes before the car from Andrzej was to arrive. Autumn wanted her to drop a block away so that no one would see the drop. She was concerned about someone following Elizabeth. She would probably never notice the car, and Autumn wouldn't be around to do anything about it. There was no reason for this wonderful woman to run into problems with what Autumn was into. Elizabeth wasn't a combatant and she was most definitely not a threat to anyone. They kissed, and Autumn walked to her hotel while Elizabeth drove off.

When she got to the hotel entrance, Autumn was met by a man in an all-black suit. He was quite stocky and shorter than Autumn, but not short. He looked shorter from his sheer size. She thought his shoulders almost looked to be half his height in width. He had probably played football at one point. Possibly professionally. The man made a motion toward a jet-black Lexus parked nearby.

"Will you be joining Mr. Christos tonight?" the driver asked in a voice made of pure bass sound.

"Why yes, I will," Autumn said with a coy smile. Time to get into character and go to work. "Nice car."

"Yes," he replied simply.

Autumn walked to the car and had to applaud the punctuality of Andrzej's people. The driver let her into the back seat on the passenger side. She folded inside and looked to her left as she was greeted by Andrzej himself. He had two champagne flutes in his hand and offered her one.

"We travel in style, My Dear," Christos said with a big smile usually reserved for sales people. "I think you'll enjoy what I have planned for tonight. I hope to surprise you with something catered to your tastes."

"Exciting," Autumn said taking a flute. "I hope it's an energetic activity. I've been feeling cooped up recently."

"Oh, then you will love tonight's activity. How long until we arrive, Theodore?" Andrzej asked the driver as he slid into his seat.

"Fifty-six minutes with the current traffic," came the deep voice of the driver.

"Perfect," Andrzej laughed as the car entered traffic on the one-way street. "We can chat all through the city. How have you been spending your time in the Gateway to the West?"

"I've been walking all through this downtown, hoping to find some real excitement. I'm not a baseball fan, hockey has finished with their season, and football has left the city entirely. I might have enjoyed watching a Rams game before they left for Los Angeles. I guess it's still early for that, but it is unavailable either way. All told it seems that this is a dull city." She took a drink of the champagne.

126

"My Dear, you must simply know where to look for your excitement," he said. The smile was still plastered on his face. It may have even grown slightly. "I take it that you enjoy the more violent sports?"

"Yes. Hard competition makes for the most exciting sports. At this point, I think I'd even watch a wrestling event."

Christos laughed sincerely.

"Then I have judged you correctly. Tonight, we're going to an underground fighting competition held by a local group. Many people compete, and magic is allowed if the two combatants agree on it ahead of time. This is the most exciting sport I have yet to encounter. I've watched similar events all over the world."

"Wow," Autumn was genuinely excited. She took another drink and smiled warmly. "This may be a very fun night. I must say, Andrzej, that night-clubs are not the most exciting form of entertainment in my eyes."

"Good for networking, though," he said draining his flute and reaching for the bottle for a refill. "I must meet with a man tonight about business, so I may slip away for a bit, but I will be back for the main event. I've heard that the main event will be one of their premier bouts. I'm anxious to see it."

"Do you want any protection during your meeting?"

He laughed again.

"No, no. I have security, My Dear. You have strong arms, that is true, but this is very important work. I'm glad, however, to hear that you want to be close to me. Your concern warms my heart. I'm very

The Hunter Overture

close to completing my masterstroke. Everything will change after that."

"Yeah?" she tried to sound interested without letting on what she knew. "Got a big money-making venture underway?"

"Oh no," Andrzej's face became serious for a moment. "Money is immaterial to what I have planned. I have far grander plans."

"That sounds very exciting," Autumn feigned ignorant excitement. She was hoping he would drop hints.

"It is," he said allowing the smile to return to his face. "Stay with me and you can join me when I'm finished. Money and the like are mere symbols of power. Unimaginative men seek those things. There is no reason to have anything in this world but pure power. When I complete my plans, the world will be mine."

"Amazing," she kept her tone slightly disinterested. Wide-eyed awe wouldn't fit the character she had been playing to this point. "Can I help you in some way? Anything this big has got to be incredible. I'd love to be involved in some small way. Maybe you can find some way to involve me."

"Oh, but you will be. You will be with me the entire way. This will be a surprise to everyone. Just be sure to stick with me. Afterward, you can be as involved as you wish."

Autumn realized that she wasn't going to get him to spill the plan here and now. He was enjoying the game too much and he didn't need her for anything. She knew she had to get over to that side of his affairs if she was to effectively take care of this problem.

She'd have to watch for some way to prove herself invaluable to him. The second major part of infiltration was finding a need and convincing the target that Autumn was the best possible way to solve it.

They continued for a while making small talk about different contact sports. Andrzej turned out to be quite the connoisseur. He knew every organization and quite a bit about most all the fighters. Autumn thoroughly enjoyed their conversation at that point. Andrzej was quite an enjoyable man when he wasn't trying to impress his lackeys. Or summon a terrible beast-from-the-depths to destroy the world.

"We're almost there, sir," rumbled Theodore's voice from the front seat.

"Excellent. Well, My Dear, let us prepare for an exciting night." He drained his flute and took both to set in their place to be cleaned later.

The car came to a stop. Autumn heard Theodore open his door before he opened hers. She stepped out followed by Christos. There was no red carpet here. Nothing marked the event at all. They stood outside an old warehouse in a rundown part of whatever town they had come to. The lot was full of vehicles ranging from large trucks to expensive luxury sedans.

Violence knew no social class barriers.

They walked toward the building and Andrzej spoke with the man at the door. He motioned, and another man appeared to lead them to their seats. He showed them down the aisle and stopped once they reached the front row. There they found empty seats next to some other friends of Christos'. Autumn had been brought along as eye candy. She had to find a way to elevate her position.

They took their seats and he began to speak with the man next to him. No introductions were made, though Autumn realized that he was the man Andrzej had come here to meet. She would have to keep an eye on him as well. He might be a second in command who could also perform the ritual; she may have found a second target. She kept eying Andrzej's rings as well. There was no shaking the idea that she knew that language, but nothing came to her. There was still no more than an itch of familiarity.

If it still bothered her later, she could get a much closer look after she took them. Of course, that necessitated her getting closer to his operation. She thought about the idea of killing them both tonight, but what if there were more? How big was Andrzej's organization? She simply didn't have enough information to judge correctly what she needed to do. Her plan continued unchanged.

The first fighters were entering the ring for the opening bout. There was no preamble, music, or announcing. This was the barest bones of a fighting organization. Autumn guessed that their appeal hinged on brutality. This group had probably experienced more than one fighter dying in the ring. Maybe they even hoped for it. A part of her wanted to get in the ring and try her hand at a fight as well. It would clear her pent-up energy.

A simple bell rang and started the match. The two men moved into the center of the ring and began to dance and circle. There was a sign up that marked this as a non-magical fight. Both men were smaller but there was no other evidence of any enforced weight classes. The feeling out process didn't last long before they jumped at each other. There was no referee in the ring and the fighters didn't seem to mind that one bit.

They began striking and the crowd went wild. One of the men showed signs of gaining an advantage, so the other man quickly took him to the mat. On the ground the advantage changed hands and the other man began to rain down forearm blows. The man on the bottom was obviously better on his feet. He pulled the man on top down to close the distance and reduce the power of his strikes. His motion was answered with a brutal head-butt.

The man on the bottom was rocked by the blow. He was already showing signs of a concussion. His will to fight was already waning. The man on top wasn't satisfied, so he delivered a few more blows before the man on bottom ceased moving. The bell rang again, the crowd cheered, and the man stood victorious. Officials entered the ring and removed the injured man while the other posed and cheered. Crowds always love a winner. Without rules fights tended to be quick and brutal. These bouts would never appeal to the masses.

All the non-magical fights moved in similar tones. There were three more of them and the crowd seemed to enjoy them well enough. However, Autumn could tell she wasn't the only one waiting for the magical fights to begin. After the fourth fight she saw the crowd break up a bit going for food, beer, and bathroom breaks. There were a few people around the ring selling booze and others taking bets. Christos was enjoying what he watched, but he had been engrossed in a discussion with the man next to him for the most part.

Autumn enjoyed the fights and tried her best to eavesdrop on their conversation, but it seemed that they had put up a magical barrier to hold down the sound. In the ring she saw that they were setting up four odd devices under the ropes on each side of the ring. The sign was also being changed. It appeared that they were moving to the magical bouts. That conversion seemed to be the impetus for the break.

Christos and his compatriot seemed to reach a mutual agreement because the barrier came down and he turned to Autumn.

"Enjoying the show, My Dear?" he asked with genuine concern.

"So far, though the caliber of fighter has been a bit lackluster," she responded, not hiding her slight disappointment. "I am excited to see the next bout, however."

"You're a true connoisseur. The magical fights are the best," Andrzej said with childlike excitement. "No offensive spells are allowed. The fighters are only allowed to enhance themselves with magic for the fight. Creativity usually decides these fights more than pure power."

"Excellent. This will make for a great show. This was a great idea, Andrzej."

He smiled satisfied in the knowledge that he had impressed her. This was the kind of match Autumn wanted to see. She figured, after his explanation, that this would be the sort she would try if she ever tried it. There was no sense in her beating men who weren't using magic. She was enhanced so she might find actual competition here. It had been a while since she had been in a good fight with a skilled opponent who could challenge her.

The first man entered. He was tall and thin, almost lanky. He wore a long and loose pair of jean shorts and no shirt to hide his thin chest from the crowd. An old man led him down to the ring. The thin man kept his head down looking at no one else. He climbed into the ring slowly. Autumn wondered how much enhancement it would require for him to be competitive. He almost looked mentally challenged by the way he moved and acted. He walked to a corner and hunched there.

The second man was shorter, but easily a hundred pounds heavier. He wore traditional fighting shorts and no shirt, which showed his lifetime of body building. Autumn knew that worked well for show and pure strength, but it could be a hindrance in a fight. Of course, she knew nothing yet of his enhancement. He could be much better than he looked. She was almost on the edge of her seat.

There were officials for this one, but they were around the outside of the ring weaving a protective magical barrier. She felt sure this was in case things got out of hand and spilled out of the ring. The two men stood in their respective corners waiting. The muscular man bounced and jumped like a child waiting to go play. The tall man simply stood there looking at his feet. He almost seemed not to understand where he was or what was happening.

The bell rang, and the heavy man jumped. He moved across the ring almost at a run. Lanky walked a few paces forward, but did nothing else. Muscles charged in and slugged him in the gut right off doubling Lanky over in pain. As he bent over he met a right hook from Muscles.

The crowd roared at the beating they were witnessing.

Muscles kicked Lanky while he was down and Lanky merely rolled away holding his abdomen. Muscles was beaming. He even stopped to celebrate a bit before moving in for the kill.

Autumn heard him yell at his opponent: "Is that all you have? I thought you were supposed to be tough." This kind of cruel competition fit his demeanor well, it seemed. He bent down and picked up the tall man and threw him across the ring unceremoniously. Lanky dropped and flopped over.

The crowd continually roared in pleasure, but Autumn failed to see any sport in what was happening in the ring. She didn't look amused at all.

"Do not fret, My Dear. This is nowhere near over. Well, maybe it is. JC is undefeated so far. That is the tall man. Pedro is new to the circuit. He knows nothing about who he faces. He has heard rumors, but that's all. Keep your eyes open."

As Autumn watched she saw JC start to talk to himself. She couldn't hear him, but he kept chanting and talking. It almost looked like he was giving himself a pep talk about hustling and not giving up. As he spoke, he became more animated. Pedro was celebrating and taunting him without paying much attention. Autumn was watching, however, and she began to understand what was happening. JC *was* mentally challenged. He must have had the mind of a young child and she thought she knew who his hero

134

might be.

As he spoke his body began to change as well as his attitude. His whole body began to fill out with muscle. It resembled the change Bruce Banner went through when he was angry. Suddenly, his jean shorts didn't look loose but tight. Even his face changed. His jaw became squarer and his bones shifted slightly to give him a different appearance. Pedro realized his mistake too late.

JC stood up tall and smiled at Pedro. His entire demeanor had changed. JC now looked cocky and sure in his movements. Pedro rushed in trying to finish it and JC hit him. He hit him multiple times and then threw him into the ropes. Real ropes aren't springy as they appear in wrestling, so Pedro didn't rebound off them. JC went to him.

Pedro moved forward to meet him and JC executed a hip toss throwing Pedro to the mat. Pedro popped up quickly. JC met him with a boot to the gut doubling Pedro over. He quickly shoved the shorter man's head between his legs and executed a powerful power bomb. Pedro hit the mat on his back with the wind knocked out of him. His head bounced viciously off the canvas.

The crowd roared, and JC celebrated through the ring.

Pedro was hurt. He lay on his back a moment not sure where he was. Autumn guessed that he had taken a lot of the force to his head and had a concussion now. JC stood by Pedro's head with his right hand open in the air. He then bent over Pedro at the waist, placing his face close to Pedro's, and waved his open hand in front of his face.

The crowd exploded, and JC disappeared… literally.

Autumn watched as she saw the ropes on one side bend then there was a pause. Suddenly she heard a loud bang and Pedro's head was bounced off the canvass, again.

Hard.

Materializing from thin air, JC stood over Pedro. JC smiled and posed a bit for the crowd who popped big for him. Pedro tried to stand back up and JC helped him onto his own shoulders like a fireman's carry. The audience continued to go crazy and Autumn joined them. She knew what came next.

JC flipped him off his shoulders and slammed Pedro onto his back onto the canvas while holding onto Pedro's head. Pedro screamed, and Autumn thought he looked like he may have received a broken back or even a broken neck.

Scurrying over him, JC lifted one of Pedro's legs, and pinned him. Apparently, this happened often because a referee was waiting. He slid into the ring and pounded his hand on the mat three times.

JC jumped up and celebrated to the cheering crowd. He danced and posed for a bit before getting out of the ring and walking to the back followed by the older man. He gave many high fives along the way. Officials solemnly climbed into the ring with a stretcher to take Pedro out on his back. She figured this might be his last bout here or anywhere.

"The spell will last for, maybe, twenty minutes more before reverts back to the way he was before," Andrzej leaned over and spoke to Autumn. "The man with him is his father. He'll collect his money and take him home afterward. The boy loves it… when he knows what's going on. That's how they pay for his medical care."

"That is an amazing spell," Autumn couldn't hide her amazement or smile as she spoke.

"It's the only one he knows. The boy is a magical savant. I'm not even sure he knows that he's using magic. With the right training he could be amazing. His raw power is quite amazing, but he hasn't the mind to learn the nuance required for delicate use. Maybe, when he was young, he could have been taught to work with his mind to heal himself."

"Wow," Autumn exclaimed. She was excited to see what the main event was if that was the opening magical bout.

The next two matches were also magical, but far more what she had expected from a magical fight. She guessed they opened with one of their best to get the crowd excited after the regular fights. Maybe JC had a bedtime he had to make so he couldn't fight later.

It seemed that time was drawing near for the meeting between the Andrzej and his guest. They were gathering a few things and standing up. There were two large men nearby who also stood. They appeared to be bodyguards. Autumn realized that Andrzej's bodyguard had not traveled here with him. That didn't seem like good practice. She began to wonder if something was wrong. She had thought that Theodore was also his bodyguard.

The four of them were walking out when Autumn saw that one of the guards had a gun out pointed at Christos. She could let him die right then, but she'd never know if she had finished the job entirely. She had no way to stay close to Andrzej's partner if that was even who he was.

In a flash Autumn was up and moving. He brought the gun level right as Autumn grabbed his gun arm. She grasped his wrist with her right hand and put her left fist straight through his arm at the elbow. It broke easily causing him to scream and drop the gun.

All three of the other men turned to see Autumn strike his shoulder, breaking it as well. The man dropped to his knees and looked at the man Andrzej was meeting and then quickly at Christos. Everyone looked down at the gun on the floor near the man. Understanding flowed over Andrzej's face as he shook his head and then nodded toward Autumn. Almost reflexively she drove her forearm into his neck snapping it. The man dropped like a dead weight.

"My god," said the man Andrzej had come to meet.

"Yes, my own guard turned traitor. What a course tonight's events have taken. Who could have predicted it all?" He looked up at Autumn. "Seems that I'm in need of a bodyguard, and you were spectacular, My Dear. Does your offer still stand? I think I may be ready to accept your qualifications."

"Certainly," she picked up his gun. "Do you want me to start now?"

"It seems that you already have."

Autumn smiled.

"Come with us please and keep your eyes open."

He looked at the other man and smiled. Seemed like Autumn had found her way in. Maybe things would all work out well after all.

CHAPTER FIFTEEN

The man with Christos seemed to be very suspect
of Autumn and what had happened. His look was one
of complete disbelief. Autumn had done nothing to
gain his trust, and she seemed to have little effect on
him in any other way. She'd have to keep her eye out
for a way to make things better if that was even a
possibility.

"Andrzej, I know that you like her, and that I'm not
the man to tell you who you should keep on your arm,
however, you know nothing about her in any real way.
How competent is she? What is her goal here? To
whom do her allegiances lie?"

"Marcus, Marcus, Marcus," Andrzej replied,
assuming a painfully patronizing tone. "I know that
she's quite capable and strong. I know that she
jumped to save my life when none of us were even
aware of the threat. I'm also a wonderful judge of
character. Remember how I gave you a chance when
no one else would? Her motivation is power. All
women want power; Lindsay is simply more honest
and open about that. She wants to be close to

someone who wields true power. Her allegiance will be mine entirely when she sees what we do during the ritual."

"But, Andrzej-"

"No!" Andrzej showed that fast anger again as he spoke. "I have made my decision and I will not have you question me. Let us go and finish our preparations. I want to be back here in time for the main event. I have a surprise in mind that will be excellent and prove many things to you."

"Certainly," Marcus replied with calm aplomb. "I'm sorry. I merely wish for you to have the best security so that all goes exactly as planned. We can afford nothing going wrong now and you are far too important to take any chances."

"Of course, I understand. Now, let us retreat and have done with business."

Autumn was relieved to find that she had so thoroughly fooled Andrzej. She would have to keep an eye on Marcus. He was not nearly as trusting as Andrzej. She was glad she hadn't tried to ally herself with his efforts. He would have taken much too long to crack. Paranoia was a hard thing to get past.

Silence marked their quartet as they moved through the raucous crowd. A man ran up to Andrzej and pulled him away to speak. Autumn stepped forward enough to catch some of their conversation. The man seemed quite concerned with the murder that had been perpetrated at Autumn's hands.

"I comprehend the situation, but I can't allow that kind of thing to continue here," the man said to Christos. "There is already enough violence in the ring."

"I understand, my friend, and I assure you that it was a one-time event," Andrzej said in soothing tones. "It is not often that my own guard tries to assassinate me. Fortunately, someone else was watching out for my well-being." He looked back at Autumn and smiled before turning back. He made a motion with his hand and suddenly she couldn't hear anything they were saying. They continued to speak for less than a minute before the man walked away and Andrzej turned back to their group.

"Let us leave for more important things. All is well, and I have arranged for the surprise I told you about."

The quartet walked out of the main door and walked along the wall to an outlying building to the East. The night was warm and pleasant, but the tension among the small cadre added a chill that could be felt by all. Once inside the smaller building the other guard locked the only door and stood by it. Autumn matched his positioning not knowing if there was an etiquette to this kind of thing. Andrzej could be quick to anger, and she didn't want to step wrong now. She kept her herself alert. She had no idea what might take place at this meeting.

The two men stood over a table set in roughly the middle of the room. They no longer guarded their sound from the rest of the room, but Autumn assumed that the room itself was blocked for both sight and sound. Marcus' guard was alert to things outside of the building. Autumn kept her focus locked firmly on the two men standing at the table. This would be her best chance to find out what was really happening.

"So, I want to move soon," Christos opened the conversation. "I'm tired of waiting. Our delay from here out only allows the Consortium time to prepare a counter measure. They may have already infiltrated our efforts. They could have been the ones who turned Kevin into a traitor. That would make sense. We must not allow that to spread. On this we are in agreement, right?" Andrzej asked accusingly.

"Agreed, but I still think that Monday is too early," Marcus remarked with visible frustration as Andrzej sighed dramatically. "Entirely too early. We must do this right the first time. You must understand that. There is no way we survive a mistake to try a second time. And we don't know who got to Kevin. We should take some time to investigate."

"I will not stop for any kind of investigation. Surely, that would only benefit those who oppose us. We know who is against us. As for your preparations, we have discussed this many time before, Marcus. I understand your fears, but we have planned this well for months. How will two weeks, or more at your pace, help anyone aside from our enemies? We must move now," Andrzej almost yelled as he slammed his fist down on the table. "Once we have completed the ritual the Consortium will be able to do nothing to oppose us. You must have faith and vision. Bravery is what will bring us ultimate power, not cowardly sniveling. We must be bold and act."

"I still have preparations that simply must be completed with the utmost care. That is being cautious not cowardly." Marcus seemed frantic to buy himself more time. Autumn began to wonder what his true motivation was. Were there preparations to complete or did he have something else in mind?

"I'm beginning to question your competence,

Marcus. Worse, however, I am questioning your fire and faith. Do you have the child?" Andrzej asked.

"Yes," he replied with more force than Autumn expected. "After the one you had fell through I think we were both glad I had prepared a backup. See, that's the kind of care I am talking about. If you'd have let Daniel guard us both, Kevin couldn't have tried to kill you. You move too fast and too sloppy."

"Those two were expendable idiots. Yes, you were smart to have multiple contingency plans. That's why I'm glad to have you along. And I feel more comfortable having two guards. Kevin's treachery has allowed Lindsay to shine through as the superior option. Now we must go for the glory. You have the plans to back us up, we have a child, and how about the location? Is it set?"

"Yes, I told you that," Marcus was having to defend himself hard. Too hard to further his argument. "Everything has been done aside from the work that must be done on the day of the ritual."

"Superb!" Andrzej said throwing his arms out wide. "Then why the additional delay? You must see my problem. I think you're merely scared and, while that is understandable, we must be the men to have courage enough to step into the new world we intend to create. We are the next true pioneers. We won't simply find a new world, Marcus, we will create one. Shape it from the old. We will carve paradise out of the garbage that is this world. This is exciting. Where is your passion?" Andrzej excelled at delivering his passion through speeches. He could rile up any crowd, but Autumn was beginning to think he needed Marcus for more than simply planning.

"We must study. We must be certain and methodical," Marcus was not buying the rah-rah speech.

"Study?" the word seemed to taste like ashes in Andrzej's mouth. "I know the ritual. I have assumed up until now that you knew it too. We have practiced. What don't you know?"

"Another rehearsal? We had a few mistakes the last time."

"You're like a cowardly woman, Marcus. You fret over the smallest details. I found that useful in the past, but now you want to waste more resources and time on yet another fake ritual. No more delays. I want to move forward with our plan. I am tired of waiting. Monday is the next chance we have and I'm certain now that we must grab that."

"Andrzej?" Autumn took a chance and spoke up from her spot. "It sounds to me as though he doesn't trust your ability to make this work. Maybe time is needed to find another second."

"Is this true, Marcus?" Andrzej looked thunderstruck having never thought of that option before. "Do you dare question my ability to wield such power?"

"No!" he glared at Autumn as he spoke. He turned his eyes to Andrzej and looked apologetic. "I simply want the greatest chance for success. This is too important to rush."

"But, Marcus, can't you see that we haven't rushed. We have taken the proper time to do this correctly. We need to move Monday. I will wait no longer. We can wait no longer. The time is now."

"If you believe it to be the best for the plan then it

shall be so. I meant no disrespect."

"I know you didn't," Andrzej said with a smile. "We are very different people. You don't have my fiery Romani blood flowing through your veins. You're more cautious. But the world needs both the lion and the rabbit. You've always been a loyal follower. This is a subject that calls for heated discussion. I would be concerned if you had no passion. Prepare yourself, Marcus, for in two days we shall achieve ultimate power."

CHAPTER SIXTEEN

They returned to the fighting arena after the
discussion. Marcus was noticeably chilly after that
conversation. Autumn would have to watch her back
now. Marcus was smarter and more careful than
Andrzej. She could only hope that he wasn't as
powerful. She had taken a chance and decided to
throw away her relationship with Marcus for a
stronger connection to Andrzej. If the opportunity
came up she could try to use what she said to convince
Marcus that she was passionate about the project, but
there was probably no chance of salvaging their
relationship.

They reached their seats while the officials were
cleaning up after the previous match. Apparently one
of the fighters had attempted an offensive fire spell.
The enchantments around the ring had rebounded it
back at him with a power boost. Four men were in the
ring moving his charred corpse out before the next
match. The audience was going wild. They seemed to
love as much carnage as they could get. The main
event would have a long way to go to top the last bout.

Andrzej leaned over to Autumn.

"That was nothing. You're going to love the main event. It's coming up next. We made it just in the nick of time," he sounded like a kid on Christmas. "Don't forget that I added a flavor to it myself."

"Sounds like that last bout was quite a show," Autumn was preparing herself for a disappointment. There was too much hype now for the next fight to live up to. "I'm afraid that you have built the next match up too much."

"It will put your concerns to rest and prove to you, me, and Marcus that I have, yet again, made a brilliant decision. Just watch. I promise that you will not be disappointed, My Dear."

He could be such a cryptic fucker.

An announcer came to the ring for the first time in the night. He climbed into the ring and the crowd calmed enough for him to do his job. He was holding a stick microphone and wearing a tuxedo. His poise was that of a man who had announced many fights in his career. Who knew there was such a position as professional underground fight announcer?

"Good evening! It is time… for our Main Event!"

The crowd roared at his delivery. He gave them a moment before motioning for calm.

"This will be a magical fight to end the night. As you know we have no official titles in this division, but there is always pride on the line in any bout. Tonight's contest has much pride to be earned. First, a man you most certainly know. He has been a part of the most memorable matches in history. He has fought all over this country and all over the globe. He is the holder of the only verified Undefeated Record known to all of mankind!"

The crowd exploded at this announcement. The room sounded like there were forty thousand in the audience instead of three. Autumn had to assume there was some kind of magic involved. Could people make that much noise otherwise? The announcer let this ride a little longer than earlier before working to get the audience down again. This man was very good at reading a crowd.

"It has been two years since he last fought in St. Louis. I'm sure you all remember that match and the fact that we had to find a new location after that," he paused for another shorter roar intermixed with laughter. "And now, the man you have all come to love. He is feared throughout the known world. No fighter has been able to weather... The Storm... of F! 6!"

There was no controlling the crowd after that announcement. As they screamed and chanted a very large man appeared in the aisle leading to the ring. He stood both tall and broad with the well-toned body of statue or a model. Autumn watched him enter and placed him at nearly seven feet tall and three-hundred-eighty pounds. He was a true beast. She could completely understand why the crowd loved this monster so much.

He walked slowly down the aisle with his arms raised to the cheering crowd. He soaked it all in as he mounted the ring and climbed in over the top rope. This man was one of the most loved fighters Autumn had ever seen. He couldn't have been more over with the crowd. Once again, people loved a winner and being undefeated was something truly amazing to be able to brag about. She couldn't wait to see who volunteered their body for destruction during this show. Even Autumn began to be swept away in the tidal wave of adrenaline.

It took several minutes for the announcer to wrest control from the crowd. Once they started to calm a bit F6 would pose and rile them up again. There was almost a game being played between the fighter and the man in the tuxedo. They both seemed to enjoy the back and forth tug-of-war with the crowd. Eventually, Underground Michael Buffer got the crowd down enough to try and announce the challenger to the crown. F6 stepped back into his corner and kept up his look of intense concentration and mental focus.

"This month there will be no open challenge," there were scattered boos and jeers. "I hear your disappointment, but we strive to offer you all the greatest fights possible. We have been offered a real challenger earlier this night." Cheers this time. "This challenger has never fought here with us before and has a record completely unknown to myself. I have been told, however, that she is a monster."

The crowd response was mixed but excited.

"She?" Autumn said aloud out of sheer surprise.

"Please welcome the challenger... Lindsay... Brown!"

The audience was still confused, but the energy made them jeer and boo the challenger to their hero. Some cheered the fact that they would see an inter-gender fight, while others cheered any potential for blood. As much as people enjoy a gimmick like an open challenge, in the end, they really want a good one-on-one match.

"What?!" Autumn turned toward Andrzej.

"Here is your chance to prove yourself My Dear."

Had he planned this all along? Had all of this been so that he could have her killed?

"How?"

"After your performance with my previous bodyguard I thought you might enjoy a real challenge. I told you I had a surprise. I spoke with the promoter when he came to talk to me about the Kevin incident. I convinced him to let us stay. I told him that he did not want to kick out the first real challenger to F6 in years. I figured this would show how good you are to both myself and to Marcus."

Autumn looked over at Marcus and he had a large smile all over his face. As far as he was concerned his problems with her were over. He couldn't have been having more fun. He made sure that their eyes locked so that she could see how happy he was that she would get what was coming to her.

She looked up at the monster in the ring and back at Andrzej.

"Okay. You asked for this," Autumn stood up and took off her coat and the gun she was wearing. She stuffed both into her bag and set it on her chair. "I'll be back."

She walked around the side of the ring away from F6 and hopped onto the apron. Many in the crowd were having trouble knowing how to react to what they were seeing. Some started to cheer when they saw that she was large and well-built while others still couldn't get past the fact that she was pretty. Autumn was large, but the beast in the ring was huge. The crowd could not come to a consensus aside from their desire to watch carnage.

Autumn climbed in under the top rope and instantly climbed onto the top rope and balanced herself in the corner. She flung her arms up and posed for the crowd. More were won over by her seeming confidence and charisma. She might be pulling a few fans, but no one intended to wager any serious money on her victory.

She saw no reason to make this feel small for the crowd. She had always loved when fighters played to the crowd. This part was all about show and excitement. She had made a great choice of a shirt for the fight, but she was regretting her choice of bras. She had not expected any athletic competition, so she was unprepared for that. The crowd would appreciate her mistake as well.

She jumped off the ropes and turned to meet the beast in the middle of the ring. She had to keep in mind that this was a magical fight so, on top of his size, he could use magical enhancements as well. She had no way to gauge his magical prowess. Or the prowess of whomever had enhanced him. He stuck his right hand out to shake her hand and she took it. Her hand disappeared into his.

"Okay, the combatants are ready," the audience barely held their calm as the announcer continued. They knew it wouldn't start until he did, but they didn't want to wait. "This is a magical fight. F6, do you want to call for a Death Match? You have the privilege as the returning champion."

His voice was like gravel and broken glass was his breakfast cereal of choice. It rolled out of him like cold molasses. "Tonight, I will be magnanimous. I choose no Death Match."

"He says no, folks!"

The crowd applauded his generosity. Many were now more comfortable knowing that he would only hurt the pretty woman in the ring... very badly. Men walked through the audience shouting odds and taking bets in the lag before the match. Autumn's chances were almost too low to be calculated without a computer.

They both retreated to their corners while the betting was completed. This would be a gold mine for the bookies, but they had started late since she had been announced late. The promoter was allowing them time to get all the action going that they could. This was probably the main income of the whole venue.

Autumn leaned over the rope and yelled to the nearest man taking bets.

"Hey, bookie!" the man turned to look at her. "I want to put four hundred dollars on myself."

"You sure?"

"Of course. Do you need the money right now?"

"No, I know where you'll be sleeping soon. I'll come get it then."

The crowd roared with laughter.

"Okay, no more bets, people," the announcer called. "It is time for this match to begin. Can Lindsay survive F6 or will this be yet another Unnatural Disaster?"

The crowd was going hoarse already from yelling so loudly. They might have nothing left for the end of the match at the rate they yelled. Autumn was calm. She had figured that she would have to work smart.

He would come out strong. If she turned out to be stronger than him then this would be easier. If that wasn't the case, she had a lot of training to fall back on. She was only a little concerned... maybe more.

F6 continued to dance in his corner. Autumn could not afford to consider him a joke in any way. With enhancement he could have numerous powers at extreme levels. She knew of no rule that said he couldn't go beyond strength and the like. She had no way to further enhance, herself so she would have to make do with what she brought into the ring. Autumn stood calmly waiting to see what the fight would bring.

The Bell Rang.

The Crowd Cheered.

F6 moved.

Those three things happened simultaneously. The big man almost leapt across the ring. He was shockingly fast for his size.

Great.

Autumn ducked to the side. She wouldn't try anything crazy until she knew better what she was up against.

F6 turned and came after her again. This time he had a better plan in mind than Hulk Smash. He had his hands up so that he could grab her when he got close. He wanted to be sure that she couldn't move away.

Autumn allowed him to get in closer this time and ducked to swing at his liver. She connected hard and felt his body ripple and bend around her fist.

He had almost no reaction whatsoever.

He was suppressing his pain reception. She now knew one of the enhancements. There was no point in trying any pain causing maneuvers. She'd have to go purely for damaging his body instead.

She tried to duck out quickly, but she had let him get very close. He grabbed her wrist and his face broke out in a big toothy grin like a killer shark.

Were his teeth filed to points?

That grin turned into confusion when he went over her head and landed on his head in the corner.

The crowd cheered her hip toss, but Autumn knew she had only achieved making some distance and him a lot of angry. His face showed no amusement anymore. He had expected to be in complete control during this match.

Autumn extended the distance between him even though he had the reach advantage. She couldn't hit him from here, but she couldn't risk his grasp a second time.

Her best chance was his legs. If she could take out his legs, then he would be taken out of the fight. F6 got back to his feet and approached her slowly. He was wary now.

Autumn lunged in and danced away when he took the bait. She wanted to keep him off balance and maybe get into his head. He tried to grab her but missed.

Autumn kept this up and after a few cycles in rhythm she lunged but dropped her level down. He jumped after her, but he wasn't prepared for her level change. He grabbed where she would have been, but not where she now was.

She took her shot and swung her right leg around to

collide with his knee. He had his legs bent so she didn't break it outright. He grunted and rolled back.

Shit.

She had gotten him with one attack but to no real effect. Now he was aware of her strategy. There was fire in his eyes, but his movement was off. She had managed to damage something.

Slightly.

Autumn grew more aggressive with her success. The crowd approved. She figured this was already longer than most of F6's fights.

Autumn landed a jab and a right hook before she danced back. He was enraged and blindly trying to grab her. His mind was on punishment and revenge. This girl had humiliated him; how dare she? Skill found no foothold in that landscape.

Autumn floated in for another attack and fell into a trap. F6 grabbed her left arm and pulled her in close. She tried to pull away, but he got an arm around her waist and one on her left wrist.

Shit. Skill had found a foothold.

With his strength and arm length he simply pulled and tried to remove her arm from her torso. Autumn could feel the enhancement to his strength. It hurt... a lot, but she held on. She couldn't twist enough to elbow him, so she grabbed one of the fingers on his hand around her waist.

With a tug she broke it backward.

He grunted and held on.

She repeated that on his next finger.

He grunted but held fast.

She grabbed the next two. F6 released his grip on her waist.

She broke both of his fingers anyway for good measure. His right hand was almost useless now. Before he could pull away, she gripped all four of the broken fingers on that hand and twisted. She was sure that he could grasp nothing with his dominate hand.

F6 pulled back his arm and inspected his now ruined hand. He looked at her hard and she knew that this had become a Death Match.

She smiled at the monster and nodded.

She moved in to quickly finish the job, but his ruined hand flew out and caught her in the right eye. That one hurt. She would have a solid black eye for that mistake. She couldn't forget that he was still fast and dangerous. Even with his right.

F6 smiled and moved to capitalize on his success. He swung out his left arm and caught Autumn with his forearm. She flew off to her left and hit the ropes.

Okay, mistakes get punished. Lesson learned.

She got up. They stood for a moment looking at each other. They had both been hurt now and neither of them was jumping to close the distance.

The crowd was rabid. They had expected a beating, but they were getting one of the best fights they had ever seen. This one was going to be talked about for years.

Autumn decided to get a bit crazy and rely on her abilities. How could he predict her actions if she had no clue herself? She shot in toward his legs expecting him to move to grab her.

He did.

She slid around behind him instead while he bent to get her. She wrapped her arms around his waist and quickly bent herself backwards taking him over in a

German Suplex.

His sheer size made that hurt.

Autumn turned on a dime and grabbed the first of his legs that she could lay her hands on. She got his right leg and pulled it straight.

She then brought her knee and her weight down on his straight knee.

It broke.

The crowd howled.

F6 began to comprehend what was happening.

He reached down and straightened his broken leg. Autumn stood back to see how this played out. Once his leg was straight he grabbed the ropes to pull himself up. Did he have healing magic going as well?

His leg did not hold.

He didn't have any kind of fast healing spell going on. Or she was stressing it to the maximum.

He fell on his left knee when his right leg gave out. He grabbed his hurt knee but looked up to see Autumn rushing in. She drove a running knee into the side of his head.

His neck bent sideways at a sickening angle and he went down. Autumn stepped back and waited. F6 wasn't moving.

After enough time the bell rang, and the announcer climbed back into the ring. He had no clue how to react to what had happened.

"We have a victor and the person who broke the world's only known undefeated streak... Lindsay Brown! The Stormbreaker!"

The crowd was not excited. Many of them hated to see such a record broken and even more were realizing how much money they had lost. No matter what people said it was hard to watch a record be broken when people invested in it. Later they would all brag about having watched it happen, but for now the mood was melancholy. Autumn climbed out of the ring with no celebration. She had a lot of money to collect.

CHAPTER SEVENTEEN

Autumn went to the bookie to collect the money, she felt, she had truly earned. There was a crowd of people around him shouting about it being rigged. People seemed to believe there was no conceivable way a woman could have beaten F6. When he saw Autumn, he had very mixed feelings. The crowd parted when they saw her. Their conviction about a rigged game and the quality of a female fighter might not be as complete as they claimed.

"I want my money," Autumn said with a slight smile. "You do remember me, right?"

"Oh, I definitely remember you. You're one of only three people I have to pay. Even with the chunk you get I pulled in more than a month's worth of takes. I don't know if I should yell at you or kiss you."

"How 'bout you pay me and leave me the fuck alone," the look on her face belied her lack of amusement for his antics.

"Fair enough. Sheesh, just tryin' to have some fun. Here," he reached in and pulled out a wad of bills and handed it over. Autumn unfolded it and counted it there. Eight thousand dollars. They really hadn't expected her to win. "Didn't mean to hurt your feelings. F6 was undefeated."

"Doesn't hurt me," she said smiling and walked back to the seats where Andrzej was still laughing heartily to Marcus.

"Am I going to receive a slap for my trickery?" he said to Autumn still laughing.

Autumn was angry, but that was not the way to play this to get what she needed.

"Andrzej, did you see what I did to him? If I were angry with you there's no way you are getting only a slap. Fortunately for you, I made a lot of money and got to take my frustrations out on someone almost my own size."

His laughter renewed, "See, Marcus? That's why she's here to guard me. Who could do that job better? Sorry about the money you lost."

"She's good. Better than I thought," Marcus said, feigning amusement. "All the more reason for you to be wary of her. You're taking great risks, Christos. Greater than I took with my money. And for both of us. When I lost, all that was taken from me was some money. Her competence and sudden appearance in your life should make you far more suspicious."

Autumn had to applaud Marcus' observations even though he was trying hard to blow her cover.

"I understand your concern, Marcus, but I have great faith in strong women. I do, however, feel magnanimous. We have something to celebrate and I want to have time for revelry. You have two additional days, Marcus."

Both Marcus and Autumn were surprised to hear

this.

"Really?" Marcus asked.

"Yes," Andrzej said to him, putting his arm around Marcus' shoulders. "I was fired up and angry earlier. I was trying to rush things. I don't agree with two weeks, but let's move it to Wednesday. That will give you a little time to feel better and it will give the rest of us time to celebrate Lindsay's victory. Come, My Dear, let us party tonight."

"Andrzej, I'm tired," Autumn sighed as she spoke. "I'm coming down from the excitement and want nothing more than to sleep. You're free to party all night, but I wish to return to my hotel. Besides, Marcus here would feel far more comfortable without me challenging his masculinity."

Marcus scowled at her but said nothing. Autumn was aware that he would spend the party trying to change Andrzej's opinion of her, but her silence would have power. She figured that any arguments that she made would only give Marcus room to argue. Best to allow him to bury his own cause angering Christos all night long. She knew she had to play this carefully. If she was right, Marcus may have made her. She had to be careful not to add to any evidence he may have. If he could question her all night long, she would eventually contradict herself enough to make his case for him.

"Oh no, My Dear. Please come," Christos said. "We will celebrate your amazing victory over the terrible F6. That calls for drinks and great reverie."

"I'm never in a party mood after a fight. Less so after that one. I want rest and time alone. That is my way."

"So be it," Andrzej said with a magnanimous sigh. "I am feeling very giving, tonight. We will celebrate in your honor. All will be well. You need to be fresh and ready to go on Wednesday. It will be then that I'll need you at your very best. You've earned a day or two off. However, I would like to meet with you before the day.

"Of course," she replied. "When?"

"Oh, I'll send a note for you."

"Lindsay?" Marcus spoke up. "Would you be willing to meet with me tomorrow? I think that, if we can speak, I will feel better about our working together."

"Certainly," Autumn replied. She could think of no way out of it. She knew it was a trap, but there was no way to escape with the time Andrzej left before the ritual.

"Excellent!" Andrzej exclaimed. "I think that's a wonderful idea. Yes, Marcus, a little time will make everything better. As you can see, once again, we work so very well together. We must never take our eyes off the true prize. Go get some rest, My Dear."

"Thank you. Can someone give me a ride back to my hotel?" Autumn asked. She was locked into the meeting with Marcus now.

"Certainly," Andrzej responded with a warm smile. "Theodore is at your disposal."

"Good night then," she said. "You know where to find me. I'll be awaiting details of the meeting times with both of you."

"Good night, My Dear," Andrzej bowed as he spoke. Some misconstrued act of chivalry.

Autumn collected her bag and left. Theodore met

her outside by the front door. He already knew what he was to do. Magic again, she assumed. She instructed him to take her back to her hotel the most direct way possible. He was quite agreeable, but he never spoke aside from direct answers to questions. The trip back was shorter than the trip out. She assumed that Christos had told him to extend it so he could have more time with her.

She thought about Elizabeth on the ride back. The thought of a massage sounded wonderful, but she could be temperamental after a night like this. There was no reason to subject the poor woman to that this early. Autumn decided that sleep was the best cure. She could contact Elizabeth later.

She woke in the morning with a fresh day ahead of her and the lingering proof of a battle the night before. Her face was puffy and tender. Her eye was solid black, and her left arm felt sore and beat. All told she felt pretty good. Experience told her these injuries wouldn't last very long.

Before any of the rest of the day could crush her plans, Autumn booted up her phone and sent a message to Elizabeth. She wanted to get the ball rolling on a plan, although she had no idea when either Marcus or Andrzej would want to meet. She then walked into the bathroom for some much-needed shower therapy. Hot water, pressure, and soap could make many wrongs right again.

After a long shower and much of the hotel's hot water she dried off and checked her phone. No message. She decided to dress comfortably today as she had some prep work to do before the big night.

She'd have to have a specific kind of store to get what she needed. She had no clue where it might be located, but she knew that a city this size should have at least one. Of course, there was the problem of this being Sunday, but she could see if one was open.

Lying comfortable on her bed, she began to search the Internet for what she needed. As was always the case, she found many pretenders but there were three very good options that looked legitimate. Two of those options were nearby so she decided to start there. Autumn preferred to leave her car at the hotel and walk. In cities it was easier to escape if need be and easier for her to tell if she was being followed.

Once her basic prep was complete she checked her messages again. Her phone was set to give her no alerts from anything. There were too many possible ways that a message or call could cause her problems. There was no message from Elizabeth. Autumn figured that her store wouldn't be open on Sunday. Google had no information about the hours, so she'd have to check in person. She turned the phone off as it had already been on longer than she liked.

She grabbed the cash she had won the night before and headed off in search of adventure. Really, this would be another shopping day but at least it would be more interesting than clothes shopping. Half a mile away was her choice for the first store. She thought it had all the marks to be what she was looking for. Inside and out it was an old antique store. The kind of store that smelled of incense and was full of items that never seemed to be bought by anyone.

That was a front, of course, the store's real business was magic. The old shopkeep sold items of power, potions, spells, and, hopefully, services. When she had found the shop on-line she had read some comments about it. When she read between the lines she gathered that he might be quite good. Autumn had no connection to the magical community here, so she had no way to verify that. She could have spoken with James, her Neolithic Consortium contact, but he would then have knowledge of what she had going on. She wanted to avoid that as much as possible.

Approaching the door, she could already see that her luck would not hold. The shop was dark inside and there was a sign on the door giving the hours. It was open until five on every day except Sunday. Of course. Well, hopefully, she could get there early tomorrow, and he could work quickly. She had thought that three and a half days would have given him enough time. She thought about the other stores, but, with what she had read, this guy seemed to be her best option. The other two had a fair number of bad reviews and she needed quality.

She booted her phone up and saw that it was ten-twenty-one. She also saw that she had received a message. She smiled as she leaned against the wall of the shop and opened it.

-Good morning, Beautiful. I'd love to meet you today for another date. Can we have enough time to go back to your room after?-

Elizabeth was very pushy for such a small woman. Fortunately, no one could push Autumn if she didn't want that and she decided she'd allow Elizabeth to push her a bit. She still didn't know about her other meetings. It was possible that neither would happen today. She thought about the consequences of telling them she had plans. Surely, no one would be surprised if the Lindsay they knew had other things going on. Of course, their communication had been very one directional.

She walked back to her hotel to see if she'd received anything. She could make optional plans with Elizabeth in case either wanted her for either lunch or dinner. She began to think of what to tell them about her plans should she need the cover. Maybe she could claim that an old friend lived in town. It would probably be better than family. She decided against any kind of business, because that could be tracked too easily. She wanted to keep that side of herself ambiguous to avoid being caught.

Arriving back at her hotel she walked up to the desk. The young girl there looked new. Maybe this was a shift no one wanted or a good place to stick new people. The girl looked intimidated when she saw Autumn standing there.

"May I help you?" she asked from the safety provided by the counter.

"Hi. Do I have any messages?" Autumn asked. "Lindsay Brown's my name. I'm in room three-seventeen."

"Let me check," the girl said and looked at the computer. After a moment she looked back at Autumn. "No. Nothing in here about a message. I haven't taken any messages today for anyone."

"Well, should someone come in, please call me and let me know. I would particularly like to speak with that person if possible."

"You could give them your room number. Then they could call you."

"No," Autumn spoke sharply causing the girl to jump. "Under no circumstances is anyone to get my room number. Is that clear?"

"Yes, ma'am."

"Good. You call me and let them speak to me."

"Yes, ma'am," the girl squeaked. "Anything else, ma'am?"

"No, thank you," Autumn said turning away and walking up the stairs to her room. Once inside she pulled out her phone and sent back a message to Elizabeth.

-I want to see you but I may have to take a meeting today as well. Yes, we can come back to my room. I'll make time. Would a dinner date tonight work well for you?"-

Again, she shut down her phone. She was excited, but that was no reason to ignore danger and change solid practices. She had more time than she had expected since Christos had extended the ritual day. She hadn't really planned on having down time during this job. She didn't have a lot to do if she wasn't working or seeing Elizabeth. Autumn had never found television or movies to be very enjoyable. She enjoyed watching football, hockey, and MMA, but those were more enjoyable at the event.

She was contemplating her dilemma when the room phone rang. She hadn't been expecting that at all. She looked at it suspiciously at first and then answered it.

"Lindsay Brown."

"Ms. Brown, there's a man here who wanted to leave a message for you. I told him you'd like to speak with him," came the voice of the girl at the desk.

"Certainly. Put him on."

"Lindsay?" Autumn didn't recognize the voice. "I'm here on behalf of Mr. Kanellis."

"Who?" Autumn asked him.

"Marcus Kanellis."

"Oh, sure," she said realizing she hadn't expected him to have a last name for some reason. "What does he want?"

"He wants to know if you would be free for lunch today," the man was trying hard to sound formal. It sounded unnatural on him.

"I think that would work. When does he want to meet?"

"He's in the car now, so the sooner the better."

Oh, making him wait would burn his ass. Autumn thought about playing the part of the woman who took forever to get ready but decided against it.

"Can you afford me twenty minutes to prepare?"

"That will be fine," he said to her. "I'll tell Mr. Kanellis thirty in case you need a bit more."

"Thank you," she said and hung up. That might turn out well. She didn't have a lot of time to prepare, but she also didn't have a lot of time to anticipate it. Keeping the meeting simple would be her best line of action. Give him very little and expect less. She merely wanted to survive this meeting without screwing up. She had most everything she needed on him. If she wasn't trying to grill him, he would have less reason to be suspicious.

She sat on the bed and checked her phone. She had a new message from Elizabeth.

-Dinner would be great. :) Do you like Mexican food?-

-Sure, as long as it's not super spicy. How about you pick me up at 5 tonight?-

She waited to see what Elizabeth responded. She had some time to kill, so she could wait a bit. Autumn wasn't a fan of all this, but somehow, for Elizabeth, it all seemed worth it.

-5 works great. I'll pick you up like before. I know where we're going so just leave that to me. Oh, and only a pussy can't handle spicy things. ;)-

-I have a meeting for lunch so my phone will be off until we meet. If anything changes I'll let you know. See you at 5.-

Autumn laughed as she turned the phone off. She was very excited about seeing Elizabeth tonight. That would be a great way to end the day. If she heard from Andrzej about tonight she'd have to say she had plans. She wasn't, however, so excited about her lunch with Marcus. She found that she couldn't trust him at all. Something about his very presence made her skin crawl. Fortunately, one lunch should go quickly enough to be tolerable. She didn't need him to love her. Hell, he had wanted the meeting. That probably meant that he had something to pitch her.

Maybe, he wanted to get her affection away from Christos. He might be that arrogant. She'd have to be careful around him.

Time to go to work.

CHAPTER EIGHTEEN

Autumn dressed comfortably for her meeting with Marcus. She had no desire to impress him, so she didn't need to dress uncomfortably. He had first met her last night in jeans, so she could aim for about the same. She wore a loose hooded sweatshirt, so she could strap a firearm to her abdomen underneath. There would probably be no need for it, but she felt more naked without one than without pants. She was certain she and Marcus would not be entirely alone. He would certainly have security or, at least, his big bodyguard.

She descended the stairs to the lobby and saw a man standing near the front door. She guessed he was the guy she had spoken with. He wasn't there last night. At least, she hadn't seen him if he had been. He checked his watch and motioned for her to come his way. She looked around the lobby and saw no one else there. She had expected Marcus to meet her with overwhelming force. His bodyguard was a huge guy. She had at least expected him. Instead she got a man who looked like a lawyer or businessman.

She walked toward the door and marveled at how
nondescript he was. His hair was brown as were his
eyes. He stood about six feet tall and had an average
build. Nothing about him stood out in any way. For
the first time in her life she had met the average man.
Something about that idea felt creepy to her. No one
was supposed to be average. Not entirely.

"You're early," he said in a bland voice that
matched his look. Anything interesting about his
voice had been added by the phone.

"I didn't need long," Autumn walked out the door
he was holding open. "Where are we going?"

"I don't speak for Mr. Kanellis unless he asks.
He'll tell you when you get in the car."

There was a simple blue sedan sitting on the road.
She wasn't sure what it was, but it looked fine.
Marcus was not nearly as concerned with appearances
as Andrzej. She stepped over to the car and the man
with her opened the back door on the passenger's side.
She sat down and saw Marcus in the front passenger
seat. The whole experience felt much less welcoming
than her earlier ride with Christos. The average man
slid into the driver's seat and started the car.

"So," Autumn asked. "Where are we going?"

"How do you feel about steak?" Marcus asked.

"I like it well enough. Do you know a good place?"

"Michael here, says he knows a decent place."

"You bet," the driver said. He even had an average
name. "It's got good food at a decent price."

"That sounds fine," Autumn said. She had no
desire to be here any longer than she had to. She
would have accepted Burger King had they suggested
it. She couldn't complain, however, because her type

wasn't supposed to like cheap things like that.

They drove on and no one said anything. Marcus wasn't starting any conversations and Michael seemed to be very careful around Marcus. There was hope that this might be an easy lunch. There was no way it would be pleasant, but if no one spoke much, it would be better. She was very surprised that his guard wasn't there. Marcus must not have been concerned that she would do anything. He was right, but that didn't seem like the most cautious option for a man who seemed as paranoid as he did.

They didn't drive for long before they pulled into the parking lot of a small local place. The building looked a bit run down. As if its peak days were fifteen years ago. The decline appeared gradual, but consistent. Autumn would never have looked twice at this place had she seen it on her own. The lot was mostly empty. She guessed that might have been part of the biggest draw. Marcus seemed the type to prefer his encounters to be private. She began to wonder if even Michael would be there when they spoke.

They all exited the car and Michael held the door for both to enter the restaurant. Once inside he walked over to the bar and took a seat. Marcus walked toward the back and Autumn followed him. She saw why the guard hadn't been there before. He was standing behind a table in the rear of the restaurant. She guessed that he had prepared things and made sure they would have privacy. That seemed far more like the Marcus she had expected.

They walked to their table and had a seat. The guard never acknowledged them, and Marcus never acknowledged the guard. A server came to the table right away bringing water, silverware, and menus. She seemed very nervous and unsure of how to act. Finally, she spoke.

"Would you like anything to drink other than water?"

"Water will be fine for me," Autumn replied.

"Same," said Marcus. He was looking at the menu already and never looked her way.

"I'll come back for your order," she said scooting away as quickly as she could.

Autumn looked at the menu and quickly picked something simple out. She had no desire for a big meal. She set her menu down and waited for Marcus to decide. She would play this as slowly as he wanted. So far, she had no idea why he had even wanted this meeting. He seemed to be as uncomfortable as she was. If she hadn't known better, she would have thought that Andrzej had forced this meeting.

"So," Marcus said putting down the menu. "Are you ready to order?"

"Yeah."

He made a motion and the server returned.

"Yes, sir," she said quietly.

"I'll have a sirloin well done with a salad and baked potato," Marcus rattled off his order mechanically.

"Certainly. What kind of dressing would you like?"

"Ranch," he almost seemed angry that he had to answer a simple question.

"And for you, ma'am?"

"I'll also have the sirloin, medium-rare, with mashed potatoes, and steamed asparagus. Thank you," Autumn tried to sound a bit kinder. It was rare that she tried to make social situations feel less awkward.

"Thank you," the woman said, taking their menus. She walked off to the back with a small shiver in her spine.

"So, now that we've ordered, let's chat," Marcus said with a wry smile that dripped with ulterior motives.

"Fine. You called this meeting," Autumn decided to play inconvenienced. "What would you like to talk about?"

"Well, you, frankly, and this situation. I'd like to get to know you a bit more. Andrzej seems to like you so much, but I've barely met you. I probably wouldn't know you at all if not for that horrific incident at the fights."

"Indeed," Autumn responded. "It was so odd that his guard turned on him there in public."

"I'm sure he was a plant from the Neolithic Consortium," said before taking a drink. Autumn wondered if it was to hide his expression. "If they know what we are doing there is no way they aren't trying to infiltrate our plans. Alexander DesChanes would love nothing more than to take our ritual and perform it himself. He hates the idea that anyone else has any power."

"Do you think so? How would he have gotten to his guard?" Autumn wanted to keep him talking. The less she said the better.

"Oh, he has people everywhere," Marcus continued. "He has both the money and the influence to get to anyone. Andrzej is entirely too trusting of people. He assumes that he's such a good judge of character, but he forgets that people can become corrupted by outside influences. Even he can."

"Do you think?" Autumn picked up on what might be the possibility here. "Could someone get to him?"

"It's possible. You've seen how he acts. He has a lot of ego. Andrzej loves the glamour and show of power. I imagine there is so much about him you don't know."

"True," she pushed. "I don't know much about him beyond what he has told me."

"Well, you know how he loves to talk about his Romani heritage and his being Greek born?" he smiled viciously as he spoke. "Well, he is Romani, but his parents are Polish. He hates it. His name is a Polish name that people often mistake for Greek. He doesn't even know the hints he gives off. He always tells stories of 'Babcia.' Did you know that's a Polish word. I'm not even sure he knows that. He tries to hide so much, but he's too lazy to do it correctly. He hates his humble past."

"Well, lots of people have a humble past, but that doesn't mean anything," Autumn spoke carefully. She wanted to stoke the fire, but not too much. "He seems proud to have come from humble beginnings."

"True, but I assure you that is all for show. He hates his roots. He talks of the Neolithic Consortium, but he's never been close to them. He applied when he was younger and was denied at the entrance," Marcus seemed to know a lot of Christos' past. "He never made it far enough to meet anyone of consequence, let alone Alexander as he says."

"He's a blow hard, sure, but he's also powerful, so he can brag a bit," Autumn hoped to push Marcus a bit more.

"Powerful, sure, like a big dog. Andrzej has no discipline. I've had to prepare most all the ritual. He fancies himself a powerful leader, but he gets everything by bribing people to be around him. His friends are all there for the money and influence of being seen with him," Marcus was in full rant mode now. "He's powerful, but he can't control it. He has dreams but no work ethic. He's brash, impatient, and headstrong. All terrible qualities for a wizard."

"Not like yourself?" Autumn asked.

"Exactly. I'm nothing like that. I'm methodical and careful. I spend time studying and preparing for what I do," he was getting worked up. She had to be careful now. He was getting angry thinking about Christos.

"Sure, someone has to be," she said. "Isn't that why you two work so well together? You have the technique and he has the power?"

"You don't think I have power?" his eyes bore down on her like lasers.

"That's not what I said," she was careful with her words, but she had expected that reaction. "You do the preparation and study, so you can better direct his power with yours."

"Well..." he paused for a moment. "Yeah. I guess that sounds about right. He needs a guiding hand and I provide it."

"Exactly," she said. "That allows you the power of two men."

The server returned with their food at that moment. She handed out the plates and they both ate in silence for a bit. She felt certain that he was thinking what she had said over. She wasn't sure why, but she

177

thought the tenor of the conversation had changed at that moment.

Autumn would have enjoyed her steak and vegetables had she not been so concerned about the tone that had entered Marcus' voice. Something told her that he had something in mind, and she knew his type of mind. There was no way he had suddenly decided they were friends from here on out. She didn't want to spark the conversation to resume, but the question hung heavy over the table. What was this power-hungry wizard thinking?

After a couple bites more, Marcus looked up at Autumn and smile.

"The food's quite good, isn't it?" he asked innocently.

"Yes, it is," she had no idea how it tasted, but why argue.

"Yes, only the best. The best food and the best company," he said holding up his water glass. "I should have ordered wine, but it'll be okay. To a new understanding."

"I'm sorry, but what understanding are we toasting?"

"Why, ours, of course," Marcus said with a smile that could freeze a fire. "I had seen you as a rival who blindly followed Andrzej, but now I see that you are so much more than that."

"Am I now?" she was scrambling in her mind to find what he had seen. What had she said? Did he think she was on his side now? Maybe, he simply thought they were now friends. That would make this whole job easier. She could get in closer to both and receive much less suspicion. She thought about the pitfalls of assuming his meaning. If she were wrong, she could feign ignorance easily... it was true. If she was right, then he would move forward with that idea. This was not her strong suit, but she thought it best to move forward. Hesitation would have been the worst thing she could have done.

"Certainly," he said after a few more bites. "I had you pegged wrong before. For that I am truly sorry. Christos finds people all the time who worship him and blindly follow his ways, but you're more."

"Oh, that, of course," she spoke feeling as though she were still behind by a few moves. What was she missing? "I am truly committed to success. Of course, I don't know much yet, but I can already see who's side to back."

"Exactly," he said with a satisfied smile. "You recognize the sides and can spot a winner. You're a strong ally to have, most certainly."

"Thank you," Autumn replied feeling better. She had won him over. "Once the ritual is over no one will be able to stop you."

"Yes. So, there are plans that must be made," he continued to eat. His posture and tone had relaxed significantly. She had managed to strike the right tone.

"Of course. Is there more that you need me to do or know?" Autumn began to calm down as well. She noticed, finally, that the food was good. Not the best she'd had, but good for a neighborhood place. "I can be very useful."

"I'm sure you can. Yes, there is much more that you can do. Of course, this is not the place to discuss it. We'll speak more in the car of the specifics. We are fairly safe here, but there is no reason to take unnecessary chances."

"Right. I feel the same way. People on the outside have no need to know our business."

"To think, I thought you were throwing a wrench in everything back at the fight. I thought you were ignorant when you stopped Kevin. Now I see that you are a far better ally than he ever would have been."

"Of course. He was obviously terrible at his position and easily corruptible. No one will get to me that way. I won't let anyone get to Andrzej on my watch," Autumn continued. She was eating while she spoke. Once she calmed down she realized how hungry she had been.

"Is that so?" Marcus spoke ice into existence. Autumn hadn't been watching him or she might have seen his mood turn, but she had been focusing on her food.

"Why, yes," she said and looked up. Immediately she saw that something in Marcus had changed. Suspicion had returned. Once again, something she had said had changed the entire tenor of their conversation. This had been a mistake. She had been afraid that a prolonged conversation could lead to problems. Now that seemed to have happened.

"I should have guessed," Marcus said quietly. Suddenly his face changed again. A smile returned, but the emotional tone never changed. The smile bent his lips but never touched his eyes. Autumn knew a fake smile when she saw one.

"You're both safe with me," she said thinking rapidly. What had happened?

"Good. That's what I wanted to hear," Marcus motioned for the server. She returned quickly. "Can we get the check, please? I just remembered that I have a meeting I must attend soon."

"Of course, sir," she said pulling out a receipt.

"My man will cover it," he motioned toward his bodyguard who was still standing nearby. Marcus wiped his lips and stood up. "We must leave."

He was speaking to both the server and Autumn. Conversation had been shut down entirely. She was still a few plays behind the game. Autumn was trying to replay the conversation as quickly as possible, but her head was still reeling from the speed of the direction changes. Not wanting to cause another issue, she stood up and followed Marcus out of the restaurant. The driver met them at the door and held it for them.

Marcus held open the door to the blue sedan, so she could enter first. Once inside he closed the door and leaned down to the window. The driver must have opened it because it dropped without any action from Autumn.

"I must bid you ado. I will see you the night of the ritual. Be well, My Dear," venom dripped from the words.

Marcus stood and walked away. She saw his guard meet him by another car. She realized then that he was taking another route back. She also realized that she had burnt her bridge with Marcus. Something had happened, and he had closed off to her entirely. The driver said nothing on the ride back. She spent the time thinking back and going over the conversation.

By the time they arrived at the hotel she had come

to a conclusion: Marcus was the one behind the betrayal. She didn't have hard proof, but it seemed the strongest assumption. She figured that he had thought she was on his side and then she had showed him otherwise. Had she been quicker in the restaurant or simply said less she might have preserved his illusion. She now had another enemy. Fortunately, she could think of nothing that would tell him of her true motivation. As best as she could tell he now thought she was entirely loyal to Christos and that he couldn't turn her in any way. It hadn't been a complete disaster, but she had managed to fuck it up more than a little.

CHAPTER NINETEEN

She continued to think to herself as she entered the hotel. She tried to understand all the ramifications of the meeting that she had come from. Marcus couldn't go to Andrzej with anything. He didn't have anything on Autumn and it might require him to reveal his own position. However, Marcus did have a new position on Autumn and he was not the type to stand back and wait. He had affected Christos' first guard. Could he do something to her?

"Of course, he can," Autumn said to herself as she closed the door to her hotel room. "He could have you killed. It's the most direct action he can take."

Something about saying it out loud made the words weigh more. The whole idea felt more real and three-dimensional. Some thoughts had to be fully realized immediately. She would have to be on guard for what Marcus might do. He had a guard of his own who could make a run at her, but somehow that didn't seem his preferred method. It lacked his kind of style. Marcus didn't seem to take much direct action. She figured he'd be more likely to try and get Andrzej to get rid of her or set a trap that would make someone else have to kill her.

She looked at the clock and saw that it was twenty after one in the afternoon. She didn't have plans for a few hours, so she decided to check out the other store downtown. It sounded far less promising, but maybe she could compare pricing. That might give her a better idea of the deal the other store offered her. Of course, reviews can always be wrong as well, so it would behoove her to check more places either way. The walk would help her expend some energy and enjoy the day a bit. She couldn't stand being cooped up for too long.

Having looked at a map on her phone before turning it off again, she set off through the street toward her second choice. St. Louis had a lot of history, but she felt little of it downtown. The whole area was more modern than she had expected. Some cites show their age and some try to hide it, but this felt different. She felt certain that there was an older part of the city that showed its age, but she simply hadn't seen it. Maybe, if she had the time later, she'd walk down by the river-front. Those were usually the older portions of these cities. Of course, history wasn't her strongest interest, so she probably wouldn't. It might depend on how her date with Elizabeth went.

The walk to the store wasn't long or very interesting. She had time to think, but nothing enjoyable to think about. History had distracted her for a bit, but her mind soon returned to the matter at hand: the ritual. She had gotten close, but there was the variable of Marcus. She felt certain she'd have to kill him, but he could throw things off so much. There was no way for her to learn anything about his plans. Any inquiries she made would give her away. All she could do was plan for many possibilities.

She reached the store and saw that it was open. At least she could do something, even if it wasn't much. This store looked different from the other had from the outside. This had the look of a head shop. When she pushed open the door she was assaulted by Patchouli and Sandalwood. Try as she might she couldn't stop herself from sneezing a couple times before she was five steps in. There were racks of weird clothes that looked like they were dirty, used, and worn but carried price tags proving otherwise. One side of the shop had a long shelving unit with oils, candles, and incense. The other side had a long glass case with glass implements Autumn felt certain weren't for the use of any legal substance in Missouri.

Behind the counter stood a tall thin man with long hair in dreadlocks. He wore a bright tie-dyed shirt and unbleached cotton pants. He smiled as he watched her enter the store. She looked around for a moment before making her way to the case. She had intended to look around a bit, but that smell was going to kill her sooner rather than later. Time to get down to business.

"Can I help you?" the guy asked when she approached.

"Yeah, I'm looking for some special service," Autumn said, realizing she had no real way to tell him what she wanted without saying it outright. All too often, when someone asked directly these shops would play dumb. Many cities had ordinances against the selling of magical items or enchantments. The people tended to be afraid of what they don't understand, so they'd rather create a black market for the items they intended to buy when they make them illegal. She could never understand why people who wanted to gamble, smoke, drink, and fuck made these things restricted or illegal.

"Umm…" he looked around. There was no one here and he had to have known that before he looked. "What kind of special services are you looking for?" He pinched his right thumb and forefinger together and put them to his lips.

"No, not like that. I need to procure some protection for myself," she said, trying to find a way to say it. "An item that could help me.

He stood up for a moment and looked at her. Once again, she realized that with her size and build, she looked far more like a police officer than a customer of this place. Her posture and bearing didn't help that at all. His face showed the trepidation he felt. She figured that the law here was much harsher on magic than weed. The fights she had attended the other night must have been heavily banned.

"I'm sorry, ma'am, but I don't know what you're talking about," he suddenly sounded formal and stiff. "Everything we sell here is on display and legal."

"Look," she sighed. "We both know that isn't true. You think I'm a cop and I think you're an idiot. I'll try and prove you wrong if you'll do the same. I don't give a shit what you're doing here. In fact, I really need you to do something for me. I think you're capable of making something that will provide me a bit of protection when spells start to fly. I've told you what I want straight forward. What can I do to prove myself?"

"Well," he stood back and looked at her. For a moment she saw a different look in his eyes. The heavy-lidded stoner look disappeared. "Okay, I'll take a chance. I might be able to help you with that... maybe."

"Good. I want something that detects magic being used. Something that would alert me to something being cast."

"That sound delicate."

"Yeah, I guess so," she said figuring he was already dickering for price. "Really, it shouldn't be that hard. I want to know if I have a spell on me or something like that."

"Without a specific target spell or even spell type it would require a lot of intricate work."

"If you're trying to get your price up, I don't really care. I need it and quickly. I'll pay, but god help you if you try and fuck me."

"Well, it could be done for a price, for sure. It'd probably take a couple weeks, but we could get it to one for the right price."

"A week?" she asked shocked at that time.

"Yeah, but that'll cost," he said growing cautious again.

"I need it by Wednesday. No later."

"Oh, Hell no. There's no way anyone here could do that."

"No one here?"

"Well..." he looked around again and leaned in close. "There's a shop about half a mile from here. It's downtown and kind of looks like an antique shop," he said whispering quietly. "The guy there is pretty good. Really, he's better than anyone we've got here. I don't know for sure what he can do or how fast, but he's the only choice you've got round here who even has the skill."

"I see," she said standing back up. "Well, thank you for your time and honesty."

"Have a good day," he said with his smile and slow persona taking back over. He had his story down as well as any amature stage star learns her lines. She had expected to use that store, but she had not expected the salesman here to send her there. She had read on-line that the old man was good. Sounded like everyone thought that.

She left the store and walked around the downtown area for a bit. There wasn't much else she was interested in, but it felt good to move. She thought about swimming at the hotel, but the pool was small, and she hadn't packed a suit. A long walk would have to do the trick. Once she saw that it was three-thirty she began to head back to her room. A quick shower and she would be ready early. She'd hate to make Elizabeth wait.

At ten minutes until five o'clock, Autumn stood in the lobby of her hotel waiting. She had seen a lot of this lobby since she had been here. For a moment she thought back to all the hotels she had stayed in over the years. She hadn't had a stable address since she'd been in the military and that hadn't been all that stable. Autumn had lived in a shit-hole apartment since she had nothing to draw her away. She had spent so much of her time deployed that she generally forgot about anything being home.

Elizabeth's small car pulled up outside the door. She shook herself out of her memories and stepped outside. Elizabeth smiled brightly as she watched Autumn walk to her car and open the passenger side door. Bending and folding once again, Autumn sat in the front seat. She had to slide the seat back, so she had any leg room at all. It helped, but designers must have assumed that tall people didn't need to purchase economy cars.

"Comfortable?" Elizabeth asked.

"Only if you stretch the definition of that word to the breaking point."

"I'm sorry," Elizabeth looked a bit hurt. "It's the only car I have."

"It's fine. I was exaggerating to a point. How have you been?"

"Better than you, judging from your eye," Elizabeth looked at Autumn closely. "If I hadn't seen you the other day I would assume you were healing from a black eye. It barely shows, but I can see it. You okay?"

"Yeah, I'm fine. I took a bit of a hit, but it wasn't too bad. No need to worry about it," Autumn could think of no way to explain the fight and her rapid healing. That wasn't how people worked outside of movies and comic books. "So, tell me about the place we're going."

"Well, it's a small local place. It isn't very fancy, but I like the food quite a bit. If you'd like to go somewhere else, we can."

"Oh no. That sounds fine. People have been taking me to too many places that have high expectations lately. I enjoy having a chance to relax a bit."

Autumn watched the city go by for a bit as Elizabeth drove. She recognized very little of this city, so she had no idea if she had been this way yet. She could have spent some time driving around, but that didn't seem a very effective use of her time.

"It won't take us long," Elizabeth said with a smile. "Did your lunch meeting go well?"

"Let's not talk about work."

"Okay, I didn't want specifics, but I'll leave the subject alone entirely. So," there was a pause in Elizabeth's words as she thought. "What do you like to do with your free time? What do you do for fun?"

"Well, I keep up on a few sports. I like both football and hockey. I watch combat sports when I can find them."

"Combat sports?" Elizabeth asked. "Like UFC and boxing?"

"Yeah. Those and any of the others like them. When I can find them, there are a lot of great groups around the world."

"What about pro wrestling?" Elizabeth laughed.

"Really, it's better than a lot of shows on TV," Autumn smiled as she settled into the flow of the conversation. "I don't care so much about what they have to say or the results, but the stunt show can be quite impressive. Some of those people are very good at what they do."

"Really?" Elizabeth asked. "That wasn't what I was expecting. I figured you'd hate it."

"As a show yes, but the athletics are there for sure. What about you?"

"Well, I travel to a lot of trade shows and conventions for work. I enjoy the travel."

"Are those fashion shows with models and such?" Autumn asked her.

"Sometimes, but more often they're convention floors where people try to sell you on a new clothing line or store concept. They aren't nearly as glamorous as movies portray them and I'm not well known enough to go to the big shows that make it to TV. I've never been on a red carpet or anything. In the end, business conventions look like business conventions everywhere."

"Okay, and when you're not at one of those?"

"Work eats a lot of my time. Outside of that I sit in my apartment and watch Hell's Kitchen and other shows to pass the time."

"Hell's Kitchen? What's that?" Autumn asked unable to get an image from the title.

"Really? You've never heard of Hell's Kitchen?" Elizabeth's shock made it into her voice. "It's a reality show with Chef Gordon Ramsay. People compete to win a position at a big restaurant."

"I see. So, they cook stuff? That doesn't sound very exciting."

"Well, sure, but it's not that simple. You'd have to see it to understand. You really don't watch TV, do you?" Elizabeth said a bit baffled.

"Not if I can help it," Autumn replied. "I watch games when I can, but even then, I'd rather go to a game. Most combat sports work off the Pay Per View system so you have to order them to watch them. I never pay attention to the commercials. When I do watch a game it's at a sports bar or something like that."

"Wow. That would either be awesome or terrible,"

Elizabeth said laughing. She turned into the parking lot of a small restaurant that looked like it used to be a fast food joint. The shape seemed familiar, but the colors were now the bright primary colors people used for Mexican places. She pulled into a spot and stopped. The lot wasn't full yet, but two cars had followed them in. It looked like it would be full as the night went on.

Autumn held the door open for Elizabeth. Neither of them commented on it, but Autumn heard a chuckle from a woman standing behind her. For a moment she thought about telling her how little of her concern the situation was but decided against it. She didn't like the idea of Elizabeth thinking she was a hothead. Instead she held the door for both her and her man. The woman gave her a look until she saw how much smaller her man looked than Autumn. It probably didn't change her opinion, but it changed her desire to express it openly.

She and Elizabeth were shown to a booth in the back of the restaurant. Autumn assumed Elizabeth had requested it, so they could have a little privacy. Water, chips, and salsa were left on their table for them when the server walked away. Elizabeth began to dig in. Autumn tried a bit of the salsa and it tasted pretty good. They ate for a moment as they looked at their menus. Autumn didn't get a lot of Mexican food, so she wasn't sure what she liked, but it seemed that most of the item used the same ingredients but in different ways. She found one that sounded like something she'd like.

"You find something that looks good?" Elizabeth asked.

"Yeah, the Carne Asada sounds pretty good."

"You ever try anything with mole sauce on it?"

"What?" Autumn looked at the menu where Elizabeth pointed out an item. "I thought they meant a little furry rodent."

Elizabeth's laugh rang out clear as a bell at Autumn's comment.

"What? No, it's a sauce. Why would you think they eat moles?" Elizabeth asked.

"I don't know. Maybe they have a lot of moles in Mexico. It would be meat, right?"

"I'm not sure I can be with someone who thinks Mexican people eat moles," Elizabeth responded.

"Well, I'm not sure I can be with someone too hoity toity to eat a mole if she's hungry."

They two of them paused for a moment before bursting into laughter. They both chuckles for a bit before calming down. That seemed to break the tension they hadn't realized they were feeling. The whole mood brightened after that moment. Their server came back while they were laughing, and they calmed down enough to order. When she left they laughed a bit more. Both were left feeling a bit stupid about how nervous they had felt before this moment.

Their laughter died down and Elizabeth took a drink. She didn't want to start coughing. The rest of the restaurant continued as if they weren't there. The world cared not about two women making a connection despite the beliefs of romance writers. Birds didn't sing and there were no fireworks. Both women calmed down and continued their conversation.

"I feel a lot better," Elizabeth said. "You have a wonderful laugh, but it almost sounds unused."

"Thanks, I think. I don't find a lot of things to laugh about," Autumn said unsure how to take that. "So, what is mole sauce?"

"Oh, well, I'm not entirely sure what's in it, but I know it usually has a smoky chocolaty taste. I like it. It adds a little heat and a lot of flavor when made correctly."

"Chocolate on pork?" Autumn wrinkled her nose. "That sounds... weird."

"Sure, but it's good. I take it you don't try a lot of new things?"

"I've never really cared much about food, really. I watch my diet for the sake of nutrition. I've spent time eating carefully and such, but food has never been all that important to me. It's simply something I need to live."

"Really?" Elizabeth looked sad for a moment. "That's terrible. I understand watching what you eat and all, but food can be so awesome. I've taken trips with the hope of eating the native food somewhere. I went to a convention in Seattle once and had to go to Pike Place Fish Market. It was awesome. I then had to go eat seafood at some of the local places. It was really good."

"I'd like to visit Seattle," Autumn said with a smile.

"Really? Did I convince you already? Because there are better food cities than that. New Orleans is amazing."

"No, I'd like to go and watch a Seahawks game there," Autumn told her. "That is, actually, my favorite team in the NFL."

"Well, what do you know? You finally tell me a favorite of yours and I know nothing about them. I guess I may have known that Seattle had a football team. I assume that the guys you date all know that stuff," Elizabeth took a drink and felt a little stupid. She had hoped to find more for them to bond on.

"It's okay," Autumn told her. "I am usually on my own in my interest. I don't expect you to know them all that well. In fact, when I have been with men, sports are usually all we have. Most of them are usually pretty dismissive of my interest as well."

"Really? Why? I always thought guys wanted to date a chick who liked sports."

"Well, the meat-heads I've been with have wanted to date women who were interested, but they wanted to know more about it. There's a macho aspect to it all."

"Yeah?" Elizabeth was a bit scared. Knowing she was the first, she was worried about how she might measure up. She knew she wasn't anything like the guys Autumn had been with before. They were probably all jocks who lifted and did tough things like watch combat sports with her. Could Elizabeth do that?

"Yeah," Autumn continued. "They assumed that I liked the team because I liked the colors or thought Russel Wilson was cute or something. It tended to be a big problem in the end. They wanted a woman who liked it but couldn't compete with them. There was one guy who split up with me when he kept losing races to me."

"Really?" Elizabeth laughed. She quickly stopped. "I'm sorry. I didn't mean to laugh."

"No, it was really funny. He would keep challenging me to races in every situation he could. Finally, when we had gone to see a college football game and had a chance to go out on the field afterward, he challenged me to race from one end zone to the other. We lined up and ran the hundred-yard race. I hit the other end zone while he was still near the fifteen-yard line."

"Wow!" Elizabeth said setting her glass down. "That's a lot faster than him."

"He agreed. He broke up with me right then and there telling me that *I* was too competitive. I was amazed and may have said a few vicious things to him."

"He sounds like a dick," Elizabeth said. "He was challenging you."

"Yeah, I told him that. He said I was remembering it incorrectly, so I told him to go fuck himself."

"Straight to the point."

"Yeah," Autumn said taking a drink. "I never could seem to find a guy who could accept that I was more physically gifted than he was. I guess that was a pill too hard to swallow."

"Well, surely, when they saw you, they knew you were strong and such."

"Of course," Autumn said flexing unconsciously. Elizabeth noticed and smiled. "They liked that as long as they were stronger. One guy tore his pectoral muscle trying to out-lift me. I never told any of them that they had to."

"I'm not a man, but I can understand on another level. I was with a girl in college who kept trying to prove to me that she was girlier than me. She challenged me on everything I did. Finally, she proved one weekend that she could pick up more men than I could. She slept with thirteen guys that weekend and sent me a tape. I was devastated at the time."

"I bet. What a cunt," Autumn said.

"Yeah," Elizabeth hid her smile. "I got her back, though, when I sent a copy of the tape to her parents."

"Holy shit, that's cold."

"They yanked her out of college right away. As the story goes, she was then sent to a Catholic College instead. I never knew what angered them more: the fact of her weekend orgy, or that she started the tape with a candid message to her 'bitch of a girlfriend.'"

"Wow. You really stuck it to her," Autumn was quietly proud of her for not spreading it around the school, but getting her back.

"Well, I just thought that her parents had the right to know what kind of education they were paying for," Elizabeth said and laughed. "I haven't thought about that in years. Her name was Christine. She was really pretty. I never cared whether she was more fashionable than me. Of course, I was just her college experiment. That's happened to me a few times."

"Really? Was that hard to take?"

"Of course, it was," Elizabeth said. "I was still young myself and thought they were serious. It really colored my views. I was young and pretty. One girl explained it to me. She said that I was easy to hide. I didn't put out a 'dyke vibe' in her words. She said she had always told her friends that we were just friends. She told me if I said otherwise she'd tell them she stopped hanging out with me because I came on to her.

She had made a point of defending me to her friends as straight. She had it all figured out well. Most weren't so organized, but probably thought something similar."

"Damn," Autumn had never thought about what it would be like going through life that way. People tended to be more careful around her because of her size and capability. Guys had challenged her before, but she could always black eyes or break noses to get her point across. Elizabeth hadn't had that option. "Well, in case you're wondering, that's not what I'm doing."

"You sure? I'd understand if it was. I don't react the same way now. I'm older and have a better understanding of the world. I don't hold it against those girls. They were young too. We were all confused. High school was worse for the confusion but more happened in college. Now my eyes are open."

"Well, I'm not," Autumn spoke with a smile that warmed Elizabeth's heart. "If I wanted to experiment I'd tell you that and I don't have any friends to hide anything from."

"Okay, that is far sadder than anything I've said," Elizabeth reached across the table and took Autumn's hand in both of hers. Autumn's hand was bigger by a lot. It made Elizabeth look even smaller and more fragile.

"What? Why do you say that?"

"You have no one? No friends at all? How can you live that way?"

"No, it's not like that," Autumn tried to think what it was like. She had spent so long living this way. "I travel all the time, so I have no time for people. I'm always going somewhere new."

"That doesn't help," Elizabeth said looking into Autumn's eyes. "That sounds so empty and hollow."

"But, I like it like that," Autumn told her. "Life is so much simpler that way."

The server came back and began to distribute plates out to them both. The food smelled great. Even Autumn was excited to try what was set in front of her. They both asked for refills and the server filled their waters. After he left they looked back at each other.

"Okay," Elizabeth said. "Let's talk about something happy for a bit. This is getting too heavy."

"I agree," Autumn said as she built a tortilla up with rice, beans, and steak. "Let's stay on the lighter side and not pick on me."

"Oh, I see how it's gonna be," Elizabeth said eating her sauce covered pork. "You're off limits."

"Sure, if you want to come back to my hotel room, I am," Autumn said with a wink.

"That's not fair. You can't hold me hostage like that."

"Sure, I can," Autumn took a bit of the wrap she'd made, winked, and smiled at Elizabeth. "I can make all the rules here."

"This seems unfair. Maybe I don't want to go back to your room then," Elizabeth let her face go stone straight.

"Oh no, I didn't mean-" Autumn was cut off by Elizabeth's knowing smile. "Fine, you got me. I can't really hold you hostage, can I?"

"I've played this game a lot, Sweet Lips. I'm pretty damn good at it."

"Sweet Lips?"

"Yeah, I tried it out, but it doesn't really fit," Elizabeth said with a chuckle.

"Is that what I have to look forward to?"

"Oh, I think you know what you have to look forward to," Elizabeth replied with another wink. "But we have a wonderful dinner to finish first."

"Thank you for this, by the way," Autumn said taking another bite. "It's really good."

"I thought you'd like it. Their food is fairly basic, but it's really good."

"Agreed," Autumn said making another tortilla. She added a bit of the salsa to this one. Elizabeth smiled when she realized how much Autumn was enjoying it.

They sat and ate for a bit enjoying each other's company and the good food. Autumn was surprised how comfortable she could feel around another person. She liked Elizabeth a lot and their interaction felt fairly natural. She hated that she had to lie to her, but there was no way she wanted to see the look on her face when she found out what Autumn really did. If possible, she would have to leave before that happened. There was no reason for Elizabeth to find out.

They passed conversation with each other through the rest of dinner. They didn't speak much. They had both been hungry and finished their food quickly. Once again, Autumn picked up the check. With the money they had paid her, she could afford to buy some meals. They walked back out to Elizabeth's car together after dinner.

"Well, is there anything else you want to do before

you head back?" Elizabeth asked.

"Not that I can think of," Autumn responded as they climbed into the small car. Elizabeth drove off heading back downtown. The ride back seemed shorter than the first. One of those odd effects of perception. Autumn rarely contemplated those things, but she felt different around Elizabeth. She felt more human with more interest in things other than her job. In fact, she was surprised to realize she hadn't thought of work at all during dinner. It was a nice break from her usual stressful thoughts and preparations.

Elizabeth pulled up to the hotel entrance and stopped. Autumn looked at her quizzically.

"Is something wrong?" Autumn asked.

"No, why?"

"You can't park here," she told Elizabeth.

"Oh, and why do I need to park?" Elizabeth asked as a smirk curled her lips up.

"Park the car and come up to my room you jerk."

"Jerk, huh? Well, I will, but you're going to pay for that insult."

Elizabeth pulled away and drove into the parking garage to look for a spot to park.

Elizabeth lay next to Autumn dozing lightly. Autumn looked over at the clock on the night stand and saw that it was after eleven. She had no idea when the party started or when Elizabeth fell into her light sleep, but she had never felt so relaxed. Despite how the day had started and that terrible lunch, she was happy with the day. There wasn't much Sunday left and she'd have to get right back into the game in the morning if she wanted to have everything ready for the Ritual. Wednesday was coming up quickly.

But, for the rest of the night, she'd let herself have a normal life. Was this how it felt? Someone great lying next to her in bed? Their night had been great from the food, to the conversation, to their activities afterward. Everything had been so pleasant and enjoyable. None of what had come to be normal in her life had happened. No fighting. No monsters or magic. She hadn't faced death the entire time she'd been with Elizabeth. Why do people want her life? Why did she hear people complain that their lives were boring? She would love nothing more than a normal life such as this.

"Hey there, beautiful," Autumn heard Elizabeth's voice wake out of her slumber.

"Hi," Autumn said, smiling at her lover. "Did you sleep well?"

"Sure. You drained me of every ounce of energy I had. You're lucky I woke up at all."

"You're welcome to go back to sleep. It's early still, really," Autumn told her.

Elizabeth raised up slightly and looked at the clock. She reached around and hugged Autumn allowing her hands to search and meander over the toned and hard body.

"No, I need to get back to my place," Elizabeth dropped back onto the bed. "It's hard enough waking up on a Monday. If you're with me I may never leave. My whole business will collapse if I don't open my shop."

"I guess I understand," Autumn made a show of frowning.

"Oh, don't frown," Elizabeth said and kissed her. "I

can come back tomorrow and bring back your smile after work."

Autumn smiled at her and the thought. Could she be happy living like this? Find herself a normal job? Would Elizabeth like her if she were normal? The whole idea seemed impossible, but two million dollars could change a lot. However, nothing about Autumn was normal. Inside or out she was not a normal person. And she never would be. Not anymore.

"I understand," she finally said. "I wouldn't want you to ruin your business for me. You go be responsible. We can get together tomorrow night."

"Absolutely," Elizabeth said leaning over and locking Autumn into a deep passionate kiss. Autumn's arms wrapped around Elizabeth and came around again. In that moment she felt so fragile. Autumn realized how careful she had to be. The weight of who she was and what she did came down like a lead anvil. She could kill this wonderful woman. She wouldn't even exert any effort. Her lifestyle would certainly kill her. How could Elizabeth survive in the world Autumn occupied? If anything, Elizabeth was who Autumn fought for.

They pulled away. Elizabeth kept her hands on Autumn and looked into her eyes.

"Are you okay? You seem off all of the sudden."

"No no. I'm fine," Autumn lied. "I'm just going to miss you."

"Well," Elizabeth gave her another quick kiss and stood up. Autumn marveled at how beautiful her naked body was. Again, however, her beauty came from her delicacy. Like a China doll Autumn would always be concerned about breaking her. "Until, tomorrow when I'll see you again."

"Certainly," Autumn said and watched Elizabeth gather her things and get dressed.

"At least I drove so there'll be no walk of shame."

"Are you ashamed?" Autumn asked.

"Not at all," Elizabeth smiled. "It's just an expression."

She finished and walked toward Autumn who stood up out of bed. Elizabeth hugged and kissed her again. It was hard to part ways. They both wanted to stay together.

"Have a good night," Autumn said. "Drive safely."

"Of course," Elizabeth replied. "You never know who's on the roads. At least the drunks shouldn't be out in force."

"Talk to you tomorrow."

"Good night," Elizabeth said and left the hotel room. Autumn sat back on the bed and felt a slight empty pang. She knew this was loneliness and that when she left Elizabeth behind it would be much worse, but she could miss out on the time they could have together. She was enjoying the way it felt to be normal for even a little bit. She thought of Elizabeth walking down to her car in the garage. She had said she didn't have much of a drive to her apartment. Autumn was also glad she hadn't walked. She wouldn't have felt comfortable with her walking home alone. She would have had to press to walk her home.

Maybe she should have walked her to her car. Would that have been the right thing to do? She had been so enamored with her own warm feelings she had forgotten her usual caution. Surely, Elizabeth could get home safely. She'd lived in this city for a long time. She knew how to stay safe. Autumn laid back down to fall asleep feeling fairly secure in her assumption. She fell asleep never knowing about the dark blue car that followed Elizabeth out of the garage.

CHAPTER TWENTY

Autumn woke up the next day a bit later than she had expected. The day before had taken the energy out of her in a variety of ways. She woke with thoughts of Elizabeth, but they were soon replaced with work. She needed to get to the magic shop as soon as possible. Andrzej and Marcus still had plans to summon a demon. There was also her suspicion that Marcus was in business for himself. She wasn't certain, but it would make sense after the meeting they had had.

She prepared for the day and ran through the meeting again in her mind. She still couldn't find definitive proof that Marcus would betray Andrzej, but she had a feeling that he had plans of his own. There was something shifty about Mr. Kanellis. She certainly didn't trust him in any way, but she was no detective. Andrzej was a terrible judge of character, but she knew that already by her own position.

Dressed comfortably in jeans and a plain T-shirt, Autumn left the apartment for the magic shop she had wanted to use yesterday. The walk was short, and the day overcast. It wasn't a bad day, but there was an ominous feel that came with the growing heat. Autumn walked on through St. Louis to the store-front she had visited before. It didn't look much different than it had the day before. The store still looked closed as she couldn't see much light coming from the inside. That was mostly because the windows were packed with odds and ends, but the effect was the same.

The one major different was that the cardboard sign in the door now said that the store was open. There was no outside light marking the status. She opened the door and stepped inside. No one greeted her when she walked in. The store's contents were particularly odd and poorly organized. A toy car resting on an old wooden rocking chair with long, decorative, wooden spoons across the arms. A cupboard with a note on it stating "toY GuNs iNside" on the front. The candles and incense were present though she never saw any, only a strong smell gave evidence.

She walked through the path that was cut through the jungle of merchandise carefully. Looking up on either side she saw large stacks of buckets, crates, and wooden boxes. It was easy to imagine these collapsing onto the path blocking any entrance or exit from the labyrinth. She had a feeling of trespassing as she traversed the maze of old furniture and items from years gone by. Autumn wondered how easily someone could get lost in a place like this. Had it happened? Had a child ever been stuck? The store itself seemed adversarial. Almost demanding of sacrifice for safe passage.

She found a large glass display case full of odd

jewelry, pens, old keys, sunglasses, CDs, and old
buttons. Behind the counter sat a small old man with
ridiculously thick glasses. He looked like a cartoon
character. His head was down, and he was snoring out
from under his fedora. He didn't fit the ambiance of
the store at all. She had expected a dark and
mysterious man who made deals with those
unfortunate enough to venture into his shop. Autumn
lightly tapped the glass top counter.

"Can I help you?" a voice replaced the snoring, but
nothing else changed about his appearance.

"I need a check performed and a charm, please,"
Autumn responded to the voice. With all she had read
and heard she didn't bother being coy about what she
wanted. There was not enough time for games.

"A check?"

"Yes," she continued. "I fear I've been the target of
an enchantment or spell. I thought that you might be
able to check and eliminate it should you find one."

"I see," came the same voice. Autumn felt sure it
was the old man behind the counter, but he still hadn't
moved the slightest bit from his position. "You sure
that I'm the man you want? That stuff's not allowed
around these parts."

"Well, I was under the impression this shop was the
best in the area, but I'm beginning to question my
judgment. I'll move along and let you get back to
your nap."

Autumn turned, and the old man opened his eyes,
slightly. He jumped when he saw her.

"Wait," he was very attentive now. "I simply
wanted to be sure that you were serious."

"Well, let's assume that I am and that I hate games."

"By the look of you I would think so. Think your man put a tracking spell on ya?"

"I'll ignore that... once," Autumn said narrowing her eyes. "Now, do your job before I move on and possibly leave you worse for having met me."

"Okay, okay. Sorry, that's just the most common concern. I get a lot of women in here who think their man has put a spell on them or want one on him. I'm not sure, but you may be the first woman I've seen who wanted anything else. Well, there's always the request for a love potion, I guess, but I get so tired of rejecting people. Come with me." He walked around the counter to meet Autumn. He could only have been five-four or so and built like a twig. He wound his way through the store with Autumn in tow. They ended their trip at a door marked "eMploYees oNlY." The room behind the door had as much free space as the rest of the store combined. Autumn finally felt that she could breathe properly.

"So, you think someone put a spell on you, huh?" he continued. "Someone with a violent purpose?"

"Possibly," Autumn spoke as she looked around his workroom. This area was well organized with things in place and surfaces cleaned off. He obviously spent a considerable amount of time working in this room and space was important. "I've been dealing with a few wizards recently and want to be careful. I'd also like to procure a charm of some sort that would block and alert me to a spell being cast on me."

"Hmm... well, the first one is real easy," his thin reedy voice proclaimed. "Let me start there and think a bit on the charm." He took off his hat as he spoke. The top of his head was bald with a ring of snowy white hair around his skull. His face was wrinkled, and his skin looked thin. Autumn wasn't sure of his age, but she would have believed that he had lived in three different centuries. His movements, however, were precise and careful despite his obviously advanced age. "Please stand over here with your legs shoulder width and your arms out from your body."

Autumn moved over and stood as instructed. She found herself hoping this guy was the real deal. He seemed odd,... even for a magic shopkeep. She would hate to have to hurt him, but she was also suspect of any kind of magic. Some of these old guys could get grabby and perverted if they thought they could convince you that it was required for the spell. She had been asked to strip for a check like this on many occasions. Those never went well... for the wizard. She watched as he picked up an old knobby wand and turned back toward her. There was a comically large crystal at the end of it.

"Okay, I'm gonna move this around you and the crystal will light up if it detects a spell on you. The color will tell me the type and the brightness the strength. Got it?" he sounded like a doctor explaining a procedure. "If it lights up we can zero in and see what can be done. Please hold still while I'm checking."

Autumn stood still while he waved the crystal around her at a painfully slow rate. He had to climb on a chair to get to the top of her. Each of his motions was meticulous but made him seem even older. He kept making odd noises as he moved his wand and his tongue was never fully inside of his mouth. He never did touch her, even though he kept the wand very close. He finished his work and it never lit up once.

"Well, either you're clear or the skill of the spell is far beyond my level," the old man said with a smile.

"That had best not be an excuse."

"No, I'm good at what I do," he told her. He set the wand down carefully and looked back at Autumn. "You do seem to be awfully angry, if I might say so."

"That's my business," Autumn wondered why his wand showed no sign of the ritual done on her before. Was that skill level high or was he a fraud? She didn't want to tell him, but it would be good to know how much of it could be detected. "Let's talk about the charm."

"You said you wanted a shield or an indicator?"

"Yes. Well, I'd really like both, but I don't know what you can do. I need to know if someone is trying to enchant me or use a spell and I'd really like some degree of protection."

"Well," he put his hand on his chin while he thought about it. "The indicator is easy. That can be a lot like my wand. The shield is a bit trickier. How powerful are the spells you are expecting to encounter? Along with that how well do you want your shield to remain hidden?"

"I really don't know about the strength. As strong as possible? As far as the effects, it is best if it remains completely hidden."

"That's a tall order," the old man said scratching his paper-thin scalp. "Without knowing the strength, it's hard to dial in the shield. It's really not as simple as physical armor. Magic is more of a wavelength. To get any kind of complete protection, many different shields are usually woven together. Calibrating for a powerful offensive spell will likely allow enchantments through. Then there's the problem of visibility. There are always effects when absorbing magic."

"What can be done that's still completely invisible?" The little man seemed to know what he was doing.

"Something meant for blocking holding, tracking, and the like could still guard against charms and be invisible," he said with assurance. "The wearer would feel effects from the more powerful spells, but a strong will could still provide protection."

"That'll have to work," Autumn told him trying to sound friendly. She felt a bit bad for being so harsh early on. He seemed very knowledgeable and relatively friendly once he was focused. "Can you do that by five on Wednesday?"

"Sure," he said with confidence. "That's the kind of intricate work I specialize in. That should be more than enough time, really. Do you want the indicator to be separate?"

"Combine them if you could," Autumn replied.

"Fine. What would you like as the item?"

"The item?" she asked.

"I have to enchant something. I can't weave magic into the air in front of you. What would you like?"

"Oh, yeah," she shook her head. The last few days seemed to have gotten to her more than she figured. "Something simple, please. Something I could easily wear without drawing attention."

"Sure, I'll see you at five on Wednesday."

The old man allowed Autumn to find her own way

out of the store which seemed to be far more accepting to her presence now. She knew magic could achieve a lot of things, but it almost seemed to give the store itself a kind of personality that moved with the owner. Maybe that was helpful to him somehow, but it was more reason for her to distrust magic all together. She wouldn't want to break into this place.

She could think of nothing else to do with her time, so she walked back to her hotel. Andrzej had said he might want to see her again before the ritual. She assumed he would reach her through the hotel again, so she'd have to keep checking on it. She couldn't imagine what he wanted from her that would come before Wednesday, but she had to appear ready. She was supposed to be his employee now. Maybe that was what he wanted; proof that she would jump when he said so.

Walking along the sidewalk she took a moment to lean against a wall to send a message. Booting up her phone she looked to see if she had received anything from Elizabeth. She had no new messages. Mondays must have been busy days at the shop. She had said that she fired Pete, so she might have more to do by herself. Autumn took the initiative to send her a message. It dawned on her how out of character this was, but she didn't care. She wanted to hear from Elizabeth.

-Good morning. How did you sleep? Hope your day is going well.-

She wrote and rewrote the message until it ended up so bland it almost wasn't worth sending. Autumn wasn't good at these kinds of domestic things and wasn't sure how it would sound. She figured she could always fix anything in subsequent messages. Having sent it she turned off her phone and resumed her walk. She wanted to get back to the hotel to check for anything from Christos.

As she walked up she saw a familiar black Lexus sitting in front of her hotel. She walked inside to see a familiar man in a black suit. She walked over to Theodore.

"Good morning," she said standing behind him.

"Well, hello," he said before he turned around. She wasn't sure, but she thought he might have jumped a bit before he turned.

"Here to see me, I assume?"

"Why, yes, I am," rumbled his deep voice. "Mr. Christos would like to speak with you. Would you be free to meet with him?

"When and where does he want to meet?" Autumn asked.

"He is outside in the car once again. He'd like to meet with you as soon as possible."

"Well," she replied. "Everyone seems so eager to meet with me so quickly. I'm dressed and ready so how about we go now and get this over with?"

"Certainly," he said stepping forward. "Follow me, please."

Theodore walked to the Lexus and opened a door for Autumn to climb into the back. Once again, Autumn saw Andrzej sitting inside with a broad smile on his face. This time he didn't have any champagne, however. She slid inside. Theodore closed the door and climbed into the driver's seat. The car was already running, so he smoothly pulled out and into traffic.

"Do you always come along to pick people up?" Autumn asked playfully.

"Theodore and I were out taking care of some other business," he smiled as he spoke. "I thought we should drop by and leave you a note. I was pleasantly surprised to see you walk up and come outside with Theodore."

"So, where are we going this time, Andrzej?" Autumn asked.

"Well, I was hoping you might join me at my residence for a little conversation," he said with a smile. "There are things in the trunk that Theodore needs to get inside soon."

"I'd rather not."

"Why not, Lindsay My Dear?" he asked looking hurt.

"I have other obligations later today. I would rather not get too comfortable and run the risk of missing them."

"I understand that, My Dear, but I assure you we will make it. I have things to talk to you about that require privacy and that is the best I can think of."

He seemed very insistent and Autumn could think of no good excuses to give him. She didn't want to go, but she would have to or risk blowing her cover.

"Sure, that makes sense," she said with a smile. "As long as I am back here by two."

"Fine fine. Theodore," he yelled to the driver. "Please take us to my apartment. Be prepared to take Ms. Brown home by half past one. We wouldn't want her to be late."

"Yes, sir," Theodore said and continued to drive.

"I don't live far from here. The drive doesn't take long."

"Well, I guess I will finally see where you live."

"I think you'll like it, My Dear," Andrzej said with a lingering smile.

CHAPTER TWENTY-ONE

They drove in silence the rest of the way to Andrzej's apartment. Autumn had never seen him so quiet. She couldn't help but think something serious was wrong. Maybe he had a heavy weight on his mind. The ritual was coming up and he considered it to be life's work. She worried, however, that Marcus had found a way to spin lunch yesterday into a story that reflected poorly on her. Could he have found a way to sink her work here?

She was surprised when they pulled into a lot by an apartment building. It seemed nice, but somehow, she had pictured Christos owing a fancier place. She had expected a house on land despite his saying it was an apartment earlier. The building looked well maintained and protected and it was inside a guarded gate and fence. Still, it was a brick building with no spectacular architecture or unique design. Somehow it wasn't his kind of place.

"I understand what you're thinking," Andrej finally said as Theodore parked the Lexus next to a blue BMW. "The building looks plain. Too plain for someone like me."

"Actually, yes. That was exactly what I was thinking," she said surprised at his insight.

"While the inside is very plush, you're right. I don't like the building or location. However, St. Louis isn't my permanent residence. I have a home in California that, I'm sure, you'd find more my style," he said standing outside of the car waiting for Theodore to get ahead of them to open the doors. She noticed that he tried to play it off that Theodore was simply faster to the door than Andrzej, but she saw him slow down to allow for that pace. "This is a stopgap for the time I'm here in St. Louis to work. This was the best location, so I had to find some place to live and this was available."

"That makes sense," Autumn responded picking up her pace to match him. Theodore had gotten far enough ahead of them. He punched in the code to the outside door and held it for the two of them. Andrzej lead the way into a bright lobby decorated in marble and weathered woods. She couldn't be sure, but it all had a slightly fake feel to it. Somehow, she thought this wasn't true marble. The building seemed to be as focused on appearances as her employer.

He punched the button for the elevator and they all stepped inside. She hated being in small boxes like this even more with people she knew as enemies, but she had to maintain the illusion. Theodore also looked uncomfortable if only because of his size. She leaned back against the polished mirrored walls as Andrzej pushed the highest number on the keypad. They traveled up quickly. At least the elevator was well maintained. There was no shake, squeak, or rattle.

The door opened onto a hallway that was decorated in a deep reds, purples, and gold. This whole floor felt like a royal court in an old movie. Autumn couldn't stand the gaudy nature of the whole thing. It all felt ostentatious and arrogant. It would be impossible not to see every member of this floor as sanctimonious and pretentious. The smile on her face never wavered, but she wondered what Elizabeth would say about the look of all this. She'd have to find a way to ask her at some point.

"Each floor is decorated in different color combinations growing plusher as the levels rise," Andrzej sounded like a tour guide as they walked down the hallway.

"It seems a bit much for my tastes," Autumn responded casually.

"Possibly," he said almost to himself. "I like the gold trim next to the purple."

"It all seems a bit much, but not bad," she didn't want to push him too far in case Marcus had said something.

"Possibly," he repeated. They reached what must have been his door as Theodore opened the door and held it for the two of them to enter. His apartment was similar to the hallway, but the color was cut with all of his decorations. The lights were colored and muted. Someone had carefully lit the entire room like a film set. The tone in the living room was that of a Romani camp around a camp fire. Autumn had no way to know how he had done it. Maybe it was magic or maybe it was movie magic.

All around the room there were old decorations and items she assumed had come from his family and the

clans they had traveled with. She wondered if he had
been given these things or if they had been stolen. It
could have made for an interesting room, but it all felt
slightly off. Something about it felt like a harsh
juxtaposition. Maybe Andrzej had come from this, but
it wasn't him anymore... or was it?

"You like, My Dear?"

"It is very unique," she responded. "I've never seen
a room like this before."

"Of course not," he said beaming. "I've collected
many personal items from my family and other
Romani clans to make this room feel like my
childhood did. We would spend most nights around a
fire telling stories, singing songs, and sharing years of
wisdom. I wouldn't trade my childhood for anything."

"I guess I never pictured Romani life this way in the
Eighties. There is so much about that lifestyle I never
knew," she tried not to sound too skeptical, but that
was part of her problem. The room felt too Nineteenth
Century to be real.

"People all over the world ignore the noble Romani
people," he said as his chest puffed out. "I have faced
discrimination my entire life for my roots. People
assumed we were thieves and killers. Few people
wanted to dig any deeper to learn that we were good
people with a rich history."

"I'm sorry, if I've ever given you that impression."

"Not at all," he turned to face her. "You have
always taken me for who I have become and never
judged me for where I started. That is part of why I
have so enjoyed your company. You live for now and
the future, not the past."

Autumn couldn't help but understand him a little

more. Her past colored her as well. The only reason people don't judge as harshly was that she could keep it hidden. Her skeletons were all interior, so to speak. Andrzej may have been a blowhard, but the giant chip on his shoulder had pushed him to succeed. Or was Marcus correct? He had said Andrzej was lying about his past out of shame. Could she trust anything either of them said?

"I've wanted to ask you about your name," Autumn took a chance. "It's very unique."

"Thank you," he loved the subject when it was him. "My parents wanted to give me something to carry with me to mark my Greek heritage."

"I'm surprised because it doesn't sound very Greek," Autumn trod lightly here. "To, be fair, I don't know the language, but all the names I've heard sound very different."

"There is a lot of diversity in that small area," he said pushing on unabated. "The Greek peninsula was the true cradle of civilization. So many things we think of as modern society began there. It is entirely too diverse to stuff into any one definition."

"That may be true," she had one last thing to say that might get her in trouble, but she needed to test the veracity of what Marcus had said. "It reminds me of names I've heard in the Polish and Eastern European areas."

"Yes, it should. You have a good ear," he was enjoying his turn as teacher. "The Greek people traveled, and everyone visited them at one time or another. In all that time, people changed their ways to take influence from the Greek people."

"That's amazing," she capitulated to his story.

Seemed that Marcus had been correct about how Andrzej felt about his name. An Internet search earlier had revealed the origins of the name and how many people thought it was a Greek name. She had wondered if he was ignorant or lying to himself. "So, what is it you wanted to speak to me about?"

"Straight to the point as always, My Dear. First, I want to thank you for saving me that night at the fights," he turned and began to walk to another room. "Please, come with me to my sitting room."

They walked into a room that was more conventionally decorated but still very self-gratifying. Here he had a few pictures of himself with people she assumed he thought were impressive. There were books all over the room. Some of them were prominently displayed so that she couldn't miss them. They appeared to be magical texts, but the way they were displayed suggested bragging. He had quite a collection that she assumed would impress many wizards. She wondered if this was his collection for his home or if he had another one.

"You see, Marcus has been wanting me to accept Daniel as my personal guard as well," he walked to a bar while he spoke and made himself a drink. He offered her one as well, but she declined. He motioned to a high-backed chair for her and took a seat with his drink in one that sat at a right angle to the one he offered. Autumn took a seat next to him. "I trust Marcus implicitly, but I believe that a second guard increases our chances of catching anything going wrong before it gets too bad. You see, when the ritual is performed our personal guards will be the only other people in the area with us. Had you not caught Kevin's betrayal, I do have some magical protections you see, I probably would have been hurt but not killed. It would be very hard for someone to truly get to me. I might, however, have had to delay the ritual for weeks and I certainly would have allowed Daniel to be our guard. There wouldn't have been time to find another. You saved us from all of that."

Autumn couldn't help but hear his tone of bragging even while he was thanking her for saving his life. Marcus was indeed correct about Andrzej's ego. She could find no limit to what he assumed he could achieve. There must have been a good reason to have Marcus around if he was willing to share any credit with another mage.

"Well, I'm happy to help," Autumn responded kindly. "I didn't realize I had done that much."

"You really are a lifesaver in more ways than one," he smiled and took a drink before continuing. "After your victory I wasn't sure if I'd thank you enough. I was so surprised you had won. Congratulations."

"Thank you," she replied a bit impatiently. Was this why he had brought her here?

"However, let me get to the point," he finished his drink and stood to make another. "I want to discuss your lunch with Marcus yesterday."

Shit!

"My lunch? Why is that?" she tried to sound normal and a bit confused.

"Yes, My Dear," he turned back with a fresh drink and sat back down. "I'll get to the point. You questioned whether Marcus was competent the other night."

"I was just-"

"I want to know whether you think he's scared. After you had your lunch, did you get any impressions of him?"

"You want to know my opinion?" she said, baffled.

"Yes, you seem to have a great judge of character as I had mentioned earlier. What is your opinion of Marcus?"

Autumn's mind was reeling. Did he know something? Was this a test to see if she told a similar story? He had said he trusted her judgment, but could she trust that? She was lying. Marcus was lying. Why should she assume that Andrzej was telling the truth? She had to move forward somehow while not getting caught. What should she tell him about yesterday's lunch? What did she want to tell him?

It was true she didn't like Marcus, but if Andrzej lost his trust in Marcus she wasn't sure what he'd do. If he killed Marcus she could then work to take out Andrzej, but what if he simply banished him from their work? She would have to take care of Andrzej before he could complete the ritual and then find Marcus before he could replicate it. Her best option still seemed to be keeping them together and, frankly, allowing Marcus' plan to move forward. Sure, she like Andrzej more than Marcus, but they both wanted to destroy the world she lived in.

"No, Andrzej," Autumn started carefully. "I don't think he's scared or incompetent. He seems confident. If anything, I think he isn't accustomed to such grandiose vision."

"Really?" he looked intrigued. "Go on."

"Well, most people have dreams, but they can't fathom truly achieving them," she was starting to roll now. She had found a line that would work for them both. "Many people would be capable of achieving greatness if only they had vision. Life teaches people to keep their feet on the ground while visionaries fly despite what they've been told."

"That makes sense," his chest was puffed out with pride. "If that is the case, then, why shouldn't a visionary find another visionary to work with?"

"At first that sounds like the way to go, but that is short-sighted," she continued. She had an entire line of argument now. "You see, visionaries tend to have the problem of missing the banal hurdles and problems. They are high in the clouds, so they might miss what's on the ground. The most successful men are visionaries, but people tend to forget their companions who had their feet on the ground. True success takes both. You and Marcus can work well together. You're differing ideas and methodologies will cause some strife, but you need each other. Each of you uniquely cover each other's blind spots."

Andrzej sat for a moment. He wasn't speaking which was making her incredibly nervous. She had rarely found a time when he wasn't talking. Sipping his drink slowly, he looked contemplative for a long moment. Was he comparing what she had said to what Marcus had said? Was he looking for problems? Had he found something? She hadn't told him anything about lunch to avoid that very problem, but that didn't mean she couldn't have hit a land-mine anyway. Why should he trust her over Marcus? He had been working with Marcus for a much longer time period.

Still the silence continued, but Autumn held strong. She wouldn't be the one to crack. She had used silence herself to break someone's confidence and cause them to confess. She wouldn't fall to the same test. Whether or not this was a test, she would match his silence. They continued to sit there until he drained his glass. Afterward he stood up and walked over to the bar. He didn't refill his glass, but instead set it down and returned to his chair. Seeing no clock Autumn had no idea how long the silence had continued, but it felt like hours.

Andrzej sat down and looked up at Autumn.

"Lindsay, My Dear, I have misjudged you," he said calmly. What had she done? What had she contradicted? How had she fucked up? "I have seen you as both strong and beautiful... but never as wise. For that I'm sorry. That was very poignant. I had never considered my situation from that side before. I knew I liked Marcus and that he was useful, but I never appreciated him as a key to my success. That makes sense, however. There is so much he brings to the table that I never realized entirely.

"I think of my vision as the most important portion, and it is invaluable, but where would we be without his research? I found the original ritual, but he performed a better translation. I found the items of power, but he recognized them for what they were. This isn't my accomplishment. No, this is our accomplishment. My greatness is built with his help. History will remember the name Andrzej Christos while Marcus Kanellis will be forgotten to the ages. However, I won't forget. I won't be one of these men who crush the backs of lesser men to achieve greatness, no. I will uplift those who lack vision. I will praise the hard working. I will elevate those who cannot elevate themselves. While people praise my name and my power I will see that Marcus is remembered."

He had stood in the middle of his speech out of dramatic imperative. After he finished he turned and looked at Autumn. She was awestruck by how he had taken what she'd said. That had been pulled out of thin air to get through the conversation safely, but she seemed to have struck a chord. She had judged Christos correctly, but she was very glad she wasn't truly working with him. The man's ego was amazing. He had taken her words and ran with them.

"I'm glad to hear you say that, Andrzej," Autumn finally felt that she could speak after his soliloquy. "I think that kind of confidence in Marcus will bring out the best in him."

"Of course. Now I see that I need to support him. Lift him up with me," Andrzej was fully back into his element now. "He is a good man, but he could be great with my help. We will achieve our goals. I will not be denied my destiny. I had always thought Marcus refused to see his, but now, because of your words, I see that he wasn't able to see that he has a destiny. I must do what I can to help Marcus become the visionary he can be."

Autumn couldn't believe how he was spinning what she had said. In fact, she wasn't entirely sure what she had said. In her mind she had said nothing more than the kind of stuff people paid to hear from self-help conferences and bought in books. All of that seemed like shit to her, but maybe it was more powerful than

227

she'd thought. Now she had to get out of here before she managed to say something stupid and ruin it all.

"I'm glad that I could help in some small way," she said. "You two seem to be doing such amazing things here. You keep saying you're going to change the world and I'm glad to contribute even a little to the cause."

"My Dear, you have already done so much. Marcus doesn't trust you, but he hasn't seen how truly loyal you are. He never told me about your dinner yesterday, so I assumed it went poorly. I had hoped to hear that you two had bonded, but instead I see that it is he and I who needed to bond further. In time he will see the depths of your loyalty, of that I am certain. Worry not, My Dear, all will work out well and you will still hold that position of power next to myself."

"Thank you," Autumn could think of little else to say. "With you on my side I have little doubt about our success."

"Indeed," he walked back over and had a seat. "How did your lunch go?"

"Well," she said realizing she wasn't getting out of this subject. Damn. "It was quiet and awkward. I think he might have been a bit jealous of me. We talked, but we couldn't really connect at all. We seemed to be on different pages the entire time. I think he's worried that I will get between the two of you."

"Of course, he does," Andrzej leaned back and tried to look understanding. "He has spent so long so close to greatness. He, of course, doesn't understand that the two of you occupy entirely different positions. Thank you for your honesty. I knew I could trust you.

I will make things better. Marcus needs a reminder of what has been accomplished and how much we have already done."

He stood up and walked toward the door.

"Please excuse me, My Dear. Theodore will take you back to your hotel. I need to contact Marcus immediately and work on this," he said with a motion of his hand. Theodore appeared on the other side of the door. "Thank you for your help. You will be rewarded in time."

Autumn stood up and walked to the door. Andrzej bowed slightly and motioned her to the door and Theodore. She walked a few steps and then stopped and turned.

"What about the ritual night?"

"Oh, I will send a car and information to you. I simply must contact Marcus as soon as possible. Good day." He walked off into the house leaving her with Theodore. She had expected to get some more information about the night. She was still running as blind as she was before. She looked at Theodore who only motioned toward the front door. What else could she do but leave? She walked toward the door and her ride home.

CHAPTER TWENTY-TWO

Once again Autumn rode back to her hotel with Theodore in complete silence. She had no need to give him directions so there was no conversation whatsoever. She enjoyed the fact that he could drive in silence. People often assume that silence was a sign of a negative feeling or reaction. Autumn spent most of her time alone and in silence. She relished her quiet time. If Theodore had nothing particularly important to say to her, she appreciated his lack of small talk. What a waste of time.

On the ride back, she used her time to check her phone. She hadn't received a message from Elizabeth, but it was still during a regular work day. Her phone told her that it was one-thirty-seven when she checked it. She had expected a message from Elizabeth by now, but she really had no idea how she was on a regular basis. Maybe she was too busy in the day. Why hold it against her that she ran a successful shop? Autumn could be patient. Elizabeth had talked about getting together tonight. Autumn decided to send her a message either way to let her know she'd be free.

Autumn had talked about possibly being busy herself. She was now certain she'd be free all night. Andrzej would be busy with Marcus and vice versa. As long as no threat suddenly broke out, she had bought herself a night, so she figured she'd let Elizabeth know. Maybe they could go do something outside. Autumn liked moving and walking. Surely there were some attractions around here that would get them out of a building for a bit. She had been sitting a lot lately.

She took some time to construct her message. She had never had to be so careful with the men she'd been with. They usually pursued her hard enough that she didn't have to work. When she did send them messages or talk to them she often didn't have to be careful. They weren't so serious that they cared all that much about the specifics. Autumn was a hot trophy to have around. That seemed to be what it always turned out to be. Once they felt that she wasn't a good show piece because she challenged their manhood they wanted out. She knew that there had to be other types out there, but she wasn't good at choosing.

She finally settled on a message and sent it to Elizabeth. She was trying to keep it all casual sounding. There was no sense in sounding too serious, but the longer she spent trying to construct the message the more serious it became. It seemed that carefully casual conversation was far more difficult than she had expected.

-Hi. Hope your day is going well. I will be free tonight after all. If you're free as well send me a

231

message.-

She wasn't entirely happy, but she couldn't fix it. This was why she didn't like this kind of thing. It was so much easier to punch things to solve her problems. Maybe she should consider throwing Elizabeth over her shoulder and carrying her away. The image made Autumn laugh and break the silence as they turned down South Fourth Street in front of her hotel. She saw Theodore's eyes in the rear-view mirror, but he never spoke. His devotion to her privacy was wonderful.

She climbed out of the car before he could open the door for her. Autumn didn't need a servant to make her feel important. She waved back with a smile and walked into her hotel. She had very little to do before Elizabeth would be off work. Autumn assumed that her shop would be open until five or six. She would probably then have work to do before she could leave. Autumn hadn't had lunch yet and she was getting hungry. She decided to meander out and get some food.

She hadn't gotten past the lobby when she turned around. There was nothing in her room waiting, so why not. She walked out onto the street and decided to look around. Why move her car when she had no specific destination in mind? There had to be places to eat around her hotel. She would follow Elizabeth's advice and try some place new. She began walking along the streets turning almost at random. A part of her wanted to get lost and drum up some action out of boredom.

She turned down another street blindly and saw a

sign for an Italian restaurant. She walked toward the
door and saw that they had signs in the window for
sandwiches and pasta. She thought a hot sandwich
sounded pretty good at that moment. Italian food was
usually pretty hearty, and she was a lot hungrier than
she had thought. She opened the door and was
assaulted with the smells of Italian seasoning and
tomato sauce. Her stomach almost carried her through
the door.

The restaurant was deceptively big inside. There
was a desk at the front with the seating area continuing
deep into the back of the building. There was a well-
dressed young woman at the desk. She grabbed one
menu and motioned Autumn to the back. Autumn
requested a booth against a wall and away from as
many people as possible. Privacy would make her
planning easier and she had reached her quota of
people for the week days ago. She had decided to use
lunch to plan for the ritual as much as she could. She
didn't have a lot of information, but she needed to
collate what she had.

The young woman led her to a booth in the very
back of the building that met her requests perfectly. It
even lay on the outside of the lit zone making it dim.
She sat against the wall with a menu and tried to
decide what to have for lunch first. Their sandwiches
sounded terrible once she looked at the choices, but
the rigatoni sounded decent. Pasta would be her
choice. She added garlic bread and an iced tea to the
order when she saw her server. Autumn figured that
alcohol would not be the best option before the big
ritual. They weren't happy that she hadn't paired her
pasta with a wine.

As she sat she began to consider the situation and
the players she knew were involved. Marcus planned
to betray Andrzej. That much was obvious to her now.
His silence to Andrzej about their meeting had cleared
up any questions she might have had. She assumed
that he meant to kill him as well. He might have to
keep him alive for some reason, but that didn't seem
very likely. She was certain Marcus intended to take
the power for himself. If he killed Andrzej that would
make her job easier. Either way he would at least have
to bind Christos to take control. She was also
comfortably certain that Andrzej had no clue what
Marcus had planned. He truly thought he had a friend
in that treacherous mage. Sad really.

She wondered what had brought them together in
the first place. She had never asked that. Andrzej had
talked so much she hadn't thought about things to ask
him. He probably would have told her, too. Marcus
seemed very competent and knowledgeable. He also
seemed to truly hate being subjugated by Andrzej.
Autumn had yet to see any real show of Andrzej's
power. She still felt he was not an impostor, however.
Were that the case someone would have called him out
by now she was certain. Both men seemed to need the
other for some reason. The speech she had given
Christos was bullshit. Without knowing much more
she guessed that Marcus had the knowledge and
Andrzej had the pure power. Andrzej seemed to
suggest something to that effect and it would explain a
lot. Marcus was probably the real architect of the
whole plan. Andrzej wanted power and was quite
naive.

Autumn would have to be certain to get both of

them. She had to assume Marcus could perform at least some of the ritual himself. Leaving him as a loose end could be disastrous in the future. Another option would be to destroy some of the ritual items. Andrzej had said there were special items Marcus had found. That could stop a ritual from ever being performed, however, that might not be enough. There could be other items that would work as well. She decided to add that as an additional act after she made sure the two mages were dead. That would require her to wait for them to set it all up to know what those items were, but it would add another layer of protection against future endeavors. It seemed to be the safest course of action.

The idea of a demon or god being called to Earth bothered her a lot. Wizards were hard enough to deal with without having help or divine power. She liked the idea of adding a redundancy factor to make sure it would be harder for another wizard to pick up the pieces. There was also the idea that she might be able to wrangle more money out of it that way. The Consortium could afford to give her some more cash.

Her food arrived, and the server sat down across from her after setting down the plates. Autumn looked up to see that it wasn't her server, but another Italian man in a button-down silk shirt with the top three buttons undone. His hair was jet black and slicked straight back from his face. He had a big toothy grin on his face as he checked her out. She could feel the slime from across the table.

"Buon giorno!" he said warmly.

"What do you want?" her voice was flat.

"A chat. Just a simple conversation with such a

beautiful woman," he had an Italian accent, but it sounded like he had picked it up from a movie, not from Italy. Autumn guessed he had never been to Europe at all.

"Why not go find one who actually wants to talk to you? I hear they don't cost too much. Just a little more than your cheap shirt. I'm busy asking my waiter to bring me another rigatoni. This one came with too much slime."

"Now, why treat me that way?" he asked, feigning being hurt. "I've come to chat and be friendly. Why eat lunch alone?"

"If you're my only option, alone is vastly superior," she said, never breaking eye contact. "Who needs friends? I've got none now and that's way too many."

"Signorina-" he said reaching forward to take her hand.

"Fuck off," her voice forced his hands back though Autumn never moved.

"Calm yourself, I come with a message from Mr. Christos."

"Why the fuck didn't you say that to begin with?" Autumn relaxed a bit. "Deliver it and get the fuck out."

"Such anger," he said, leaning back in the booth. "He wants you to be at his complex by nine tomorrow night."

"I thought he said Wednesday. Tomorrow's Tuesday, jackass," Autumn was smelling a rat.

"The ritual will begin Wednesday morning, but the preparation will begin tomorrow night."

"I see..." she said still unsure about the whole thing. Why had he chosen a different way to deliver the message? Why deliver it so soon after she had left? Why not send someone she recognized, like Theodore? "Why did he send you?"

"After you left he changed the time he wanted to have you picked up," he said. "Theodore had other tasks to do and I was nearby, so he sent me."

"Changed it, huh?" Autumn asked.

"Yes," he said nodding his head. "You left the apartment and he went looking for Mr. Kanellis. On the way he realized that he needed to change the time and asked me to tell you."

"He never told me a time. What kind of shit are you trying to pull?"

"I see," he said with a chuckle. "He must have thought he had. He was all worked up over something you had told him. He seemed very excited and scatter-brained. I assume you know him well. He can be... eccentric."

"That is true," she responded. He knew a lot about what had happened recently, and his story seemed plausible, so she decided to listen, but she'd try to keep her eyes open. If it was a trick, it would be best if she knew when it was coming. "That does sound a bit like Andrzej. Okay, what's the new time for the first time?"

"He'll provide a car from your hotel at seven-thirty. That way you will be on time."

"Fantastic," Autumn told him stoically. "You've done your job. Now, fuck off and send my waiter back."

"I can easily see what he sees in you," he stood up. "But a bitch will always be a dog."

Autumn considered turning his head around on his

shoulders but decided to let him walk away. She wasn't sure what all was going on and she couldn't afford to set anything back or get herself removed from the inner circle. That annoying man could have been a test from Marcus to try and get her out of Andrzej's good graces. Marcus could have that kind of information if he had spies in Andrzej's home. That seemed to be a very likely possibility.

After a few minutes Autumn's server returned as asked. She requested another plate and laid into him for allowing that to have happened. She had wanted a quiet lunch to get her thoughts together. So far, she had gotten nothing together. Her mood was taking a rapid nose dive as the day wore on.

When her food arrived it was brought out by the manager. He apologized profusely and offered her dessert on top of no charge for the food. Autumn declined the dessert. She informed him that she wanted only to be left alone to think. She still had time to plan, but it was coming quickly. The more she thought about it, Wednesday morning seemed like the most reasonable time to perform a ritual like this. It would have to be pulled when the rest of the world was asleep. Fortunately, she had started moving so early. There wasn't much time left.

CHAPTER TWENTY-THREE

With her lunch being a total disaster, she decided to get back to work for a bit. Before she left the restaurant, she checked her phone but found no new messages. She hadn't really expected there to be one in such a short time, but she had to check. At this point she only expected to hear from Elizabeth after five tonight. Until then she had a lot to do with a whole day being cut off her time-line. The first thing she needed to do was take care of the charm.

She walked back to the antique shop she had visited earlier that day to speak with the old man. Maybe something could be done to get it done tomorrow instead of Wednesday. As she approached her hopes sank. The lights were out, and everything seemed closed down. She checked the door and saw a hand-written sign there giving her the story. This wasn't making her feel any better.

SoRRY we're closed. Please coMe bacK toMoRRoW afteR 3.

She almost punched the door. She'd have to come back tomorrow, but would that be enough time for him to work? She had hoped she could pay him to work through the night. She'd have to try showing up early. The sign said three, but maybe she could catch him coming to work. Otherwise she'd have to come at three and see if she could get him to work late and finish it. She didn't feel very comfortable going into battle without the proper equipment.

She walked away from the store in a terrible mood. Had she been thinking correctly, she would have tried to get the detector finished a day early. She was usually so careful about these things, but she had assumed it would take him a while to work. If she'd tried for Tuesday it might have been done. Now, she'd have to set her plans to account for not having the detector or shield. All she could do now was prepare for that possibility.

She walked the downtown area for a few hours with no distractions. The look on Autumn's face told anyone nearby that she needed to be left alone. Few things put her in a worse mood than a job turning sideways. It was still redeemable, but how much harder would it be now? She had a lot of information giving her a leg up on most everyone, and she was fairly sure she knew more of the plans than any other person. Andrzej didn't know about Marcus or her and Marcus didn't know about her.

It seemed probable that Marcus was behind the guy in the restaurant, but he could have been from Christos. That was a real possibility, but it didn't feel right. He knew all the right things to say, but he didn't seem like the kind of guy Andrzej would send. He had a very proper appearance to maintain and that guy was little more than a used car salesman. He seemed far more likely to work for Marcus. She'd have to keep her eyes open. Marcus could be trying to get rid of her.

After walking around downtown Autumn found herself back at her hotel. She hadn't intended to head back so early, but it was a good time for it anyway. She climbed the stairs to her room and checked her phone once inside. Still no messages. She had returned after four and hoped for something. She figured she might as well get ready in case they did get together. Her mood was in the tank, so she hoped she wouldn't be a downer all night. Surely, Elizabeth would be able to lift her spirits.

She showered and dressed with nothing else to do but wait. She finally settled back and switched on the TV. She tuned in to ESPN and listened to commentators prattle on about which NFL teams were going to be strong this season. She usually hated listening to the off-season prattle, but there was nothing else. They couldn't really know anything at all, but these guys had time to fill. They had to come up with words to say about every possible subject. The only real reporting in their work lasted less than six months.

With the TV set for background noise she thought about the ritual. Throughout all this no one had told her shit about the actual ritual, so she still had no idea how she'd handle things on the day. Andrzej had said that if she hadn't shown up Marcus's guard would have been the only person present when they performed the ritual. So, she assumed that there would now only be four of them. That would give her a lot of space to work.

Or would it? How rigid was her part in it all? Maybe Andrzej had a specific place for the guards to stand. That would also mean they could more easily focus on what she was doing at any moment. If one or two could be there she figured she wouldn't have anything to do with the actual ritual. If she would have had a specific role in the proceedings, she would certainly have to practice. How big was the area? Where was it? Inside or outside? With everything she knew there were still so many questions. Maybe, she wasn't as well informed as she had first thought. No matter how she sliced it, this was still going to be rough.

She checked her phone after five-thirty and still had no messages. This added another level of anxiety. She had freed up her night, so she could see Elizabeth again. It was getting late enough that she should have heard from her. Autumn tried to think back to things she had said to see if she'd said anything wrong. Had she insulted her at some point? She hadn't thought so, but she wasn't good at this. With no forward momentum possible on the Elizabeth front, she returned to work, but she could only spin her wheels there as well.

Finally, she stood up and went for the door. She would walk over to the shop and see what was up. She got downstairs before she realized how bad that sounded. Elizabeth was a full-grown woman. How controlling would it seem to have Autumn show up at her door because she hadn't received a message? Of course, Autumn was accustomed to being able to control the situation. How often had she been in the driver's seat in her own life? Here, she had opened herself up and given some control to someone else and that was leading to the problem.

She took a deep breath and turned around when she heard a voice behind her.

"Ma'am?" Autumn turned around to see the woman at the desk leaning over it and motioning to her. Autumn walked over to the desk to see what she needed. "Hello, ma'am," the woman continued.

"What do you need?" Autumn asked her.

"You have a message that came in a little bit ago."

"Why didn't you call me?" Autumn asked.

"I thought you were out. I was going to catch you on the way in," she said apologetically. "I'm sorry."

"It's okay. What's the message?"

Here," the woman handed her an envelope. It looked very similar to the one she'd received before from Andrzej. It also read *Lindsay* in careful print on the outside. Autumn took the note.

"Thank you," she said and left. The woman looked a bit concerned that Autumn had said nothing to make her feel better, but she never her feelings. Autumn was too wrapped up in her own concerns to notice.

She walked back to her room and opened the note.

Lindsay,
We're going to proceed tomorrow night with preparations for the ritual. I want you to arrive here at 9. To that end I'll provide the same car and Theodore to pick you up in front of your hotel at 8. After tomorrow you'll be a part of history.

Andrzej

She read the note twice. Something wasn't quite right. It sounded close to the first note, but not quite the same. Was he excited? Was this another trick? Of course, she had burned the first note and envelope, so she had no way to compare the two. This one also contradicted the man in the restaurant, but hadn't she been expecting that? Seven-thirty or eight o'clock? Not much difference, but too much to not consider.

If someone were trying to set a trap they'd surely want to come at the earlier time. If she left at seven-thirty she wouldn't be here for the eight. The more she thought about it the more she thought one of them was Marcus and the other was Andrzej. She would have expected Marcus's note to have come after Andrzej, but then she remembered that the slime-ball had said that the time had been changed. She figured that Christos didn't know about Marcus' message since that would change the whole thing.

Why hadn't Marcus stopped Andrzej from sending the second note? He had done well to control the game to this point. Surely, if he planned to get rid of Autumn, he'd find a way to stop Christos from sending any more messages that might contradict his. Hell, he could have simply said he would send the note and then destroy it. It all seemed too easy for such a major mistake on his part. Was there a third party working against one or both of them?

Stop.

She sat down on the bed for a moment. How deep
into her own head had it all gotten that she was
questioning the conspiracy around the conspiracy?
She was beginning to see ghosts all around her. She
was starting to feel like Jay Cutler dropping back
looking for pass rush instead of trying to play. Once
she started down this road it became entirely too easy
to keep going. Soon she'd see everything as a sign of
conspiracy. Was Theodore involved? Was Elizabeth
involved? How far could she crawl down the rabbit
hole?

Autumn laughed out loud. She had to release the
tension. Pulling her phone up she checked for
messages. Nothing yet. Lying back on the bed and
turning the TV on again, she tried to focus on ESPN
for a while. She needed to clear her mind. Becoming
paranoid wasn't going to help. Soon she'd be making
all the wrong assumptions and end up all too
ineffective.

She checked the channel guide and saw that Hell's
Kitchen was on. She flipped the channel over and
watched a repeat. They were running a marathon of a
previous season and she thought it might be something
she could talk to Elizabeth about. For a time, she
watched people cook and snipe at each other over
every conceivable thing. She had no idea why
Elizabeth liked this so much. Autumn would have
preferred to watch the contestants fight for the prize.
While watching chefs cook some special dishes she
fell off into an uneasy slumber.

CHAPTER TWENTY-FOUR

Autumn woke up around one in the morning. She hadn't been aware of how late it had gotten until she checked her phone. No messages had come in and it really dawned on her what had probably happened. It all made sense and she had to admit it. Elizabeth had probably thought about all they had discussed and realized it was best for her not to go any deeper. Autumn had told her she was lying and hadn't given her any idea when she might tell her the truth. Elizabeth had every reason to protect herself. Autumn thought about the stories of the girls in college and how that must have hurt. Why wouldn't Elizabeth work to prevent that happening again?

On top of that, they only had a fun and physical relationship. It was obvious that Autumn was going to bounce after this job was done. She hadn't made any effort to hide the fact that she intended to continue roaming. It simply didn't make sense for Elizabeth to hang on. She wanted a life and really had one here. She had her own business and it seemed successful. How stupid would it be for her to throw all that away

246

to be with a woman she had met only a couple days prior? Ridiculous. Autumn knew Elizabeth was too intelligent for that, so she had probably disengaged before she became too attached. It only made sense.

Autumn turned her phone off without sending any more messages. There was no sense making this any worse for Elizabeth every time she saw another message from Autumn. She took her clothes off and lay back in bed. If she didn't have the rest of the job ending tomorrow she would have loved to get a drink. She had no idea how late she could have gone out, but bigger cities tended to have later hours. None of that mattered now, however she had a big day coming up and this might be the only sleep she'd get for a while. The shop's hours started at ten in the morning. Autumn set an alarm for five.

She planned to stake the place out before it opened. Maybe she could catch him coming to work so she could ask him about speeding it all up. She feared that three would be too late. He might be able to move faster, but there was such a thing as asking too much. She would be entirely willing to pay for his time. She hadn't seen an apartment above the shop, so she didn't think he lived there. Thinking about the layout, she'd have to circle the place and check for a rear entrance.

As she continued to think about the hours she would spend waiting in the morning she settled back into sleep. Her mind never allowed her to rest well; there was too much anxiety and concern for the ritual. So many things could go wrong. In fact, there were far more ways it could go wrong than right. That made sleep difficult.

The clock on the night stand blared at five waking her immediately. Autumn slept very lightly even when she was sleeping well. No one would catch her unaware while she slept. Normally, she didn't get or need much sleep, but occasionally she would allow herself to get more than usual. It might help cover the times when she received much less. Her job didn't have a regular schedule.

She cleaned up and prepared for the day. The big trials would begin at seven-thirty, but she had a lot to do before that. By five-thirty she was out of the room and heading for the street. She figured that the old man did his work in the room he had checked her in. If that were the case, he would have to come into work to get things done. She had no idea how early he might come in, so she needed to get there early.

Briskly, she walked through the early morning dark to find the shop. Cities looked different in the early morning. At night they were full of excited people ending their days. Clubs bustled, and people ran around finding their entertainment and vices. The silence of the morning allowed the truth of the city to come forward. Appearances washed away as those who had nowhere to go found a place for the night. Animals came out to pick the bones of last night's excesses. Few people were out and those that were tried to evade notice. It felt like the city itself resented the people and demanded silence for a time.

Autumn never broke that silence as she didn't speak, and her shoes made no noise. She could feel the accusing gaze of the city upon her. She was out too early for its taste. The people were supposed to stay locked away for a bit longer and she was breaking the rules like a petulant child. She met no one on the street as she walked. The air was chilly and the sky clear though it would probably be warm later. The sun had yet to poke up over the river. The moon was waning in the sky, but its light was still bright, and she couldn't see any stars for the street lamps.

She reached the block and walked around the back. There she saw many unmarked back doors. There were other businesses on this block, but the antique shop must have had two of these doors at least. She had the problem now of knowing which door he might use. She could have broken in and waited inside, but he would certainly have magical locks and protections set. He had more than enough skill to protect his business. That would also destroy any goodwill she might have built up.

She walked around the building again and tried to figure out exactly which rear doors might lead into the shop. Judging from the dimensions of the store she tried to work out how much of the back it covered. She walked back around and looked at her best guesses. One of them had a lot of rust built up on the hinges. She figured that door had gone unused for a long time. The other looked like it had been used recently, but she saw spider webs covering the door's top corners. The web looked old and abandoned. This door hadn't been opened last night when he'd left. She walked back around the front.

He probably entered and exited through the front and took the trash out the back. How much trash could one man generate in one day? She could imagine that he made much, really. It may have been a few days before he had to take it out. If she was right, she'd only have to watch the front. Of course, he could do anything. All she could do was wait for him to show up. She hadn't eaten or drunk anything that morning since she could handle being hungry better than needing to use a restroom. She didn't want to leave her post until she was ready to walk away. This was too important.

Autumn held on until after ten-thirty. There was never any sign of life in the shop. Before leaving she walked around to the rear and checked those doors as well. There was a new web up on the door, but that was the only change she saw. She didn't think he had come in the rear entrance while she had been watching. The sign on the door was the same, so she figured the only thing she could so was wait until three.

She left the store and her frustration grew. So many things were out of her control. She had to wait and hope for things to work out. Autumn was not a hopeful person. She checked her phone but wasn't surprised when she hadn't received a message. By now she was certain Elizabeth had moved on. She was disappointed, but it was for the best. Saying goodbye would have been hard and needlessly painful. Elizabeth was a smart enough woman to know that.

As she meandered downtown in search of an outlet for her pent-up energy, she came across an old gym. It looked very rundown and no effort had been made to hide its age. There was one window on the street and from that she could see equipment, bags, and a mocked-up ring. She couldn't believe her fortune. Autumn had found an old-style boxing gym at the perfect time. As she looked there were people inside and it seemed to be within operating hours. This would work greatly to help her burn all her excess energy.

She opened the door and was assaulted by the smell of hard work and testosterone. There were a few men working around the equipment, but not nearly as many as the gym would hold. Most of the equipment look old like the building and was in the early stages of disrepair. This gym had passed its heyday, assuming it ever had one, and found itself on the later end of decline. No reason not to get a workout before it all decomposed in a week or two.

Autumn had no membership, but she saw no one who looked official, so she figured she could avoid capture for one session. She'd simply act like she belonged and see how far that would take her. Hotel fitness rooms were never useful to her. The weight was too low on any machine they had, and it was rare to find weight machines in the first place. Treadmills and bikes wouldn't do the trick for any real workout. She wanted to really work up a sweat.

She grabbed a stained white towel off the rack by the door and walked over to an unattended bench. She decided to work some weights, but to avoid the bags and ring. Heavy bags were a quagmire of problems for her. Rarely did anywhere have a bag heavy enough to provide her any real resistance. Even then, if she became too aggressive she tended to destroy them. She was hoping to go unnoticed here today, so that wasn't a risk worth taking.

Finding a large rack of plates, Autumn began to load the bar for a few warm-up reps. She figured that

two-fifty would be a good starting point. She hoped
that the equipment would hold up well because she
wanted a real workout without causing destruction.
The bars and bench looked old and there were spots of
rust from lack of care. No sense going nuts with the
equipment yet.

A large man, bulging to the point that he must have
paid someone to keep his head shaved so well,
sauntered over to see what the new woman was doing.
He inspected the bar and stood by as Autumn sat on
the bench. She wondered if he was someone official
but figured that he was no more than some 'roid case
who thought he ran the place. Great.

"Hey, Babe," he said, flashing his biggest smile.
"You actually planna lift that or you just setting up
that bar for me?" He chuckled at his clever wit.

Autumn chose not to answer. She really had no
desire to get into anything with this joker. Maybe if
she left it alone and let him make his jokes he'd walk
away when it stopped being fun. She lay back on the
bench and positioned her hands on the bar. He leaned
on the bar and looked down at her.

Damnit.

"You new 'ere, lady? Not just anyone can lift 'ere.
This is Bruno's Gym and I'm Bruno. I gotta clear
everyone who works 'ere. Got that?"

"Fine," she sighed. "I'm in town for a few days and
hoped to get a workout in. Good enough?"

"I don't know. You look like ya may not know
whatcha's doin. Why doncha show me those big pecs
before I letcha lift this much weight," he laughed
again. "You really know how much this is?"

"Two-fifty."

"Good," he smiled as he spoke to her. "Can you lift that much? It's a whole lot and I'm worried 'boutchyour safety."

"I'll out lift your ass," there it was. Autumn was getting mad now. She had wanted a nice workout alone and now she had challenged some guy to a contest. Damnit.

"Yeah?" he laughed. "Fine by me. You keep up with me and I's got no problems witcho workin' here. Move over, Babe, I'm first."

Autumn sighed again and stood up. Well, she had started it. She could have tried to defuse the situation, so she could have a nice quiet workout, but she had to challenge the guy. These assholes always made her so angry that she had no more than a hair trigger the moment she saw him. Now she was entirely too competitive to back down, so she'd have to teach him a lesson.

Bruno sat on the bench and made a show of stretching and preparing. He made sure to flex and show off as much as he could in the process. Finally, he leaned back on the bench and planted his hands on the bar. With a smooth and easy motion, he lifted the bar and completed three reps before replacing it in the rests.

Bruno stood up and made a great show of wiping down the equipment for Autumn to use. "'Ere you go, princess."

Autumn sat on the bench and leaned back. She planted her hands again and lifted the bar up above her. She performed ten smooth and easy reps before gently placing the bar back in the resting position.

"Show off," he said, still smiling. "Oh well, you

wants to go up now?"

"You going to try and keep up with me?"

Bruno laughed, "Okay, honey, let's go. Wow me."

Autumn walked over and grabbed two twenty-five-pound plates and added them to the bar. She could see that it took Bruno a moment to do the math. He moved his lips quietly while he added the numbers.

"That's three hundred if you have a problem with the math," Autumn couldn't help but taunt him.

Most of the rest of the people in the gym had migrated over to see what Bruno was doing. There was a growing buzz in the room as they realized that he was in a lifting competition. The buzz grew when people began to spread that it was with the tall lady standing by the bench. There were only a few people by then who took their own workouts seriously enough to keep going. Everyone else wanted to see a show.

Bruno lay back under the bar. Now, he was in full show off mode. He had a reputation to uphold and he loved the pressure. He placed his hands on the bar and yelled as he lifted three hundred pounds off on the rests and onto his giant arms. He worked five reps this time breathing loudly before dropping the bar back onto the resting place.

He popped up and the small crowd applauded. Few could have moved that bar and Bruno had done it easily. Though no one there had heard the setup, they had all heard that Bruno was challenged by this chick who thought she could out lift him. The other men were laughing and waiting to see how Bruno would handle his victory.

Autumn took the bench again and slowly lay back.

She carefully placed her hands again on the grips of the bar. The bar came up smoothly with no noise from her and again moved through ten reps before coming back down on the pedestals. She quietly sat up and looked at Bruno.

He chuckled, "Impressive, princess. You's pretty strong, I'll give ya that. Wanna keep going or you hitcho limit? I understand if ya has."

"You asking to quit?"

His face shifted when he realized what she was saying. The audience gasped at the audacity of this chick.

"I was tryin' to be nice. Put fifty more on."

Autumn half smiled at his anger. She changed out plates to get three-fifty on with a better arrangement. She had learned long ago to be very careful with her arrangement and to conserve space. The bars only had so much space to hold weight. And she tended to add a lot.

When she finished Bruno pushed her aside and dropped his weight onto the bench. He performed a well-practiced breathing ritual that, apparently, informed the crowd that shit just got real. Finally, he lay back and grabbed the bar. Yelling again, maybe louder, he threw the bar off the rests and onto his outstretched arms. He did five reps again with heavy breathing and grunts. He stood after he replaced the bar and the crowd cheered. He took the time to high five his fans and bump chests with some of the larger men.

Autumn watched the reactions with curiosity. None of these other men were winning anything. She guessed that on any other day Bruno would be bullying them to prove himself, but they probably had to kiss his ass on a regular basis to feed his massive and unstable ego. How could they cheer him? She kept thinking they should want him to fall. Of course, that would probably have consequences for the patrons here as well. Too bad.

Autumn lay down again, placed her hands, and did ten smooth reps. She stood up to no applause. There were some shocked faces around the crowd, but no one seemed happy that she had kept this contest going. She had been having fun for a while, but the whole thing had escalated so much that there was no joy left here. She figured that it was time to speed the process up and get this over with.

"You nearing your max? What is it? Four? Four-fifty?" Autumn put no effort to spare his fragile ego. Her tone was as accusatory as possible.

Bruno had to stay cool for the crowd, but it was obvious that he was both angry and surprised. This should have been over. He had not been prepared for a real contest. Of course, he'd never live it down if he lost to a girl. His tiny mind was beginning to roll around the implications, but it would be a while before he understood.

"Four-fifty, huh? What say we skip straight to five?"

"Now you're talking," Autumn smiled. He was trying his best to outmaneuver her mentally. She found that the saddest part to watch.

They both worked together this time to get the plates arranged. Bruno may have been an ass, but he took lifting very seriously. Bruno taxed his mind again for the math. He was very careful to be sure it was five hundred exactly. Autumn felt certain they were near his max. Impressive indeed.

He dropped onto the bench and performed his ritual again. Were the weight higher Autumn might have questioned magic. However, Bruno was being very careful now. He motioned to two men in the small crowd and they stepped to the bar. His acolytes took up their position with directed and rehearsed precision. Autumn felt sure they had been in this position before. Bruno wasn't entirely stupid though he was too proud and boastful for his own good.

He lifted the bar with help and did three slow reps. When he returned the bar the crowd loudly supported him. Many of these people had never seen someone lift so much. There was a different buzz in the crowd after that. That may have been the most they had ever seen, but the chick didn't look nervous. These meatheads had no clue how to process the information.

Autumn calmly lay back on the bench again. The whole bench was wet now from Bruno's sweat. He was no longer taunting her or taking time to clean. This was serious. Autumn thought that she would have no choice but to take a shower after this. She had no desire to smell like Bruno all day.

She placed her hands as before and saw that the same two guys stood there to spot her. She had expected them to stay away but then she saw one of them smile as he realized that when she dropped the bar he'd get to lift it off her chest. She suppressed a shiver.

Autumn lifted the bar with no help from either of the spotters. She performed the same smooth ten reps she had been performing the entire time before replacing the bar. She sat up and stood to her full height and looked at Bruno. He was scared now and trying not to show it. He knew he couldn't go on much further.

"Okay, lady. So ya fancy yerself the next Chyna? Let's set this bitch for five-sixty-five. Whadayasay?"

"Fine," Autumn replied flatly.

Bruno was locked in now. He had expected she was near her limit too and hoped it was lower than that. He began to load the bar the way he had the one and only time he had managed five sixty-five. He was working hard to stay calm while he did. The buzz grew through the crowd. People had heard he did this but hadn't seen it. Autumn allowed him to load it however he liked. This was his big show. As she listened to the buzz she began to hear some dissent in the crowd. Some had less faith in their man than others.

Bruno sat on the bench and again went through his ritual. It was like a security blanket for him. It took him long enough Autumn began to wonder if he was trying to think of a way to chicken out. When he lay back and placed his hands the crowd went silent. Two men were added to the spotting crew. Autumn didn't know if they were needed or if this was more theatrics to add to Bruno's mystique. The additional men stood at the ends of the bar on each side. The gravity in their faces made her think this was serious.

Bruno finally yelled, and the four men worked in concert with him to get the bar onto his outstretched arms. There was applause, but the crowd was still saying nothing. Bruno slowly lowered the bar and bounced it off his swollen chest as he worked to throw it up. The bar moved slowly, but, to the big man's credit, he got it all the way up for one unassisted rep. The four spotters helped him replace it. When the bar came down on the rests the crowd exploded.

Bruno stood, and people crowded around him. Everyone was amazed by what the big man had managed. People passed on kind words and platitudes about how amazing he was. People patted his back and felt his muscles while he flexed and smiled. Bruno stood and soaked it all up. This was why he did most everything he did.

While they crowded around Bruno and he talked of how he was naturally gifted before all his hard work, Autumn lay back on the bench almost unnoticed. She positioned herself carefully for balance and waved off the one spotter who had stayed by the bar. His eyes grew to the size of oranges as he realized what she was about to accomplish.

Autumn lifted the bar smoothly off the rest and the spotter jumped sideways and yelled for everyone to hear.

"Jesus Fucking Christ!"

The crowd turned, and jaws hit the floor. Bruno dropped to his knees as he realized he was defeated. Soundly defeated. They could only watch in awe as Autumn, having balanced the bar carefully, did ten reps with only her left arm. No one could truly believe what they were seeing.

She caught the bar with her right hand for stability and placed it back down smoothly. When she stood up calmly no one said anything. What could they say. What they had witnessed was impossible.

"Well, thanks for the workout. Think I'll go get a

smoothie," Autumn turned calmly as she spoke and walked out. She threw the towel into a bin across the room as she left. That took care of some of her anxious energy. The rest would be channeled into her business tonight.

CHAPTER TWENTY-FIVE

Autumn returned to her hotel after the gym for a much-needed shower. Bruno was a heavy sweater and she had worked up a bit of her own to go along with it. She still had a few hours until the sign said the shop would be open again, so she could take care to not smell terrible when she arrived. No one from the desk stopped her on the way in. She was surprised by this since it seemed someone was always leaving her a message of some sort. Relief flooded her system when she realized she had some time to herself to clean up and prepare.

The night was looming ever closer and she still had a lot of things to get straightened out. She'd have to consider her options while she cleaned off the steroid sweat from the gym. She should have done a second set with her right arm. Symmetry and all. She peeled off her wet clothes and couldn't help remembering the gym. Thinking about it, she realized that she had gotten very aggressive at the gym. Even at her size and build most men didn't take her seriously and that burned.

Autumn had spent most of her life compensating for people's expectations. From the time her parents had died people spent time and effort telling her how she should be reacting. Somehow, she was never sad enough, happy enough, or even weak enough. When she played sports, she was told not to take it too seriously because there were no good professional sports for girls. When she learned martial arts they always tried to frame lessons as an attack by a man trying to take advantage of her. When she joined the Marines, she was told she should get married and have children instead. Was it any wonder she grew to be angry and cynical?

After her shower she looked at the clock and saw that she still had an hour until she had to leave for the magic shop. She wanted to get to the shop before three in case he showed up early at all. Any extra time she could give him might prove valuable to his getting it done on the new schedule. It was possible for her to work without the detector. She had spent most of her jobs working without any magical gear, but this time she worried about the amount of magic around. With two wizards with their own motivations, she felt she needed to know when the magic started flying.

Having the job to do helped her keep her mind off Elizabeth. Autumn was disappointed, but she knew it was for the best. Fortunately, she wasn't too attached yet no matter how it felt. Her feelings on the subject felt foreign to her. Usually, these things had little to no effect on her, but somehow this felt different. The whole situation was different so that might be leading to the whole problem. She preferred to think about the job, because she could accomplish something in that arena. She still had some control over how the night would play out. The situation with Elizabeth had been taken by someone else and Autumn had little choice left. In the end, she decided that was what led to the different feelings. She hated lacking control.

Back to work she began to consider her choices. There were different scenarios ahead of her, but she didn't have full information about any of them. Her first option was how to handle Marcus' betrayal. That one seemed the easiest. She decided to wait and see if Marcus betrayed Andrzej. Not if, but when. Marcus might do that killing for her. She figured she could only get off one or two shots so, if Marcus took care of Christos, then she could save those for Marcus. Autumn was sure there would be security all over the area, even though there would be only four in the ritual area, so she needed to get the job done quickly so she could be prepared for the fallout. She'd have to try and control that whole situation quickly.

Marcus was certain to have his bodyguard there. He had wanted Andrzej to use the same guy so there was no chance he wouldn't be there. As concerned as they both have been about this ritual, there would have to be a small platoon of other security people. Someone had to take care of the area or building or wherever this would all be taking place. Andrzej had probably hired all the security, but Marcus was smart enough to get them on his side before he tried to kill Andrzej. That might have been part of what he needed the additional time to do. No matter where she stood with the other security she was certain she'd have to kill Marcus' bodyguard.

No matter what happened Marcus had to be target

one as soon as Andrzej was dead. He was simply too powerful to allow any leeway at all. Autumn decided to take both of her forty-fives. She wanted all the ammunition she could carry in case it became necessary. She could carry them openly since everyone there would be expecting her to be armed. She'd look more out of place not carrying. That would make her plans easier since it required no trickery.

The positive possibility was that the other guards might not get involved if both wizards died quickly. Chances were they were no more than hired guns. There was also the possibility that there wouldn't be other security, but she couldn't count on those options. The bodyguard was certainly loyal. He was a large man who was most assuredly armed, and he was probably magically enhanced as well. He might even have been a mage himself. Autumn had never seen him use magic, but she had never seen him do anything. Even if he wasn't, she was certain that Marcus could manage to enhance him easily.

The charm she hoped to have made would help to some degree if the spells began to fly. Autumn could do very little against magic. That was her biggest weak spot in a situation like this. If all went well Marcus would kill Andrzej and the ensuing chaos would make a perfect cover for a couple well placed shots. She'd have to watch him closely and be in position to move quickly once it all went down. With the mages down, she felt she could handle the humans who stuck around.

After the targets were down she could work to destroy any items that looked important and powerful.

At least she could do that if she didn't have to make a quick exit. Destroying those could end any part of the ritual still open after she took out the wizards. Once she had all of that under control, she could concern herself with the rings and any other proof she deemed necessary. After the deed was done and she was still alive she could worry about her pay. Doesn't matter what the payout is if she died in the process.

Autumn wasn't entirely satisfied with the amount of uncertainty in her plan, but it was all she could put together with what she knew. She had no idea where it was happening or what the grounds looked like. She didn't even know if it was happening inside or outside. Usually, she preferred to stakeout the location and make more specific plans, but there was no opportunity. She'd have to fly blind and trust her skills.

CHAPTER TWENTY-SIX

Autumn looked at the clock and saw it was one-thirty. If she headed out now, she could watch the shop in case he showed early. She rose from her position on the bed and strapped on one of her guns, put on her boots, and took off for the magic shop. She still had to hide her guns under her coat since she was walking around St. Louis. She'd have to wait for tonight to cease her concern for concealment.

The walk wasn't long, and she had grown accustomed to it by now. The store was open when she arrived so that was her first positive mark for the night; the old man hadn't tried to run. He must have shown up early. The sign was no longer in the window and the door was open. She was kicking herself for not showing up earlier. That time might end up costing her. There was a young man at the counter talking to the old man when she traversed his maze to the counter. Autumn gave them space and browsed the store for a bit. She hated it when people would hover near her.

The young man reminded her of a boy she had

dated in high school. That felt so long ago now. Autumn thought back to the days when sports and her training were the most important things. She had dated him her senior year and he was the longest relationship she had ever had. He had been the blond quarterback for their high school team. Autumn had tried, but she couldn't get onto the team. Even then she could lift more than many guys in school. However, despite her strength and athleticism, her gender made people nervous when considering her for a football team.

They had been what people might call a power couple at the time. Lance, his name was actually Lance, had their lives all figured out. He was going to UCLA on a football scholarship. Autumn was supposed to follow him. He'd be drafted to the NFL, he hoped for the Cowboys. They'd be married during his first season and then start having kids while he started winning rings.

All went perfectly until Autumn decided to join the Marines. He couldn't understand why she wanted to deviate from the plan. He tried so hard to convince her that there was no future in the Marines. His argument was solid except for one hole; he had no answer for what Autumn was supposed to do with her life. He assumed that having and raising his kids would be enough to make her happy. He didn't understand why she left him that night.

For all she knew that young guy talking to the old man could be Lance, but she doubted it. That kind of thing only happened in stories. After he left, Autumn approached the old man. He smiled when he saw her approach. That was her second positive of the night.

"You're early," he said still smiling. "Do you need to add to the order?"

"No, I received some bad news and I am hoping you can help me," Autumn tried to sound pleasant, but she was fighting her usual methods of intimidation and force. "The day has been moved forward. Is there any way I can take possession today by five?"

"That's a tall order," he said with his hand on his chin.

"I understand that and I'm willing to pay more. I tried to show up and tell you as soon as I knew, but you've been closed."

"Yes, I have…" he paused almost to Autumn's breaking point. Her patience was running thin. "Fortunately, I've been working on your very item. I had a few things I was going to do with it tonight, but I could finish it earlier. I would need until five, but I think I can get that done."

"Really?" Autumn was amazed. This old man was great. He had given her the best news she'd heard in a long time.

"Yeah, come back around five and I'll have it for you. I hope everything is alright," he said looking concerned.

"That is still left to be seen."

Autumn left after that and decided to get some food before the night. She had grown hungry after the gym and knew it could be a long time before she ate again. This time she didn't try anything too odd. She found a Subway that was downtown and ordered a sandwich, soup, and a drink. No one bothered her here and nothing unusual happened. With the last week as it had been, she was happy to deal with the normal.

She checked her phone while she ate for both the time and any messages. None had arrived as she had come to expect. She kept her eye on the time, so she could get to the shop slightly before five. After that, things would go off quickly. Her night would begin before the seven-thirty arrival and probably not stop until this job was over one way or another.

She finished her food and meandered back to the hotel one last time. She had time to kill and decided to spend it in her room. She had no reason to, but she had no reason to do anything in particular until five. She continued to watch ESPN and think about the night ahead of her until she left for the shop. She was ready to get things going. Autumn has never been comfortable with anticipation.

Her nerves burned with anxiety as she, once again, walked through the human-laden streets of downtown St. Louis. She quietly watched different people as they walked by. None of then knew anything about the destruction coming their way. Would they believe it? Would any of them wish to help if they did? She figured most of these people would choose to believe everything was going to be fine even if she were to explain it all.

The job of assuring that safety had fallen to her and she intended to complete her task.

Once again, she traversed the labyrinth to his counter. He stood behind it beaming proudly as she approached. His face may have been old, but he did not look tired or worn out as he stood there almost giggling.

"You've come back for your charm?" the old man

said, practically giddy.

"Did you think that I wouldn't?" Autumn said, confused.

"No, I'm very proud of my work on this one. I think you will love it."

"Great, tell me about it," Autumn said and leaned on the counter giving him her whole attention.

"Right. So, first, I made it a ring. I figured that rings are easy to carry and inconspicuous. Other jewelry falls off too easily. I couldn't remember if your ears were pierced so I avoided that."

"Good, they're not," Autumn frowned slightly as she responded. "So far, so good."

"It will provide complete protection from simple charms like sleep and basic illusions. With a strong will you'll be able to shake off stronger charms and suggestion spells. You seem to have the will needed to make that quite useful."

"And it has no noticeable effect when it provides these protections?"

"Correct," he smiled and seemed almost to vibrate with excitement. He was quite proud of this part. "When magic is dissipated the energy has to go somewhere. Usually, I convert it into light so that it's harmless, but in your case, I have converted it into heat. It may hurt a bit, but it won't be seen. That is why the limitation is small spells. Otherwise it might start a fire. Now, there's also a mental projection of magic that must be dealt with. Light usually works here too. That's why everything lights up, but I got clever. I channeled the mental part out through an olfactory effect. Your ring will produce a smell."

"What smell is it?" she said screwing up her nose

unconsciously.

"That depends on the spells used and the smeller herself. It will translate to something the smeller associates with that spell. Most people, however, are not suspicious of random smells. That's the best part. Smells tend to float through the air and we all tend to ignore them when they are out of place."

"That sounds acceptable," Autumn said with a slight smile. She was very impressed with the little old man's abilities. This had been the best decision.

"But wait! There's more," he said with a knowing smile. "The ring has three charges in it capable of blocking very powerful spells. This will cover powerful offensive spells and the like. These charges will give off both light and sound when used. However, they are triggered only by your conscious will. You just have to hold the ring out toward the spell and clench your fist. I wanted to provide you with something more, but I figured you'd want a trigger on it. You'll have to know the attack is coming, but it's better than nothing."

"Wow. Yes. That sounds like a very elegant solution. I must say that the stories I read were not wrong about your skill. Thank you for your foresight. What about the magical detector?" Autumn stood from her leaning position. She was truly amazed at the work he had achieved.

"Ah, yes. This was simple." He pulled the ring out for the first time. It had three bands in tricolor gold braided around each other with a clear stone embedded on the top. There were some words engraved on the inside. "The three bands cover the three separate functions. The gem is clear now. When it detects magic the gem will not shine but appear to be a different colored gem. A charm will make it look red while an offensive spell will make it look green. I have a paper with it all written out for you. I thought that might help."

"Excellent. You've outdone yourself. Thank you, now, how much does this cost?"

"It really wasn't that bad. I already had a ring that would work. I closed the store for a while, but it's not like I get a ton of business, really. I would say it's very reasonable at fifteen hundred dollars."

"I see... is cash acceptable?"

"Ah- yes. Very," he smiled wide.

Autumn counted out the bills from her payment. The price was low for all he had done. Lower than she had expected or thought was fair. However, no one had ever accused her of being fair to anyone. She paid his price, collected the ring, and looked it over. It did have an elegant, almost regal, look to it. It wasn't the kind of ring she would wear normally, she didn't wear jewelry normally, but it would be almost unnoticeable. She slipped it on her right ring finger and it resized itself to fit. That aspect of magic items was great and very hard to become accustomed to.

"Is that all?" Autumn asked him.

"Is there something else you want?"

"No, but this seems easy and cheap. I'm waiting for the rest of the price. There has to be a catch somewhere."

"Ah," he nodded slowly as he spoke. "I'm not really in this for the money anymore. I have no kids, so there's no one who wants whatever money I can accumulate. I work because it's what I do, and I find it interesting... sometimes. When someone provides me with an interesting challenge or something new I am just so excited to try it out. I guess you can call it my challenge me discount. Does that make sense?"

"Actually sir, it does," she smiled at the old man. "Thank you for your hard work and skill."

She left the shop and decided against checking her phone for any messages. It was time to stop being a silly school girl and accept life. She'd let Elizabeth leave gracefully. Autumn walked back to her hotel to prepare any last things for the night. She arrived before six and the first car was set to arrive at seven-thirty. It was possible that Andrzej had changed his mind for one of the two cars. No matter what, she figured that she should check them out and find out what she could.

With her new ring on and the small list out she approached her room. Now she could find out if the letters had placed any spells on her room. Her door was clear according to the gem in her ring. Opening the door, she passed inside keeping her eyes open. The stone never changed color at all. As best as she could tell the letters had simply been letters. Standing there she wasn't sure if she was happy or disappointed. The whole thing was absurdly anticlimactic. Even though she didn't want there to have been a spell, it was a letdown anytime something went against expectations

Autumn wanted to be sure all her equipment was proper and functioning. She had already checked and thoroughly cleaned both of her Colts, but she checked them again almost ritualistically. Few things could hang someone out to dry like malfunctioning gear.

She was careful to properly prepare them. Caring for her equipment was relaxing and calming before tonight's action. She loaded four magazines all together. Each one held seven rounds with one chambered ready to go. Two she loaded into the guns while two went into her coat pockets.

She had decided to keep the coat for the night. It had useful pockets and it didn't really get in the way. The coat covered her legs down to her knees, but it was loose. She preferred to keep her pistols strapped to her thighs. They were easy to reach and the didn't get in her way. The coat provided cover while walking around the city, but she would not want to depend on that for long.

She wore stretch denim jeans. They still felt sturdier than other pants but allowed her more freedom of movement in a fight. She didn't take to the trend of tight pants. She wore a man's style that was loose. She always laughed when she thought about doing her job in tight leather. It might look good in a movie, but she would tear them open trying to move in a fight. She went with a tight, knit, turtle-neck shirt. She preferred some neck covering in these situations. Not much reason for it, simply a preference. Again, she paid little attention to her hair.

Her boots were thick soled combat boots. She had found nothing better. They were water-proof, warm, and had great grip. She had tried steel toes before thinking it might be a good idea, but she found that her feet were stronger than the toe of the boot. She no longer looked for it but didn't care if it was there. Autumn had never broken a bone since they had upgraded her to her new body. From what the scientists had said she was stronger than steel. They had said that the structure of her bones involved tungsten-carbide and carbon nanotubes.

Autumn decided against a bag. She didn't want a lot of things to carry. If she needed to carry things out she could probably find a bag or simply use her pockets. If she needed to take anything large she might be able to steal a bag from one of the security guys. Either way the less she went in with the better in her mind.

She took the time to modify her coat to tear away if need be. She had popped the stitches in the shoulders. That would take away anyone's ability to use her sleeves as handles. She was concerned that she might have her blind prep skills tested on this one. There would be a lot of power floating around and she had very little knowledge. Because of that she was taking every precaution she could think of. The separation is in the preparation, a coach had once told her.

Once she had finished all her preparations she left via the back exit of the hotel. Walking around the block she looked for a spot to hide. There was a low wall at the UMB Bank across the street that would provide her with some cover provided the driver wasn't looking too closely. Autumn could then see or be sure what the first car was all about. Best case scenario she figured it was meant to delay her or keep her away. In the worst case someone was probably supposed to kill her. She had her money on the second one. Either way, if it didn't have Theodore in the driver's seat she had no intention of getting into the car.

She waited patiently for fifteen minutes. A dark

blue car pulled up that was highly similar to the one Andrzej had sent before… but only similar, not the same. Of course, he most likely had more than one car, but the note had said the same car and driver. She looked in the window at the man driving the car. Bingo! She had seen him before. It was Marcus' bodyguard sitting in the driver's seat. She felt certain then that he was there to kill her. Why send his personal guard if there wasn't dirty work to be done?

Autumn stayed where she was and watched to see what would happen. It seemed that she had figured correctly on Marcus' plan. After another twenty minutes the black Lexus from before pulled around the corner. The man in the blue car never acknowledged it, but he pulled away and drove off. He must have realized the ruse had failed. He would certainly report this fact back to Marcus. Autumn smiled.

Not that easy, douchebag.

She emerged from her hiding space and walked across the street. Theodore looked surprised and oddly relieved. He had been waiting outside of the car, but on the wrong side of the vehicle. He took it all in stride and opened the door for the back seat.

"Ma'am," he rumbled as he held the door.

Autumn opened the door for the passenger seat and climbed in. Andrzej was not in the vehicle this time. She had figured that he wouldn't be. There were probably all sorts of preparations to be done. Theodore sat in the driver's seat and looked at her.

"I don't like to be treated differently. I'm sure you understand that."

"Yes, ma'am," he smiled, but there was a touch of real emotion at the corners of his eyes. Autumn liked him.

He drove off without another word. She began to wonder how much information Theodore had. There would really be no reason to tell him anything specific. She also realized that it would be safer for him the less he knew. If he knew nothing, then Marcus would have no reason to kill him... aside from petty spite. He probably had a lot of that. Theodore focused on transporting his cargo safely to its destination.

Autumn relaxed a bit and tried to track the route he was taking. Not knowing the city well, she was soon lost in a jumble of lefts and rights. She had no context to go with the directions. Soon thereafter she gave up mapping and simply looked at the scenery. It was always possible that this would be the last ride in a car that she'd ever have.

CHAPTER TWENTY-SEVEN

The car pulled to a stop in a small gravel lot. Autumn looked around, but she could see no building nearby. There was a thick wooded area surrounding the lot and the road approaching it. She did see a path from the lot leading into the wooded area that disappeared at the tree line. The lot already had a significant number of vehicles in it, though it wasn't full. She guessed they might have been the last to arrive at the party. There it was. The blue car from the hotel in the lot. Surprise, surprise.

Theodore made no moves to exit the vehicle so Autumn followed suit. She looked down at her ring and saw that the gem appeared to be yellow. The note had said that yellow meant a tracking or locating spell. She also smelled the faint scent of dog fur. Not entirely unpleasant. Magically activated scented candle. The old man could make millions.

After a few more moments, Theodore turned to Autumn.

"Ma'am, they are expecting you. That path ends at their location, but I can't follow or lead you there. I haven't been cleared to leave the parking lot. From here out you have a higher clearance than I do. I won't open your door for you."

He smiled again as he said this last bit.

"Well, seems that you may have the better situation here. And thank you."

"I just drive the car," he said with a smile that agreed with everything she had said. Autumn really did like Theodore.

"Stay safe, Theodore."

"Teddy."

"Teddy," she smiled. "Oh, who does that dark blue car over there belong to?"

"That? That's one of Mr. Kanellis' cars. That driver is a lot like me. No clearance."

"Really?" Autumn asked. "Because he's not in his car."

"Must be pissin in the woods," Teddy said with an odd expression. She thought she might have detected worry on his face, but it was hard to tell for sure.

"Dangerous around here. Probably not a good idea."

"Yes, ma'am. I'll be stayin on the gravel," he smiled again. "You enjoy your hike through them dark scary woods."

"You're all heart, Teddy," she said with a laugh. "You ever play football?"

"Left tackle in high school and college. Never went beyond that."

"Too bad. I bet you were good at protecting your QB."

"Never gave up one sack in my entire career," he smiled wide again.

"I bet you didn't. Protect yourself tonight, Teddy," Autumn said as she got out and walked over to the path. She walked by the blue car but there was no driver there. She figured that the bodyguard wasn't the normal driver. So, it was Marcus' car that had been sent before. He probably wouldn't be too happy to hear the news she hadn't gotten into it, so she'd have to be careful from here on out. Marcus may have figured out she knew something or at least he may have come to heavily suspect it. Comforting thought to have as she disappeared into the tree line.

The path was narrow and quite dark with trees covering most of the sky. The Moon was full, but so were the trees in summer. Much of the bright light still couldn't reach the ground. The path was rough here. There were many pits and holes that desperately tried to twist and break ankles in the dark. Again, Autumn was glad she never tried to wear heels on the job.

As she walked she glanced at her ring. She saw that the ring would appear red quite often. The whole area was probably flooded with magic by now. She could only assume that their preparations involved weaving spells all over the landscape. It probably wasn't safe at all to step off the path, so she'd have to accept that she had entered magic country now.

Autumn was surprised how many times the path curved as she followed it. It must have been fairly long. She had expected a straight path from the lot to wherever she was going. Still, she had no idea what to expect as she continued to walk. A while back the gravel had stopped and the new path seemed less worn. She wondered when it had been carved and by whom. Could Andrzej have made it for tonight? Was this part of the prep they were speaking of? There was still a lot of leaves, twigs, and debris on the path. Not many had traveled this yet.

Finally, she cleared the tree line and entered an almost cavernous clearing. The bright sky against the trees that completely lined it led to the look of a ceiling in a room. The bright Moon overhead was made even brighter because she had grown accustomed to the dark of the woods. There was a fire that lit the clearing as well as a few men helping to arrange some items in the clearing according to Andrzej's orders. Autumn tried to pay attention to them all. Any one of them could be a powerful item she could destroy or steal.

However, the obvious focal point was an area at the north end of the clearing. There were two pedestals standing five feet tall anchored to the ground ten feet apart. The ground between them appeared to be meticulously cleaned. In front of them was a large stone altar. It looked to be about five feet long and maybe four feet tall. The altar must have weighed tons.

On top of the left pedestal sat a large blue orb. There seemed to be a light emanating from within the orb. On the right pedestal sat an old and large skull. It couldn't have been human, but it was closely related. The creature that had originally used it was probably twelve feet tall assuming similar dimensions to that of a human. It had a similar shape and face of a human skull, however.

Autumn chose not to approach Andrzej right away. He seemed to be quite busy and she used the time to get her bearings in the clearing. She could finally begin to gather information about the location. This was the spot they had chosen... or possibly made. It was large enough that if she were to stand at one side of it and take a shot with a pistol at the other she would stand a good chance of missing. She'd have to stay closer to be sure. Autumn was an accomplished marksman, but at fifty yards a handgun shot became tricky. This was not a time for her to get proud and try something difficult. She needed to be sure.

Finally, she saw an opening with Andrzej and approached him. He turned toward her when he saw her walking up. There was a large smile on his face and sweat on his brow.

"Lindsay! I now feel much safer. Was your trip pleasant?"

"Yes, thank you," she tried to keep her tone pleasant. She was supposed to be excited about all of this. "Theodore is quite good at what he does."

"I agree. He has been with me for some time. I think I'll keep him around even after this is all done. Though I don't know that I will need a car anymore."

"So, what is the setup? Where will I be in comparison to you tonight?"

"Straight to business. Just what I have come to expect from you," Andrzej put his hand on her shoulder. "I will be there. In front of those two pillars. That is the most important spot. My concern is from the South. That is where the parking lot and path is. I have men scattered throughout the forest on the North, East, and West."

"Why leave the circle open?" she asked him with genuine curiosity.

"If there is a weak point then you know where the attack will come from."

He was trying, but he had a lot to learn about security. Autumn wasn't concerned about outside interference, however. She was certain that Marcus would have that under control even if Andrzej was clueless. Autumn knew that the real danger would come from within the clearing. Outside pressure might even be a welcome distraction, but anything else would probably get in the way. That was why she hadn't wanted the NC to become involved. That and it might give them a reason to lower her pay.

"Am I free, then, to patrol the clearing as I see fit? I want to be sure."

"Absolutely, My Dear. You're free to do what you think is best. You and Daniel are to assure that no one, even yourselves, comes within a ten-foot radius of myself, Marcus, and the pillars. Do you understand?" his tone was grave. "Do not enter that area for any reason. That will throw everything off. Other than that, I have complete faith in you."

"Clear," Autumn was nodding her head as she answered him. "You will not be hindered by myself or anyone outside of that area."

"Excellent. I knew I'd made the right choice. The only people inside this clearing will be you, me, Marcus, and Daniel. I know very little about Daniel, but he's always been very loyal to Marcus and Marcus is, in turn, very loyal to me. He's an odd man and a chronic worrier, but he's very attentive to details. Keep us all safe and we will all be together in the new world."

"Certainly," Autumn nodded and walked off.

Andrej was very naive for a madman. She had always pictured his type to be more paranoid... like Marcus. She decided to walk around and find good spots. It would make more sense to know multiple angles than to have one spot alone. She could then move around tonight and alleviate concern about her actions. That should ensure her a better chance to create distance between herself and Daniel when everything went down.

She began to walk all around the clearing, inspecting it for exits and entrances along the way. She might have to run into the woods for cover. She was no forest tracker, but she could move well enough through a wooded area when she needed to. She could neither see nor hear the men in the woods. so she had no idea how far away they were. She might have to think about taking to the trees for cover. People rarely looked up when searching for things. The treetops might also be safer if there were magical traps set out.

As she continued to pace the clearing from different angles, Daniel approached Autumn. He moved with the security of a man who had been very large his whole life. He was a dangerous man and he knew that fact very well.

"Hello," he said as he stopped a few feet away from Autumn. He had a very stiff demeanor almost like a robot of some sort. Autumn wondered how long ago he had been his own man.

"Hi," she kept her tone even and her face impassive. "What do you want?"

"You are also guard?"

"Yes."

"I'll be watching you also."

"Same to you, dude."

"I no trust you. Free will taints your judgment."

"Uh-huh," she cocked her head slightly as she spoke. "That's quite a philosophy you have there. That all you have to say?"

"Yes," he turned and walked away after delivering his message. Autumn had no idea how to interpret what had happened. She'd have to keep a very close eye on him as well tonight. He was obviously severely loyal to Marcus, but it might go deeper than that. She then elevated him to target number two right after Marcus. She couldn't help but wonder what kind of magical creature Marcus had created in Daniel.

She watched him walk back to the exact spot he had been standing before and retake his post. He stood unmoving, watching the clearing. His only action was to sweep his vision from one side of the clearing to the other slowly. He kept that motion up like a security camera. She had never seen a guard quite like him before.

CHAPTER TWENTY-EIGHT

Autumn continued to move around the clearing like a caged panther. She was looking for good lines-of-sight and locations for attack should different options become necessary. Andrzej was oblivious as he proceeded with the preparations for the ritual. His focal point was the area around the two stone pillars and the altar. That seemed to be his top, and only, priority. As Autumn moved she kept an eye on the ritual prep as well. She grew to be certain that destroying either the orb or the skull would be advisable. Both would be preferable. She wanted to stop anyone from performing this in the future as well.

As she watched Andrzej, Autumn saw Marcus speaking furtively to Daniel. He looked at and gestured toward Autumn as he spoke. When he saw her watching he broke off from his conversation and moved toward her. He moved like a man trying to project as much power and influence as possible. Autumn caught herself wondering how banal of a childhood he had had. He'd given her the whole line about Andrzej, but Marcus acted like average was the worst insult that could be leveled at him.

Autumn brought her focus tight. Now was the most important time to keep up the act.

"Miss Lindsay," with his words came a large fake smile. "How does this Midwestern night find you?"

"Fine," she said cautious of how he would treat her after their lunch. It had obviously changed his view on her, but how would that manifest itself?

"Good," he continued to smile. "I am indeed glad that you could make it tonight. Andrzej seems to like you so. He feels better and works better when you're around." Marcus drew in close and lowered his voice to the barest of whispers. "I do not. I am certain that you're up to something. I can sense some ulterior motive in you. I'm not sure what it is, but I'm watching."

Seemed that she was right about Marcus' suspicions.

"Yeah? Sure, that you aren't projecting?"

"I have ways to handle people who oppose me," the threat dripped out of his mouth in his still quiet tone.

"People who work for you too. How heavy are the enchantments on your pet goon over there? Can he even breathe without your magic?"

"You're out of your depth," Marcus kept his eyes locked on Autumn's as he spoke to her. "Andrzej may like you well enough, and that has kept you alive to this point, but should you get out of line suffer no illusions that he will protect you from what is to come. As for my people that is of no concern of yours. I have ways to make you heel as well when the time comes. Play nice and behave yourself and you may yet survive this night."

Marcus stepped back and straightened his robe.

"You be sure to keep Andrzej safe tonight," he spoke at his previous volume. The smile instantly returned to his face. "Tonight, he is the most important man on the planet."

"Sure, Marcus, I'll take care of *anyone* who tries to bring him harm." Autumn and Marcus locked eyes for one last moment and she knew that he had understood her.

Marcus walked over to the columns to help Andrzej finish the ritual preparations. Autumn began to move again, but her mind was occupied with what Marcus had planned for tonight. Did he have some great plan to control her tonight or was he simply referring to Daniel? Had he a plan to take control of her and make her one of his? He seemed to have great confidence in his guard's ability even though he had watched her beat F6. Autumn began to hope she'd get a shot at the great mechanical monster. He might be more of a challenge than Bruno or even F6.

She was not certain Marcus knew what she was doing or even if he had any specific ideas. As far as she could tell, he thought she was there to protect Christos, but for some reasons of her own. With his paranoia she was surprised he hadn't jumped to the correct conclusion and guessed she was from the NC. Of course, it was possible he had. and he was playing his card close to the vest. She couldn't afford to make a lot of assumptions now. She'd have to stay prepared for whatever he had planned.

She heard movement in the woods and saw one of the security men walk out into the clearing. He ventured over toward Andrzej and Marcus with caution. Apparently, they too had been told not to violate that area. Autumn moved in closer to overhear what they all had to say.

"We've searched the woods for a mile around the area. We haven't found anything at all."

"Excellent," Andrzej said and turned toward Marcus. "These men you suggested are very efficient and thorough. I'll have to continue to use their services as we move forward. They could make the kernel of an excellent military force."

"Yes, I've found their skills to be invaluable to me when I've needed them." Marcus spoke with a smug air of superiority that struck Autumn further. He acted as though he was the man in charge. The more she saw, the more she realized how naive Andrzej must be. Marcus had the bearing of a villain from a melodrama. He reminded her of Khan from her father's favorite movie.

The security force was certainly in Marcus' pocket. There was no doubt of that fact. Autumn would have to be prepared to deal with them quickly. Her plan for an escape into the woods might be the best option. She could take to the trees, move quietly, and avoid overwhelming numbers. Her pity for Andrzej at that point grew, though she began to think he had it coming. What kept him so blind to the obvious deception in front of him? She couldn't imagine being so blind.

"Sir, if you have no other specific instructions, I'll instruct my men to take up their patrols of the woods right away."

"Certainly," Andrzej responded crisply. "I trust that you know best how to keep anyone away from this area. It would be catastrophic should anyone interrupt us once we've begun. Nothing must happen," Andrzej told him with his usual flourish. There was a sense she got from him that he felt he was always on stage. His life was a performance for an audience no one else was aware existed.

"Yes, sir, absolutely," the man snapped and marched back into the woods as only a man playing at being in the military could. Autumn could see that he wanted to join but couldn't for some reason. She guessed he had a bad attitude. Guys like that always seem entitled to their opinions and ideas even though they are often wrong. He was the kind of guy who would tell his superior to "fuck off" at the worst time and then whine about the Court-Martial.

Marcus and Andrzej continued their prep. They seemed to have a lot left to do and it felt like hours had already passed since she had been here. Autumn kept no watch and she had not brought her phone. There was no reason to have any gear she didn't absolutely need. She wondered how much longer the whole process would take.

Her anxious energy was building as time passed. Autumn hated waiting at a time like this. She knew what needed to be done, and she only had to make decisions when events unfolded. Waiting for others to act was entirely contrary to her nature. She began to contemplate doing it before the ritual started. They couldn't continue if they were dead. She should be able to get close enough. There was no way she couldn't get off two shots before the mercenaries got to her. Daniel might be an issue, but she could deal with that. Then there was the possibility that either or both of the wizards had a magical shield that she couldn't see. If she failed, she'd never get another shot.

No, there were too many possibilities this early. She'd have to wait until they were further occupied. She needed the distraction. Daniel might fall apart once Marcus was dead, but she couldn't count on that fact. If she waited for the betrayal she might have one less target and chaos to boot. Autumn was fast, but she had yet to see what Daniel was capable of. Magic was a hell of a drug. Best to never assume superior fire power, so she'd have to use overkill force if possible.

Andrzej and Marcus changed. They seemed to be growing more serious. Autumn heard Andrzej's voice boom out over the clearing. He was using magic to enhance it.

"Ten minutes until we begin the ritual. Everyone make ready. Any delay will be met with grave response. We move to change the course of history tonight. Everyone here will be part of the new world. Rejoice at your fortune and new position. Reflect on the world as it was and is now, for tomorrow the Earth shall be born anew and we shall all stand astride it as the new rulers."

There it was. Not much time left. Autumn made one last visual pass over the whole area. She located Daniel and saw that he had done the same. He was in the same spot as before, still unmoving. Autumn moved away from him but kept to a line where she could maintain a shot on Marcus. Autumn chose to walk a pattern over the grounds instead of standing a post. At each turn on her path there was a spot she had marked for a possible shot. Moving would make everyone present expect her motion and help obfuscate her true intention. The longer it took to notice her after Marcus died, the better.

After his death she would be noticed. Daniel would be problem number one. The mercenaries would be a distant second. Many of them would probably flee after they lost their paycheck. She couldn't count on that, but it was probably true. Daniel had to be dealt with quickly, so she could get out fast. If she moved swiftly, she might be able to cause more chaos by blaming Andrzej for Marcus' death and Daniel for Andrzej's. Then, they would understand Autumn killing Daniel. It was risky, but it could work.

If she could muddy the water with the regular human mercenaries, she could buy time. That was going to be the biggest commodity tonight: time. She had to do as much damage as possible in as short a time as possible. If she could get them to search the woods for her, she might be able to circle back and destroy the items. That might even be something she could do after they had left entirely. That destruction had to move down her list of priorities. Time would be too short for her to figure out how to destroy them while being hunted.

Daniel had no visible weapons, but she'd try to get out before any real investigation could take place. She'd have to do a lot of fast thinking once the bodies began to stack up. The best course of action was to not engage the mercenaries at all. Let them decide what to do. If she could get out quickly, they would find chaos in the clearing and make their own decisions. Even if they chose to blame her and chased after her that might allow for time to deal with the rest and escape. Getting back to town was something she'd have to figure out later. She wasn't even sure where she was, and Teddy probably wouldn't want to help her after she had ruined his perfect sack record.

Autumn watched the two wizards move into their ritual positions. Andrzej stood between the pillars and in the area between the altar and the columns. Marcus was stationed to his left near the altar. He seemed to have a supporting role in the whole process as far as she could tell. She would have to stay alert. Autumn had no idea when Marcus planned to betray Andrzej. She didn't know what he needed Andrzej to do first, so she couldn't gage his opportunities.

The show was about to begin.

CHAPTER TWENTY-NINE

There was no audience here and time meant nothing to Andrzej this night. Neither the stroke of midnight nor the full moon was a factor in how this ritual moved forward. Christos was making his grab at ultimate personal power and nothing was going to delay or hurry him at this point. Once both he and Marcus were on their marks he began with the ritual.

Andrzej began by chanting in a language that Autumn didn't understand. He began to chant slowly and quietly. There was a rhythm involved, but it was slow. After a minute or two Marcus joined in the chant in a different language. At least Autumn thought it sounded like a different language. She knew neither of them, so it was possible they were the same, but something about the sounds made her think they were different. Marcus matched Andrzej's rhythm and volume surprisingly well. Autumn saw energy begin to draw around the blue orb. It seemed that small flecks of light were moving toward it and it began to glow brighter with the accumulation of those flecks.

She looked and saw that nothing was yet happening with either the altar or the pillar with the skull. The blue orb was their sole focus at first. The glow was growing very slowly, and their chant was not picking up pace much faster, so Autumn had a feeling they were in this for the long haul. She continued to pace her patterns around the clearing. She wanted to change nothing she was doing until the last moment.

The problem with acting now remained the same as before. While she was certain she could get one of the mages and reasonably confident that she could get the second as well, she saw no way to get out of this alive if she were to try. She could try to go after Marcus first and claim betrayal, but she'd have both Daniel and Andrzej on her. She had no clue what Andrzej was capable of or, for that matter, Daniel either. She also felt certain that if either lived the ritual would continue. If not tonight, then another night soon.

Autumn glanced back at Daniel to see if he had changed at all. It was almost impossible to believe that any living being could remain so completely unmoving for so very long. Even when people stood still they would sway or twitch or sneeze or even blink. She wasn't certain that Daniel had done any of those things... ever. Autumn strongly questioned his humanity. Kanellis must have hit him with some extremely potent enchantments. Of course, that was assuming he was ever human to begin with.

Autumn peeked down and saw that the ring was changing colors. It now looked more like a multicolored gem with different facets showing different colors. It must have been reacting to the ritual being performed. She guessed that it was never intended to be around magic like this. Maybe there was no other magic like this. Either way, she figured that her early warning system wasn't going to help her much on this one. Hopefully, the protective qualities would still be of some use should magic start flying.

The blue orb's glow seemed to be increasing faster with the tempo of their chanting. Autumn kept moving as the glow grew to light the area and then grew beyond. The light seemed to expand exponentially. It reached the level of a bright spotlight when Autumn became concerned with the power being gathered. With that much could it be destroyed? She began to think she should destroy the skull before they powered it. There might be too much power flowing around for her plan to move as intended.

Maybe it was time to throw out the possibility of survival. With the lesser god to be summoned no one had much chance including her. She hated the thought of taking suicidal action, but it wouldn't be guaranteed. She might be able to destroy the skull and kill one of the wizards before escaping. Maybe the rest could be left to the Consortium to handle. What good was two million dollars if the world ended?

She moved toward on side to line up a shot at the skull when a silvery sphere flashed up around the pillars, altar, and both wizards. What fresh Hell was this?

Marcus began to chant in English. Autumn had trouble making out the meaning of the words, but they were spoken in English. She was perplexed as to how that could be when she saw a small boy stand up from behind the altar. He was rubbing his eyes like he had woken from a very deep sleep. The chanting continued, and the boy ceased movement as he fell completely under the thrall of Marcus.

Shit!

Clare had said that there were other kids and that they were to be sacrificed. The sacrifice of children had completely passed out of her mind. Autumn watched as the boy ceased movement exactly like Marcus' bodyguard. Was this the ritual he had performed on Daniel? Marcus continued to chant for a moment longer in English. Energy drew to the silvery sphere along with debris from the surrounding area. Everything physical that touched the sphere was vaporized.

Shit!

She'd lost her chance entirely. The sphere remained translucent, but the barrier seemed more tangible now. That sphere looked to be a powerful shield erected around the ritual. Is that why Andrzej wasn't strongly worried about complete protection? Autumn began to wonder if there was anything she could do to break it. She had encountered shields before and then it had taken a magical method to break through. She had no magical methods available to her here. Could her ring help? She had no clue.

But Andrzej had been concerned about safety. If this shield was going to be up the entire time no security at all would be required or, at least, more magical security would be required. Maybe there would still be an opening at some point. Maybe the shield couldn't be maintained through the whole ritual. Maybe Autumn was simply speculating because she felt she had lost her chance and failed.

"Climb onto the altar now," Marcus commanded the

boy.

The boy moved very unnaturally as he climbed onto the large stone rectangle. His eyes showed no recognition of anything happening around him. He had trouble climbing something so tall, but he continued with no concern for cuts, bruises, or injury. The boy stood on top of the altar when he was done. Autumn could see blood coming from his elbow and both knees. The scene was amazingly unnatural seeing a child bleeding with no reaction.

"Take your shirt off and lie down," came the next command.

Mechanically, the boy pulled his shirt off, sat, and then lay down. Autumn saw how small and fragile he looked against all the power being slung around by the two wizards. Once he was down Marcus tied him down to small points on the sides of the altar. Marcus had returned to the chanting. There was a loud hum from all the energy, so she could not make out the words any longer. She had no clue what language he was chanting in anymore.

Andrzej continued to chant unabated. His focus was absolute. She saw now why two were required for the ritual. The glow of the orb continued to grow, but at a much slower pace. It seemed that Andrzej was nearing completion on the blue orb. His chanting was fast and loud, but Autumn could not hear it over the hum of energy. The sphere might have been dampening sound to some extent as well.

Marcus reached into his robe and pulled out a large old dagger. The blade looked to be silver and there were jewels and runes all over the handle and blade. Marcus continued to chant as he held the blade out as if offering it and the child to the god they wished to summon. The boy hadn't moved the slightest bit as he lay on the stone altar. Marcus moved slightly to stand over the boy's thin chest.

Marcus' mouth stopped moving and the boy began to stir immediately. His head turned, and he quickly realized he couldn't move his arms or legs. He started to panic against his bonds, but he got nowhere. Autumn couldn't hear his screams over the hum, but she was certain he was screaming. The boy looked up at Marcus pleading when he noticed the dagger. Marcus raised it slowly holding the boy's gaze. The boy realized what Marcus had planned and redoubled his futile efforts for freedom. A smile spread wide across the face of the wizard as he paused with the dagger floating above the young boy.

Autumn could not help but understand the boy's position. She had been there before when events were changing everything, but you don't have enough power to change the outcome. She didn't know if he had parents or what his home life looked like, but she was certain he was hoping someone would save him. *"I'm not strong enough, either, son,"* Autumn thought to herself. In his story the villain was too powerful to overcome.

Marcus' mouth spread as he laughed manically. He brought the dagger down fast while he laughed. His skill was apparent. This was not his first murder. The blade slid easily between the boy's tiny ribs and found his heart on the first motion. He began to thrash against his bonds but only for a moment before he grew still. Leaving the dagger in the boy's chest Marcus reached down and pulled up a silver bowl.

From what Autumn could see there were already some small organs inside the bowl. She figured these were from his earlier experience in child murder. This was why the children had been taken. She had managed to save only one of them.

Kanellis began to cut the boy quite specifically to let the blood flow out. He held the bowl at the corner of the altar and the blood ran to it. There must have been channels carved into the stone. Autumn had not inspected the altar closely earlier. Marcus showed great patience as he collected as much as he could. Andrzej continued his chant seemingly oblivious to what had occurred on the altar. The atrocities before him had no effect.

The sphere was no longer growing brighter or larger, but, instead, it was throbbing in space. There was a pulse to both its size and illumination. Marcus lifted the bowl and Autumn could see that the organs were soaked in blood. He turned and began to walk to the skull. As one wizard raised the bowl over his head the other drew his chant to the climax of his long crescendo.

Andrzej almost screamed, and Marcus poured the contents of the bowl carefully onto the skull.

The blood and organs were absorbed by the skull.

The entire contents of the bowl disappeared into the dread item. Marcus carefully poured it all losing nothing to spillage before stepping a few paces toward Andrzej when he was done. Once back Christos' voice boomed out over the land louder than humanly possible with his final phrase. With that the sphere pulsed and then it too was absorbed into the skull. For but a moment at the end of that, the clearing flashed as bright as day before returning to the dark of night. Both men watched as both items of power glowed brightly on their pedestals.

Andrzej relaxed a moment and turned toward Marcus. There was a broad smile on his face as he realized what they had accomplished. He appeared to have put most all the power he had left into that spell. It had obviously taken a lot out of him, but he was supremely satisfied with his results. He looked like he could already conquer the world until he saw Marcus. Andrzej's smile seemed to be slapped from his face when he saw the wolfish grin on Marcus'. The dagger was in his hand again and he looked hungry like a shark. First Andrzej seemed confused and then his face morphed into one of terror.

"Why, Marcus?" Autumn heard him say as silence once again returned to the night.

"Why not? Why should I share power under you when I can control it by myself?"

Three things happened simultaneously at that moment.

Marcus yelled: "now, Drake!"

He threw his left arm out toward Autumn throwing a wave of force that hit her squarely.

He plunged the dagger down, with his right hand, into the chest of Andrzej killing him instantly.

Autumn flew backwards and slid to the edge of the clearing on her back. She hadn't had the ring ready, so she couldn't block the blast. The force used was intense to have moved her like that. Autumn recovered quickly to survey the field of battle. Everything had changed completely. All her plans were dead. She had been out maneuvered completely.

Marcus was bending over the body of Andrzej removing the rings from his hands. She watched him put them on himself. The smug look of self-satisfaction was permanently plastered on his face. Daniel had moved to a position closer to both Autumn and Marcus. She would not be able to get to Kanellis now without going through Daniel. Behind the unflinching guard stood a man with a gun and the game changer.

So many of her questions were answered in that nightmarish moment.

One of the mercenaries had come out of the woods. In his arm was Elizabeth with a gun against her head. Her hands and feet were bound, and he had her on her knees. In a flash Autumn jumped to rage as every nerve in her body burned. She would not be too weak to save Elizabeth.

She started to move when she heard Marcus boom over the clearing.

"Now, don't be stupid. Even you can't get to her before Drake here can pull that trigger. You have no reason to do anything stupid. I have nothing against her and if you make no move now you can both still walk out of here alive and well."

"Lindsay!" Elizabeth yelled. They had not chosen to gag her.

"Hold on," Autumn called back to her. She turned to Marcus. "You fucker."

"Sure. That's fine. Call me what you want if it makes this easier for you. The simple fact is that I'm in charge here. Andrzej is dead and I'm in control. I had hoped you could be swayed, but this works just as well. Now, do as you're told so Daniel here doesn't have to destroy you in front of this woman."

This was a first for Autumn. She suddenly realized how much she cared about Elizabeth. She had never been in a situation where someone held her with a hostage. There had been times before with her SEAL team, but they had all signed up. They knew the risks. Autumn had brought Elizabeth into this. If anything happened to her it would be all Autumn's fault. She understood completely why she had instinctively avoided any connections to other people.

She knew that she couldn't trust Marcus. He had betrayed his partner bare moments ago; what would stop him from lying to Autumn? There were far too many reasons for him to kill them both. Not the least of which: he enjoyed it. Could she afford to wait for an opening?

On the other hand, she couldn't allow this madman to finish the ritual. If Andrzej had been correct, the power he would have obtained was monumental. Marcus couldn't be allowed to control that kind of power. There was also the demon he planned to summon. She had no clue if these were two separate facts or the same, but neither could be allowed to happen. Either way this situation felt world ending. She had to try something.

And maybe something stupid.

"And if I refuse?"

"Then Daniel gets to take care of you while I finish my work here. I'll be magnanimous and allow the girl to live and watch Daniel destroy you. I may even let her watch me complete my work. As you can see there is no win here for you. No way out. You are not the hero here. Do the smart thing: step back and relax. This will all be over soon enough."

Finish? She still had some time, then.

"Well, Daniel, you want a shot at the championship?"

"You must be dumber than I gave you credit for," Marcus shook his head while he spoke. "Fine, Daniel…"

The brute perked up when Marcus said his name.

"Finish this bitch for me."

CHAPTER THIRTY

Daniel began to stalk toward Autumn. She quickly rose to one knee and drew both of her Colts. In the same fluid motion that brought them out of their holsters she aimed at the brute and unloaded all sixteen rounds and ejected both magazines. He might be large and enhanced, but sixteen forty-five caliber rounds will slow down anything.

She never found out.

A bright glowing barrier appeared in front of the monster and each round stopped cold when they hit. All their energy was converted and expended as harmless light and a dull thud. Marcus had his left hand out and he was once again laughing.

"You're so predictable. Such a small imagination."

"Fuck you," Autumn said flatly and holstered both firearms. She rolled to her left and onto her feet. She had no time to reload and take any more shots. Daniel was drawing close. He moved more fluidly now. Marcus must have allowed him some control back. He was taller and larger than Autumn, but she was getting used to that. Taller than F6, but not quite as meaty. This could be rough.

"Fuck it." Autumn charged in. There was no time to measure her opponent. She needed to end this quickly. She put her strength and weight into it and speared Daniel at the waist. She planned to lift him up and slam him on the ground.

She hit and stopped dead. He stood still.

What? How?

He quickly grabbed her around the waist and lifted her into the air. He brought her up entirely over his head and brought her down on her back.

She landed hard, expelling the air from her lungs.

Taking a quick breath, Autumn rolled to her right in time to miss him stomping down where she had been. She checked and saw that Marcus was still watching. She had no clue how much work he had left to do. She was running out of time.

She performed a kip-up and rolled forward to create some distance.

Daniel stomped forward while Autumn stood to meet him. Once he drew close, she dropped down and swept his leg out from under him.

Gravity propelled Daniel backwards, so she pounced on him as he was falling. From her mounted position she began to rain down rights and lefts onto his face. He blocked and moved so none of her blows landed clean.

She kept up the pressure trying to keep him pinned down. Eventually, some of her shots should get through his guard. Though she would tire sooner, she had to go full energy. Counter-punching took too long.

Daniel bucked his hips up throwing Autumn

forward to the ground. His strength was incredible. Autumn landed on her hands and knees and threw a mule kick blindly backwards.

She heard a grunt and felt something solid under her heel.

She quickly stood up and turned. Autumn was heavier than she looked, but he was immensely strong. She needed to stay out of his grasp. Her speed would be the better asset it seemed.

He closed the distance again while Autumn began to formulate a new plan. He also seemed to be trying to end the fight quickly. The pace stayed high on both sides.

She knew that she had to both free Elizabeth and take back her advantage. She couldn't take her time with this fight. Even aside from Marcus she had no clue how much endurance Daniel had.

Autumn allowed Daniel to drive her back a bit with a flurry of rights and lefts. She dodged and weaved so nothing landed. He had skill, but it wasn't his strong point.

Autumn ducked and battered him with a few rapid shots to his abdomen. Each connected, and she finished it off with a sideways blow to the inside of his left knee.

He grunted and came down on his hurt knee. She came up as he came down with an uppercut to his chin. She felt bone under her fist.

Daniel's head snapped back as she belted him, but his left hand shot forward and grabbed her left leg as well. He pulled in and took her swiftly off her feet.

Planting a foot on her abdomen he stood with her left leg in his wide hand. He pulled up while holding her down with his foot. It hurt, but he was inefficient. That was the only silver lining to be found here.

Autumn's knee and hip burned from the force exerted. Did he have the strength to remove her leg? She couldn't afford to give him the time to prove it.

She did the first thing that came to mind. Autumn thrust her right leg up into his crotch.

He held onto her leg, but the force of the blow took him off his feet and threw him backwards.

Autumn pushed up quickly with her arms and came around over top of him in an arc. She landed with her right knee directly on his face. That shot seemed to hurt him. Something cracked.

Daniel let go of her leg when Autumn dropped a few forearms onto his face for good measure. He seemed to be feeling a bit more of what she was doing as she aimed for the fragile facial bones.

He tried to grab her again, but she had figured that out and moved before he got there. She stood up and felt pain in her left hip.

Great.

She had her back to Drake. Glancing around quickly to judge direction and distance, she also checked on Marcus. He must have lost interest in the fight. He had returned to casting his spell.

Shit. Or maybe not.

Daniel climbed back to his feet. He charged her like a rhino. Rage and pain were his driving motivations now. She wondered when the last time he had felt pain was.

Autumn stood her ground as he charged in. She let him draw close before she turned, grabbed his arm, and yelled, "Elizabeth! Get down!"

Autumn's hip toss threw Daniel over herself backwards. Autumn landed on her side. Elizabeth fell forward onto her face when Drake tried to put a hand up to stop Daniel. His hand was no match for the monster that landed on top of him.

Autumn drew a Colt from its holster as she stood and took a magazine from her pocket. She walked forward and drove the magazine home and racked in the first round.

A few steps from the pile of men she saw Drake's head and fired two rounds into it unceremoniously. He twitched with the shots but made no other movements at all. She had no clue whether Daniel's weight or her shots had killed Drake and she didn't care. She fired one toward Daniel, but he rolled off the pile before she had a solid aim.

He was still quick.

Tracking his movement, she fired again. The second shot hit him in his left leg. He grunted again and stood up. He must still have significant pain dampeners running. She wondered how much of this he had felt so far.

She fired three more shots rapidly at his torso. He turned missing two of them but the third struck him in the lower rib cage area. He was bleeding, but still moving. She dropped the gun as she dodged to his left to miss his next blow. He was favoring his injured left leg, but still strong.

Swinging out her leg, she connected with the bullet wound in his left leg. Daniel dropped to his knees in front of her so Autumn straight kicked him in the spine driving him face down on the ground.

Again, she pounced onto him but got his back this

time. She quickly grabbed his left arm down by his waist. Planting her right foot in the center of his back, she rotated his arm close to his body one hundred eighty degrees over his head like turning a big wheel.

As she turned it around, she felt the tendons and cartilage stretch, tear, and then snap preceding the bones around his shoulder cracking under the pressure. This caused him to release more than an audible grunt. She was overtaking his pain dampening magic, finally.

Daniel put his right hand down to push himself up. Autumn kicked the arm out from under him and grabbed his wrist. She stretched it out to his right side straight and planted her left foot on his shoulder. She then torqued his arm back, over his back, over her foot until it lay flat.

This time, when she felt the tearing and breaking, he screamed. She stepped off the big man with no functional arms and turned him over onto his back. Autumn reached down and picked him up by his throat. He was little more than dead weight, as she lifted him up until he was looking in her eyes. She saw fear.

"I'm still the reigning, defending, and undisputed champ," she smiled. "And you lose."

Autumn punched into his torso under his rib cage and dug through layers of muscle and organs to find his spine. She put her hand around it and snapped it to the side severing all connection from that point down. His body shuddered and went limp. Autumn dropped his paralyzed body and turned to face Marcus.

"Good fight, but you're too late," he said, as he made a cutting motion with his hands between the pillars. As he did a cut appeared in space that widened into a round portal. She could see something behind him through the portal, but her mind could not make sense of what it was. Marcus jumped into the portal and disappeared.

Autumn turned and strode triumphantly over to Elizabeth. She found a knife on Drake and used it to cut her bonds.

"Are you okay?" she asked her freed lover.

"I-you-"

"Yeah, now you know a bit about what I do. Here," Autumn took the ring off her finger, wiped it clean on her pants, and gave it too Elizabeth. "Take this. It can protect you. If it turns green someone is using magic to attack you. Hold your fist forward clenched and it will protect you."

Autumn loaded the last magazine into the Colt she had left.

"Take this as well. It's ready to go. Point and pull the trigger's all you have to do."

Autumn stood up and marched toward the portal.

"Wait," Elizabeth called out as she followed Autumn.

"Stay here." Autumn took her coat off and gave it to her. "I have to finish this." Again she started for the portal.

"Lindsay…"

Autumn stopped again and turned back before she entered the portal.

"Autumn. My real name is Autumn Graves. Sorry you had to find out this way. But I want you to know."

With that she disappeared into the portal and another world.

CHAPTER THIRTY-ONE

Autumn stepped through the portal and her world view irrevocably changed. She found herself in a large cavern somewhere... else. Alien. The air felt heavy and almost acidic. She turned for a moment to look back at the portal and she could see the world she left behind before a blue barrier closed like an iris over the portal. She could see nothing through the barrier, yet it didn't appear to be solid matter.

Putting her hand on the barrier, she noticed that it felt solid and slightly tingly. There almost seemed to be a mild electric current flowing over its surface. It didn't react to her touch though. Looking at it she could see no way to open it. There was no signal on the side or trigger around it. She figured that it must have a magical mechanism. When she found Marcus, she could get the answer from him. She'd have to before he died.

Time to end this.

She turned again to take in the details of the new world she had entered. The cavern was huge. She could see the ceiling and side walls, but there was so much space inside she couldn't see the end of the cavern. The walls were a variety of stone she couldn't identify. She could only assume that it was really stone. There was a slight blue tint to the rock that seemed to glow. Autumn wondered if there were gems in the stone reflecting some light source. Maybe the light emanated from the stone. Nothing made sense.

She realized then it was reasonably well lit in the cavern though she could see no light source. She looked all around the room, but there seemed to be only an ambient glow. The walls had blue running through them, but the light in the room was not entirely blue. As she peered around the room, there were some plants or, at least, things that looked like plants around. The floor was flat, and gravity seemed to be similar enough. Autumn couldn't feel a weight difference, but she had no idea if she would feel it or not.

Where was this place?

"Welcome, Lindsay, to the Divine," she heard Marcus' voice before she saw him. "First, let me give you kudos for defeating Daniel. You are quite surprising. Andrzej was a better judge of your ability than he was of my character. I would guess that the same quality that made you able to withstand that fight is what is keeping you alive now.

"The atmosphere in the Divine is toxic to mortals. I am protected by these." Marcus held up his hands and showed that he was wearing the rings that Andrzej had worn. "These are the Hunter's Rings. Together they protect any individual deemed strong enough with the Hunter's Armor. Your interference made me decide to use these to finish the ritual here.

"I'm amazed how well you're holding up. Though your ability to withstand the atmosphere means that you will have the honor of being the first victim of Koracus O'Dein. I have almost completed the spell that will allow me to control him. I have already summoned him. Watch and you shall see me use a demon to become a god."

Marcus turned back to the cyclopean depths and began to chant. Again, she didn't recognize the language, but it somehow felt more natural here than on Earth. Those words didn't belong on Earth. Autumn had begun to think of this place as somewhere not on the planet she had come from. She could feel the environment attacking her subtly. She was holding up well now, but it would get to her eventually.

She had an idea.

"Marcus!"

He turned after a moment to see her crawling along the ground toward him. She was coughing and in obvious pain. He watched for a moment laughing.

"You're strong my dear, but not even you can survive here without protection. Judging by your state I'd say you have a few minutes of intense pain left before you die. You should have listened to me and left. You could have had a few more days ahead of you."

He turned back to the depths and resumed his otherworldly chanting. Perfect. She stayed low to the cavern floor in case he looked back again, and she began moving swiftly toward him. His chanting grew louder, providing her with cover. His focus was held firmly on the depths in front of him and the rhythm of his chant. Marcus began to move his hands around in patterns as energy began to collect around him from the room.

Autumn drew close to him before she slowly stood. She made no startling movement to avoid drawing his attention. She stood behind him towering over the short dark wizard so focused on his magic. Painfully slowly, she drew as close to him as she dared. She watched for her opportunity and it finally came when he raised both hands over his head in some grand gesture.

Her hands shot forward and grabbed both of his hands, one in each of hers. Autumn crushed the small bones easily. Her hands were larger than his, so she was sure to completely smash both of his hands down to the wrists. He screamed as she pulled the two rings off his now boneless fingers. Marcus dropped to his knees in pain.

She walked around in front of him. He held his arms limp resting his destroyed hands on his thighs. Tears were streaming down his face. His teeth were clenched in pain and rage. He could no longer focus enough for a spell.

"How? You were-"

"Acting," she responded flatly. "Simply acting. These are mine now."

"But Koracus O'Dein is on his way. You can't stop him. Only I know the spell. My control is the only hope you have for survival."

"Too bad. Maybe these will help me."

"You aren't a wizard," Marcus pleaded with her. "How can you hope to master the Hunter's Rings?"

"Let's find out," she said as she looked at the rings.

They were glowing slightly as she looked at them. The writing was more pronounced and glowed green. She couldn't understand it. Maybe it felt at home in this realm. She slipped the two rings on her middle fingers.

The rings appeared to glow very bright and then Autumn was lifted into the air. As she floated up off the ground, her arms were pulled from her sides. The force wasn't heavy, simply irresistible. She was stretched to resemble a less severe *Vitruvian Man*. In her mind a series of images, questions, ideas, and dreams passed between herself and some outside force. Consciously, she had no idea what information had passed, but she knew it had what it needed. Light began to coalesce around her as Marcus watched in shock.

"How? How are you doing that?"

Autumn felt herself being encased. Marcus saw silvery metal encircle her and wrap around her to form a loving shell. It started at her feet and moved up her legs to her body. The metal formed armor around her with articulation points around her joints. It seemed to be carefully layered to allow her to move well while within it. The plating had a mirrored finish that was black with green at points along the way.

Flowing close to her body, the armor formed up her torso before sliding out her arms. It wasn't form fitting, but it didn't allow a lot of extra space. She still looked human inside of the armor, but her gender was no longer easily visible. The magic was sealing her completely inside of the magical metal.

Autumn felt the helmet form around her head and for a moment her vision went completely black.

Suddenly her world lit up as a heads-up-display lit up in front of her. She had a complete view around her at least as wide as it had been with no helmet at all. She could see Marcus well before her and the utter shock on his pocked face. The atmosphere was working quickly on him. The view was the same as her vision, but she saw many new informational icons around her field of vision. They were translucent colors and she currently had no idea what they meant.

Marcus watched enthralled as she slowly floated back to the ground and regained control over her movement. Autumn looked at herself as well as she could. The armor hugged close to her form though she could feel no tight points that seemed to restrict her movement. The colors were not much for camouflage. At least not on Earth. Her left hand had a well-articulated metal glove completely covering it. She moved her hand and it felt natural. She even maintained the ability to feel to some extent, though not as well as her ungloved hand.

Her right hand felt different. When she looked she saw that, starting at her elbow, her right arm ended in a large cannon about a foot longer than her arm had been. It shined sliver with lines and points of green along the way. She moved her arm and the cannon didn't feel too heavy and the movement felt as natural as a large cannon could.

She looked again at Marcus still kneeling on the stone floor. His whole body was paying the price for the atmosphere in the Divine as he had predicted. He seemed not to notice as his entire attention was focused on Autumn with awe and terror.

"The Hunter's Armor," he uttered with his mouth

agape in awe. "How did you access it?"

"I guess I have been deemed stronger than you."

"But-" he was cut off by a large crashing sound in the distance drawing nearer. "Koracus."

"How do I send him back?"

"You can't now. It's done," his pain was obvious in his voice though there was a smile on his face. "Despite all of this you will die here anyway. He will escape this realm and terrorize Earth. You have doomed the entire world."

"No, there must be something I can do."

"You don't get it. You're not strong enough to fight him. I lured him from the depths. I had a spell to control him, but no one can oppose him. I could've used the rings to close the portal. He will get through that portal and then life as we knew it will end. You can't win when there is no game to play."

"Tell me how," Autumn commanded him. "There must be someone or something you care about."

"Die Hunter. I hope he tortures you for eons in these depths."

Marcus closed his eyes and he seemed to drain of energy. His skin turned ashen and thin like paper. Slowly his skin began to float away on some slight current flowing through the cavern. It began with his skin, but every layer of his body floated away with the current. Another loud crash shook the room and scattered the remaining ash to the breeze. Marcus was gone entirely.

Koracus O'Dein drew close.

Autumn couldn't leave here without doing something to stop him. There had to be a way to leave him trapped in this accursed realm. She ran toward the sounds of Koracus. Better he never entered this room.

She moved easily in the armor. Her speed even seemed to be enhanced as she moved. She was surprised how smooth and quiet running felt. This armor felt completely tailored to her needs. It felt natural.

She crossed the cavern toward the sound and the unseen far wall. As the wall came into view she saw another blue barrier over what looked like another portal. She still had no idea how to open it. When she reached it, she again tried pounding on it thinking the armor would allow her access. It didn't.

She punched it with her right hand and then stepped back. She had a cannon on her arm and no idea how to fire it. She stepped back and felt around inside. There was no trigger that she could find. She stretched her arm forward and aimed at the door. She began touching anything inside she could, but nothing triggered a shot. She focused forward and tried to think of how to make it shoot.

She got a vision of a blast firing from her arm.

As soon as she thought that the cannon fired an energy blast out at the door. Upon impact with the barrier, it opened to another room. Thought. The cannon works on thought. She would have to find time to practice with this. It could save her life. If she survived this day.

She jumped through the door and landed kneeling on one knee.

Before her stood a beast at least fifteen feet tall. It was bulbous and large with ram's horns on its head. It walked on two legs that were shaped more like a goat's rear legs but thicker. It had two arms that seemed to resemble human arms though they were powerful and ended in claws. The head was vaguely humanoid. The bottom jaw jutted out more and it had no hair at all. Its eyes were yellow and had pupils like a cat's. The skin covering the whole beast was grey-green and pebbled like a reptile.

Autumn stood and pointed her cannon at what she assumed was Koracus O'Dein. When it looked upon her, it roared to bring down the cavern. It obviously wanted her dead.

The feeling was mutual.

CHAPTER THIRTY-TWO

For the first few moments they stared at each other. Locked in hatred and rage at this meeting and their cross purposes, they broke the communication barrier quickly and completely. The tension was palpable. Autumn broke first.

She charged in straight at the beast training the cannon on its torso. As she did the screen icons changed to new icons she didn't yet understand and then a cross-hair appeared in her field of vision. That she understood perfectly. It pointed where the cannon did and moved as her head and body did. She had never seen a display so fast and accurate.

She fired multiple shots at the creature while she ran.

No icon that she saw looked like an indicator of power or ammunition, so all she could do was hope that it could go for long enough for her to figure something out. She ran as fast as she could straight at it while it simply waited for her to come to it. The shots she peppered it with seemed to keep it in place, but it stood its ground as she came.

When she reached the beast, Autumn dropped into a quarterback slide straight through its long thick legs.

Siding along the ground, she cleared its legs she flipped onto her stomach and used her left hand to stop. She stood and jumped as one fluid motion onto the back of the monster. There she found bony protrusions from its back. She latched onto one and raised the cannon in front of her display.

The creature seemed to be slower than she was. That or it didn't consider her enough of a threat to move quickly to deal with her. She'd show it who wasn't a threat. It hadn't learned what a threat looked like yet.

She wanted a more powerful shot and tried to think of a way to charge it with more energy. As soon as she did, energy began to build around her cannon where it began to glow. She saw the glow increase as she allowed it time to build.

Koracus O'Dein tried to buck her from its back but Autumn held her grip tight while the energy built. She only allowed the energy to build for a couple seconds fearing losing her shot. She jammed the cannon down against the beast's back and fired the energy.

The force of the blast kicked the creature forward onto its face. An unexpected side effect, however, was that the force blasted off the bony protrusion Autumn had been holding throwing her back off.

She rolled to her feet as she hit the ground. Autumn felt powerful in the armor. It seemed to enhance her already extraordinary abilities so that her agility and strength made her feel invincible. She leapt again to get onto its back. Maybe she could finish this quickly.

The monster turned and grabbed her out of the air.

She pounded on its arm, but it smashed her body against the cavern floor. The armor protected her although she still felt the blow. Its right foot came down stomping on her entire torso. Its size was going to be a factor.

Not invincible.

The giant foot continued to press her down into the stone with increasing force. Autumn tried to press back against it, but she couldn't keep a grip or gain leverage from her position. She charged the cannon and aimed for one of the joints in its leg.

Its anatomy was hard to discern, but she assumed that it needed that particular joint to stand. She fired and hit the joint on the leg not pressing her down. The monster stumbled back releasing her from its foot.

Autumn rolled and leapt up, but Koracus recovered quickly as well. Before she could take an advantage, it grabbed her again and flung her into a pillar across the room.

She had showed it enough to show its speed.

It had learned she was a threat.

Her body crashed through the stone completely and continued unabated into the wall on the other side. She felt the stone give underneath her body and the force. That hurt.

She knew she needed to retake the initiative. The aggression of the beast had to be met or surpassed for her to even have a chance. She could not afford to stay on the defensive.

It charged forward.

Autumn charged the cannon.

Once it was five feet from her, she released the

energy at what she assumed was its face. Her aim was on target.

Koracus was blown off its feet while Autumn stayed up. She ran forward maintaining a continuous rapid fire.

The moment before she reached it, right before it could grab her, she began charging the cannon again and leapt. She performed a flip through the air positioning herself upside down right over its head. She aimed and released the charged blast into the top of its elongated cranium.

Autumn landed behind it while the blast hit squarely on the top of its head between the horns. Her aim was true, and she was landing shots, but she had no clue whether it was hurting the monster or not.

Autumn charged again and stood giving Koracus a chance to turn around. She leapt again, going for another shot overhead. It was ready. Its powerful arm swung in an arc over its head catching her squarely. The force of its blow was immense, and Autumn flew off.

There was no wall nearby and Autumn was able to maneuver in the air to land in a three-point stance. The force, however, continued to push her backward in a slide. She had her cannon up the entire time firing at the beast.

Had to maintain pressure.

Her outstretched left foot hit a wall stopping her momentum. Feeling a bit drained, Autumn wondered if she had an armor breach. She felt tired. Either the fight was taking its toll already or something else was draining energy from her. It was the first moment she felt there was a real time limit to this battle.

Autumn stood and charged forward again hoping the creature would try to predict her motion. She fired a few shots and began to charge again as she ran. When she was close, it took the bait. Rapidly, it moved to pick her out of the air while she slid under again. She watched and saw her opening. In her slide she released the blast up into what passed as a chin for the monstrous demon.

Its head snapped up as she had hoped, and it collapsed. The problem was that it fell backward... the way she was sliding.

The monster landed on top of Autumn with a thud.

Pinned between two bony protrusions like the one she had shot off, Autumn latched onto them and went for a ride when the horror stood.

She charged the cannon and punched into its back again and again with the cannon. The creature turned and bucked. Autumn slid around its body by the bony protrusion she had in her one hand.

Koracus grabbed her body in its claws and began to tug. She held fast to the bone making it decide how badly it wanted her removed.

She saw the protrusion began to tear off its body. Goddamn this thing was tough. She held strong while she watched it tear its own body apart to remove her.

The bone in hand, it pulled her around to look at what it had. Thinking quickly, Autumn jabbed the sharp end of the outcropping into the arm that clutched her.

She fell to the floor without the bone. She heard a low growl at the wound.

Rolling forward from her spot, she jumped back onto its back and returned to her previous spot with a more tenuous grip.

She pounded its back a few more times with the cannon. Finally, she saw that she had broken through the skin to some degree. Quickly jamming the cannon over the opening, she released all the energy she had built.

She knew she had hurt it that time. It shrieked in a high pitch.

It then vaulted up slamming its back, and Autumn, against the cavern ceiling. She had not expected that and her grip broke. She also hadn't expected the long fall to the floor.

Somehow, she was not full of celebratory feelings. This did not feel like a win.

She moved to get up and continue when the beast kicked her across the cavern floor. She flopped, slid, and tumbled across the cave before slamming into the wall. She couldn't let this end this way.

Autumn stood defiantly.

Not in this hell world. She would not fall here... to this.

Charging the cannon again she began to stalk toward the creature with hate burning in her eyes. The beast returned the act with as much hate for her as she had for it.

Autumn leapt up and forward landing on the creature's face.

It reached up and grabbed onto her with both claws while she grabbed hold of the horn on the left side of its head. It pulled her, but she pulled its head along with her.

She punched her right arm forward and fired the charged energy directly into its left eye.

The creature roared in rage and pain. There was no doubt she was hurting it, but it was hurting her as well. This was proving to be a war of attrition. A short one, perhaps.

Its grip faltered for a moment, so she renewed her grasp on its horn and charged the cannon again.

It tugged at her body. She felt herself stretch and bend, but Autumn refused to let go. This had to end.

She continued charging.

This time she began to furiously smash the cannon into the creature's teeth. Chips and various fluids sprayed off in all directions as she continued to hammer at its maw.

Finally, it opened its mouth and her arm went deep down its throat. The beast chomped down on her right arm which, in turn, went numb.

Victory flashed in the clear eye of the demon. Had it been capable of a smile, one would have spread across its horrible face.

"Undisputed champion!" Autumn screamed

She released the charged blast.

The behemoth opened its mouth as its head snapped back with the force of the shot. Autumn released the horn, so she could drop to the floor and begin a new assault.

The creature did not release its grip on her body.

Instead, it threw her with incredible force toward the back wall of the room. She flew toward the wall too fast to try to stop. She saw a portal in front of her and pulled her numb right arm forward with her left and fired many shots at the door.

It opened, and she continued through it.

There was no ground for her to land on. Instead

there was a hole she tumbled down. She bounced off one wall and then another before she hit the floor hard.

She looked up to see Koracus O'Dein fly over her deeper into the cavern. The last blast must have registered serious damage.

She'd settle for a count out.

Autumn's eyes closed for a moment.

Autumn opened her eyes and realized that she'd lost consciousness. She had no way to know how long she'd been out. Hopefully it wasn't long. There was still too much to do.

She looked up to see where she was. The fall had been fifteen feet or so though it had felt longer than that. Looking at the walls she could see they were rough so climbing might be possible. Of course, with only one good arm that might be difficult. The armor seemed to have saved her life, but she couldn't count herself as out of the woods yet. Autumn stood up and took stock.

Her right arm was still numb, and the rest of her body registered differing levels of pain. She had never gotten her ass handed to her like that before. She smiled a wry smile realizing that it took a demon to really kick her ass.

No time for pride; she was in a hole on another world.

Looking up the distance didn't seem that great.

Autumn leapt up and landed on solid ground. She still had her powerful agility... for the most part. Looking around she realized that she had a new problem. There were four portals available to her and one that was covered by stone from a recent cave in.

328

Judging from the direction that was the one she had come from.

Fantastic.

Behind her was another large cavern that she really didn't want to explore. She was done going where no man had gone before. Autumn was ready to go home. The cavern looked much like the ones she had been in before and she realized that getting lost was her biggest problem now. She had to find a way out and she would begin with the four portals before her around the hole.

She knew that Koracus wasn't dead and that, while the portal to Earth remained in existence it could try again to get out. She wasn't sure she could fight it again and survive. If she could get out and destroy the items of power, she might be able to close the portal and end its chances to get in. She seemed to have no better option than trying each door before her and hoping.

There still might be time… but not much.

She took tentative steps and moved her body all over. Aside from her numb right arm there seemed to be no major damage. None of her bones felt broken and she could still walk and jump. Something here had drained a lot of her energy. She felt incredibly tired. Drained.

She looked at the doors around her.

"No sense putting this off any longer."

She lifted her right arm with help from her left to aim the cannon at the first door. She thought and fired.

CHAPTER THIRTY-THREE

Autumn entered the first door and she could see another portal across the small room. The rock here was the same as the others so only its size gave her any idea that it wasn't the same one she'd come through. She entered the room and walked across. Maybe she'd get back to the room she had come from through this. Could caves have hallways? She hoped.

She blasted open the other door and looked through. The next cavern had a huge drop off. She looked down and saw that the floor in that room was maybe sixty feet below her. It seemed to lead deeper into the whole complex. As the floor dropped down the tone of the rock seemed to change to a reddish tone. She also felt heat coming up from the lower area. As she watched there seemed to be movement on the cavern floor. Autumn had no desire to meet anything else that called this place home.

Traveling back across the small room, she opened the barrier there. Exiting the first door she hoped it would be as easy as that to eliminate the incorrect options. What if there was no correct option? No, she couldn't let herself think that way. Her negative thoughts were evidence of her exhaustion. She had to keep moving. There were still three more doors before she'd have to find another option.

She marched to the next portal to the left of her first choice. Autumn took care to stay out of the pit she had originally fallen into. It took up a lot of the space between these doors. Holding up the wounded arm, she fired once again at the barrier forcing it open. She stepped into the next room when she saw that it was quite large.

Damn.

She'd have to search through this one. Her biggest hope was that it ran alongside the one she had fought Koracus in. She might see signs of the struggle or even a door leading to that room. That thought brought with it the reminder that Koracus was still alive and out there somewhere. She had hurt it, but she doubted that she had dealt a killing blow. She knew nothing about this cave system, so it was always possible that she could circle around directly into its waiting jaws. Then there was the possibility of something else like it.

That was a chilling thought.

No! Autumn couldn't begin to traverse down that road. That only led to fear and she couldn't give in yet. There was still work to be done and she had never given up on a job yet. There were people counting on her even if none of them knew it. She kept searching the room for an exit.

Staying close to the wall would make it easier for her find the exit back if she needed to return. Slowly, she kept walking for quite a while searching. This room again felt almost infinite in size. The light here was less extensive. There seemed to be pockets of esoteric light and Autumn never felt like a member of the right club. Her HUD gave her the ability to see in the dark to an extent, but she could easily miss details. She couldn't afford to waste time in another pit.

She continued walking hoping that the barrier would glow bright enough to let her see. She heard scratching noises in the center of the cavern. They sounded far away, and she could see nothing that far away. Was there other indigenous life here? What would that life look like? Would it be hostile to her? Most indigenous life on Earth had no desire to attack humans. Would that be true here in a realm that gave life to actual demons? She could think of no good reason, including curiosity, to find out what other creatures could live in the atmosphere here.

Autumn tried her best to move silently along the wall. Now was not the time to announce her presence. She kept her right arm pointed toward the wall, so she could keep her bearings. She'd never been a spelunker, so she had no idea if this was the best decision, however she could think of no other way to tell where she was going.

Wait!

In front of her she could see a blue light. The glow was faint, so she was still far away, but it looked like the barrier over a portal. She kept herself calm. She couldn't get crazy now and draw the attention of whatever was making the scratching sounds to her left. This was no time for risk. She kept her pace and silence the same as she watched the blue light grow brighter.

It was a door. Once she drew close enough she broke into a run and pulled the cannon up. She fired and ran toward the door. She had to leap at the last moment to avoid falling into the pit again. She hit the other side and landed without grace on her face.

She had walked in a complete circle around that room wasting time. Her spirits sank. How much longer did she have? How quickly could Koracus heal? Would it even return? She had nothing but hope and fear vying to answer that question. She needed to keep moving. Autumn stood up and turned to see the five doors. The portal with the cave-in still seemed the right one, but she could see nothing of the portal now. Normally she might have tried to clear it, but it could take too long, and she was not certain her body would hold up under the strain.

The next door was to the left of the cave-in. It lay across the pit from her position.

Shit.

Her rash actions and fear had led her to this spot. She'd have to jump once again. The opening of the pit looked to be about twenty feet. She backed up to a spot she could get a running start and fired at the door. As soon as she thought of the shot she began to run. At the lip of the pit she leapt and flew through the open portal right before it shut. She landed in a heap on the stone floor. Her right arm took the brunt of the force.

Autumn's vision swam for a few moments. She couldn't keep exerting herself this way. She might end up finishing the job that Koracus had started. Waiting a few minutes, her vision cleared and she stood up. This room was, again, reasonable bright for being underground. She surveyed it well. There was no fight damage and the room wasn't very large. Again, she knew it wasn't the cavern she had fought Koracus in. It had to be the door blocked by the cave-in. Koracus had probably caused that when he had flown through.

She saw two portals on opposing walls in the room. At least that was a hopeful sign. She could move forward. The cave-in door had been to the right of this one so she went to the portal on that side first. Maybe this would lead her directly into that and she could go home. As she neared she noticed that the barrier over the door looked different. It had a red tint to it. As she got closer the barrier seemed to get brighter.

She stopped ten feet from the door and raised up her right arm. The numb feeling had returned after the flash of pain from her fall. She wasn't sure which she preferred. She fired at the barrier and her shot was absorbed. She fired a few more times and the same thing happened each time. Autumn charged a shot and fired that. The door glowed brightly, but still absorbed the energy.

Damnit!

This door wasn't going to open. Had she known magic she might have had a way to open it, but she knew no spells. She could think of no other way to open the door.

Shit.

She stomped angrily across to the other side but saw that it was red as well. She fired a few test shots to be certain she missed nothing, but the same thing happened.

Shit.

She walked back to the door she had entered. There was only one door left after this one. Soon she might have to consider clearing the stone from the fifth door. She had even less desire to go deeper into the cave system. Further in meant further away from where she had entered. Becoming lost became a foregone conclusion after enough time. She had to try and keep going back.

Autumn blasted open the blue barrier.

Walking out carefully this time Autumn could see that there was a narrow path from this door to the last one around the pit. She carefully sidled along the wall. A sound drew her attention. On the other side of the pit there was a spiny creature moving along the floor. It looked like a large hedgehog. She guessed that it was two feet long and the top most spine was eighteen inches off the ground. It seemed not to notice her at all, so she chose not to engage.

She hoped that was the extent of other life she would find here. Autumn had no desire to play biologist. Or worse still, anthropologist. She turned back, raised her cannon, and fired at the door. The barrier slid open as all the blue ones she had run into thus far had.

- -

She proceeded into another large cavern. This one was massive in length alone. The sides were maybe ten feet apart and the ceiling was about the same in height. The room was well lit, and she had little choice, so Autumn followed the path. It curved multiple times to both the right and the left. She might have been deluding herself, but it felt like she had walked to the right more than the left.

In this hall she saw a few more of the hedgehogs. She waited to see what they would do. Showing little interest in her, they seemed to be searching for food. She watched as one walked to one of the walls and then simply walked up the wall as if that was normal. She slid past it choosing not to engage any of them. She had no clue if they had any way of hurting her, but that question needed never be answered. She kept walking to the blue door at the end of the long hall.

Her right arm was still numb, but when she lifted it with her left she felt a bit of a throb deep inside. Autumn had no clue what that might mean aside from some injury, but it felt a bit more normal. Maybe her increased healing was being dampened by the atmosphere or even the armor. It was obvious that humans were never meant to be in this place. She blasted the barrier and it opened.

-Autumn-

She walked into a small round room with a few of those spiny creatures. She wondered if they had hidden from Koracus when he came through. They now seemed to be coming back out. That or they were never in the caverns she had fought him in. She saw another door on the other side. Moving carefully through the room, she never felt any real threat from these creatures. They seemed as harmless as anything here could be. Some species of scavengers.

She blasted the door and walked into another small room. No, that wasn't entirely true. There was a path at the end that curved off and seemed to lead up. She walked through a hall not much larger than herself. It ended with a six-foot wall. The opening wasn't large, so if she moved closer to look over the wall she would be standing in a hole in another room. She walked forward and crouched to stay out of view from anything that might be there.

Taking a breath she popped up fast landing on the floor in a kneeling position with her cannon held out before her. She found herself in yet another grand cavern. How long had she been in this cave system? Time was entirely lost to her. The armor seemed to have no clock or at least nothing with a time that she recognized. Either way it would be easy to lose days here. Couldn't focus on that. She stood up and began to look around the room. Once again it was well lit with the same slightly blue light.

There was a familiar feeling here. Something recognizable. But she had been in so many caverns that they were all looking alike to her. She saw more of the hedgehogs. Lots of them in pockets all around the large room. They seemed to be feeding on something. She walked over to one cluster and saw that they were indeed feeding on something. There was some fluid on the ground and chunks of something.

Koracus' blood.

Autumn spun around and looked at the room. She felt dizzy at the sudden fast movement. Dropping to one knee again she took a moment to breath. Her exhaustion was continuing to build. Was the armor simply extending her time here? Was she still on a time limit that was drawing rapidly to the end?

-Autumn Graves-

She thought she heard something. Almost a thought on the wind. It sounded familiar but strange at the same time. Was that how death would approach? No light or memories, but a gentle voice in her head? Autumn made herself stand up and survey the room. Death would not take her easily.

Even Death itself would have to fight to take her.

The creatures seemed to be eating what was left from the fight. Maybe Koracus was a predator and these were the cleaners that came behind it like ants or beetles. Could demons be no more than part of a different ecosystem? Autumn mulled that over as she continued to search the room. She saw the shattered pillar she had been thrown through. Looking at it she could understand why she was so hurt. The column was large, and she had gone completely through it. Maybe she had massive internal damage.

She could see the spots in the floor and ceiling where her body had been used to pound divots. She did see the spots where she had caused damage to the demon, but it may have been stronger. Was Koracus hearing death as well? She decided that it would be easier for her to accept death if she had brought death to the monster as well. That seemed to be pride speaking, but pride might be all she had left.

Autumn dropped to her knees involuntarily. Her body felt so weak. The pain continued everywhere but her right arm. There the pain was coming back but it was fighting its own battle to return. She knew she was tough, but even she had her limits. She was still human, right, and humans died. There wasn't always going to be a way to escape death. She had fought a demon. Something man had feared as far back as memory existed. Could even Autumn survive a battle with something such as that?

-Autumn, please!-

Wait!

That pleasant voice wasn't death. She recognized it.

That was Elizabeth. And she sounded scared. Had she followed Autumn into this Hell realm? How could she still be alive? Autumn had to find her. She picked herself up onto shaky legs.

Unsteady as she was and with her arm numb, she had to keep going. People were depending on her. Elizabeth was depending on her. She couldn't allow Koracus to get out of this place. What had Marcus called it? The Divine? It didn't feel very divine to her. Autumn pressed on. Once the job was done she could lay down if that was her fate. But not before.

As she walked toward the end of the cavern, she let her mind wander. Elizabeth had not asked for this, yet she was still calling to her. Few people had ever achieved being on Autumn's list of people she liked. Fewer of them survived. How toxic was her presence? She continued to shuffle on weary legs. The cavern floor sloped up. She hadn't noticed the slope before. Now it was another hurdle she had to overcome.

-Autumn, where are you?-

The voice energized her. She could see the door against the wall. Finally, she had reached her goal. Not much longer and she would be able to escape this place. Autumn no longer cared about the money or what other people might have been involved. She wanted to see the sun again. If she died it would be next to trees on Earth. She would feel the wind on her face once more. Her body felt heavy as she raised the cannon to aim at the barrier. She felt slow and sluggish.

She fired, and the portal opened... on another cavern.

What?!

No. It wasn't possible.

Wait. Yes, there had been another cavern. She had entered into one cavern and then chased the crashing noises to find Koracus. This was the room where Marcus had died. She remembered how large the first cavern had seemed. She would have to trek across it again. She was close, but not at the goal yet.

There were lots of the spiny creatures here. She was beginning to think of them as this world's bugs or rodents. They were spread all around the room feeding. She guessed they'd all found bits of Marcus and were cleaning up. She also saw some odd bat-like creatures hanging on the ceiling. Seemed that the longer it had been since activity the more life came out. There was apparently an entire world of new beasts here. She hoped they all had no desire to fight.

-*Autumn, please come back.*-

The voice was louder now. Much louder. She could tell easily, now, that it was Elizabeth. The sweet tones of her voice had been marred by tears. Was she hurt? Scared? The mercenaries were still there. Autumn had hoped that they would leave when they realized they weren't getting paid, but that may not have been the case. Surely, they didn't think Elizabeth was involved. Maybe someone thought she would make a good hostage. That was how Marcus had used her.

Her legs firmed up a bit as her will hardened.

Autumn tried to move faster, but there simply wasn't much fuel left in the tank. What would she be able to do when she arrived? She didn't have any weapons. Would the armor stay with her? That was her best hope. The sight of her might be enough to send them away.

Autumn allowed her right arm to dangle as she shuffled along. Dodging the creatures made her task harder and longer, but she felt that a fight would be worse still. The bat things weren't bothering her... yet. Good news. The room was indeed as large as she had first perceived.

One of the bats flew down toward her.

She was caught off guard and fell to her side to dodge.

The creature never flew closer than ten feet. It landed near a pack of the spiny beasts off to her left. She was jumpy and overreacting. Standing again took great effort. Her armor seemed to be weighing her down now. Even the size of her own body seemed to be fighting against her forward progression.

The door!

She could see the blue of the barrier. Off in the distance she could see the shimmering blue glow of a door that must have been where she had entered. That was her way out. Earth, her home, lay on the other side. She wondered if that was how it felt in space. It looked to be only a hundred yards away. In any normal case she could sprint that in seconds on any normal day. Now, however, she had to drag her body forward with great effort.

There sounded a loud roar in the depths behind her.

Koracus O'Dein!

-Autumn!-

Terror behind and home in front. This would be the most important touchdown in human history.

She dared not look forward. Autumn kept moving. One foot forward and then the other. She dared not check her progress... or lack thereof. Keep walking like all of life depended on it. She couldn't give up. As long as she kept moving she could keep the drive alive.

Always play to the whistle.

The floor inched forward at an agonizing pace. Autumn had increased her speed as much as she could. She could feel the weight of this realm coming down on her. It felt as though the whole Divine was trying to stop her from reaching her goal. That was what she needed... an enemy to hate.

"Fuck you. No realm is going to beat me. I'm Autumn Fucking Graves Goddamnit! I'm not losing to you!" she screamed in her helmet.

Her pace increased.

There was another roar. It sounded closer, but still not in this cavern. Autumn finally looked up from the floor to see where she was.

Thirty yards to go.

She could do this. She no longer moved with her head down. Her will was renewed. Autumn drove herself forward with everything she could find within herself. She would not let that creature end her life. She had fought a demon and lived. That was the story. It would get no second chance at her or even a first chance at her world. That son of a bitch stayed here.

The roar came again, and she heard screeching and scrambling from the other creatures in the cavern.

They heard it too and were getting out of the way. She couldn't blame them. They were too weak to stand. Most things were. The smart money would always be on Koracus O'Dein.

Autumn realized that she had started to drag her left leg a bit. It happened when she started moving faster. Her entire body was sending nothing but pain to her brain. The answer it received was "shut up and move faster." She trusted that this was helping. She knew no other way.

Ten yards to go. A first down.

She could feel the rumblings of the beast drawing near. How far away was it? She dared not waste time looking back. Keep trekking forward. That was her single-minded obsession.

-Autumn, please come home. I can hear something coming out.-

Elizabeth could hear the roars and rumblings. Of course, she was scared. She should be. Autumn was scared too. Elizabeth sounded desperate and terrified, as any person would when they heard a real demon roar. The portal was only feet away. Close enough. Autumn began to lift her cannon. The weight was oppressive, but her right arm seemed to be screaming in pain. Feeling had come back. That meant that some strength had come back. She still had to lift with her left hand, but the pain was a good sign. She saw the cross-hair rise in front of her, painfully slowly, until it was on the barrier. She thought.

A blast fired out, but it was visibly weaker than before. For a moment she was certain that it wouldn't be enough. The door wouldn't open and Koracus would crash into the cavern. In her state she couldn't pretend to fight it. She would die.

The shield slid away as all of them had before and the portal opened. She could see Earth. Three men had ahold of Elizabeth and they were pulling her away from the portal. They turned as the portal opened to see Autumn standing there in her armor with a large cannon pointed at them.

"Fuck this!" she heard one of them scream. Agreement came from his cohorts.

They released Elizabeth and ran off into the forest like rabbits.

Elizabeth dropped to her knees awestruck and horrified at the thing before her. There was someone in weird metal armor with a cannon pointed in her general direction. Had things become better or much worse? The black and green made it look ominous and the battle scars made it look violent. Some alien from space had come out of the portal.

Had it been making those horrible sounds? The roar had seemed larger than this being.

The cannon dropped, and the being stepped forward out of the portal. She watched it reach forward with its left hand. The fingers crossed the barrier, but the metal did not. Human skin showed from underneath the armor as it penetrated the barrier. Elizabeth watched as a muscular human arm came out of the Hell portal in front of her. The arm was beaten and bloody. She moved forward as its legs gave out making it fall forward onto Earth.

Elizabeth saw Autumn's head emerge from the helmet falling forward to the ground. She wasn't strong enough to catch her, but she broke her fall to decrease the force of the landing. Once she was down,

Elizabeth pulled Autumn the rest of the way out of the portal.

It remained floating there, but she could no longer see what was on the other side. It had closed on the other side barring vision. Elizabeth didn't know that, but she was glad not to see what had made those sounds.

"I've got you. You're safe now," Elizabeth spoke softly to the woman in her arms.

Autumn's eyes snapped open.

"No, you aren't," she pulled herself up as she spoke. Elizabeth was amazed that she could move at all. Blood had dried in streams down her right arm. She had taken a lot of damage to her arm. Most of her body that Elizabeth could see was covered in cuts and bruises. Her clothing was torn and barely hung onto her body. Autumn looked like she had been in a war and Elizabeth wasn't sure who had won. That was terrifying.

"I have to close the portal. It's coming?"

"What? The wizard you went in after?"

"No, Koracus O'Dein," Autumn's voice was frantic.

Elizabeth had never heard that name before, but her body reacted immediately. The fear hit her like a bucket of cold water. This creature seemed to scare her down to her very DNA. Whatever it was had to be stopped. She watched as Autumn lurched to her feet and over to the glowing skull on the pillar.

Following her, Elizabeth tried to make sure she didn't fall. She knew nothing of what was going on, but if Autumn was this determined and afraid she would help her however she could. She watched

Autumn plant both hands on the skull and instantly some kind of energy began coursing through her body.

Autumn shook and bit off a scream as she tried to pull against the energy. The harder she pulled the more it shocked her until she had to release the skull. Her right arm had recovered some, but it wasn't as strong as before. She was injured and this one would take time to heal, but she knew she had to close that portal.

Koracus roared again. It was close.

If she couldn't lift the skull off the pedestal, then she'd have to go with plan B. Autumn bent and threw her hands out wide. She brought then in hard smashing some of the stone in the pedestal making pits. With handholds created she grabbed them and began to pull.

Elizabeth couldn't believe what she was seeing. The pillar was between four and five feet tall and it looked like solid marble or granite. Despite that, she watched this woman she had met not three days ago grab the stone where she had broken it and begin to strain. The corded muscles all over Autumn's toned body strained and stood out as she began to lift the pillar.

Slowly at first the pillar came off the ground. It sped up when it broke off from the base it had been attached to. Autumn stood to her full height with the stone in her hands. The whole scene was surreal as Autumn walked toward the glowing blue orb and the portal didn't close but shifted shape in space. This activity once again opened the portal. As soon as it opened Elizabeth saw the most horrific sight she could have ever imagined.

She knew what would haunt her nightmare for the rest of her life.

There was a huge beast on the other side. It was tall and shaped like some hellish impersonation of something on Earth. She saw that it also looked beaten. It had fluids dried on it, one eye was out, and its teeth were broken. Its throat looked burned from the inside. Had Autumn fought that? Had she done that? Was that her war? The creature was no more than ten feet from the open portal.

It roared loudly. Nothing on Earth could have made that noise any more than it could have hoped to resist its power.

Autumn lifted the pillar over her head. Koracus began to reach through the open portal as Autumn swung it down smashing the skull into the blue orb. She dropped it as she swung. The collision caused a massive flash of light and an explosion. Autumn lost track of the world for a time.

The light dimmed, and Autumn was still alive. The land around her along with the trees seemed to be blasted and highly damaged. Standing in the same place and position she could see the fading shimmer of a glowing orb around her. Her nose filled with the pleasant scent of roses and lavender. She followed the glow to its source and found a thin arm that ended in a fist sticking out from between her legs.

Autumn noticed something pressing against her ass. She turned her head to see Elizabeth on her knees in one of the most bizarre poses she could imagine. Elizabeth slowly opened her eyes and looked up at Autumn.

"The ring worked."

Autumn couldn't believe what had happened. She smiled, laughed, and her body collapsed down into Elizabeth's arms.

"Is it over?" Autumn asked barely above a whisper. Exhaustion flooded over her body as the adrenaline drained.

"Are you wanting to destroy something else? It looks like you stopped everything bad from happening, but there're still things around that're intact. I could try to drive a car in from the parking lot." Elizabeth was smiling as she held Autumn.

"Stop it. You saved us from the blast."

"I saved you?" Elizabeth interjected. "I was just lucky enough to be behind you."

Autumn giggled. A sound that was unnatural to her. She was surprised to hear it come out.

"Are you all done here?" Elizabeth asked, stroking her hair.

"Yeah. This one's all done. The world should be safe once again," Autumn tried to give a big smile, but she wasn't sure if her mouth moved at all.

"Good. I'll help you to one of the cars in the lot, so you can help me steal it. I figure you might know how."

"I heard you," Autumn's voice was growing weaker.

"Yeah? I hope so, I'm right here."

"No, in the cavern. I heard you calling me from the other realm. I heard you calling my real name. I followed the sound back to the portal. It sounded wonderful."

"Wow," Elizabeth said, unsure how any of this had worked. "I do prefer it to Lindsay. You don't quite look like a Lindsay Brown."

"Be quiet and kiss me," Autumn said and passed out. Elizabeth continued to hold her and stroke her hair.

"Sure, just as soon as you wake up. I think you've earned the rest."

CHAPTER THIRTY-FOUR

When Autumn opened her eyes again she was lying in bed in her hotel room. The light was soft and soothing. Her bed felt like the most comfortable place on Earth at that moment. Though, her body still hurt, she could feel herself healing and her strength returning. Slowly surveying the room, she saw Elizabeth sitting in a chair reading a book. It was a picture far better than the light or the bed could have possibly felt.

She looked over the top and saw Autumn's open eyes. Elizabeth gently closed the book and set it upon the small desk nearby.

"Hello," Elizabeth smiled as she spoke. Her eyes looked tired. "Are you finally awake? Feeling any better?"

"Yes, to both," Autumn's voice was harsh and quiet. "I'm feeling much better now than I did when a monster was trying to beat me to death."

"Makes sense. You wouldn't allow me to take you to a hospital. I thought you needed serious medical care. If I hadn't felt you breathing, I would have thought you died."

"I'm sorry I've caused you so much trouble," Autumn said, looking down a bit as she spent a moment trying to imagine how this had all felt for Elizabeth. She would have no way to know what was happening or what had happened. She had, most likely, the worst day of her entire life and then saw some impossible shit no one has ever been meant to see. What must have been going through her mind?

"Oh, no trouble at all," Elizabeth spoke with a warm tone matching her pleasant smile. "I've seen what you do to people who oppose you. I just agreed and helped you get back here. You weren't entirely with it at any point."

Autumn closed her eyes and took a deep calming breath.

"Thank you," her voice sounded stronger though she could feel the emotion in it. "I'm sorry you had to see that. I'm also very sorry that monster kidnapped you. That must have been terrible for you. I'm doing much better now, and I'll recover just fine all because of you. You can leave." Autumn never opened her eyes as she spoke. She was afraid to see a look of fear and horror on Elizabeth's face. Autumn couldn't bear to see Elizabeth look at her as a monster.

"Are you sending me away?" Elizabeth barely choked out the words.

"Don't worry. I won't hurt you or come after you. You have nothing to fear from this particular inhuman monster."

"Oh, shut the fuck up and open your goddamn eyes," Elizabeth almost yelled at the top of her lungs.

Autumn looked up to see Elizabeth crying and

staring her down.

"Did I-"

"Shut up. Shut the fuck up. You didn't do anything to me but insult the woman I have rapidly come to care deeply for and then try to send me away."

"I just-" Autumn tried to talk.

"I said shut up. Do you know what that means? It's my turn to speak now," Autumn saw fire in Elizabeth's eyes as she spoke. "Yes, I saw what you do. I saw you fight and destroy a man, the man who kidnapped me. Yeah, sure, I won't say that wasn't more than a bit scary. I've never seen anyone capable of doing what you did to another human being. I've also never met someone I felt deserved it so much.

"I then watched you jump into an unknown tear in the world to stop a madman from destroying that world. You didn't hesitate or cry. You showed no fear. I couldn't even bring myself to contemplate what was in front of me, but you simply did what true heroes do: you tried to save us all. I have no clue what happened in there. You jumped in and then you came out beaten and bloody like ten minutes later."

"Ten minutes?" Autumn said in shock.

"Yeah. While you were gone I thought about you and what you'd done. All the great and all the scary things. I realized something then: I wanted you back. Simple," Elizabeth's anger morphed into caring and fear. "I could've walked away, but instead I began to call out to you. I wanted you to know I was still waiting. I was scared you might not come back. Terrified, really.

"Then those guys came out of the woods. They looked around, saw me, and began talking about holding me for the money they were owed. I tried to threaten them, but one came up from behind me and took your gun. I'm sorry about that; I'm not as strong as you. Honestly, I don't know who is. But, then you showed up. You were standing in the portal threatening them and they knew not to fuck with you. Anyone would.

"When you came out I thought again that you were dying. You looked terrible, but you said the world wasn't safe yet and went to work. How much did that pillar weight? A thousand pounds? Tons? I couldn't believe what I was seeing. However, I knew it was real and I knew everything was going to be okay. You know why?"

"No," Autumn could say nothing else.

"I wasn't scared because Autumn Graves was there to save the world by doing the impossible. You were right when you said you aren't Wonder Woman, I just never knew before what it meant to be Autumn Graves. I've never felt as safe as I do around you. Most people never get a chance to meet anyone who is truly amazing. I have, and I don't want to let her go."

Autumn couldn't believe what she was hearing. No one had even spoken of her in tones like that. Sure, people have marveled over her strength and more than a few men have fawned over her body, but this was different. Elizabeth was more invested.

"I'm dangerous, Elizabeth," Autumn finally said after some time. She tried to keep her voice even and calm. She didn't want to sound too emotional. "I was in that other realm for hours. I killed Marcus with my bare hands as I killed those others. I then took his rings and fought a demon; the one you saw there at the end. Life around me will never be secure or stable. I roam the country taking these jobs for money. Do you see that? I'm not a superhero; I'm a bounty hunter. Someone paid me specifically to kill those men and I intend to take the money."

"Good," Elizabeth spoke with vengeance in her eyes. "They destroyed my shop when they came and kidnapped me, so we need some kind of income now. I still intend to have pretty things."

"You were captured simply to get at me. If I hadn't been in your life you'd still have your shop and your livelihood. You never would've been in the danger that you say I saved you from."

"So those guys were trying to call a demon here because of you?"

"Well, no. I was hired in response to their plan."

"Exactly," Elizabeth crossed her thin arms and stood as she spoke. "When given the chance to go to the moon you don't stand on Earth and complain about the risk of flight. I can never go back to my boring life if I don't try to follow this amazing one. If you don't want me to go with you I understand. I don't have much to offer.

"I will leave if you ask me to. I'll respect your wishes and I won't be mad at you either. I'll be disappointed, sure, but not angry. In fact, if you find me again I'll probably be available to you. I can't imagine ever being able to say no to the most amazing woman on Earth. How could I?

"However, I really don't want to leave you," she paused with tears in her eyes as she steeled herself for what might be the worst news of her life. "So, tell me, are you sending me away?"

The question hung heavily in the air as Autumn considered it. This wonderful woman deserved better than hopping all over the country in almost constant danger. Autumn's life would probably lead to her death. Elizabeth was a big girl and could make decisions for herself, but was she truly thinking about this one? There was so much about Autumn's life she could never understand until her life was again in danger. Could Autumn live with herself if something terrible happened to her? So many possibilities poured through her mind.

"Fuck it!" Autumn said, her face forming a small smirk. "Who am I kidding? Get over here. I don't want you to go anywhere but with me."

Elizabeth ran over and leapt into bed hugging Autumn's bruised and beaten body. Autumn tried to hide the wince from the impact.

"I noticed that I'm no longer dripping blood and it isn't dried all over myself."

"Well, I couldn't have you bleeding all over the bed," Elizabeth answered. "I thought you were broke and I'd get stuck with the bill."

"Did you? So, you took it upon yourself to clean me up?"

"Sure did. Checked as best as I could to see if you were broken or hurt too badly too."

"Oh? Did a thorough inspection did you?" Autumn asked as her smirk grew.

"Well, I was concerned for your wellbeing," Elizabeth had a "hand caught in the cookie jar" look on her face.

"Of course. How thorough?"

"Well, I did realize that you might send me

away…"

Autumn sighed, "you couldn't help yourself could you?"

"Have you seen yourself?"

"That's no excuse. I was unconscious after saving the world."

"I didn't hear you saying no," Elizabeth said her face turning red.

"Oh, I see that I'm going to have to watch you extra closely."

"You know it," Elizabeth beamed as she spoke.

"I think I can live with that."

Autumn and Elizabeth kissed each other deeply sitting on the bed. Neither woman had ever felt quite how they did in that moment.

CHAPTER THIRTY-FIVE

Two wonderful days of recovery later Autumn and Elizabeth were on the road together to go back and talk to Clarence and Thomas. The time had come to collect her payment for the job done. This one had been ugly, and she was ready to move on. The drive through Missouri would have been quite dull but bright company made it all a lot better.

"So, I've been a bit afraid to ask, but how exactly did you get me back to the hotel?" Autumn asked before they had completely left St. Louis.

"Took you long enough."

"Come on, my mouth has been busy," a smile formed on Autumn's mouth as she spoke. "Not like you have been in any position to answer."

"True," Elizabeth giggled. "Really it worked out well. I looked around for something to roll you onto and drag, but there wasn't much left intact after the explosion. I then ran to the parking lot hoping to find a car I could drive into the clearing. That's when I ran into Theodore."

"Really?"

"Yeah," Elizabeth sounded cheerful. "He was crouched by a car looking confused. When I came out he called out to see if I was you. I told him no but that you were alive and needed help. He jumped."

"Really? Theodore?"

"Yeah. He told me that you'd treated him well and he was supposed to take you home. I was extremely nervous for a short time. He seemed too loyal."

"You thought it was a trick?" Autumn asked her as they hit open road.

"No," Elizabeth turned serious for a moment. "I thought you'd fucked him. I was afraid you went back to your old ways. He said that if you were alive then his perfect sack record was intact. I don't know what that means, but I was jealous."

They both laughed as they sped along. The conversation felt too normal for the events that had taken place. The new normal of their lives was a bit jarring.

"I hope you realized-" Autumn was interrupted.

"No, I asked him. Turns out Theodore has a wonderful wife and two kids. Said you aren't his type."

"Is it bad that I'm a bit insulted?"

"Yes. Now shut it before I cut you off."

"Good luck trying."

Elizabeth gave her a wry smile and stuck her tongue out like a small child.

"So, anyway... he came back to the clearing and helped me get you to the car. He was willing to drive you back as well. We both wanted to take you to a hospital, but you would argue. We weren't sure you were entirely conscious, but neither of us wanted to face you if you became angry so we took you back to the hotel. I distracted the desk clerk while Theodore got you onto the elevator. I ran after him and we got you to the room. The rest you know."

"Wow," Autumn couldn't hide her surprise. "I wish I could have thanked him for his help."

"Oh, there will be time. I still have insurance to deal with over my store. I was thinking of giving him some money to say thank you. He said one of his little girls was in the hospital a lot. A spinal problem at birth. He really seemed to be a loving father."

"Oh," Autumn smiled as she spoke. "We'll see to it that she's taken care of. I am amazed at him. I hope to see him again."

"I'm sure we will," Elizabeth said. "Oh, one odd thing he did say. I had meant to ask you about it."

"Okay?" Autumn's curiosity was piqued.

"He mentioned it when we were getting you into the car. He said: 'I'm glad I overheard Marcus' plan to pick her up early. Christos had accepted it, and everything would have gone to shit if she weren't here.' What did he mean?"

"Wow," Autumn said to herself. "I was told by one of Marcus' men that someone would pick me up at 7:30 while Andrzej sent Theodore at 8. I think Marcus was going to have me killed."

"How did you know to wait?"

"Someone else sent me a note saying they were Christos. It seemed odd then, but I accepted it. Once I saw Teddy in the second car I knew I'd done the right thing."

"I guess the note came from Theodore, then?" Elizabeth asked.

"I guess so. I wonder how much he knew."

"Enough, that's for sure," Elizabeth replied.

They drove on chatting and enjoying the day until they were about an hour away from their destination. Autumn had to break the conversation and bring the mood down with business.

"So," Autumn's voice turned grave. "These people I'm going to be meeting with are not the kind of people you want to meet."

"Oh?"

"Yeah. I was originally hired to find this man's daughter, Katie. She'd been kidnapped for ransom by two dippy young wizards who were working for Andrzej. You remember me telling you about him?"

"Yeah, he was the dick trying to destroy the world, but not the dick that had me kidnapped. Too many dicks in this story."

"None of us knew that they were connected to Andrzej at the time," Autumn told her.

"I won't ask you what happened to the wizards."

"Good. Thank you."

"Did you find his daughter?" Elizabeth smiled hopefully.

"Yes, but she had already been killed by the two mages."

"Oh," Elizabeth looked down as she spoke. "I'm sorry."

"There was another dead child and a young girl who was still alive. I think she was being held for the ritual. Clarence, the man who hired me, wasn't happy with me. He blamed me for his daughter's death. I don't think he ever wanted to see me again, but he had ties to the Neolithic Consortium. They hired me to go after Christos."

"Wait," Elizabeth stopped her. "The banking conglomerate hired you to kill a wizard? I think they might own the bank that loaned me the money for my shop."

"They do a lot more than banking. It's also a front for a huge organization of powerful wizards. I've heard they're the most powerful group of their kind in the world. I don't know if that's true, but I can believe it."

"Wow," Elizabeth was in a bit of shock. "I've heard the conspiracy theories about them running the world, but I've never paid attention to them. There's so much about this world I don't know shit about. I never really had much of an opinion on the whole magic thing. I just knew I couldn't do it."

"True," Autumn said as she thought about what she knew. She then thought about how much she didn't know which was so much more. With that she was still an expert compared to Elizabeth. She was seeing this all for the first time. "They may not be too happy with me now."

"Why not? You did what they hired you to do."

"Yes, but to prove the job was done they wanted me to bring them the two rings that Christos had been wearing." She held one hand up showing Elizabeth the ring on her finger.

"Well? You still have them, or at least one. I don't understand what the problem is."

"Yes, but I have no intention of giving them up," Autumn's voice was firm and unyielding. "I want to find out more about them. They gave me the ability to survive in the other realm."

"That armor you were wearing?"

"Yeah," Autumn nodded her head. "They produced that."

"And if you don't give them to this guy he won't pay you?"

"Maybe," Autumn said with a nod. "I don't think they want to pay me at all. I still have a feeling that they expected me to die on this one. Rich people don't stay rich by giving money away."

"Are the rings worth forfeiting however much you were getting paid to keep?" Elizabeth asked calmly.

"I could really use the money. It would make things a lot better and I have been recently informed that my girlfriend is a gold-digger."

"Hey! I'm high maintenance, thank you very much. Get it right," Elizabeth crossed her arms and nodded. "Seriously, though, how much was it going to be?"

"A lot."

"How much?"

Autumn paused for a moment. "One million to kill Christos and another million for Marcus."

"Holy shit!"

"Yeah," Autumn nodded more as she spoke. "That would go a long way. They gave me half a million already for taking the job to get me started."

"Fuck! I didn't gouge you nearly enough that night in my shop. I let my pussy do the talking."

"Thanks."

"What?!" Elizabeth was in too much shock to keep her volume down. "I gave you the hot girl discount. I didn't know I should have given you the rich girl tax too."

"Well, I'm glad I know where I stand with you now.

Also, good to know what you consider to be a hot girl discount."

"Just sayin' I lost my shop and now I have insurance to fight for god knows how long over my payout. Good thing I picked a rich girl to fall for."

"I'm sorry about that," Autumn sounded quite sincere on the subject. "I never thought they'd come after you. I hope you really do understand how dangerous traveling with me could be."

"I know. You've told me. That's the price I'll have to pay to fall for you. Apparently, my heart isn't very logical. First occurrence of that in history, I'm sure."

"I hear your sarcasm, but I'm being serious. My work is dangerous, you've seen that. You're choosing to pick up and go with me but I'm not sure you even can be making an informed decision. I'm worried about you."

"I am too," Elizabeth responded. "You think your work doesn't scare me? I saw that thing on the other side of the portal you closed. People make movies about horrors like that. That kind of thing scars people for life."

"Yes, it does," Autumn paused for a moment after speaking. "You can still leave, you know. That offer still stands. I can take you anywhere."

"For you, you idiot. I'm afraid for you not of you. I know you're amazing and all that, but it doesn't mean that you're invincible. You won't say it, but whatever happened to you in that other place scared the shit out of you. You're the most amazing person I've ever met, and you just go racing into danger that kills regular people and cripples superheroes. Without even a second thought, you just jumped."

"I have to do what I do. I could never be a salesperson or secretary. I don't normally play hero."

"I get that. It's part of what makes you who you are. I don't want you to change, but it still scares me. What scares me more is the idea that one day something will be too much for you. We're all doomed then. I have to help you so that never happens."

Autumn smiled, "I can't imagine changing, so you're stuck with me the way I am."

"Glad we worked that out," Elizabeth managed to put a period on the whole subject. "Now, what are you going to do about this Clarence guy?"

"I don't know. I'm hoping to deal with Thomas instead. He's more reasonable."

They drove on for a while in silence. Autumn tried to think of something she could say to Clarence and Thomas. She needed the money, but there was no way she could give up the rings. She had seen the other realm and some of what it had to offer. There was no way she could give up the only weapon that gave her the ability to combat that. Koracus surely wasn't alone there and he might not even be the alpha predator.

Autumn had never been one to give up on anything that made her stronger. Her whole life had been a struggle to become as strong as she could. Now she had found another entire realm of creatures that might be vastly more powerful than she was. How could she hand over the only thing she had found that made the fight even possible? She had to be able to compete.

Autumn's GPS told her to take the next exit to get back to that small town from days ago when this all started. She never imagined when she took that job how this would all turn out. What had started as a simple rescue job had turned into a world threatening ordeal. She didn't feel ready to play at this level. That time felt so far away now. It seemed her life had changed, and she was somewhere entirely new with new rules she didn't understand.

"I think it might be best if you stay in the car. There's no reason for them to know anything about you."

"This is your job, so I'll play it however you think is best," Elizabeth felt relieved to not have to deal with these guys. "Please remember that I'm here to help if you need me."

"Thanks," Autumn said and pulled off the road and into gas station near the interstate. She reached back into her bag and pulled her phone out. She powered it up hoping this would go quickly. Searching through the prior calls she found the number to call and pressed redial.

It rang once.

"Done?" came the voice from over the line.

"Yes."

"Good. Come back to town and we'll find a time and place to meet."

"I'm already in town," Autumn said quickly. "Meet me where we made the deal before in ten minutes."

"Wait, what? I can't be ready that quickly," she finally recognized the voice as Clarence's. "I need time. You were supposed to call when you were done. Or check in with James."

"Why? You knew what was coming. Ten minutes or I start making this very difficult for everyone involved."

Autumn ended the call.

"Was that necessary?" Elizabeth was perplexed.

"I don't want him to have time to prepare. Wizards are most dangerous when they have time. Now, let's go to the hospital."

The two of them sat in the hospital parking lot for longer than ten minutes waiting for Clarence. Autumn was certain this was a power play, but she was still nervous about the other possibilities. Wizards could do almost anything given the time to prepare. The longer it went the more she wondered what he had planned for that day.

Though she doubted that Clarence was a world beater like Andrzej or even Marcus, she felt certain he must have a certain level of skill. He held some rank in the Neolithic Consortium and they were very protective of their ranks and who was allowed in. She felt certain he must have had something to offer them or else they wouldn't allow him to do any negotiating.

After a few more minutes, twenty in total, another car pulled into the lot and parked near Autumn's Toyota. She stepped out of her car and walked around the back to the red sedan next to her. Clarence stood up out of the car and walked to the rear to meet her. He had a big smile on his face that looked held on by glue.

"Hello," he tried to sound friendly but hurt. "I'm not sure why you're using these pressure tactics. We hired you and you did the job. What's the problem? We should both be happy everything worked out. I had expected to hear from you before you left St.

Louis. I had at least expected to hear from James."

"Why?"

"The bank manager?" he looked confused. "Your contact? That's why."

"Oh, yeah. Him. No, I cut him out."

"I see. Well, if you had contacted me I could have saved you the drive."

"Clarence," Autumn stopped him. "I don't trust you and you don't like me. Let's stop pretending those things aren't true. I don't know for sure that you had some sort of plan to fuck me, but I feel much better doing this on my terms. Now, where's my money?"

"That's just it," he dropped his fake smile. "You didn't give me enough time to get it for you."

"It's been days since you hired me. Well, since Thomas hired me. Where is he, by the way?"

"He had stuff to do," Clarence sounded a bit unsure. "He left me to handle it all. Now-"

"Days. What would a few more hours have done for you?"

"Well," he was growing visibly annoyed and nervous. "I didn't take the money out then. I wanted to wait to hear from you. I never heard from James, so I had no clue about your progress. Now, if you have the rings we can get everything taken care of. Maybe tomorrow-"

"Shut your lying mouth. You and the Consortium can put that kind of money together like I can find a five-dollar bill. What the fuck is going on?"

"Well, we have to have proof first. Was it just Andrzej or were there more involved? What do you have to show for it? Where are the rings?"

Autumn held up her right hand displaying one of the rings.

"That enough? There was one other mage working with him named Marcus Kanellis."

"Really?" he looked genuinely surprised. "I've heard of Kanellis. I can't believe he'd work for anyone. He seemed like the lone wolf type."

"He didn't. He planned to betray Christos and take over the whole operation. I had to deal with the whole thing making it an additional one point five million you owe me."

"What proof do you have that Marcus is dead... or even involved? We can't simply take your word about all of this. The Consortium needs concrete evidence, you see. James would have been able to help you provide proof. I could still contact him and see what he could find out. His verification and the rings should cover everything we need."

"Fuck James," Autumn was growing frustrated with every passing word from Clarence's mouth. "You're just trying to draw this out. I bet people in your organization already had an idea that Andrzej had help and who that was. Make a call."

"You may be right. I can make some calls and work on getting that verification. It may only take a few hours. At the same time, I can work on the money. I'm sure by tomorrow we can have this all worked out to your satisfaction."

Autumn could see where this was going, and she couldn't stand it any longer.

"You fucking bastard," her tone turned icy. "You're planning to stiff me and don't have to the balls to say it."

"What? Stiff you? No, I just have protocols that must be followed. Oh, and I need to collect those rings."

"Why?"

"What? Well," he paused a moment. "I need to take them for authentication. Have to be certain they're real."

"Oh, so now you want to authenticate them? What happened to tomorrow? Surely a process like that will take days. You didn't think this out very well. You're planning to fuck me, Clarence, and you're not my type."

"Well," he tried to straighten up as tall as he could. "We don't really have any written contract, now do we?"

"I knew it. You fucking coward."

"You started this. I've wanted to get this taken care of, but you've been making this difficult from the beginning."

"I want my money… now."

"Lindsay, it just isn't that easy. I have due diligence and protocols to follow. I's to dot and T's to cross. Working with an organization as large as the Neolithic Consortium means that there's a lot of red tape. I can't make the kind of unilateral moves you are wanting. Look-"

"If you say 'I'm on your side here' I will bend you into a pretzel of shattered bones and punctured organs. You aren't strong enough to fuck with me," her frustration was turning to anger with rage on the horizon.

"See, now you're threatening me," Clarence said as a sharkish smile spread across his face. "I don't think

we can do business any longer under these conditions.
I told them you couldn't handle this kind of work.
You just aren't civilized enough to do this kind of
high-end work."

Autumn moved in fast and grabbed both of
Clarence's wrists. She began to apply pressure when a
man materialized out of thin air twenty feet from them.
He stood a bit over six feet tall and wore a meticulous
suit perfectly tailored to his body. His hair was dark
aside from the perfect graying at his temples. His face
was hard and set. He was obviously unhappy about
something as he strode toward them.

Great. More wizards.

"Clarence! What is going on here?" he said in a
rich and refined voice suitable for addressing any
council in the world.

"Alexander!" Clarence had a confused look on his
face. He looked both hopeful and terrified. Autumn
was no longer his focal point. "Help me, please."

"Why?" he stopped walking a few feet from the two
of them. "From what I can tell you were trying to
cheat Ms. Brown here out of the money she has
earned. You also seem to be preparing to cheat me out
of the money given to you to pay her for her services
and time."

"No! Never. I tried to get confirmation of her
successful completion of the job. She could be
bragging or trying to cheat you."

"Oh?" Alexander asked. "Did you think to check
in? Thomas has been waiting for your call. He has
already been informed of both the deaths of Andrzej
Christos and Marcus Kanellis. The Orb of Nied and
his skull have been destroyed. Our people have

captured a few mercenaries who have been questioned. We have also summoned a being from the Spirit who said a woman of great power accomplished the deed. That woman has been described by multiple beings as resembling Ms. Brown."

"I didn't know," Autumn never released the pressure and Clarence was almost crying now. "Please release me."

"Ms. Brown," Alexander turned to Autumn and spoke. "If you would be so kind as to release this man I will see to your compensation personally."

Autumn released Clarence from her grip. He stumbled back a few steps holding his hands close to his body. Autumn kept one eye on Alexander. She had heard of him before but never thought she'd meet him. Could he really be the man behind so much power? He looked rich and powerful, but that was not the same as the kind of power he was said to wield.

"Now, Mr. Bradshaw, please get the case with the money you were entrusted with."

"What? You're just going to pay her after what she did to me? You can't let her disrespect the Consortium like that."

Though Alexander's volume only raised the slightest amount the effect was considerable.

"You dare question my actions and motivations?"

"I-"

"Stop," Alexander's command was sharp and left no room for compromise. "I told you to produce my money. You have failed to yield results. Am I now to assume that you no longer have the money here? Have you failed so greatly at such a meager task? How else am I to interpret this situation?"

"She failed!" Clarence screamed. "My daughter died because this bitch failed. I refuse to reward her for causing the death of my daughter."

"You refuse? *You refuse?!*" Alexander extended on hand forward to Clarence and he was swept up into the air with ease before slamming on the ground where he remained pinned. "Since when has it ever been your place to refuse my command?"

"I-I wasn't refusing you..."

"I gave you an order. You said no. Have I gotten the order of events incorrect?"

"It's not- I just- What about my daughter?"

"What about her?" Alexander's tone was flat. "You were the one dealing with those degenerate wizards. You became entangled with them. Your daughter's life is on your own hands. After you endangered her life you then chose to involve Ms. Brown here to repair the situation you had so thoroughly destroyed. You expected her to cover your failings as both a father and a wizard. Once again you displace your own miserable faults onto another in the cowardly hope of escaping consequences."

Alexander lifted his hand casually and Clarence rose up off the ground and floated over to Alexander. Clarence seemed to be incapable of resistance.

"Mr. Bradshaw, I have a very important question for you. Depending on your answer this may be the penultimate question of your meager existence. Think carefully before you give me your answer. Where is my money?"

So strong was the chill in his voice Autumn almost believed he had cast a freezing spell of some kind with his words. She wasn't sure if Alexander was using magic for the effects to his tone and person. If so, it seemed so easy for him to use.

"My wife has it," Clarence broke down in front of Alexander. "We had planned to run after we received the call from Lindsay. I'm supposed to buy time here and then meet her to run."

"You are honest, thank you. However, honesty will not set you free. Clarence, I detest every attribute of what passes for your character. Your position with the Neolithic Consortium is terminated along with your membership. Now, where is your wife?"

"Rolla. She should have a hotel room in a few hours. We were going to meet at the Sirloin Stockade tomorrow at the latest."

"She will have a meeting as planned, but it will not be with you."

Alexander closed his hand into a fist. Clarence rattled silently for a moment after which he never moved again. It was obvious to Autumn that Alexander had ended his life, but she could not figure out what he had done. Alexander then turned to Autumn.

"I am sorry. Allow me to retrieve your money."

"I appreciate that, but I'd rather not wait for you to go after Mrs. Bradshaw when I could go after her myself."

"Oh no, you misunderstand me. I will pay you here. Mrs. Bradshaw will be taken care of by myself."

Alexander walked over to Clarence's car and opened the trunk. He cast a quick spell and opened a portal to somewhere in the trunk space. Autumn could see a large room and a man on the other side. The man stood looking at Alexander as if this was how they did business normally.

"What can I do for you, sir?"

"Please bring me a case with two million in cash. Be quick but count carefully."

"Yes, sir," the man scurried away.

"Not that I want to look this horse in the mouth, but the deal was for an additional one point five not two."

"Of course, and I appreciate your honesty. However, I wish to compensate you for your trouble with Clarence. He was my responsibility. I make mistakes rarely and wish to make up for one now."

"Thank you," was all Autumn could say. She was still unsure how to take this man before her. He seemed professional and even friendly, but she had seen what he was capable of. It would not pay to get too close to someone like that.

"I hope to foster a good working relationship between us. You do exceptional work and I would like for you to consider more work from us in the future."

"Possibly," Autumn wasn't sure she ever wanted to be around this man again. "But right now, I'm ready to finish this job and take some time for myself."

"Of course. And such a wonderful lady to take that time with as well," he bowed slightly and looked back into the portal. He seemed to have figured everything out. Alexander reached in and took a large steel case the man on the other side was handing him.

"Counted and accounted for, sir."

"Excellent as always. Thank you," Alexander said as he took the case and closed the portal. He then closed the trunk and turned to Autumn once again. "Here you are."

She hesitated for a moment about the case. She made a habit of never trusting wizards, but she had never met one of such casual power. If she refused him she could make a terrible enemy. She could always ditch the case later.

"Do not worry, Autumn, I have done nothing to the case," he said as if reading her mind. "However, if you'd like you can move the money to another vessel."

"No," she said taking the case. "How?"

"I know many things"

"None of your people knew."

"It was not my place to share your secret with them," Alexander's sincerity was obvious. This man was amazing and terrifying.

"Well, let this be my show of faith to you," Autumn told him.

"Thank you," Alexander looked surprised.

She opened the case and peeked in enough to see the piles of cash.

"Thank you for making this right."

"Of course," his pleasant tones sounded soothing. "Please keep this in mind as future work comes around. Now, go enjoy your vacation."

Autumn didn't respond, but instead turned and walked to her car. Alexander turned and began to walk as well. At the car Autumn looked back and Alexander had disappeared. She opened the back door and dropped the case on the seat. She walked up and climbed into the driver's seat.

"I hate wizards."

"All set, then?" Elizabeth asked.

"Finally."

"So, we're rich now?"

"What's all this 'we' stuff? I can afford a crazy celebrity relationship now."

Elizabeth looked her in the face and almost cried before Autumn broke. She laughed hard. Harder than the joke was merited. Elizabeth punched Autumn in the arm, winced, and pulled her fist to her face.

"That was supposed to hurt you."

"Yeah, sorry," Autumn's laughter renewed.

"That wasn't funny. Since when do you make jokes?"

"Since I became a millionaire and am about to take a beautiful woman on a much-needed vacation wherever she wants to go."

Elizabeth smiled, "let's go somewhere warm."

"You just want to see me in a bikini."

"I want you out of one more... but yeah," Elizabeth winked.

Autumn put the car in gear and drove off. She had a few ideas of where to go next.

I hope you have enjoyed the first book in The Hunter Symphony.

Autumn Graves returns in the second novel in The Hunter Symphony:
The Hunter Sonata

If you can't wait for more of this world please check out Trevor Harrison
in
Poison Magic.

Please rate and review this book to let others know how it is and so that it's easier to find for new readers. Help other people to enjoy as you have.

For additional information and to join my mailing list please visit
Mattoon Underground.

Thank you.

Printed in Poland
by Amazon Fulfillment
Poland Sp. z o.o., Wrocław

65102043R00213